THE *Unexpected* FALL

ANNA SALCEDO

For all of us who have dreams that feel impossible to achieve. Don't give up. You can do it. I believe in you.

Playlist

"Waiting Here" by Jake Isaac
"Empty" by The Cranberries
"Father" by Demi Lovato
"By Your Side" by Sade
"When He's Done" by Tei Shi
"You Sang to Me" by Marc Anthony
"Quizás Si, Quizás No" by Los Toros Band
"Cater 2 U" by Destiny's Child
"Black Dog" by Led Zeppelin
"i love you" by Billie Eilish
"I Can't Quit You Baby" by Led Zeppelin
"Jungle" by Jimi Hendrix
"The Few Things (With Charlotte Lawrence)" by JP Saxe
"my future" by Billie Eilish

Synopsis

G enesis Gonzalez has spent the last two years trying to prove herself at Siren Music Records. Despite her dreams of creating music, she's been stuck as an assistant who spends most of her day answering emails, taking notes in painfully long meetings, and avoiding Will Kobayashi, the six-two bane of her existence.

She was just about to throw in the towel when her job announced an opportunity that could change everything—a work contest that would allow two employees the opportunity to have their song on the label's highly anticipated collaborative album, which features music from all their hottest artists. Getting her name on that album would almost be a guarantee that she'd finally get to say good-bye to being an assistant and hello to producing music. But her plans take an unexpected turn when she finds out that she gets paired with Will, who she is humanly incapable of getting along with.

They have three months to create a song that will impress the record label enough to make both of their dreams come true. But the one thing Genesis could've never seen coming is that the only thing harder than getting along is not falling in love …

Content Warning

Sexual situations, mention of parental death,

parental infidelity (spoken about).

1

It was official: heels were now at the top of my list of things that deserved to be wiped from humankind.

I scrunched my toes up in my stiletto heels, quietly letting out a hiss of pain as Doug droned on about the quarterly sales at the front of the room. My feet were in absolute pain. I was almost positive that I'd lost feeling in my pinkie toe at around ten a.m., but that had become a common occurrence these last few days, so I wasn't too concerned. My only concern was how I was going to get out of this chair when the meeting was over. Maybe I could pretend to be writing up notes when everyone left so that I could be the last one to leave and give my feet a few extra minutes of reprieve.

Taking a quick glance at Mr. Clements, my boss and pseudo-dictator, I quickly crossed that idea out. If he saw me writing notes after the meeting was over, he'd just say that I couldn't keep up and start questioning if I was "fit" for the job. Never mind the fact that he'd be pretty useless without me.

"Thank you, Doug," Mr. Wilson, the executive we were presenting to, said. He cleared his throat as he looked through some papers in his folder. "What are the projections for sales in the upcoming quarter?"

"I can answer that."

It took every ounce of willpower in me to hold in my scoff at the sound of that smooth, deep voice. Will Kobayashi stood up to his full six-two height, commanding the room with his three-piece suit, easy confidence, and annoyingly chiseled jawline. I quickly looked away when I saw his head move in my direction, as if he'd heard the miniscule sound that escaped from my throat despite my every effort. Instead, I looked toward Cora, who was sitting in the seat next to Will, brown curls framing her beautifully delicate face.

She shook her head slightly, a small, amused look on her face as she mouthed, *Stop*, at me, eyes comically wide.

Cora was one of my best friends and the closest person I had at work. After nearly two years of working here, I could honestly say that I wouldn't have made it as long as I had if it wasn't for her.

I blinked innocently but turned back toward the front. Cora understood me in a way that only my family ever had.

The truth was, I had what my sister, Alejandra, liked to call RBF—also known as resting bitch face. I struggled with making friends, and if my RBF didn't deter people from talking to me, then my inability to do small talk definitely did. I didn't want to be that way though, and I'd been working hard these last few years to change that. In this industry, you needed to be charismatic, someone people felt like they could come to, and most importantly, you needed to make a positive impression with the right people, or it could leave you stuck at an entry-level position for the rest of your career. Nearly two years into my entry-level job, and I was starting to worry that I'd sunk my career before it even started.

Despite what some of the men in this office thought, I didn't want to stay an assistant forever. I wanted to be in the studio, producing music and writing songs. That was where I belonged, not behind some desk, answering inane emails or picking up my boss's dry cleaning. Unfortunately, it wasn't easy, getting into this business, and it was even harder when you were a woman. I'd worked with countless unsigned artists and bands on their demos during my college days and even occasionally outside of work if I had time. But when it came to my job at the record label, I was perpetually stuck as an assistant in the marketing department, far, far away from any music studios.

"What sponsors do we have lined up for the Music for the Cure benefit concert next year?"

I felt someone press down hard on my foot, and I winced as my already-throbbing toe flashed with a sharp pain. Mr. Clements was staring at me impatiently, and I realized with a start that they were waiting on me to answer.

"We have Coca-Cola, Spotify, Hyundai, and Verizon so far," I said to the room. "We also have at least a dozen small indie companies that would like to sponsor, and we're in talks with Chipotle and McDonald's as well."

I could feel Will glaring at me from across the table, but I refused to look toward him. I knew that if I did, he'd just be giving me his *you don't belong here* glare, and I was in no mood for his crap right now.

The meeting went on for another forty-five minutes, and I diligently took notes, mostly because I didn't want Clements to step on my foot again if he thought I wasn't paying attention.

When the meeting was over, I slowly started stacking up my papers, adjusting and readjusting the stack. People began to filter into the halls, talking quietly among themselves, and I used every opportunity possible to nod hello and throw smiles around as they filtered out, anything to avoid getting up.

"Move my two o'clock to tomorrow," Clements said, standing over me. "And get me Luigi's today. I'm in the mood for some scampi."

I nodded, trying to keep my face pleasant and not irritated at all. Countless hours in front of the mirror had helped me a bit in making a purposeful effort to appear happy. "Yes, sir."

He walked away, dismissing me in his usual manner. There'd been times when he'd walk away from a conversation, even as I was mid-sentence, because as he loved to remind me, time was money, and he didn't see the point wasting it on people who weren't going to help him make money.

I slowly stood up, my feet feeling slightly better after sitting for a long period of time. But there was still that dull pain underneath, hovering. Letting me know that it wouldn't take long for the pain to return in full force. I walked slowly to the door, silently debating with myself on whether I should switch to my slip-ons that I had in the bottom of my desk drawer for emergencies, when I heard someone clear their throat behind me.

I knew that voice like I knew the back of my hand, and so, I ignored it. I continued walking, slowing my gait to an even slower speed when I heard his impatient sigh behind me. My lips ticked up into a smile. Maybe something good would come out of these heels after all.

"Are you trying to break a record for slowest walker?" his voice rumbled behind me.

Despite the little voice in my head that told me to just keep walking, I stopped and turned around. Will towered in front of me, eyebrow cocked slightly.

He looked at me and every inch of his face said, *I'm here to ruin your day.*

I hated him and his stupidly handsome face. With his light, unblemished skin that didn't look like it'd ever seen a pimple before, big dark-brown eyes, and a jaw so sharp that it could cut glass, the guy looked like a Japanese supermodel just waiting to grace the covers of *GQ*. What was worse was his muscular build was firm without being overly so. His broad shoulders filled out his button-downs nicely—not that I'd noticed or anything—and you could tell that he must work out from the way his shirt seemed to hug his biceps and arms.

I looked at him, still not eye-level, even with these heels. "Some people like to enjoy the time they have away from the desk. I know that's a hard concept for you to imagine, what with your *stellar* work ethic."

4

There was no way he missed the sarcasm in my voice, but he didn't comment like I'd expected. Instead, he stared down at the ground, a small furrow between his brows. I began to follow his line of sight and scowled when I saw that he was staring at my heels. Again.

He'd made no comment these last few weeks about my new change in foot apparel. But he'd noticed. Most days, I had to not look at him because I could read the amusement and confusion on his face, like he couldn't tell if he should laugh at me or get me checked out by the company doctor.

"What?" I snapped, unable to help myself after he said nothing for another long minute. My impulse control was shockingly low around Will, which was probably why we struggled with being in the same building with each other. I was already hard to like, even when I tried hard to be likable. Who could like me once I stopped trying and had the filter of a two-year-old?

He slowly looked away from my heels, an exasperated expression on his face. "Why do you wear those things when they clearly make you unhappy?"

"It's called fashion," I said, exaggeratedly batting my eyelashes. "Don't you remember, I only got this job because I want everyone's attention?"

"I don't think you're garnering the type of attention you think you are," he commented plainly, ignoring my jab at words his coworkers frequently said, words he'd agreed with. "You've been limping this entire week. Every time you stand up, your face scrunches all up in pain, and you glare at everyone harder than usual."

"You're one to talk," I retorted. "All you do is glare at people."

"That's not true. I get along with everyone," he said. Then, with a pointed look, he added, "Well, almost everyone."

I ignored the hurt that his words had caused because that pain was stupid and made no sense. Instead, I turned around, dismissing him.

I took my first limping step when he spoke up again.

5

"I've been thinking," he said, deep voice taking on a casual tone. "I've never seen you wear heels once in the two years we've been working together. Even when we have events, you'll wear something with a chunky heel, but stilettos? Not even once."

"Your point?" I spat, hoping to God my light-brown skin hid the rush of heat to my face.

He shrugged, his face giving away nothing as his eyes seemed to bore into mine with an intensity that made me want to look away. "I have a theory, but I want to hear the words from you. Why the change, Genesis?"

I turned fully around, prickles of irritation flashing through me at the sound of my name coming from his lips. "Why are you so fixated on my choice of footwear?" I asked, crossing, and then uncrossing my arms in front of my chest. A smirk of my own played at my lips. "Do you have a foot fetish? Because if so, I want nothing to do with that."

Will let out a tired sigh, his dark eyes looking up toward the ceiling, like he was looking for something. Patience maybe. Lord knew how many times I'd looked for it when I was talking to him.

"Your deflection won't work. I know you too well to fall for it."

"You don't know me at all," I said, voice rising with anger. I immediately clamped my mouth shut, mad with myself for showing any emotion and for letting him get a rise out of me yet again.

Will's head rocked back an inch, such a miniscule reaction that I wouldn't have noticed it if we weren't standing so close. He studied me with that calm look in his eyes, the one that said he understood me. That look that made me want to scream because he didn't know me at all, and he'd made sure of that. As if he could read the words screaming in my head, his jaw clenched, full lips pressing tightly together and—

Wait, how did we get so close to each other?

I took a step back, releasing a breath as quietly as possible, trying to slow my racing heart and thoughts. "I don't have to explain myself or my choices to you or anyone. If I want to wear stilettos to work, then that's what I'll wear. And if I want to wear slippers, then I'll walk around here in them, and no one can say a damn word about it."

His brows rose. "You're right."

"This has nothing to do with you," I pressed. "Nothing I do is ever with the thought of you in mind. Ever."

"I never said you did," he said, voice icy and cold.

"Good."

I turned back around, ready to be done with this conversation. I had a list of things I needed to do before I could even think about taking my lunch break and wasting time with Will was only delaying things.

"Tiffany was wrong." I paused at his words and glanced over my shoulder at him.

His eyes never left mine as he said, "Your work will speak for itself. Her tricks do not need to be yours."

"I don't know what you're talking about," I said weakly, hating the rush of embarrassed heat that washed over my body.

A few weeks ago, I'd gotten some "friendly" advice after one of our Monday team meetings.

Tiffany, who had started as an assistant for another department head a measly six months ago, was given yet another opportunity to work on an upcoming campaign. I guessed I couldn't hide my disappointment or frustration because at the end of the meeting, she walked over to me and let me know that perhaps I, too, would be offered an opportunity to work on a campaign if I only showed a little more effort. In the looks department.

"Wear a pair of heels once in a while," she offered with a sweet smile that didn't quite reach her eyes.

I wanted to snap at her, to tell her that she sounded ridiculous and the fact that she thought wearing heels and a tighter skirt would help me get into more meetings was sad—not to mention, disgusting.

But instead, I'd taken her advice. I had a few pair of heels in the back of my closet that had been collecting dust, and I figured, *What the hell?* I didn't doubt that Tiffany wasn't being sincere in the slightest, but what did I have to lose? Clearly, there was something she was doing right that I wasn't, and maybe the heels made the difference.

I knew it was stupid, and I'd felt so dumb the moment I walked into work with them on, but I was stubborn and didn't want to admit that I hated wearing heels and desperately wanted to take mine off and throw them in the trash. The more Will and the other men stared at me like I had three heads every time I walked around the office, the more I was determined to keep the heels on.

God, this whole ordeal was ridiculous and exhausting. And the fact that Will knew about it made me feel humiliated for reasons I didn't want to examine.

I turned back around and continued walking toward the exit.

How did Will know about my conversation with Tiffany?

The image of him and Tiffany laughing at my expense, smirking over how stupid I must be for thinking I could possibly get into a meeting just because I wore some heels entered my mind and made my hands clench into shaky fists. I walked as quickly down the hall as I could without making it look like I was rushing, just trying to make it to the elevators so I could get off this floor and away from Will.

"So, I'm right then," he called out just as the elevators came into view.

Don't turn around, I told myself sternly, but the bigger part of me that didn't want him to have the last word couldn't resist. I looked back at him as I continued walking.

"Think whatever you want," I said over my shoulder, putting as much confidence in my voice as I could muster. "What you think of me stopped mattering a long time ago."

I didn't wait to see his reaction to those words, opening up the stairwell door and exiting.

It was only after I started walking down, when my anger and embarrassment had time to start cooling off, that I realized I was now forced to walk down fifteen flights of stairs.

"*Dios*, when will my suffering ever end?"

8

2

I hadn't always hated Will.
When I'd first met him, my second day of work at Siren Music Records, I'd stupidly wanted to be his friend.

I walked into a meeting a few minutes early and quietly took a seat at the far end of the long conference table, feeling more than a little unsure about my place. I heard a roar of laughter, and I turned toward the sound at the front of the room and noticed how everyone was looking at one man who towered a bit over everyone. He had his black hair cut short, nearly a buzz cut, and his bright white teeth seemed to twinkle off the overhead lights as he smiled.

It was obvious that he was the center of his group's orbit. The way they were all angled toward him, leaning in like they wanted to hear more of what he had to say. I stared at him and felt strangely entranced, too. For the first time, I wanted to willingly try my hand at short talk. With him, I had the feeling small talk wouldn't be dreadful at all. There was something about the light in his eyes when he talked to them; he wasn't just saying things to fill the silence or to gain attention. I could tell that he genuinely enjoyed talking with them and wanted to hear what they had to say. Which, as a rule, went against everything that I believed about small talk and why I found it so useless.

Samantha, a new assistant who had started with me yesterday, walked in, and she froze at the entrance of the door, looking uncertainly around the room. I was debating on whether I should call out her name when Will smiled brightly at her and waved her over to join him and his colleagues. She stared at him with wide eyes as he introduced himself and the rest of his colleagues to her, and within minutes, she was smiling, shoulders relaxed, and she looked like she belonged at this company, just like the rest of them.

Watching the way he interacted with them all, I got the feeling that he was someone who went out of his way to be kind to everyone. I sat there for a few more minutes, arguing silently with myself on why I should get up and try to make friends at work even though every other part of me felt very much out of my element and would rather start setting up my notebook for notes on the meeting.

I kept to myself—always. I'd gone through all of high school and most of college without interacting with classmates unless I had to. I had my goals, and I didn't want or need people walking in and out of my life to distract me from it. At previous jobs, I'd been commended for my dedication and focus, but I knew from the many complaints—whoops, I meant, "concerns"—of my family members, that it was also one of my faults too. Outside of family, I didn't really have any friends. I had people I got along with from previous classes but no one who really knew me.

Remembering my promise to try more, to make roots at this job and build connections, I slowly rolled my chair back and stood up. I pulled my shoulders back confidently, readjusted my gray skirt, pressed down on my white button-down shirt, and strode over to their group. But when I went over to introduce myself, Will didn't wave or make me feel welcome in the group. No, instead, he stared at me with an incredulous look, smile slowly leaving his face as he looked at me like he had no idea where I'd come from. I stood there, feeling like an idiot, and quickly introduced myself to the other people in the group, who all gave me plain smiles and nods. Even Samantha, the traitor, looked at me like she didn't want to associate with the girl who'd ruined their fun vibe.

Thankfully, Clements barked my name across the room, and I had a reason to quickly leave.

Ever since that first meeting, I got the distinct feeling that Will went out of his way to ignore me. He wouldn't look at me if I talked or walked into a room, and the rare times he did look at me, he'd stare with something that almost looked like frustration or anger in his eyes. I was confused and more than a little hurt by his obvious dismissal of me. I didn't know how I could've been so wrong about one person. Even though I didn't have many friends, I'd always thought I had an excellent judge of character. Clearly, I'd judged him entirely wrong.

After about a month at the job, I'd gotten no closer to making any friends at work and resigned myself to just focusing on impressing my boss and trying to form connections with people who could potentially help me in the future with my career.

On one particular day, I'd been walking quickly down a hall of conference rooms when I heard someone mention my name from a room that had the door opened a crack. Unable to help myself, I'd stopped and peeked into the room, seeing a few guys from the team sitting together and eating lunch in the conference room. Among them was Will.

"I don't know what possessed him to hire her as his assistant," Will commented, wiping his hands on a napkin. He looked bored with the conversation, glancing at his watch every few seconds, like he had somewhere else he'd rather be.

"The girl is like a robot," Gregg, one of the accountants on the team, said with a laugh. "I don't even think I've ever seen her eat. She just runs around all day, like she's got a match lit under her ass, and she only talks about work."

"Fuck, but what a fine ass she's got," another guy said, licking his lips, and the other guys laughed.

Will, I noticed, didn't join in on their laughter and pressed his lips into a thin, hard line.

"Who cares what she looks like?" Will said abruptly. "She should've never been hired in that department to begin with."

I moved away from the door, anger coursing through me. What an asshole. What had I ever done to him for him to dismiss me so quickly, other than try to be his friend?

And that other jackhole, Gregg. I'd been helping him finish up collecting some data for his quarterly charts this week even though I didn't need to, and it made me have to stay an extra hour later to catch up on my own work. But he'd been nice, and I'd stupidly thought maybe I'd have someone to at least wave to in meetings instead of sitting by myself like the loser who got picked last in gym. Strike two for me and my horrible attempts at making friends. This was why I didn't bother trying.

I heard them start laughing again in the room, chairs rolling back on the hardwood floor, and I quickly walked away, blinking away angry tears. Because that was what they were. Anger at stupid men who clearly thought the only thing good about me was my body and not the hard work I'd been doing these last few weeks. I might not have been perfect at my job, but I was trying, and I was dedicated to proving my worth to my colleagues. I didn't know why I was surprised by their conversation. Men were just one degree away from farm pigs most days, and no amount of education could change that.

Ever since that day, I'd stopped trying to make friends with people on my team. And I especially didn't try with Will. When I saw him, I didn't make an effort to hide my dislike of him. If I had to talk to him, I made sure my words were professional even if my tone wasn't. Nearly two years later, and we'd been forced to interact with each other nearly every day, but our interactions stayed the same. Restrained dislike, sarcasm, and silent, tense conversations that never seemed to end.

I glanced toward the coffee shop's big storefront windows, shaking myself away from all thoughts of Will and the past. He already haunted me at work. I didn't need him to take up more space in my brain when I hadn't even walked through the doors at work yet.

A moment later, the bells of the coffee shop rang as the door opened, and I smiled as Cora rushed in, looking feverish. Her light-brown skin was slightly red from the December cold, and she shook snow off her boots as she walk-hopped toward me.

"I'm so sorry I'm late," she rushed out, hands reaching toward me. Not for me, but for the extra-large black coffee that I'd already bought for her.

I handed it to her, and she reverently held the cup in her hand, pulling it toward her nose as she took a sniff, exhaling happily.

"My God, you are such an addict," I said fondly, eyes softening as I watched her excitedly gulp her coffee.

Cora had been my third and last attempt at making a friend at work, though I hadn't been the one to initiate the friendship at first.

She found me outside the office building, desperately trying to pick up the stack of papers I'd dropped as they blew everywhere. Without a single pause, she began chasing the flying papers with me and didn't stop until we collected every last one. I thanked her profusely as I secured them back in my bag, exhaustion no doubt written all over my face.

She just smiled and introduced herself. "You look like you're having a bad day. Let me get you a coffee."

And even though I'd already resigned myself to being on my own, I went anyway.

And the rest, as they say, was history.

Cora wasn't the type of person who walked into your life and disappeared. From that very first day, she'd been tenacious in her quest to being my friend. When she'd said she wanted to be friends, she'd meant it. She'd shared her favorite coffee shop with me—this small little store on the corner, called Tom's Drink and Shop, a few blocks from our job—and said that we should start every morning with coffee together. We swapped numbers and proceeded to chat as if we'd known each other forever, and without me even thinking about it, I'd begun to look forward to work. Nearly every day before work, we'd meet at the coffee shop, get coffee together, and talk about everything and nothing as we walked to work.

And I loved it.

"Okay, now that I've gotten my coffee, let's talk about work," Cora said, tugging me toward the exit.

"You couldn't possibly mean the holiday party, could you?" I asked with a dramatic gasp. "The very one we've talked about nearly every day for the past three weeks?"

"Yep," she answered happily, grinning wide.

Cora was sunshine in a bottle, the optimism to my pessimism.

The moment we stepped outside the coffee shop, a strong gust of wind smacked into our faces, blowing our hair everywhere. *Carajo,* there was nothing worse than a New York winter. It was too damn cold in this state, and no matter how many years you'd lived here, you never got used to the cold after the warm summers.

"All I know is, if I'm going to this thing, you'd better not abandon me," I warned, pulling my scarf tighter against my neck. "The last thing I want is some drunk douche in the HR department trying to hit on me again."

Cora winced slightly but nodded. "Oh! How long do you think it'll take Mr. Sandston to get drunk and start promising promotions to everyone?"

I laughed, remembering the drunk older man from payroll who'd been so drunk that he gave us all a speech on how we deserved a raise and he'd make it happen even if he had to forge the CEO's name on the checks himself. It'd been a nice thought, but the executives had not been amused and quickly had Mr. Sandston packed away in a cab.

"If they have the top-shelf tequila again, I give him less than an hour."

The holiday party wasn't technically mandatory, but it was certainly encouraged that employees attended. This year, they were making a big deal about their theme, Ugly Christmas Sweaters, and promised there'd be plenty of fun games and prizes to be won at the party as well as a big announcement they would be sharing for the first time with us. Last year's party had turned out to be a lot more fun than I'd thought, but that might also have to do with the all the food and drinks I'd consumed on that day. Nothing persuaded me to do something I didn't want to do more than food.

"All I'm saying is," Cora began as we walked to one of the front glass doors to our work building, "we have to win at least one of the prizes. I heard they're giving out top-of-the-line equipment across the board. Electronics, kitchen supplies, even music equipment."

That piqued my interest. As a hopeful music producer—on a budget—I was always on the lookout for affordable equipment. One of my bass synthesizers had started acting wonky lately—not to mention, the mics could use an upgrade. Even though work kept me insanely busy most days, I still spent most nights working on my music. Creating new sounds, working on lyrics to accompany a melody that had been playing in my head all day at work. It was the one time during the day where I felt truly comfortable and happy. When I had my headphones on and was sitting in front of my equipment, nothing could touch me.

"Okay, so win the contest and get free food." I listed out our game plan.

"And free drinks!" Cora added with a fist in the air.

I shook my head, amused as she practically skipped to the turnstiles and began singing "It's Beginning to Look a Lot Like Christmas." The security guards stared blankly at her despite her infectious smile, but when she pulled a box of cookies out of her bag and held it open to one of them, he smiled softly in thanks and took it.

Cora brightened and shouted, "I love Christmas time!"

We still had the whole workday to get through, and she was already starting with her impassioned declarations.

This was going to be a long day.

3

The holiday party was in full swing.

Everyone was wearing their ugly Christmas sweaters that ranged from kind of cute to truly hideous and should be burned immediately. I had on a green-and-red Baby Yoda ugly Christmas sweater that had been getting compliments all day. To the surprise of no one, most people had heard of Star Wars. Or at the very least, thought Baby Yoda was the most adorable thing they'd ever seen. Cora, on the other hand, had on one of the ugliest sweater's I'd ever seen. It was white as snow and had all sorts of Christmas decorations stitched onto it—tree ornaments, little golden bells—but the worst was the big Santa head with a long beard made of white string that she had stitched smack-dab in the middle of the sweater. The thing was creepy as hell with its beady black eyes, but Cora was in love with her sweater. Said she'd made it herself and wanted to do this every year.

I was already planning out the intervention for next Christmas.

"Cora, come on," I said, trying hard not to whine. "We've been saying hello to a bunch of people for the last thirty minutes. I want to eat! There's a buffet, and it smells so good. Let's go grab some food and find a table to sit down."

The venue that the company had rented out was only a few short blocks from our work building, so most people had walked over after work. The place was one open floor, big enough that one hundred fifty people could be walking around and you didn't feel like you were stuck on a rush-hour subway car. From top to bottom, the place was decorated like a Christmas wonderland. An enormous white Christmas tree with so many decorations on it that it must've taken them hours to put it together sat at the back of the venue by the small stage. There were tables organized all along the walls of the floor. Most looked like they were stations that were set up for Christmas games, but I saw a few that looked like they were information booths on different departments of the company. Music was playing softly from the speakers above as people conversed and seemed to be truly enjoying themselves. The one nice thing about these parties was that you saw people from all departments really interacting with each other. There were no mean-girl cliques at these parties, not when alcohol helped loosen everyone up.

Cora fixed one of her ornaments that had been lying sideways on her sweater. "Okay, fine. I think I've tortured you for long enough."

I sighed in relief, and with my arm locked with hers, I began to speed-walk toward the buffet on the other side of the room. The setup was insane. It looked like one of those all-you-can-eat buffet tables that just never ended. And the closer we got to it, the stronger the smell of the food became until I could hear my stomach grumbling over the music.

"I think I'm in heaven," I sighed, eagerly grabbing a plate from the end of the table.

I immediately began filling my plate with food as I walked around the buffet. Chicken wings, mac and cheese, wraps, rice—there wasn't a single thing on this table that I didn't want on my plate. I just hoped the food tasted as good as it looked. You never knew if a person believed in seasoning their food or not, but I was so hungry that it could taste like a dirty concrete floor and I'd probably still think it was the best thing.

My plate was heavy by the time I made it to the desserts section of the table. I nearly groaned when I saw the wide selections of cookies and cakes. Cookies and cream cupcakes; five different flavors of cookies, ranging from chocolate chip to snickerdoodle and even an ice cream station. How was I supposed to pick just one?

I looked at my completely full plate that had a small tower of food, and with a mumbled, "Fuck it," I reached out for the throng in a nearby cookie bin. But right when I went to pick it up, another hand snuck in and grabbed it at the same time as me, our hands colliding.

"I'm sorry," I said with a laugh, turning to look at the person next to me. My smile dropped when I saw who it was. "Oh."

Will towered over me, wearing a bright red-and-green Christmas sweater that had a strange-looking elf on it with the words *I'm Dreaming of a Dwight Christmas* above it in big white letters. How this man made an ugly Christmas sweater look sexy was beyond me.

His face gave nothing away, as usual, as he quirked an eyebrow, staring pointedly at my feet, and replied, "You look … comfortable."

I'd worn heels to work but switched out of them for the party in favor of my favorite black slip-on shoes. Today was the last day before our very short Christmas vacation, where we'd get a four-day weekend, and I'd already decided that come the New Year, I'd move on from this stupid plan. I wanted to end it now, but I couldn't after our conversation. I didn't want Will to think he'd had any sway in what I did or chose to wear.

Even though he clearly does? a voice in my head said, but I swatted it away.

Shut up, stupid subconscious.

"What is your sweater supposed to be?" I asked instead, amused. "An off-Broadway version of *Elf?* You'd think they're paying you enough to afford the real sweater. Your namesake would be so disappointed in you."

His mouth opened, and he blinked. "You've never seen *The Office*?"

I narrowed my eyes, staring between his face and his sweater. "I've heard of it."

"But you've never seen it," he commented in that smooth, deep voice that made me want to strangle him. It was his *why am I not surprised* tone, and it drove me crazy.

"Sorry I don't watch overhyped crap on TV," I replied sarcastically.

"You're wearing a Star Wars sweater," he responded dryly with a pointed look.

"Ugh!" I groaned loudly. "Why am I even *talking* to you?" I turned back around, snatched the tongs from the bin, and quickly put two snickerdoodle cookies on my plate.

"Here," he said, handing me another plate. When I continued to stare at him suspiciously, he sighed and said, "Your plate looks like it's seconds away from snapping in half. Put this one underneath to help balance out the weight of all the food."

"I don't need your help," I grumbled stubbornly but took the plate anyway. Because, fine, maybe he was right.

I juggled with trying to place the empty plate beneath my tower of food without dropping it all, and a moment later, I heard Will's mumbled, "Stubborn girl," before my heavy plate was lifted entirely from my hands.

I stared up at him with wide eyes, mouth opened and ready to demand my food back when he shifted the plate to one hand, and with his other hand, he gently maneuvered my hands till I had the empty plate lying flat on my open palms. I was so shocked by the almost serene concentration on his face and the way my heart had kick-started into fast drive at the brush of his fingers that I didn't even fight him. His eyebrows sort of scrunched together, like he was thinking about something hard as he maneuvered my hands onto the plate, and I hated that I wanted to know what he was thinking. A moment later, he pulled away, and my eyes jerked away from his hands to his face, but he was an impassive wall of stone once more.

"Get ready," he murmured. A second later, he carefully placed my plate of food in my waiting hands.

I gripped the plate in my hand tightly, mouth opening and closing silently.

He must be drunk, I thought to myself with a shake of my head. Or maybe I was drunk and had made this entire interaction up in my head.

"You ready?" Cora said, walking up to my side. She looked up at Will and smiled hesitantly. "Hey, Will."

He nodded, dark eyes not leaving mine. "You're welcome."

I felt my face get hot, and I thanked God for the millionth time that my light-brown skin would protect me from looking like a flaming tomato. "Technically, I never asked for your help."

He shook his head with a sigh and turned to Cora. "Make sure she doesn't make herself sick with all that food."

I scowled. "I'll be fine."

"Where's your plate, Will?" Cora asked with a small frown.

I looked down and noticed for the first time that he didn't have a plate. Had he given me his? But what was he doing at the end of the buffet with an empty plate?

"I ate already," he replied shortly. He glanced at his watch before jerking his head in a tight nod. "Enjoy the party."

"You too!" Cora said brightly. "And thanks for having my back in today's meeting with Harrison. I swear he only questions *my* slides whenever we present."

He gave her another tight nod and looked toward me. I pointedly ignored him, turning my head to look back at the buffet. After a long moment, I watched from the corner of my eye as he turned stiffly and walked away. I frowned before shaking my head and looking away from his retreating form.

"Let's go eat," I said and began walking in the opposite direction.

"I'm surprised the entire buffet table wasn't overturned with the two of you over there," Cora commented lightly.

I rolled my eyes. "Trust me, five more minutes in his presence, and it would've been. I don't know how you work with him every single day without wanting to pull your hair out."

"He's actually really nice," Cora responded, placing her plate on an empty table not too far from an exit that looked like it led to the restrooms. "I keep telling you I don't think he hates you. The way he stares—"

"Nope," I cut her off. "Not everyone is meant to be friends. And Will has made it very clear that he does not want to be friends with me."

Cora sighed heavily but didn't argue. We both dug into our plates, and Cora switched the conversation over to the many activities they had stationed and what prizes—I meant, "presents"—were available.

"I think I want to play Conversation Bingo," Cora said, pointing to the sheet we'd gotten when we first walked in.

There were times and games listed out so that you had an opportunity to pick and choose which activities you wanted to participate in.

They had games like Santa Limbo, Stocking Guessing Game, and even board games, like bingo. I had a few that I wanted to check out, but Conversation Bingo was definitely not one of them.

"You might be on your own with that one," I said, taking another bite of the mac and cheese on my plate. It wasn't the best I'd ever had, but it certainly wasn't the worst.

"I saw a Keurig coffeemaker at that table," Cora said, tapping her finger on the paper. "There's no way I'm not going home with that baby."

"I might try out the stocking game while you do that." I bit into a cookie and nearly moaned out loud at the taste. I was starting to feel really full, but there was no way I wasn't going to eat these cookies. My mind suddenly remembered Cora's words from earlier. "Hey, what happened in your meeting today? The one you thanked Will about?"

Cora sighed. "We had a meeting with Harrison, our Assistant Director, and he tried to criticize my slides during the presentation."

I narrowed my eyes. "What do you mean?"

"He said he wasn't sure that he believed my information was accurate and then asked if I had anyone look over it," she answered with a shrug. "Will stood up for me, said that I was one of the best on the team and that my numbers were always accurate. Harrison didn't really like that, but he never argues with the guys, so he let it go."

"What a sexist dick," I grumbled. "I hate that you have to deal with that kind of crap! Why are so many men intimidated by a beautiful, intelligent woman?"

"Probably because they think we can't be beautiful and not an airhead," Cora said jokingly. I didn't smile, and she reached over and gently squeezed my forearm. "Honestly, Genesis, it's fine. I'm used to it."

"That doesn't make it okay," I argued, putting my hand on top of hers. "I hate the sexist men at this job. Let's kill them all."

"Meh. They're not worth the prison time," Cora said with a wink, and I begrudgingly smiled.

We spent a little while longer sitting at the table, chatting and people-watching as Michael Bublé's *Christmas* album played in the background. At one point, I got up to get us drinks and then got sucked into three different conversations about the season finale of *The Mandalorian*. But these were conversations I didn't mind getting sucked into because I could talk about Star Wars and *The Mandalorian* all day, every day. I was a Star Wars fangirl through and through.

An announcement went off about the start of the Christmas games a few minutes into my conversation with Jerry from legal affairs, and with a quick apology, I rushed back to the table and to Cora.

"You'll meet me at the Winter Kisses table in an hour, right?" I confirmed, taking another sip of my drink.

She nodded, eyes roaming the room as she was no doubt already thinking about her prized gift. "Yeah, I'll see you then."

We went our separate ways, and I made my way to the first game, the Stocking Guessing Game. There were a bunch of people there, everyone laughing and in excited moods as they listened to the woman in front of the table explain the rules. I had more fun watching other people try and guess what were in the stockings than actually playing the game. I didn't guess correctly, but the girl who did was so excited that I couldn't help but feel excited for her too. Afterward, I made my way around a few more tables, mostly watching other people play and talking about the game with a few people who seemed nice.

I was feeling pretty good when I made it back to the Winter Kisses table an hour later, Cora already waiting. She was holding her coffeemaker with a wide grin, and I clapped for her.

"Wow, you actually won," I said, impressed.

"Of course I did," she answered confidently. "I said I would, and once I put my mind to something, there's no stopping me."

I smirked. "Okay, well, put your mind to winning this game because they're supposed to be giving away a new synthesizer."

"Got it," she said with a nod.

"Hello, everyone. Welcome to Winter Kisses!" a man announced loudly. "My name is Chris, and I'll be leading this game. Okay, to start, I need everyone to get into teams. I've already made four teams of four based on who signed up. When you hear your name, please raise your hand."

He began to call out names, and my eyes widened a moment later when I realized Cora had gotten called for team two and I hadn't.

"Don't worry," she said smoothly. "It's better this way. That means two possibilities of winning."

I nodded, and with another smile, she raised her hand and made her way to the front. Of course, I was in the last team, and Chris ushered the remaining people over to an empty table that had a basket filled with mittens in the middle. I looked over at the other tables, trying to see if I saw any familiar faces. I saw one guy from the social media department that came to meetings occasionally in group three, but most everyone else seemed to be from different floors of the company. Must be higher-ups. I turned back around and nearly groaned out loud when I saw Will shaking hands with one of the guys at my table, hand on the chair next to me.

"Are you following me or something?" I sighed tiredly as I watched Will take a seat at the table.

The other members of the team looked between us with raised brows, and I quickly threw them a forced smile.

"I didn't plan this," was his only reply, pulling a pair of black leather gloves from the center of the table. He began to methodically put one glove on at a time, his long fingers yanking at the material until I thought for sure that it would rip at the seams.

I eyed his hands one last time before grabbing my own pair and putting them on. "Don't mess this up for the rest of us."

"I'll try my best," he said, looking surprisingly serious.

A moment later, his mouth tilted on one side in amusement. My eyes traced that smile of their own accord, and I noticed with a small jolt of surprise that his lips looked incredibly soft and masculine. Like they could hurt and soothe you, depending on the pressure he applied when he kissed you. I shook the thought off quickly, nose wrinkling in disgust.

Dios, the alcohol must be hitting me harder than I'd thought.

His lips tipped higher, a small chuckle leaving his mouth, and my eyes finally shot back to his. Smug male satisfaction was written all over his face. "Try not to let my good looks ruin your concentration, Buttercup."

I scowled at the new nickname, face turning hot. "You could never. And don't call me Buttercup."

"Okay, attention, everyone!" Chris, the moderator, shouted. "When I say go, the first person may begin to unwrap their chocolate candy. Remember that you only have three minutes, and then you have to pass to the person on your right after you've had your turn. Most of all, have fun!"

People cheered, and I focused on the bowl that was sitting in front of the one other woman on my team. I glanced at her name tag; it read *Debra, Human Resources*. She looked buzzed, eyes bright as she made a joke about starting us off strong, and I had a bad feeling we weren't going to be starting off strong at all.

"Three … two … one. Go!"

"Go, Debra!" I cheered, clapping in my green mittens.

Everyone began laughing as she tried to unwrap the Hershey's Kiss with her mitten-covered hands, only to have it keep falling onto the table. It took her more time than I would've wanted, but she finally got it unwrapped with an excited scream and pushed the bowl to the person on her right. Will.

He picked up the wrapped Kiss in the bowl and began slowly trying to peel it from the top. His tongue peeked out of his lip as he tried to pull the top string down, only for the entire chocolate to fall onto the table and roll onto the ground.

"One more minute!" Chris shouted, waving his phone in the air.

"You're going to make us lose!" I growled, frustrated.

I was too competitive to play team games and having Will on my team erased just about all my sportsmanship. I was on the edge of my seat, leg bouncing as my eyes moved from his fingers to Chris with the stopwatch.

"Such words of encouragement," he admonished in his deep voice. He looked up at me, the corner of his mouth slowly tilting up into a smirk. "Perhaps I could do this better if I heard you cheer for me the way you did Debra."

"Stop looking at me and focus on the game!" I nearly screeched. "Go! Go! Go!"

His smirk tugged higher on his face, like he was seconds from laughing out loud. He peeled off the wrapper with quick fingers and tossed the Kiss into one bowl, passing me the other bowl. "Good luck."

I quickly picked up a Hershey's Kiss and began trying to peel the wrapper off. The stupid thing immediately fell out of my hand, and I had to bite down on my tongue to hold in my scream of frustration.

I had just picked it up from the table when Chris shouted, "Time! Everyone, please put your hands down. I will come around to do the tally."

I tossed my gloves into the basket, sighing heavily. There was no way we won this game. My only hope was that Cora's team had better luck than me.

I stared down at the white table, glaring so hard that I was surprised I didn't burn a hole through the damn thing, especially when Chris took our tally and mumbled, "So close."

"Okay, and our winners are …" Chris did a little drumroll on his table that everyone quickly followed along to. Well, not everyone. Not me. "Team number three with three Hershey's Kisses unwrapped!"

Everyone clapped, and I joined in as table three whooped and cheered, high-fiving each other. Chris went on to explain that everyone got a free pair of mittens for playing, and team three could meet him at the front of the booth to claim their prizes.

"Good game, everyone," Will said smoothly, scooting his chair back.

Everyone began talking to each other as they slowly got up from their chairs.

I picked my mittens back up from the basket and shoved them in my pants pocket. I turned to leave when I felt a hand lightly touch my elbow. I didn't have to turn around to know who was bothering me. Two conversations in one night? We had gone eighteen months not standing six feet near each other if we could help it, and suddenly, he had a lot to say at a stupid Christmas Party.

"I'm not in the mood, Will."

Will crossed his arms across his broad chest, eyebrows raised. "The game was supposed to be fun."

I gave him a forced smile. "It was."

"So then, why do you look so miserable?"

"I always look this way when I'm around you," I said flatly. The game was fun, but I'd been too invested. Once you'd been presented with the idea of having something better, you couldn't help but feel slighted when it was yanked away from you. I wasn't typically such a sore loser, but losing in front of Will was making my cranky meter go haywire.

I shook my head, trying to pull myself out of my pity party. It wasn't a big deal. I'd been saving for a few months anyway; I'd just have to be more tenacious about saving if I wanted to replace it that badly.

Good-bye, lunch dates with Cora.

His gaze sharpened. "What was that?"

I shook my head, not realizing I had said that last bit out loud. "Nothing. Forget it."

It was time to stop drinking and to stay far away from anyone who wasn't Cora until this party was over. I turned away, looking for her, trying my best to ignore the presence of the man standing next to me. I inhaled, smelling a hint of his cologne and hating that a part of me wanted to lean closer to distinguish the scent.

"Genesis …"

I ran my fingers through my thick dark-brown hair, feeling the long strands land against my shoulder blades as I backed away from him. "I liked it better when we didn't talk to each other unless we had to. Let's keep doing that."

I caught sight of Cora's horrendous sweater and quickly walked away. I reached her side when I heard the music turn off, followed by someone tapping into a mic.

"Testing, testing," someone said over the speakers. The man laughed loudly, causing more than a few people to wince as the audio feedback made a high-pitched sound.

I glanced toward the front of the room and saw two men standing on the stage, one in a suit and one in blue jeans and a sweater. The man in the Christmas sweater and jeans was holding the mic, long, thin gray hair to his shoulders, and I realized with a start that I knew exactly who that was.

"It's Steve Pratt," I whispered urgently to Cora.

She craned her neck, standing on her tiptoes to try and see the stage. I gently maneuvered her to my left, and she smiled in thanks before redirecting her gaze back toward the stage.

Her eyes widened. "That's not just the owner. The CEO is with him too."

I eyed the man in the suit. He had such a severe face, all hard lines and sharp cuts. It was one you didn't forget, like when you saw a da Vinci sculpture for the first time. I'd only seen him a handful of times from far away since I'd started working at this company, but from everything I'd heard about him, he was not a man you wanted to mess with.

"We wanted to take a moment to thank all of you for coming tonight and celebrating with Siren Music Records," Steve said, big smile on his face.

Everyone began clapping and cheering, and he put his hand in the air, nodding cheerfully.

"As you might know, I am Steve Pratt, owner and founder of the company. Beside me, I have my right-hand man, Jameson Harris, who works above and beyond at the head of the company as our CEO."

People once again began clapping, though I noticed that Jameson Harris didn't smile. He just nodded, all business.

"Damn, I'd like to climb that man," a girl standing in front of us said, fanning her face.

Cora and I shared a look, and Cora began quietly giggling. I bit my lip to hold in my laugh, taking another glance at the man in question. Steve Pratt wasn't in bad shape for his age. With his relaxed personality and seemingly inexpensive clothing, he had the whole *yes, I make more money in one day than you make in a year, but I'm just like you* look going for him. But I somehow doubted that was who the girl was talking about. Not when the CEO was standing up front, looking like a reformed mountain man. He looked like he couldn't have been older than mid- to late-thirties with a tall stature that even from here, I could tell wasn't within the average height for anyone. He had a close-shaven beard and light-brown hair that was probably the only part of him that gave any hint into him not being a robot. His hair was thick, the wavy strands the most unkempt thing on a man who looked like he had been carved into a statue.

"As you know, each year, Siren Music Records releases an album as part of our Music for the Cure project. This year, we are hoping to bring awareness to lupus disease, and a portion of our profits made will go to the Lupus Foundation of America," said Steve, pausing to let everyone clap before he continued. "This year, we are going to do things a little bit differently. Every year, this album features songs from our top-selling artists, who all come together to tour for three months across America. For the first time ever, we are leaving one track open for an undiscovered artist, perhaps maybe even an undiscovered artist who has been sitting in our laps this whole time and we didn't even know it."

He had a wide, cheeky grin on his face, and more than a few people started talking quietly, trying to figure out what he was saying exactly. I looked at Cora, brows bunched as I recalled his words.

Was he saying he was open to signing a new artist? Did we have to find the artist?

"There will be a contest," Jameson spoke into the mic, voice a deep rumble. "We will be offering employees the opportunity to submit a demo of their song that they feel should be the last track on the album. One song will be chosen, and that person will be asked to join the concert in the summer."

"Yes, but this isn't open just to singers. We want any hopeful music creators of any kind to enter as well!" Steve announced loudly. "Two musically inclined individuals will be paired together to make a song that you will submit to the company in three months. The producer will be credited on the album and could potentially even get a contract to work in one of our studios."

"That is something that will be determined based on many criteria. One of which will be your standing with the company," Jameson added, a stern look on his face as he spoke to the crowd. "Anyone who enters the contest is expected to continue giving work their one hundred percent focus and hard work. On top of personally going through each of the submissions, I will be checking in with your supervisors and looking over yearly evaluations. It does not matter if we like your demo. If you are found to be slacking at work, even something as trivial as being late too many times, you will be disqualified."

"Yes, yes, all true," Steve agreed with a wave of his hand. "However, we will also be giving each team two hours in the studio each month. Time slots will be appointed when we announce the teams. I've got to admit, I'm very excited to see what everyone comes up with. This feels very CBS *Survivor*, doesn't it, Jameson?"

Jameson stared at him with the look of someone asking for patience after a very long day.

I turned to Cora, squeezing her hand in mine. This was … huge! I couldn't believe the company was really giving their employees the chance to have a song on one of their highest-selling albums of the year!

"You have to enter!" Cora practically screamed, bouncing on her toes. "You have so many beautiful songs. There's no way you wouldn't win!"

My heart was beating hard in my chest, and I felt like my mind was racing a mile a minute. The cautious side of me wanted to remain realistic, to look at all the rules and variables, but it was no match for the desperately excited side that felt like the dream that had been floating away these last few years was finally within reaching distance once again. I couldn't contain the electrified smile that spread across my face.

"This is my chance, Cora. If I can get my name credited on that last song, I could get a job in the studio!" I exclaimed, unable to contain my excitement. My cheeks were pulled wide in a smile as I continued, "I could finally produce in a real studio and not in the corner of my room with my shitty equipment, making songs no one would ever hear."

"Hey, I love your music!" Cora protested, hazel eyes bright on mine. "I can't wait to hear someone singing one of your songs. Will you remember me when you're famous?"

I laughed, pulling her into a hug. "I'll make a room in my mansion just for you."

Steve and Jameson explained more details about the contest—that the sign-up would go out after the Christmas break on Monday and we'd hear back about teams sometime in January. I listened halfheartedly, the sound of my heart racing in my ears drowning them out as my mind focused on only one thought.

I'm going to do it. I'm going to win that contract. Good-bye, office job. Hello, dream job.

4

A fter last night's announcement at the Christmas party, I
was a bundle of energy. I'd barely slept more than four
hours last night, spending half the night going through song
ideas I'd written down in my music journal or half-finished
melodies that I had recorded with my equipment and never put
words to. I had plenty of songs that I'd made throughout the
years, but I had a feeling that whoever I worked with for the
contest, we weren't going to be able to use them. From what
they'd said at the party, we would probably have to start from
scratch. Besides, those songs were way too personal to just be
sung by anyone.

I had no idea who I'd be working with, but in most cases,
music partnerships worked better when it was collaborative.
Every artist was different. Some would tell you a certain feeling
they wanted to convey; some had fully fleshed-out ideas or
even lyrics. Sometimes, you really had no idea what you wanted
to make, and you'd have to spend hours just to figure out what
your music wanted to say, what part of yourself it would pull
out of you.

I was excited to start something new, to see what song would come out when it was just me and the music. I was nervous too because I needed this to be the best song they'd ever heard. I needed it to stand out above all the other demos, but I also knew that I couldn't start doubting myself now, or I'd be a mess before they even opened the applications.

Today was Christmas Eve, also known as *Nochebuena*, and for my family, it was the day we gathered for celebrations. Most of my family members lived in New York with some scattered in the nearby states, so we saw each other pretty frequently— too frequently in my opinion. Even my family members who lived in Dominican Republic, like my mom, made it a habit to come up a few times a year, and if they couldn't come to visit, they would be FaceTimed into nearly every gathering.

Truthfully, my family didn't need an excuse to get everyone together and have a party. One time, we'd had a party because one of my uncles got a new TV. It wasn't even anything fancy. He'd just upgraded from a thirty-two inch to a forty-inch, but everyone went over and had to see it. The next thing I had known, there had been a full-blown party happening in his backyard that didn't end until after three a.m. when two of my cousins got into a fight that somehow resulted in a broken table.

Even though my family drove me crazy with how loud and nosy they were—we didn't call my *tías* the Dominican gossip girls for no reason—I couldn't imagine spending the holidays with anyone else.

"*¡Que bonita!*" Tía Louisa smothered me with kisses, hugging me close at the front door. "*Y tu hermana?*"

"She should be here soon," I replied in Spanish.

My sister had left the house before me to exchange gifts with a friend and said she would meet me outside Tía Louisa's house, but unsurprisingly, she was running a few minutes late.

Tía Louisa took my jacket from me and hung it on one of the hooks by the door. She tried to take the bags of presents from me, but I held on with a shake of my head.

She sighed and asked, "Can I get you a glass of water?"

"Please, Tía, I know you've been running around all morning," I said with a soft smile. "Come sit. I'll get you a glass of water."

"¡*Agua*!" Tía Louisa laughed loudly. "*Niña*, you know better than that. It's a time to celebrate! Bring out the good drinks, hmm?"

I laughed and ushered her into the living room with the rest of the family. It took me about ten more minutes to make my rounds around the room and say hello to all the family before I was able to walk down the hall toward the kitchen.

Tía Louisa had a nice two-bedroom apartment in East Harlem, also known as *El Barrio*. It wasn't anything fancy, but it had a big enough living room that we often had get-togethers at her place. Today, she had the place decorated top to bottom in Christmas decorations. There were also, at minimum, fifteen baby Jesus statues in the living room alone, and every square inch of the walls was covered in family photos.

I entered the kitchen to find my mother and one of my tías chopping away at some vegetables and messing around with the stove. My father had three sisters and two brothers—not to mention, the many tías that weren't my aunts by blood or marriage, but because they were close friends of the family. My mom had only one sister who lived in New Jersey, and both her parents still lived in Dominican Republic and did not have visas, so we didn't see them quite as often as we did my father's family. My paternal grandma was practically a surrogate mother to my mom, and even after my father had died, everyone still treated my mom like she was a part of the family.

"Dinner's almost ready, *mija*," my mother said, smiling.

She was as beautiful as ever. Her dark brown hair up in a fancy bun that probably had more pins in it than I did articles of clothing on. Her light-brown skin was shining in the hot kitchen, and even though I knew she had to be sweating, her makeup was perfectly intact.

I hadn't seen my mom in nearly six months since she'd had to cancel her plane ticket to come visit in August because her mom had gotten sick. She was only staying for a few days until she went back to the DR, where she'd been living for nearly a year now.

I missed being able to see her all the time, but she was happy there in a way she hadn't been in a while. She'd left the apartment for Alejandra and me, but we kept things exactly the same. If she was happy, then I was happy.

"Tía Louisa is trying to get drunk again," I said in answer, walking over to give her and my aunts a kiss.

"Make sure she doesn't drink too much. We're going to the Midnight Mass tonight," my mom reminded me, half-listening as she listened to Tía Irena's story about some doctor's appointment.

Tía Louisa tended to forget where she was when she got drunk, and after last Christmas's debacle, it wasn't a bad idea to have someone looking out for her.

Every year, no matter whose house Christmas Eve dinner was at, we always ended the night by going to Midnight Mass at the closest church. Growing up, it was always weird, having to explain to people that I celebrated Christmas on the 24th and not the 25th, like everyone else. For my family, December 25 was a regular day, where you just lay around, ate leftovers, and relaxed at home.

"Do you guys need help in here?" I asked, starting to roll up my sleeves on my red sweater dress. "I don't mind—"

"No, no," my mother said, shooing me. "Go out there and spend time with *la familia*. And find out where Alejandra is."

"I'm here, *Máma*," Alejandra shouted, breezing into the kitchen with her boyfriend, James. Her brown skin was red from the cold outside, but as always, Alejandra looked beautiful. "I'm sorry we're late. The trains weren't working, *tú sabes*."

Alejandra and James walked around the small kitchen, giving hugs and kisses to everyone before finally making it back to where I stood. Somewhere between entering the kitchen and making their way back to the kitchen entrance, both Alejandra and James had taken off their coats. Which meant I could see their matching sweaters. Alejandra's was more like a sweater dress since it went up to her mid-thigh, but she wore leggings underneath with cute boots that really made it work. My sister was tall—five-ten—and all legs with a slim build. In terms of looks, we didn't have many similarities. I was barely five-six, and while we shared a membership in the itty-bitty titty committee, my hips and ass weren't exactly in the slim category. We did, however, share the same nose and smile, though Aleja probably used the latter more than I did.

Tonight, however, I couldn't hide my grin when they came up to me, especially when I saw James scowling at me.

"Love the outfits, guys," I enthused, hugging first Alejandra and then James. "Really, James, no one can pull off a navy sweater with red reindeer on it quite like you."

"Don't tease him, Genesis," Alejandra said, kissing James's cheek.

He wrapped his arm around her waist and squeezed her to his side.

Alejandra continued with a dopey smile, "He's wearing it to impress Mom. You know how she likes shit like that."

"Still no guy for your family to torture?" James asked me with a smirk. "I need someone to talk to at these things, who isn't one of your aunts, asking when we'll have babies."

"Aw, poor baby," I replied, rolling my eyes.

"There's this cute guy at the restaurant who I think you'd like," my sister commented with a sly grin. James gave her a look but wisely said nothing. "Stop by on Sunday. He's working on my shift. I'll introduce you to each other."

"You know I have no time for a relationship right now," I said with a sigh.

"Okay, then meet him for a quick hook-up," she replied with a shrug. "I'm sure he'd be down."

"Not interested," I answered, glancing back to make sure our mom and tías weren't listening. "Now, stop talking about sex when all our super-religious and hypocritical family members are around. The last thing I need is for Tío José to start talking to me about the sanctity of marriage, as if we don't know he cheats on his wife every time he goes to the DR."

James choked on a laugh, and Alejandra nodded with a dramatic sigh.

"Ah, gotta love family gatherings. Do you think Julia's baby daddy is going to start drama again? I really hope he doesn't break down the door like he did last year at Tía Clarissa's house."

"You didn't hear?" I asked, exiting the kitchen with them. "They're back together now, and he'll be stopping by later to go to church with us."

The living room was crowded with family members sitting on the sofa, children on the floor, and folding chairs placed all around the four corners of the wall. Everyone was talking over the loud television, and yet I knew without a doubt that if I tried to turn it off, I'd be met with shouts of protest and flying *chancletas*. A few younger cousins were on the floor, playing a board game, and began shouting for me to join them, but I waved them off when I saw my cousin Yari sitting next to our *abuela* on the couch.

Yari was twenty-four, the same age as me, and was my favorite cousin and one of my favorite people in general. We used to spend every summer together at our abuela's house when we were kids and weekends at her place when my mom had to work. As we got older, there were even times when she'd stay at my place for days after getting into a fight with her mom. We were as close as sisters—hell, she *was* my sister as far as I was concerned. And I hadn't seen her in over a month, ever since we'd said good-bye at the airport before she flew off to Europe in November.

"Oh my God, Yari, you dyed your hair!" I shouted over the blaring sound of *Laura* on the TV.

Yari's normally dark brown hair was now a dirty-blonde, and she pulled it off really well.

"*Prima!* I've missed you." Yari jumped from the couch and into my arms. Literally.

Even though I should've known she'd do something crazy like that, I was unprepared and stumbled as I tried to carry her weight. Yari hugged me close and gave me a bunch of kisses on my cheek, laughing when I started protesting and trying to squirm away. Many of my family members were laughing and shouting in Spanish about how cute we were, which really just encouraged Yari to start hugging me even tighter and dramatizing her whole act like she was a Broadway star.

"Okay, okay, enough, you little slob." I dropped Yari's legs, and she slid back to the ground, grinning. "I think you got your lipstick all over my face."

"You know you missed me, *puta*," Yari said affectionately, hugging me again. "My God, you look so different off of FaceTime. Have you lost weight?"

"*I* look different? You're the one who dyed your hair and got a tan, all in the span of the one week I haven't talked to you," I said with a laugh.

"Psht, girl, you know I had to come back to New York, looking good," said Yari. "Especially since Ricky started texting me, saying he misses me."

"Ugh, please don't tell me you're going to get back with that douche," I groaned.

The Europe trip was originally supposed to be a couples trip with Yari's boyfriend, Ricky. But then she walked into his apartment a week before they were supposed to leave and found him in bed with some chick he swore was just a friend— cue the eye roll here, folks—and despite his begging and pleading, Yari broke up with him and said she never wanted to see him again. She still went on the trip though, all on her own. I'd wanted to go with her, to use it as an opportunity to get a much-needed vacation, but unfortunately, the only way I'd get that much time off was if I got fired.

I linked arms with Yari, and we started walking to the bedroom Tía Louisa used as a guest room now that Jessica, her daughter and one of my cousins, had moved out. Yari knew I needed more details, and there was no way we'd have any privacy with our nosy family members always listening in on our conversations. We passed by Alejandra and James, who were talking to Tío José, and I had to hide my smile behind my hand when I saw James sending me a pleading look. There was

39

a good chance Tío was probably preaching to them about some verse in the Bible and he'd hold them captive until dinner started.

"No way am I getting back with that fucker," Yari answered vehemently, closing the bedroom door behind her. "He cheated on me with some Boricua from his building. What, he thinks because it's been a month, that I got over that shit and he's going to just hop back into my bed?"

I jumped onto the bed, flopping onto my back, and I felt the bed undulate underneath me as Yari joined me. "I know he hasn't been sitting at home, moping for you. Remember the video Aleja sent me that I sent you of him in the club? He was all over that girl, and Aleja told me she saw him leave the club with her."

"Oh, I remember," Yari said matter-of-factly. "That's why I'll meet up with him and let him see me with my new hairstyle and beautiful España tan, and then I'm going to tell Ricky to go fuck himself."

"*Vaya con Dios, puto*," I said somberly, making us both crack up. "Ugh, I've missed having you here. Work has been horrible, and Aleja has been gone all the time lately. She's always sleeping over James's house. I'm worried she's going to fail out of her first year of college."

"She's been with James since high school," Yari pointed out and then paused, looking pensive. "You think they're the real deal? It's been what, three years since they got together?"

"Yeah, just about," I agreed. "She loves him a lot, and I can tell he loves her too. He's annoying, but in a way, I kind of see him as a brother, you know? I just hope he never hurts her because it would literally crush her."

"From the way I've seen James around her, it's him that we should be worried about," said Yari. "That girl has his balls in one hand and his heart in the other."

I smiled, thinking of how inseparable those two were. "As long as she's happy, I'm happy."

"It's too bad I'm off dating; otherwise, I'd ask her to hook me up with one of his brothers," she joked. "Man, I'm tired of these dudes playing me. Dominican men are just not worth it."

"Aww, but then you' ruin abuela's dream for us to marry one of our Dominican *hermanos*," I teased.

"I love being Dominican, but these men are nothing but dogs," Yari argued. "Shoot, I know you're not judging me because you've never dated a Dominican."

"Hey, I dated a guy who was half-Dominican," I refuted. "Granted, it only lasted a few weeks, so I'm not sure it counts, but still."

"Evan?" Yari scoffed. "That definitely didn't count. You were, like, fourteen, and you didn't even want to kiss him because his lips were always chapped and cracked."

"Oh my God, eww," I said, cracking up as the memories came flooding back. "I completely forgot about that. I think I spent most of those three weeks running away from him than actually spending time with him. I only went out with him because you'd teased me for not having my first kiss yet."

"Hey, don't act like I peer-pressured you," Yari defended with a grin. "You could've picked any number of guys in our class, but you decided to pick the most awkward-looking one. That's on you, prima."

I rolled my eyes before sitting up at the sound of a knock on the bedroom door. The door opened before we could say anything else, and Yari's mother peeked her head inside.

"Hey, girls, the food is ready," Tía Celia said smiling. "Genesis, you look so beautiful, darling. How are things going at the music company?"

"Thank you, Tía," I replied, standing up to give her a hug and kiss. "They're good, just working as much as I can."

She frowned softly and ushered us out of the room. "*Niña*, you shouldn't be working so much. You're young; don't forget to have fun and go out. Is money tight?"

"No, it's nothing like that, Tía," I lied smoothly. "I just like having the extra wallet money. Besides, you know my music equipment isn't cheap. Plus, there's a new club that just opened in the city that I've been dying to go to with Yari, and you know how she loves to go all out whenever we go somewhere."

"Hey, why go out if you're not going to make it memorable?" Yari said, shrugging. "I like to look my best; you never know who you're going to meet."

Tía Celia smiled, wrapping her arm around Yari's shoulders and hugging her to her side. "Ah, Yari, *te quiero*."

"Love you too, Mom," Yari said with a grin.

I smiled to myself as we made our way into the dining room, all the family already seated, the food spread on the table. I took a seat next to Alejandra in the corner near the kitchen, and Yari took the seat to my right. There weren't enough seats for everyone to sit at the table, and truthfully, the apartment wasn't big enough for the amount of people here today, but that never stopped my family from trying to have a meal together.

With everyone talking over one another, it took a while before every family member was able to get a plate with food on it. After Tío José said the prayers—Aleja, Yari, and I had all shared sarcastic looks between each other when he talked about following God's commandments—everyone quickly dug into their food.

"So, were there a lot of cute guys in Spain?" Alejandra asked, glancing at Yari.

"The guys in Spain are sexy as hell," Yari said with a wink. "After the first guy asked me out, I was like, *Ricky who?*"

We all laughed.

I ate more of my food, silently listening as Yari told us story after story about the cute guys in Spain and all the hilarious dates she'd been on. I was so happy for her, and I could tell that this trip had been the break she'd needed.

"But in all seriousness," Yari said, putting her plate on her lap, "the whole trip was an amazing experience. I feel like my perspective on life is so much different. I'm so grateful—you have no idea."

There were loud bursts of laughter in the room as my family listened to a story one of my uncles had shared. I saw my mother laughing loudly, her head resting on Tía Clarissa's shoulder. It made me smile to see that everyone was having a good time.

"Alejandra," Abuela called out. "How is school?"

Our grandmother only spoke Spanish, but besides the younger kids, everyone in the room was conversing in Spanish.

"It's good," Alejandra responded back in Spanish with a small smile. "I've already signed up for classes for January."

"When are you two getting married?" another aunt asked her, pointing toward James beside her.

James looked to Alejandra in question since he couldn't understand what they were saying, but she ignored him, squirming uncomfortably in her seat.

"Tía." Aleja tried to laugh it off, but Tía Maribel continued, bringing attention to the other family members sitting next to her.

"I think it's better you get married and start a family," Tía Maribel continued with a shake of her head. "You don't even know what you're going to college for; it's a waste, I think. Better to start young so that you have more energy."

"Tía, stop," I snapped, getting angry. I could see that Aleja's cheeks were a light pink as she tried to laugh off the conversation.

"Genesis," my mother said sharply.

"She can't talk about Alejandra like that," I argued.

I stood up, plate in hand. I should've known they couldn't go one gathering without criticizing at least one of us.

"Okay, everyone, calm down," Abuela said, putting her hand up. "I'm sure Maribel didn't mean it like that, Genesis. I love that you're so protective of your sister, but niña, you have to respect your elders, hmm?"

I was still mad, but I nodded my head anyway, clenching my plate in my hand.

"Why don't you play us some music?"

"Okay," I agreed after taking a deep breath.

I put my dish in the sink, washed my hands, and then made my way into the living room, where the upright grand piano was. It had been my father's, and it was the piano I had watched him play on, and the piano that had started my love for music all those years ago. I had spent more hours playing on that piano than I did probably anything else, including sleeping. It used to be at our place until a few years ago, when we'd needed to get our floors redone and had Tía hold it for us, and, well, it just felt right to have it here.

I sat down, and with a flex of my hands, I began playing Mozart's Sonata No.16 in C major. It was a simple piece, one that I had learned at a very young age, but I knew that my abuela loved it because it reminded her of my father. He'd taught me a lot of little pieces, and I'd picked them up quickly—mostly because I'd spent hours practicing while I used to wait for him to come home.

I went from Mozart to Chopin and even a few pieces from my favorite soundtracks like *Pride & Prejudice* and *Wakefield*. I loved music in every form, and I wanted to create it in every way. Sometimes, I imagined one day composing for films, but truthfully, all I wanted was to hear a song that I'd created playing on the radio. Thinking about that made me think of the contest at work, and I felt a burst of excitement race through my heart.

I started to smile as I played "Dawn" from *Pride & Prejudice*, as it reminded me of Elizabeth, my favorite heroine in any book or movie. I got lost in the music, playing whatever struck my mood, and soon, the sound of my family's chatter eased away until all was quiet. My world was nothing but the music, and I felt so safe. I could almost feel my father's presence with me on the bench, cheering me on as I learned a new piece, giving me his undivided love and attention, even when I got frustrated and wanted to give up.

My father was the reason why I played. He had been a musician, played lead guitar for a bachata group with a few of his friends as well as written all their songs. My first memory wasn't of a person, but of a pair of hands wrapped around a guitar, singing softly to me as I lay in bed, fighting off sleep so I could sing one more lullaby with my dad.

Music was the gift my father had shared with me; it was in my DNA. I'd learned how to play the piano at three, sitting with my father at the piano while he taught me simple chords. As the years went on, his lessons on the piano turned into guitar and countless other instruments; we'd spend hours playing music together, singing until my voice got hoarse. My father had been gone a lot on gigs, but whenever he had been home, he'd always spent time with me and an instrument.

I switched to one of my original pieces titled "Hope," a piece I'd composed for my abuela when she became depressed after the fifth anniversary of my father's death. I was only seventeen at the time, but to this day, it was still one of my favorite pieces I'd ever composed because of what it meant to my abuela. It started off sad and a bit slow, but it soon turned uplifting in a way that always reminded me that no matter how dark a cloud was, the sun always found a way to shine through. It was my way of telling my abuela that no matter how much it hurt to have him gone, he was still with us every day. And that he would never be forgotten.

The thing I never told her, that I never told anyone, was that it was a lie. Watching my mom turn into a shell of who she had been after he died had been years of cloudy skies. When he'd died, it was like a big part of her had died too. And even though those sunny days had eventually come, where she picked herself up off the floor and tried to keep living, she was never the same. None of us were. Even now, I missed him like he'd left only yesterday.

It hit me suddenly that this was yet another Christmas where he was gone. There had been so many that sometimes, it was hard to remember if he'd ever been there. Twelve years gone, and I didn't think it'd ever feel normal that he wasn't here with all of us.

My father hadn't been a perfect man. Even though I would give anything to spend even one more minute with him, to be held in his arms, I never tried to make him out as some kind of saint, like some of my other family members did. Because the thing was, my father had been flawed, just like so many others. He was human, and he was selfish and hurt my mom so many times, but the thing I didn't think he'd ever realized was how he was hurting me and Aleja as well. Every time he cheated on Mom, he was cheating on us too. It had been so confusing for me to see someone who said he loved my mother but continually hurt her. I'd cry for my mom, feel helpless when she wouldn't get out of bed, as my father had left on another one of his gigs, like he'd taken her will to live with him in that van. She'd eventually get up, say she deserved better, say she was a strong and independent woman who needed no man, and yet when he rolled back into town, she sang a whole different tune. With three simple words, he'd have her wrapped around his finger. Until she found out about the next woman. And then the cycle would continue.

Love was a hell of a drug. I'd learned that from a young age and taken that lesson very seriously. I had no plans of ever letting a man have that kind of power over me. As far as I was concerned, the only love I needed was the love of my family.

I had just finished the last note in the piece when I felt someone hug me from behind. I didn't have to turn around to know it was my abuela. I inhaled, smelling my abeula's favorite perfume, the one she'd been wearing for years and made me think of home. I turned, wrapping my arms around her, her body feeling so fragile in my hands.

"*Gracias, mi preciosa nieta*," my abuela said, her eyes a bit watery. "He would be so proud to see the kind of woman you grew up to be."

"Gracias, Abuela," I said softly, hugging her tightly.

I saw that some of the family had moved into the living room while I was playing, and they all started giving me praises for the music.

"Come, take a break," my abuela said. "Alejandra's going to put some music on from her laptop."

I nodded, and after softly closing the cover for the piano, I got up and went searching for Yari and Alejandra. I passed by my younger cousins, who had moved on from their previous game and were now playing Monopoly on the floor.

I carefully stepped over their bodies when I spotted Alejandra, Yari, and James huddling over the laptop in the dining room. An old Romeo Santos song was playing through the speakers hooked up to laptop, the upbeat music making me want to dance.

"You guys look like you're taking this whole DJ thing a little too seriously," I commented lightly, and they all turned to look at me.

"We're trying to find this one Spanish song, but nobody knows the title," Alejandra explained. "So, we're Googling the lyrics we know to see if anything comes up."

"Found it!" Yari exclaimed, pointing to the screen. "Add it to the playlist, and we're good to go."

I moved closer and saw that they had made a Christmas playlist filled with a bunch of songs—both English and Spanish. But mostly Spanish. The song they were looking for was called "*Quizás Si, Quizás No*" by Los Toros Band. There weren't many songs on the list that were actually about Christmas, but that wasn't really the point of the playlist. It was about finding good songs that people wanted to sing along and dance to. It was about finding songs to make sure everyone was having a good time.

"We still have three hours until we have to go to church," Yari commented. "Anyone want to get drunk off eggnog?"

James laughed. "Is going to church drunk a good idea?"

Alejandra, Yari, and I all looked at one another before simultaneously stating, "Yes."

"The Mass is long, and it's also in Spanish," Alejandra said, running her fingers through the light-brown hair on the top of his head. "Trust me, you're going to need the eggnog to not fall asleep."

"Just don't act stupid, and you'll be fine," I added. "Half my family will probably be tipsy, especially my uncles. Sometimes, I think they use the holidays as an excuse to drink, I swear."

"I think every family does that," James commented. "Hell, as a country, we celebrate St. Patrick's Day and Cinco de Mayo every year, and yet ninety-five percent of the population thinks of those two holidays as nothing more than holidays to get drunk and act stupid. Nobody's interested in recognizing what we are celebrating and why those days are important. Or any holiday for that matter."

"Damn, James." Yari whistled, looking surprised and a little bit impressed. "Now, I don't even want to drink the eggnog anymore because you have me feeling bad. I love Jesus; he knows I do. Happy birthday, Jesus!"

"Yeah, thanks for calling us out for the hypocrites that we are, James," I joked, and if I'd had a drink in my hand, I would've raised it in toast to him. "How about we play something to help pass the time?"

"I wasn't trying—"

"It's okay James. We're just messing with you," I said, giving him a small smile. "But you are right. Holidays shouldn't be about getting drunk, especially not religious ones. It should be about spending time with the people you love … and I'm not sure about you guys, but there's nowhere else I'd rather be and no one else I'd rather be with than the people in this room. You're my family."

James nodded, putting his arm around Alejandra's shoulders, and she smiled at me in thanks. After giving each of them a hug, Yari left the room, only to reappear a moment later with a deck of cards.

"Okay, I'm thinking we kick this back to some childhood favorites and play War," Yari said, grinning. "Afterward, we can do Goldfish, Slapjack, and even Bullshit!"

"And then can we get some milk and put it on the table for Santa?" Alejandra said in fake wonderment. She gasped. "Oh, and maybe we can try to stay up extra late and listen for Santa on the rooftop!"

Yari laughed, sticking her tongue out. "Don't pretend like you didn't believe in Santa until you were thirteen years old."

"Babe, really?" James said with a laugh. He kissed her softly on her full, pouting lips and said with a soft grin, "I thought I was the only one."

Her face lit up, and they all immediately started up a debate on how old was too old to believe in Santa and if he was ever real, all the while, Yari started handing out cards to play the games.

Yes, I thought to myself with a grin, *these people are my family. And thank God for that.*

As promised, when I checked my work email on Monday morning, there was all the information for the contest application in our weekly newsletter. The person in charge of the newsletter was no doubt channeling Steve's energy as there were no less than ten exclamation marks in one paragraph but I didn't mind. Because I was feeling very exclamation-mark happy myself right now.

"What kind of information are they asking for in the contest application?" Cora asked as we walked into the conference room together.

We had our weekly Monday morning briefings together since the marketing, finance, and social media teams all shared the same floor. These meetings were mostly useless, just a time for them to go over any company updates and reminders on the biggest clients that we were working with for the week. All the teams worked with different clients at all times, and if we went over every client, we'd be here all day, so we still had to have our own individual department meetings later today.

"They asked about experience, credentials, stuff like that," I explained, fighting the urge to take my phone out of my pocket and reread the email again. Unfortunately, I had a gray pencil skirt on today that had the world's smallest pockets, which made taking my phone out nearly impossible, which made the decision to keep it in my pocket a much easier one. I really didn't want to spend another five minutes trying to squeeze it back into the pocket. Not when I wasn't confident that one wrong push could end with my making a hole in the damn thing.

"They also asked about which genres you preferred to work in, and there was a link to fill out a questionnaire about yourself."

"Like a personality quiz?" Cora asked, sipping from her coffee.

I shrugged. "I didn't click on the link, but that would make sense. They're trying to pair people based on who they think could be the most compatible."

"Cora! Genesis!" Bill greeted as he took a seat across from us. "How was your Christmas?"

Bill was probably one of the nicest guys at the company and worked on the marketing team with me. He was in his late forties, and we had initially bonded after I complimented a family photo he had on his desk while I waited for him to fill out some forms for Clements. Ever since that day, he'd made it a point to talk to me whenever he saw me, mostly about how his ten-year-old twin daughters were driving him crazy. I loved how much he loved his family, so I didn't mind hearing his stories.

"Hi, Bill!" we said in union, waving.

Bill had light-blond hair that was balding slightly in the middle of his head and a medium build that gave me big adorable-dad vibes. When he turned in his chair, he swung the chair too hard and kicked me with his foot.

"Oh shoot. Sorry, Genesis," he said with a laugh. "You know I'm such a klutz with these darn chairs."

I smiled. "It's all good. How was your Christmas with the girls? Did they like the monster trucks?"

"Oh, yes, they loved it!" he enthused. "But I didn't think about how they are remote-operated, and now it moves around the house at all hours of the night. The girls think it's funny to scare me half to death with them. Nearly stepped on one yesterday and busted my ass."

Cora laughed. "Those girls sure are something."

"Don't I know it," he said with a proud smile. "And how was your Christmas? Did you have a good time with your families?"

"Oh, I had the best time!" Cora exclaimed, eyes shining with excitement. "Some of my family came from Puerto Rico, and my aunt made the best coquito in the world, you have to try it!"

"What is it?" Bill asked, taking out a pen to write the name down.

"It's Puerto Rican eggnog," I explained as she helped him spell the name. "It's really good, especially if you like a sweet drink."

Cora nodded. "I'd bring some to work, but, well, it has alcohol in it, and truthfully, there's no more left at my apartment."

I shook my head, amused. "Well, I didn't have any coquito at my Christmas this year, but we had lots of good food, and one of my uncles dressed up as Santa for my little cousins at the end of the night. It was cute to see how excited they got."

"That sounds real nice—hey, Will!" Bill called out cheerfully.

Will sat down a few seats from us, wearing one of his usual black button-downs tucked into his black work pants that looked like it had been tailored to fit his body perfectly. So annoying. His dark hair was swept back from his face, not a single hair out of place on his head. I'd bet he never had a bad hair day.

"Good morning," Will greeted with a nod in our general direction. He took out his tablet and began scrolling on it, no doubt trying to get some work in before the meeting started.

"How was California?" Bill asked with a big grin. "You must've been happy to be in that California heat for a few days."

"Among other reasons," Will answered smoothly, and I fought the urge to roll my eyes.

Bill nodded. "Right, right. Your family all lives down there, right? Did you enjoy your Christmas with them?"

I glanced over at Will, surprised. I hadn't known his family lived in California. His skin did look a bit tan, a red hue to his cheeks.

Maybe he got sunburned while he was down there, I thought with glee.

When I saw Will turn toward me, I didn't look away, like I usually did. I just continued staring, like I was dissecting a frog and the frog really grossed me out. Which wasn't hard to do because thinking about frogs really *did* gross me out. Why were they so slimy? Yuck.

Will answered Bill's questions but never looked away, a small smirk playing on his lips. "I had a great time with my family. We ate lots of Hershey's Kisses while I was down there since my family had a jumbo bag to finish off. It actually made me think of you, Genesis. I know how passionate you are about that chocolate snack."

My eyes narrowed slightly. "Knowing you, you probably hogged the whole bag for yourself and didn't share with your family at all."

"I'm a team player," Will answered easily. "I know that's not a term you're familiar with. Shall I define it for you?"

That motherfucker—

I took a deep breath, my hand fisted in the fabric of my skirt. *Do not engage. Do not engage*, I repeated to myself, even as I threw daggers at him across the table.

He was not worth it. I was in a good mood today. My dreams were on the right track, I'd had a great four-day break, and I would not let Will ruin my good mood.

"A team player is defined as someone—"

"I know what that phrase means," I snapped, fighting the urge to stab that annoyingly gorgeous face with my pencil. "Cora, will you please tell your coworker that Merriam-Webster called, and they said he should stick to his day job. That is, if he can even manage that. How sure are we that he can count to ten?"

"Uh, I'd really rather stay out of this," Cora answered nervously, hands raised.

"I can count just fine," Will answered over her, voice echoing in the room as people talked around us. "Shall I give you an example? Days Genesis Gonzalez has worked at Siren Music Records: seven hundred and thirty. Days that she has presented in a meeting: four."

The room was quiet, as if everyone had stopped talking, and I didn't have to look around to know that we had the attention of every person in the room. I heard someone snicker, and it took everything in me to not get up and choke that sound out of whoever had done it. I didn't realize that Will had been keeping tally of my work, but I shouldn't have been surprised. Of course he had, probably for a moment exactly like this. To throw it back in my face, to point out how little opportunity I was given, and how I was always regulated to basic administrative details around the office despite the fact that I'd been here longer than more than a few of the people in this room. And I knew why. I'd fucked up *one time* on a presentation that Clements had allowed me to lead on. Just once, but that was all it had taken for him to write me off as a complete fuckup and treat me like I was a kid playing dress-up. When he let me lead, it was only because he had to show to his higher-ups that he was giving me the opportunity to grow. But he didn't actually believe I'd do a good job. Even when I kicked ass on the next two presentations, it was like it didn't matter. He'd already made his impression of me, and he didn't want to change it.

"Good morning, everyone," Lewis, the head of the accounting department, said as he walked into the room.

Clements, head of marketing—my department—and Thompson, head of the social media team, followed behind him, and everyone quickly sat down and diverted their attention from Will and me.

But I could forget what he'd said. And I couldn't answer the way I wanted to because that would most definitely get me fired, so instead, I did the only thing I could think of. I pretended to scratch my forehead, and when I was sure no one was looking, I extended my middle finger against my temple so that it was directly pointed at Will. He rubbed his hand across his mouth, and with a shake of his head, he turned back to his tablet. As if I were the one being childish. Okay, maybe I was being childish with that move, but he'd started it!

I groaned, flipping open my notebook. I sounded like a damn five-year-old, arguing with myself.

"I'm sorry," Cora whispered, brows furrowed in concern.

I shrugged, brushing off her words. "Don't apologize for him."

After the morning conference, Clements sent me on errands around the office. My day-to-day work usually consisted of mostly administrative work and very little direct contact with the clients. What I typically did versus my actual work description were two very different things. As a marketing assistant, I was supposed to be playing a role in many different aspects of marketing, ranging from updating spreadsheets and doing behind-the-scenes work for meetings to communicating with clients and even assisting and attending promotional events. I might answer some emails, but I'd been to very few of the meetings, especially if they took place outside of the office. The only times I left the office was to run errands for Clements, like getting his lunch or whatever else he wanted but was too busy to do. Things that were not a part of my job, but

I did them anyway because I didn't want to complain or give him another reason to dislike me.

Truthfully, I didn't enjoy my job. It wasn't fulfilling, and I felt stuck. I'd wanted the job because I thought any job in the music industry was better than none at all, but now, it felt like the longer I stayed here, the less I believed in myself, in my ability to make it in this industry. Before finding out about the contest, I'd been debating on looking for a new job in the new year. But now, I felt like I needed to hold off, to see if there was finally a way in at this company.

Siren Music was one of the top music label companies in the country, number one on the East Coast. It was the place to be, the company that could take anyone's career to the very top. I'd seen it happen with countless artists and producers. The thing that I loved about this company was their ability to find hidden talent or a hidden sound and make it mainstream. They didn't sell what mainstream was playing; they made the trends that mainstreamed followed.

I wanted to be a part of that.

Not by working in their marketing team, but by working in their studio, making that music for them.

You will, I reminded myself, hefting Clements's dry cleaning higher on my arm as I walked quickly down the hall and toward the elevators. Fortunately, the elevator doors were still open, and I was able to get onto an uncrowded elevator.

Unfortunately, Will happened to be on this elevator.

"You do realize your job is not to be his personal assistant, right?" Will said with a raised brow.

"You do realize what I do at work is none of your business, right?" I responded, pressing the floor button a few more times even though it was already lit.

He shrugged, leaning a shoulder against the wall behind him. "It just seems like you would rather spend your time picking up dry cleaning than being an actual part of meetings."

"You have me all figured out," I said with an eye roll. "I'd actually applied at the dry cleaners down the street, but they weren't hiring. Working here was a last resort."

"A new dry cleaner opened up in my neighborhood. I can put in a good word for you," he offered, tone serious.

We stared at each other, another stare-off that would likely result in one of us having to give up when the elevator doors opened. It wouldn't be me though. I'd walk backward if I had to. I wasn't going to lose again, not after this morning. His gaze snapped away from me sharply, and I blinked in surprise at the flash of emotion that had crossed his face, the way his eyes had seemed to darken.

"If he was going to let me present in those meetings, he would've done it by now," I said, surprising myself.

"So, just like that, you give up huh?" he asked with a shake of his head. "If you want something to happen, make it happen."

"That's so easy for you to say," I argued, voice rising in the empty elevator. "You don't get treated like you're just here to look pretty in a room filled with egotistical assholes who think their every idea is the best one."

"Make yourself stand out," he pressed. "If you lie there and let him treat you like that, he's never going to stop. You need to show him you're an asset. Unless, of course, you're not—in which case, enjoy being as assistant forever. Not sure how long your new high-heel obsession can last on that pay though."

The doors opened to our floor, and I stomped out and walked straight to my cubicle without a backward look. Screw Will and his stupid opinion. It was easy for him to talk when he'd had it all handed to him so easily. He moved around this place seamlessly, like freaking Jesus walking on water. Everyone liked him, everyone respected him, and when he had an idea, no one asked him what his credentials were. No one asked if he was even qualified to be talking in the meeting.

In our last meeting, one guy had looked at me and said, "Aren't you the coffee girl?" when I raised a concern about their marketing strategy toward different demographics that went against the research we'd done.

So, screw Will and his stupid opinion. Screw them all. Because one day, I would be bigger than them all, and they'd be sitting at their desks, wondering how the hell they'd let someone like me sit in the small cubicle at the back of the room.

6

The next evening, I spent hours just sitting at home, playing my guitar.

I'd been working on a new track for a few months now, one about August summer days and that feeling of change waiting around the corner and the mix of anticipation and dread that you felt about it. Music was the one thing that I could never get tired of. It was the one constant in my life. I loved playing music, but what I loved even more was being able to compose it. To take a few chords, to take a feeling, a fleeting thought, and create something bigger than me. It was the most satisfying feeling to be able to put together a song and know that it was a piece of me that would always live on. My thoughts, my feelings, my experiences were out there; they'd happened, and they existed forever in time, in a three-minute song.

Slowly, I switched chords in my song, my fingers moving without conscious thought to form the D chord and then the G. It took a half-second to realize I was playing "Twinkle, Twinkle, Little Star," and I began to smile, eyes closing as my mind wandered.

Growing up, some of the first songs that I'd learned to play on any instrument were lullabies. I remembered my father used to sit with me at the piano as we practiced for what felt like the millionth time that day, and maybe it was.

He could tell I was getting tired because the next thing I knew, he was singing the lullaby, but he was singing it all wrong, the words completely ridiculous.

"Fickle Pickle, drives a car," he sang, and I stopped playing and started giggling immediately.

He told me, "Sing with me, mi corazone. *Music doesn't always have to be serious; it should be fun too."*

And so we'd spent the last hour of that practice and many more in the future just being silly with music, making up the most ridiculous lyrics for whatever song he was teaching me for the week.

"Twinkle, Twinkle, Little Star" forever became "Fickle, Pickle Drives a Car," and as I began to sing it out loud to myself, I was struck by how a memory could make me smile and also so sad at the same time.

I missed my dad, and I couldn't help but wonder how many other songs we would've created together—silly or not—had he not died. Would he have ever made it with his group, his songs playing on the Spanish radio station like he'd dreamed? Would I have made different decisions in my life if I'd had him to talk to, to guide me through my music as the only person who really understood what it felt like to live and breathe with this ache bellowing for the melody in my soul?

I used to talk to him all the time about my dreams, about how I'd write songs for his group one day, and he'd tell me, "You're going to write songs for people much bigger than me, my little star."

I guessed I never would because that Genesis had died when my father died in front of me at only twelve years old. So much of who I was, was tied to him, music, and his death. It was like looking at two different versions of myself and asking them to coexist. I'd never know what life would have looked like had he lived. I could only imagine, but even then, it felt like a sad sort of torture to do so. There was no use in thinking about what-ifs, especially when it would never happen.

I played and played my music, switching from song to song without pause. I went through the nursery rhymes and lullabies, played some of my dad's original music before looping back to my own. The more I played, the more everything else just faded away. I felt light, happy. In those minutes where I played, my reality didn't exist. Work stress was momentarily gone, worry about my sister disappeared, and my dreams didn't feel so far out of reach with a guitar in my hand and my songs in my ears.

I switched to a new song when Yari came over, using the extra key that she had. She walked into the living room and sat down quietly as I sang a song I'd written a few years ago called, "First Heartbreak." The lyrics told the story of how heartbreak touched a child who waited on the steps for a father who would never return, about a child who heard her mother crying through the thin walls in her room for a man who would never stay.

Darkening skies, tearstained cheeks,
But what was love, without your first heartbreak?

I sang the last note and gently rested my hands on the strings.

"God, I hate how beautiful your voice is," Yari said with a sad sigh. "It should be illegal to have a voice like that and not sing all the time."

I placed the guitar back on its stand and laughed. "Gee, thanks."

Her blonde hair was down in waves, tanned skin flushed from the cold. Her makeup was, as always, on point, and she looked flawless even though I knew for a fact that she barely gotten five hours of sleep last night. But Yari was the type of person who could get two hours of sleep and still look beautiful.

"I really don't know why you're not trying to make it as a musician," she commented, sock-covered feet lying on the coffee table in front of the sofa.

"Because I don't want to sing, duh," I said playfully with a smile. "Anyway, how was work?"

"About as exciting as it ever is, working at a dentist office," Yari said, flipping her hair over her shoulder. "Someone came in with their tooth in a glass of lemonade and wanted us to reattach it. They were very upset when we explained that it needed to be in milk, not lemonade, to successfully have a chance at reattaching the tooth."

"Yikes," I said with a wince. "Please tell me it wasn't a front tooth."

Yari nodded, tapping one of her canine teeth. "They were in a bit of denial and left to get a second opinion by a 'real' dental establishment. Let's just hope he doesn't come back in tomorrow with that glass of lemonade."

Yari worked as a dental hygienist in a dentist office in Queens. She'd been working in this field for a few years, but she'd just recently finished her degree and finally gotten promoted to her official job, which meant a lot more money too. Working in a dentist office had made Yari the unofficial dentist of the family. Everyone came to her with their teeth and oral concerns, and I honestly didn't know how she didn't lose it with all our family sticking their open mouths in front of her face all the time.

"Enough about work. Tonight is movie night!" Yari cheered, clapping her hands. "Where is Aleja?"

"Alejandra said she would be here in a few hours, sans boyfriend." I added when I saw Yari's question forming on her lips.

"Shocking," Yari joked. "I thought they were, like, superglued to each other or something."

I made a noncommittal sound and stood up to grab the television remote. "I'm not even going to start up that conversation again. Let's just be happy she's actually coming."

"Fair enough," Yari said. She watched as I clicked into Netflix on the TV. "Can I pick the first movie? I *am* doing your nails for you for free after all."

"And I'm straightening your hair," I returned but passed her the remote anyway.

Yari grinned and blew me a kiss before turning her attention fully into picking a movie.

Our girls' nights usually went something like this: we'd start off with just watching movies and basking in *our self-care on a budget* portion of the night, like painting our nails and doing face masks. Then, somewhere along the way, we'd add some alcohol to the mix, and somehow, no matter how the day had started, we *always* ended up drunk and giggling about shit that was nowhere near as funny as we thought it was.

It was the best.

Sure enough, three hours into girls' night, and as Yari did our nails, we were shouting over the movie as we tried to say the words to one of our favorite movies, *Pride & Prejudice*.

"This is my favorite part!" Aleja shouted, waving her hand in our faces, one of which was holding a flat iron. "No one say it but me!"

"Bitch!" Yari argued with a grin. "You can say the line, just don't burn my face off with that thing."

My sister recited Darcy's famous declaration of love, ignoring Yari completely.

I played along, joining my sister in quoting the movie in a deep voice, smiling when Yari pretended to swoon.

Yari sighed dreamily. "I love Mr. Darcy so much. If only there were men like him around still."

"He's one of a kind, I'm afraid," I agreed.

"I don't know. I've always been more into Mr. Bingley," Aleja mused. She turned her attention back to Yari's hair, and I passed her the next piece of hair to straighten. "He's so sweet and kind. There's something attractive about a man who is so obvious about his love for a woman. Every time he looks at Jane, he has hearts in his eyes. He's just ... perfect."

"Probably because we're so used to seeing guys playing games nowadays," Yari joked. "Which is funny if you think about it since society insists that women are the ones playing games. We give our love freely; men are the ones who put stipulations on who and when they'll give affection."

"Not to mention, they always have an excuse for their shitty behavior but expect us to just get over it whenever we express feeling hurt," Aleja shouted.

"If we're going to start a conversation about how fucked up men are, I'm going to need a drink," I declared, standing up and fetching the bottle of wine from the kitchen. I brought three wineglasses and plopped them onto the table beside the couch.

"Well, we're going to need more than one bottle of wine to get through tonight." Yari laughed, filling her glass to the top.

I couldn't say I was surprised by the turn of events; after all, it wouldn't be a girls' night if there wasn't some good old-fashioned boy talk.

"Yes, I've missed this!" Alejandra squealed. She plopped against our recliner seat, Yari's hair forgotten for the moment. She opened and closed her fist, her arms outstretched like a greedy five-year-old. "Pass me the wine, please and thank you!"

I eyed her for a second before filling her cup halfway. "I can't take care of both of you tonight, so try not to get too drunk."

Alejandra huffed but agreed, taking a small sip from her glass once I passed it to her. "So, what should we talk about first? Biggest dick we've ever seen? Best sex? Worst?"

"Wait, wait!" Yari exclaimed, jumping up. She placed her glass on the table. "I say we make this fun! Let's put a bunch of questions in a bowl and then play Spin the Bottle. Except every time the bottle lands on you, you have to answer a question."

"What is it with you and games?" I quipped. Aleja pouted, so I sighed heavily but added, "Count me in."

We quickly got some paper and wrote a bunch of questions down. I wrote some funny ones and some questions that were more serious. I just hoped I didn't get any of my questions.

"Okay, I'll spin first," Alejandra volunteered as we all got situated on the floor, an empty bottle in the middle of our circle, our glasses of wine beside us. She sat up on her knees and spun the bottle, and we all watched with rapt attention as it slowed, slowed … and finally stopped on Yari.

"Fuck, how did I know that would happen?" Yari laughed. She picked up a crumbled piece of paper from the bowl and read it silently to herself.

"¡*Dime!*" I said curious.

"If you could have one last romp in the hay with the last guy you had sex with, would you?" Yari read out loud. She scrunched up her nose in distaste. "That would be a hell no."

"The European men didn't satisfy you?" Alejandra asked, wagging her eyebrows.

"I didn't sleep with any of them," she admitted. I'd already known this since we'd talked about it before, but it was news to Aleja. "I kissed plenty of guys and went on a lot of dates, but the last guy I had sex with was Ricky."

We all stayed silent for a moment, processing. It could be so hard to move on even if every part of you wanted to. For me, I didn't let myself get attached to guys because I knew that when they left or when things got bad, I didn't want to care; I didn't want to be hurt and crying over a broken heart. For Yari, she gave her all in her relationships because she loved being in them. She was a relationship kind of girl. She might love to have fun, and she might be putting on this whole act like she was done with Ricky, but I knew her well enough to know she was not even close to being over him.

"Well, you know what they say," Alejandra said, raising her glass in the air. "The best way to get over him is to get under someone new."

"Hmm … well, you see, that won't work because I like being on top," Yari responded, doing a little dance in her seat, and we busted out laughing.

"¡*Wepa*!" I shouted, drumming my hands against the floor. "Okay, let's keep this game going! Yari, spin the bottle."

She took the bottle and spun it, and of course, it landed on me.

I grabbed a random paper and read it silently to myself. *Fictional character you'd spend a night with?*

"One guess who wrote that question," Yari joked after I read the question aloud.

Alejandra bobbed her head. "I am awaiting your answer, dear sister."

"Are we talking animated characters or ones from books, TV shows, or movies?" I inquired.

"For the sake of being scandalous, let's narrow it to animated characters," Alejandra declared with a fiendish grin.

"Then, I'd have to choose Dimitri from *Anastasia*," I said after thinking for a long moment. "He's cute but not a pretty boy, and he'd know not to get attached."

"Ugh, you are so annoying," Alejandra said with a huff, and I grinned.

I knew she'd wanted me to pick some Disney prince and talk about true love's kiss, but she should also know me well enough to know that I'd never do that.

"If you don't like my answer, then you shouldn't have put the question in the bowl," I said simply.

"Blah, blah," Alejandra responded with a wave of her hand.

I spun the bottle, and it landed on me once more. "Oh, come on!"

I picked up a paper and read it aloud, "*What's your deepest fear?*"

There were a lot of things I was scared of, but most of those weren't things so much as situations. I was scared I'd never make it in the music industry. I was scared that something would happen to my family, and this time, we wouldn't be able to put the pieces back together. I was scared of love. I was scared of heartbreak. I was scared of the future. I was scared of the past.

I feared the unknown.

"My biggest fear," I said drawing it out, "is that I'll wake up one day, and Alejandra will have tried to cut my hair again."

They laughed.

Once, when we had been kids, Alejandra had been on this kick that she wanted to be a hairstylist, like one of our aunts, and wanted to start cutting hair at her salon. Our aunt, of course, said no, but Alejandra was determined to show her that she had what it took. And so, while I was sleeping, she decided she'd give me a haircut to showcase her talent. Her plan, she'd said, was that I'd wake up with this amazing haircut, and everyone would be so amazed and proud that our aunt would have no choice but to mentor Alejandra at her shop.

Obviously, things didn't work out so well.

She chopped off half of my hair in the worse kind of zigzag pattern, and I had to cut my hair to my shoulders in order to fix the uneven cut. To say our mom was pissed would be an understatement. I had been mad, too, but I'd ended up liking the new haircut, so I had gotten over it pretty quickly.

"When you have a dream, you have to chase after it," Alejandra said with a grin. "Even if everyone, including the scissors themselves, are telling you not to."

I laughed. "Well, you know now, Aleja. If you're ever tempted to cut my hair … don't."

The game went on, question after question, and time seemed to fly by in a mingle of laughter, confessions, and smiles.

"*Craziest place you've had sex?*"

"Janitor's closet," Alejandra answered with a dopey look on her face.

"Ugh, enough with the lovey-dovey eyes," I joked, flicking her on the forehead.

She stuck her tongue out at me but spun the bottle.

"*Favorite sex song?*"

"I hate this with everything inside me," Yari said, "but 'Take You Down' by Chris Brown."

"*Best orgasm you've ever had?*"

"The ones I give myself," I answered easily, tossing the paper onto the table. It wasn't a complete lie; some of my top orgasms had happened with me, my vibrator, and my imagination.

"*If you could go anywhere in the world, where would you go?*"

"France," Alejandra answered decidedly. She went to drop the paper on the table and then paused, a small frown on her face. "No, wait. Actually, I'd choose Costa Rica. It looks so beautiful in pictures, and the water is so blue."

On and on, the questions went until the bowl was empty, and I felt almost dizzy from the wine consumption and laughter. Alejandra, of course, got drunk, and after having a thirty-minute conversation with her on why she couldn't sleep in the hallway outside of the bedroom but rather her own bed, I was able to get her tucked in and comfortable.

Yari was buzzed but not as bad, and as I placed a cup of water next to Alejandra's bed with some Advil, I heard her come in quietly.

"You're so good with her," Yari noted, watching my sister sleep. "I don't know that I could have the patience of always having to take care of someone."

I studied my sister, and even though she was eighteen years old, I could see flashes of her at three, seven, ten years old, always trailing me, always leaning on me for comfort and direction. When our father had died and my mom stopped leaving her room, it had been me who got her ready for school, made sure she did her homework, and ate her food. It had been me who made sure she took her showers, wiped the blood from her scrapes, soothed her when she had a bad dream, wiped her tears when she was sad.

"She's my sister," I said simply. "And I love her. No matter how old she gets, I will always be there for her."

Yari rubbed my shoulder before laying her head on it in silent comfort. We stood there for a long second, both lost in our own thoughts.

Eventually, when my eyes started to feel bleary with tiredness and my feet began to ache, I closed her door and walked slowly down the hall.

"Let's go to sleep," I said. "It's going to be a long day tomorrow."

7

L ife seemed to move in a slow-motion blur as I waited for the next contest email and to find out who I would be working with. When I wasn't running errands around the city for Clements, I was at my desk in my small corner cubicle, headphones on as I listened to music, updated spreadsheets, and answered emails.

The new year had come and gone, and fresh on January 1, my trusty—but flimsy—synthesizer had decided that it was not interested in joining me in the new year and died. Just my luck and probably an omen of what this year would have in store for me. Broken synthesizer meant good-bye to cafeteria food during lunch and hello to an instant cup of noodles at my desk. With any hope, I'd be able to save up enough money to buy a decent one in a couple of months.

My phone buzzed on my desk as I finished eating lunch, and I glanced at my screen to see a text from Cora.

> *Cora: Hey, can you stop by my desk real quick before heading into our two o'clock meeting?*

Me: Yeah, I'll head over now.

We had a meeting with a client who we wanted to work with us for a Valentine's campaign we'd be running next month for an artist's album. It was crazy how the new year had just started, but we were already working months in advance. That was the thing about marketing; you were always thinking about the next big opportunity to promote something, and most times, you were so wrapped up in the next big project that you didn't even get to enjoy the hard work you put into each of the campaigns.

I walked across the floor, moving past most of my coworkers in their cubicles, hard at work in front of their computers. I exited our department, the glass door quietly closing behind me as I made the short trek down the hall, past the elevators, past the hallway that led to the conference rooms, and instead kept walking straight to the other side of the floor, where the finance department was located. Marketing had offices and cubicles on the left side of the floor, and finance was on the right. You had to walk past the elevators to get to either department, and it was separated by a glass door on each side. The conference rooms were a separate hall that faced directly in front of the elevators.

Even though we worked on the same floor, entering into the finance department was like being in a whole different world. Instead of small cubicles that covered the majority of the open floor, like in my department, most of them had their own private offices. There were a few who had a desk area in the open space, but even that was an upgrade from my workspace. Cora was one of the few who did not have her own office even though she definitely should, but she'd made her desk look cozy and very homey. She had a little plant on her desk and a few trinkets that she'd gotten from friends and family. Her desk was tidy and neat, like it had come straight from an IKEA showroom.

Cora waved when she saw me, hand reaching inside one of her desk drawers for something. I leaned my hip against the side of her desk and watched as she pulled out her secret stash of mini cupcakes that she liked to save for stressful days.

"Oh my God, thank you," I rushed out, immediately taking two cupcakes from the container. I quickly unwrapped one and shoved the entire thing in my mouth, moaning softly at the taste of the sugary-sweet frosting on my tongue.

"I had a feeling you'd need a sugar intake before this meeting." Cora smiled.

"I've gotten too spoiled, eating lunch with you in the cafeteria," I admitted after I swallowed the cupcake down. "These noodle cups are just not doing it for me. I'm hungry not even twenty minutes after I've finished eating my lunch."

"Those things are so bad for you," Cora said with a shake of her head. "The sodium alone ..."

"I like them," I answered with a shrug. "And it's a cheap lunch, which saves me almost fifty dollars a week that I would've been spending on lunch."

"Is it really necessary to get that synthesizer?" she asked with furrowed brows. "Can't you still make music without it? You have, like, fifty different pieces of equipment at your place. Surely, something else can replace it."

"Of course I can still make music without it," I explained. "But it's a great piece of equipment to have when you want to create a new sound. I'll have to save regardless, so I might as well start now, and maybe I'll be able to start eating with you by spring."

"Spring!" Cora exclaimed, surprise coating her face. "It'll take you that long to save? How much does this darn thing cost?"

"Probably not," I admitted, smiling at Cora's inability to curse. "But I also want to buy a new drum machine, so I figured I'd just knock them both out now."

She shook her head, brown curls brushing against her cheeks. "Man, I hope that stuff is worth it because with the amount of sodium you'll be eating these next few months, the least of your worries will be your music."

My music said everything I couldn't. When I was feeling happy or sad or angry, a lot of the times I didn't know how to express myself. But then I would sit down with an instrument and my computer, and I could process it all. It was my form of therapy, my way to release. There was no price you could put on that for me. With or without the equipment, I could still make music, but if I wanted to make music to send to music companies, I needed more than just a simple guitar recorded over some lyrics. I needed to be able to show my music range, my ability to work with all sorts of equipment, but even more, my ability to create a song that would sell.

"Don't be dramatic. I'll be fine," I said with an eye roll. I smiled though, warmed by her concern. "I'll switch it up, I promise. I'll do homemade sandwiches and leftovers from the night before, too, and a bunch of other stuff."

She nodded, looking appeased. "If you ever need the money, I don't mind—"

"I know," I said cutting her off. "And I appreciate it more than you'll ever know, but I want to do this my way first."

"Cora," Will spoke from behind me, and I jumped slightly, caught off guard.

I turned and saw that he was standing by his office door, looking one hundred percent pissed off. His thick, dark hair was brushed back from his face, but there was a strand that curled ever so slightly over his forehead. He was wearing a white button-down today with a light-gray pinpoint tie and navy pants. I didn't even bother glancing down at his shoes, as he always wore black shoes, not that I could necessarily blame him. Men didn't have quite as many options for shoes that were work appropriate as women did.

Just like I'd promised myself, I'd stopped wearing heels to work and gone back to my flats and cute booties with the new year. My feet were still thanking me for my decision, and I wasn't sure when they would forgive me for wearing stilettos to work. Today, I had on a long-sleeved, maroon-colored sweater with a high collar and simple black work pants and booties. I'd done my usual light brush of makeup, donning concealer, mascara, and a pink gloss that I'd borrowed from Alejandra this morning. I wasn't a big makeup person, but I almost never left home without at least putting some concealer on to hide the lack of sleep I got most nights.

"Ready for the meeting?" Cora said brightly, standing up from her desk. "Do you have their file in your office, or should I get it from the records room real quick?"

He turned his head slightly, his sharp cheekbones on display, and a moment later, he lifted the file in his hand in answer. His eyes landed on me. "Genesis."

"Good to see you, Will," I lied with a big smile. I ate the last bite of my mini cupcake and turned to Cora. "You ready to go?"

"I didn't realize we were looking for a new assistant in our department," Will commented, arms crossed over his chest as he leaned against the doorframe of his office. "Should I let Derek know he's being let go?"

And *this* was why I usually had Cora come to my desk.

Will always had to make a comment every time I came over here, as if he needed to remind me that I didn't belong here and never would.

"I know how much it would make your day if you could see me sitting across your office, ready to answer your every whim," I said airily. "But that day won't be today. Or probably any day. Because I would rather quit my job than have to answer to you."

He stared at me impassively, his jaw clenched for one long moment. "You say the sweetest things to me."

"I know, right?" I replied brightly. I began walking toward the exit with Cora, thrilled at finally getting the last word in and stumping Will.

"I'm a little disappointed to hear we won't be replacing Derek," he said, not raising his voice even a little bit, and yet his words stopped me in my tracks all the same. "If you were working in my department, I would work you so hard that you wouldn't last a day."

I turned toward him and watched as his eyes lifted quickly toward mine, eyes a shade darker than their usual dark brown. He hadn't moved a single inch from the door, arms still crossed and shoulder leaning on the doorframe, but there was something about his body language that felt different. Tense. Like a lion watching its prey, waiting for the perfect moment to pounce.

"Not likely," I said with a scoff, ignoring the way my heart began beating a bit faster in my chest. "If I worked in your department, you wouldn't know what to do with yourself."

"Oh, trust me," he said, voice deep, "I'd know exactly what to do."

I shifted slightly, reminding myself that, like everything with Will, he was just trying to get me riled up and mad. He seemed to get some perverse pleasure out of seeing me lose my cool, probably in the same way that I got a satisfying kick out of pissing him off. I'd never known one person who could make me feel this level of irritation until I'd met him. To think that I'd almost double-majored in accounting instead of business. Then, we could've really worked together, and that would've been a disaster straight from hell.

I rolled my eyes and turned to Cora, who was staring at us with raised brows, light-brown cheeks slightly flushed. I gave her a look and said, "Coming?"

She nodded, taking one last glance at Will, and mumbled, "Funny choice of words, *chica*."

When we stepped out of her department, the door closed behind us.

I took one look at her and said, "Don't. Just … don't."

She sighed, like what I was asking her to do was a huge burden. "That was …"

"Will being Will," I said firmly. "He always has to have the last word. Next time, you're meeting me at my desk, cupcakes or not."

Cora stayed quiet, and we made a right when we got to the elevators and went down the long hallway to the conference rooms. It didn't take long for us to get to the conference room we'd be using for the meeting, and when we stepped inside, we found the room filled with people already sitting at the table. Clements was seated at one end, glasses on his face as he read over some papers, and I internally groaned. I'd been hoping to talk with Cora for a few more minutes before the meeting started, but now, I'd have to join Clements and hope he didn't add any more things on my list to do before the workday was over.

"Good luck presenting," I said softly, giving her a small smile. "You're going to kick ass."

Cora smiled, and we went our opposite ways, her sitting toward the front of the table with her department coworkers and me walking toward Clements, who was sitting at the opposite corner of the room. I pulled out the chair next to his and slowly sat down, mumbling a quick hello. I put my notepad down and glanced at what he was reading and blinked in surprise when I saw it was my report of a market study we'd done last month. He'd written all over it, circled some words, scribbled in the margins with words too small for me to read from my seat. He'd been making me write up summary reports of these studies for months, but not once had he ever made any comments about them. I'd assumed he wasn't even reading them, and it was just something he made me do because he liked to make sure I was busy at all times.

He looked up, and I knew he could read the surprise on my face, but he didn't react to it. "Give me the rundown on the client."

I sat up straighter and immediately recited all the information I'd memorized about Henrietta's Jewelry & Co. "Henrietta's Jewelry & Co. is a jewelry manufacturing company that was founded in 1965 by Joseph Grant. The company started off as a small business in Georgia that quickly grew in business and became one of the most successful jewelry companies in the United States. It now has over two thousand chain stores all around the US and Europe. They specialize in jewelry but also sell stationery, china, personal accessories, and last year, they debuted their first line of fragrances."

He nodded. "And why are they a company we want to work with?"

"Their fragrance line has been a huge success with the eighteen to twenty-four demographic, and that is the demographic we are marketing to with Jenny Sky's music," I answered. "Their fragrance line is all about sophisticated meets sexy, and Jenny's latest song in their commercials could bring a boost in sales on both sides. She also has the social media following and look that we could utilize as a pitch for more money in the contracts. Jenny's team said she was open to a personalized fragrance with their company for the right price."

"What Jenny's team does with her personal fragrance idea is up to them," Clements said dismissively, taking his reading glasses off. "The company wants us to market her album in a Valentine's Day campaign collaboration, and that's what we'll bring up in today's meeting while going over contract details."

I nodded, making a quick note to myself to quit while I was ahead. That note lasted all of thirty seconds before I opened my mouth and tried again. "I've been thinking about the best way to reach our target demographic, and I had an idea—"

"That's enough, Genesis," he said briskly, closing the folder with my report on the table. "I need you focusing on taking notes for this meeting. Make sure you have them typed up and on my desk by the end of the day. I also need …"

On and on he went, and I sighed internally, nodding along and writing down my new agenda items. At least he'd been reading my reports, and if he hadn't been saying anything about them, then it must mean they weren't terrible, right?

Baby steps. It was all about baby steps with this job.

The universe hated me.

It was official. I had to have done something bad in a past life because it seemed like this current one was intent on making me miserable in every way that really mattered.

"I don't think deleting the email will erase what it said," Cora said softly somewhere to my right.

I'd always liked to think of myself as a realist. Someone who lived very concretely in setting realistic expectations and goals and dealing with my problems head-on. I wasn't a big fan of letting the pieces fall where they may or hoping for the best when life threw me a curveball.

And life had just thrown me the shittiest curveball.

I was talking a curveball so shitty that when it hit you, it felt like you'd been knocked over by a ten-wheeler. Music and family. The only two things that really mattered in my life.

And now, one of them was being threatened.

"I don't think breaking your cell phone will do the job either."

I put my head in my hands and tried to pull myself together. Even though my cubicle was at the back of the room, there were still plenty of people working around me, and the cubicles weren't exactly the most private spaces. They were eight-by-eight feet, and the walls were thin as hell.

"Genesis, it's going to be okay," Cora said gently, her hand hesitantly rubbing my shoulder.

"How could this possibly be okay?" I said into my hands. I lifted my face, so she could hear me better. "I'm going to have to give up the biggest opportunity I've been given thus far in my pathetic music career, and chances are, I'll never get another one like it."

I slumped in my chair, aware I was being extremely dramatic, but considering the circumstances, I felt it was warranted.

After waiting another week, the email from the CEO had finally come through with the next steps in the contest. He'd sent individual emails out to each person with a short introduction, a very thorough list of rules and requirements, and then at the very bottom of the email, he'd listed the name of the person I'd be working with along with an attached bio about the person.

And the name attached to my email was none other than Hikaru Kobayashi. Also known as Will, motherfucking bane of my existence. The one person it was physically impossible for me to be in a room with and not argue with. The whole thing made no freaking sense. They'd made it seem like they would be pairing us at random, but even though we were in different departments, we worked on the same floor! I'd assumed I would be paired with someone from *any* other department on *any* other floor.

But I'd gotten Will.

Other than a short, *As a music producer, we think you will work well with Hikaru, who is a talented artist and has years of experience with songwriting as well.*

First of all, since when did Will have musical aspirations? Second of all, there was no way in hell we'd ever work well together, and almost anyone in the building could attest to that.

Hadn't Jameson Harris talked with our direct supervisors? Surely, they would've told him how bad of an idea it was to pair us together.

Then again, I wouldn't put it past Clements to purposefully sabotage this opportunity for me. I'd bet he'd probably laughed when they told him I was entering the contest and brushed the whole thing off.

My fingers squeezed down so hard on my thigh that I had no doubt it would leave a bruise.

Deep breath, I reminded myself.

I took a deep breath in through my nose, and when I slowly let it out, I unclenched my fingers from my thigh.

"You don't have to give up the opportunity," Cora reminded me, voice hesitant. "You could ... you could try working with Will—"

"Cora," I cut her off sharply. "I guarantee you that would only lead to disaster. In fact, I see it leading to my termination because I would literally kill him on the first day of practice."

Cora sighed, and I turned to look at her. She was sitting beside me in my small cubicle, her fingers playing with the fabric of her navy-blue turtleneck dress. "What are your other options though? Other than dropping out of the contest?"

"I don't know," I admitted, feeling frustrated and trying hard not to take it out on Cora, who was only trying to be a good friend. "Right now, I want for this to all be a horrible nightmare and to wake up to the sound of my alarm going off and the email to have not been sent out yet."

Surely, things would change tomorrow. Maybe Will would demand a new partner, or someone would have dropped out of the contest, so they'd need to do a quick switch with the contestants, and I'd be moved to work with someone else. I brightened slightly, heart racing with the possibility. Yes, that could happen. It was a completely plausible situation. In fact, I'd bet it had already happened.

Cora looked at me suspiciously. "What are you thinking?"

"I've just decided I'm going to be optimistic about this whole thing," I said, sitting up straight in my seat. I began rearranging my desk, fixing stacks of paper, wiping the keyboard free of any dust or crumbs, a small smile on my face.

"That's great!" Cora exclaimed, relief on her face. "I knew you'd come around. Working with Will won't be so bad, I promise. You guys will figure things out."

I was tempted to tell her my plan, but I knew that she wouldn't understand. Cora always saw the positive in every opportunity, a *glass half-full* kind of girl. There were times when I couldn't understand how we'd become such good friends because our personalities were so different. But it worked for us—until we got to situations like this. Where Cora wanted me to just let things happen and I needed them to go my way— and if they didn't, I did everything in my power to try to change the course of action.

"Thanks for being here for me," I said, giving her a smile. "I need to get back to work, but we'll talk later?"

She gave me a quick hug around my shoulders and stood up. "Of course! Text me if anything else happens!"

I nodded, and with a wave, Cora began her walk back to her desk. When I saw her leave my department a minute later, the door closing shut behind her, I sat back in my desk chair and turned on my computer. It took a few minutes for the thing to turn back on from sleep mode, but as soon as it did, I pulled up a Word document and began to make a list.

How to Lose Will as My Partner in the Contest:

1. Email Mr. Harris and inquire about a potential need for a partner in the contest and my availability to fill said role.

2. Request a switch.

3. Convince Will to drop out of the contest, which will get me a new partner.

4. Get Will fired, which will get me a new partner.

5. Convince Will to quit his job, which will get me a new partner.

On and on my list went as I continued to work on it throughout the day. I had gotten to fifteen different ways to get out of being partners with Will before the day was even over. Looking over the list, I knew that some ideas were more believable than others, but nothing could be overlooked in the initial phases.

After narrowing down my list to my top three ideas, I began to write out detailed plans of action for each of them. Each plan had its own individual backup plans that would allow them the maximum amount of opportunity to work before having to move on. My hope was that this would take no more than a week of time, and then I'd have plenty of time to get a new partner and maintain my opportunity at having my song on that album.

"What are you doing?"

"Shit!" I jumped out of my seat and quickly turned my monitor off, my heart beating wildly in my chest.

I turned around, and Will was standing at the entrance of my cubicle, his winter coat and bag clutched in one hand as he stared down at me.

"What are you doing here?" I demanded, looking around the room and taking notice of how empty it was. One glance at the clock on my desk indicated that it was already five thirty, way past the time to go home.

"I'm here to talk about the contest." He casually pulled on the sleeve of his navy-blue suit jacket, face indecipherable. "You know, the one you were writing a thesis on your computer about?"

I felt my face get hot with embarrassment. "I don't know what you're talking about."

Will gave me a look that told me he did not believe me for a second. "Great, so then you're ready to talk about our music."

"Well, actually ..." I trailed off, thinking about plan A on the list. "I wanted to talk to you about that."

Will stared impassively at me. "Go on."

"I was thinking," I started with a hesitant smile.

His eyes dropped to my lips and narrowed.

"We both know that we don't work well together and working on a song would be disastrous. Instead of pretending otherwise, why don't we both put in a request for a different partner?" I felt my speech getting faster, the longer I talked, wanting to get all of it out before he shut me down. "I heard that Calvin is participating in the contest, and you guys get along so well. I bet he would agree to work with you in a heartbeat. That way, we both get a fair chance at winning this competition, and no one gets hurt."

Will stared at me quietly, his face giving nothing away, even as I could tell he was thinking hard about something. "No. You're my partner in this competition, and I'm not working with anyone else."

My face fell. "Why not? Are you really telling me that you think we would work well together? Us working together is an almost guarantee that we'll lose."

"Did you even read my bio?" he asked. When I didn't reply, he muttered something under his breath. "Music is a huge part of my life. It's very important to me, Genesis. I've been playing music for as long as I can remember, and I still play it now, every chance I get. I play with a band on most weekends, but I also do a lot of gigs, just me and my guitar. This isn't something I do just for fun; it's my dream. And just looking at your bio that was sent out, my gut says you feel the same way."

I stared wordlessly, processing his words, and trying not to look completely shocked. I hadn't known any of those things about Will, and I didn't know how I felt about it all. I'd always tried my very hardest to not let Will invade my thoughts when I left work, but the few times that I had thought of him, I'd always thought he was someone whose idea of a chill night was doing people's taxes for fun as he watched *Jeopardy*. Never in a million years would I have thought he had a musical bone in his body.

"I didn't know that you'd double-majored in business and music technology," he said, voice strangely soft. "Your bio says that you've worked with a few artists already on the side and won a bunch of awards in school for your music."

I sniffed, looking away from him. "Yeah, well, there's a lot you don't know about me."

"Then, give me the opportunity to know you," he pressed. After a long moment of me staring at him in suspicion, he added, "For the sake of the contest."

I sighed heavily, looking back toward him. "We don't like each other; there's no way we'll be able to do this."

Will stared at me, determination in the set of his jaw. "We'll make it work."

I shook my head, shoving my stuff into my bag. "I don't want to be Debbie Downer, but it would be a disaster, Will. This isn't *Camp Rock*. We're not living in a feel-good movie. Two people who dislike each other as much as we do are not going to just figure it out and magically get along."

"Think about what I said," he said firmly, eyes scanning me as I pushed my arms through my coat.

"Think about what *I* said," I responded.

"There are only two options here." Will's eyes never wavered from mine. "We either work together or you drop out of the contest."

I ignored him, squeezing past him toward the elevator.

"Let me know your answer by tomorrow," he called out behind me.

I didn't bother answering. There had to be another way.

9

There was no other way.

I'd stayed up half the night, picking apart the email, and spent my entire morning commute on the train, trying to find a loophole, some way for me to switch partners, but to no avail. My choices were work with Will for three months or drop out of the contest.

And even though a big part of me felt like there was no use in even trying to make a song with him, I knew I had to try. Because if I never tried, I'd always wonder *what if*, and this was one what-if in my life that I could control. That didn't mean I wasn't convinced that this wouldn't be a disaster. Because every which way I looked at it, I couldn't imagine how we could get along for one day, let alone three months.

I'd worked with musicians I didn't like, but it was different when you didn't know them and didn't have a history. In the past, I'd always been able to stay professional, even when someone was being rude and often trying to swindle me out of my song because they'd be the ones "to make it popular" and shouldn't I just be happy with hearing my song being played at live events? I knew I was no big shot—yet—but I also knew my worth, and my songs were worth a lot more than fifty dollars. But again, I'd been able to push through and work with them and create some of my favorite songs. While no band I'd written a song for had made it big yet, they had their own following, and I often went to their gigs to check in and watched the crowd go crazy for a song that I'd written. I kept those relationships going because even though we weren't close, we shared a connection through music, and that wasn't something you let go of so easily. Or at least, I didn't.

The thought of building any sort of relationship with Will, especially one wrapped around music, was so ridiculous that in any other instance, I would probably laugh. I wasn't sure how I was going to remain professional when my mouth seemed to have a mind of its own whenever I was around him. Add in knowing that Will would argue with me over every word and beat of the song, just for argument's sake, and I was right back to worrying about the state of my sanity by the end of April.

Not to mention, the chances of us actually winning and having my first official song on a major record album that would be listened to by millions were looking slimmer every minute that I thought about this predicament.

But it was fine.

It might not be the situation that I'd expected, and it might make things harder, but when had anything ever happened for me easily? I'd work hard and make it happen, just like everything else I'd ever accomplished in life. I'd had my pity party for one yesterday, and now, I needed to keep going despite this very big bump in the road.

The first email from Will came at ten thirty in the morning.

I'd just sat down at my desk after a short meeting with Clements in his office when I both heard my computer go off with an alert and felt my phone vibrate in my pocket.

When I clicked on the email, I didn't even fight the scowl that swept across my face as I read it.

From: wkobayashi@sirenmusicrecords.com

To: ggonzalez@siremusicrecords.com

Subject: Contest Response

Good morning.

As we spoke about yesterday, I am awaiting your answer pertaining to the contest. Are we working together, or are you choosing to give up on this opportunity? I await your answer.

Best regards,

Will Kobayashi

Finance Analyst

Siren Music Records, New York Location

My fingers were flying across the keyboard the moment I read the last sentence, not even letting myself think about what I was going to say.

To: wkobayashi@siremusicrecords.com

From: ggonzalez@siremusicrecords.com

Subject: Re: Contest Response

Good morning.

I hope you are in good health. I seem to be dealing with a case of short-term memory loss. Could you kindly refresh my mind on our last conversation? Is this a knitting contest that we entered? I've always wanted to learn how to knit, but I can't see why I would choose to work with you.

Warmest regards,
Genesis Gonzalez
Administrative Marketing Assistant
Siren Music Records, New York Location

I smirked, feeling all too proud of myself as I began to respond to other work emails. I just finished answering one email about the stats on a social media campaign we'd run last month when I saw Will's name pop up at the top of my screen. I debated on jumping right into it but decided to be a good employee and get through a few more work-related emails before reading his response. My leg bounced as I read and responded to email after email, my mind already conjuring my next response to whatever his reply was, and when I finally got through my last work email, I quickly clicked on his unread message and read it.

From: wkobayashi@sirenmusicrecords.com
To: ggonzalez@siremusicrecords.com
Subject: Refreshing Your Memory

Genesis,

It is interesting how you seem to go through bouts of short-term memory at the most random times. Is this like that time you experienced a short-term memory loss and only forgot my coffee order during our quarterly meeting last year? For your safety, I think you should get that head of yours checked out.

As I'm not sure just how much was erased from your mind, I will give you a short summary that will hopefully jog your memory. We both entered a music contest that the company had opened to their employees. We were paired together to create a demo that we will submit to the company, and they will choose one song to include on their upcoming Music for the Cure album. This opportunity also comes with the potential of a contract for the producer—that would be you—to work with the company on future projects.

You have not yet agreed to work with me on this opportunity for reasons only you can answer. My guess is, you are intimidated by my talent. While I cannot promise that my talent won't awe you into feeling inferior, I can promise that I will be supportive of your talent—or lack thereof—and do everything in my power to win this contest.

Whether you are interested in winning is something that remains to be seen.

Regards,

Will Kobayashi

P.S. I would recommend Dr. Shari on 15th and 3rd for a neuro consultation. I wish you a speedy recovery.

To: wkobayashi@siremusicrecords.com

From: ggonzalez@siremusicrecords.com

Subject: Memory Has Miraculously Reappeared

Hello,

Thanks for that very detailed refresher and your sincere concern for my health. It always amazes me how … thoughtful you can be. While my memory is still a bit hazy, I don't remember your lack of musical abilities being a reason to feel intimidated so much as skeptical. Regardless, the situation is fresh in my head, and I am up to speed.

As always, it's been a pleasure, speaking with you.

Sincerely,

Genesis Gonzalez

I waited a few minutes to see if he would respond, but surprisingly, my inbox stayed empty. It didn't take long for me to get lost in the busy flow of work, and before I knew it, the morning had flown by, and I was taking my thirty-minute lunch at my desk, Cora joining me as we did some light shopping on my desk computer.

"I wish I had the legs to pull off this dress." Cora sighed sadly at my computer screen.

"You can pull off anything you want to wear," I said, looking at the emerald-green dress on the screen. "And there's nothing wrong with your legs."

"I'm short," Cora complained with a pout. "These legs get me where I need to be, and I'll love them for that, but they sure don't do me any favors when I'm standing next to leggy blondes at the bar."

I winced.

Yeah, I knew that had happened to Cora on more than one occasion. Being only five-two, she was struggling to meet average height, even with heels on. Last weekend, she'd gone to a bar with some coworkers, and she'd said that she saw a really cute guy, but he literally stopped talking to her mid-sentence when a beautiful, tall redheaded woman walked by and left her side to try and talk to her.

Honestly, men were trash.

"Why would you want to be with any guy who wasn't completely enamored with your beauty from the moment he saw you?" I asked, taking a bite out of my sandwich.

Today was a homemade turkey sandwich with cheese, tomato, and some lettuce, but if I was being honest with myself, I'd give anything for a chimichurri right now. I'd been daydreaming about that burger the entire week, and there was a great little Dominican food truck about five minutes from the job that made the best chimi burger I'd ever had in my life. There was something about the seasoning in their burger that I still couldn't figure out, but it had my mouth watering for more every time.

Cora shrugged, staying quiet. Her arm brushed into mine, pulling me out of my food daydream. "How about these boots for you?"

She must have taken control of the computer while I was dreaming about chimi burgers because we had left the dress section of the website and were now looking at shoes. The boots in question were thigh-high black boots with a thick heel that screamed my name.

"I like them, but I have enough boots in my closet to last me a lifetime," I admitted. "Besides, they aren't on sale, so I can't convince myself that it's worth the buy right now."

Cora leaned back in her chair, raising her arms above her head in a stretch. I watched as she began cleaning up her lunch and glanced at the clock. I had a meeting with some of the members on the digital marketing team later today, and I had to make sure I made time to get everyone's coffee orders situated and the reports printed and organized for each member.

"I say you bookmark the boots and buy them for yourself as a little treat," she said, tapping the top of the computer monitor. "What's the point in working if you don't get to buy the things you want?"

I opened my mouth to respond when I saw a tall figure in the corner of my eye, and while I couldn't see his full face, I knew that sharp jawline well enough to know exactly who it was. I turned my head and found Will standing at the entrance of my cubicle, annoyingly handsome and looking entirely unsurprised to see Cora in my space.

"Is the meeting about to start already?" Cora asked Will, quickly picking up her phone and tablet.

Will shook his head. "No, we still have a few minutes. I'm here to talk to Genesis."

"Oh," Cora said slowly, turning to look at me. I shook my head slightly, and she nodded and turned back toward Will with a smile. "I'll see you in a few!"

Will stepped out of the cubicle door so that Cora could leave, and I waved as she all but ran away. He silently stepped back in, eyes cataloguing every inch of my desk area. It was a small cubicle, so it didn't take him long to look around and make whatever judgments he was quietly making in that head of his. I thought he'd make some comment about the online shopping that was still on my computer screen, but surprisingly, he said nothing, looking around with a clinical, almost-detached eye. Like how I imagined he shopped for furniture or groceries. No outward show of emotion, but you could almost smell the disapproval rolling off him as he watched people sit on the furniture at the stores or the little kids tossing the box of sugary cereal in their cart.

I thought about the last time Alejandra and I had gone to the mattress store two years ago and how we'd spent over an hour just lying on all the beds and bouncing from one bed to the other, giggling like a bunch of five-year-olds as we made up elaborate stories about what kind of sleep each mattress would offer us. Beds that were too firm would give us early back problems, Alejandra had said decidedly, and would give you dreams about sleeping on clouds. I nearly smiled, just thinking about that day, and I knew without a doubt that had Will been there, he would've scolded us the entire time.

"Not that I don't love sitting here in silence with you," I said dryly, "but do you mind telling me what you want, so I can go about my day?"

He looked away from one of the photos on my desk—one of me with my sister and Yari at her high school graduation—and looked at me with that same expressionless look on his face. "Don't tell me your amnesia has come back for the second time today."

I narrowed my eyes. "It hasn't."

"The contest," he said bluntly with a wave of his hand. "Yes or no?"

No, I wanted to say, *because agreeing to work with you would feel a lot like agreeing to go back in time to work on the* Titanic *even though I knew what the outcome would be.*

"Yes," I said stiffly, fingers clenched.

He nodded, a small flash of emotion darting across his features before he was back to his aloof, cold self. "I have only one rule if we're going to do this."

I crossed my arms across my chest, already on the defense as I waited for him to continue.

"You need to give this opportunity one hundred percent of your effort. This competition is important to me, and I won't have you quitting on me."

"Finally, something we agree on." I stood up from my chair and looked at him head-on. "I will give my all to this contest for the next three months. All I ask is that you do the same."

His sharp cheekbones seemed heightened as he stared down at me. "Then, it's settled." He put his right hand out toward me, like we were shaking on a deal. "We're partners."

"*Temporary* music partners," I amended, staring warily at his hand.

After an awkward moment, where his hand did not move, I hesitantly put my hand in his, eyes locked on him. It felt like my hand was engulfed in his, and when his hand squeezed mine, it was like an electric shock went straight up my arm and through my body. I blinked, taken aback, and noted belatedly that I could feel rough calluses on his fingertips, probably from years of playing a string instrument. I quickly yanked my hand away, forcing all thoughts unrelated to music away.

"Is there anything else, or can I get back to my day?"

He hesitated, lips parting for a moment before he shook his head and stepped back. "We'll talk soon."

I said nothing, eyes tracking as he walked out of my cubicle and out of my line of sight. I slumped back into my seat, rubbing the palm of my hands across my eyes until I was seeing bright flashes of fireworks behind my eyes.

My heart beat loudly in my ears as I replayed our interaction over and over in my head. Music partners with Will. What a nightmare. What a total and complete nightmare.

We're going to win this contest, I told myself, instilling confidence into each word until I felt grounded once again. *Winning is the only thing that matters.*

I was in a weird mood the rest of the day.

I couldn't help it. Even though I was dealing with my new reality, I was having a hard time accepting it.

During free moments at work, I reread through every single email or form I'd received or sent since the contest had been first announced in December. I thought about my career—both with music and at Siren Records—and I knew that no matter what, I wasn't ready to give up on my dream.

I'd worked my ass off since I was five years old to become the musician I was today. I'd worked hard my whole life to get good grades, to win the scholarships to go to the prestigious music schools, and to win the awards that would help me obtain a dream that had always been just shy out of reach.

I'd gone to NYU with a full ride in their music program and still managed to double-major in business and take more classes than was probably legal. But I'd done it even if it'd meant taking six, sometimes seven, classes a semester, even taking the max amount of classes during the summer and winter breaks. All while still making music on the side, building connections with other musicians in my university and in the city, grabbing at every opportunity to make music, even when nine out of ten times, it amounted to nothing.

All of this was written in my bio for this contest and had been shared with Will. All the awards I'd won, all the projects I'd done—both at school and on the side—my degrees, all of it.

I'd hesitated at first when I was filling out the application because I didn't want to seem like I was bragging, but then I'd thought, *Fuck it. Why shouldn't I brag?*

I'd just never thought the person who'd be learning all this about me was the one guy who constantly toed the line between enemy and work colleague.

I blasted music in my ears the whole way home, simmering as the music sang along to my mixed bag of emotions. I started with some Slipknot because everything about their sound sang to me in moments like this and moved on to some Korn and Disturbed. I needed heavy drumbeats and low guitar riffs that were balanced with gravelly, deep voices that made me want to jump into a mosh pit and fight out all my uncertainties and frustrations. I might have been sitting in a smelly, packed train underground as a man's muffled demands for justice tried to pierce through my noise-canceling headphones, but in my head, I imagined the stack of reports I'd had to print, staple, and collate for fifteen people and visualized ripping up all the papers into a million little pieces, tossing them all over the room until it was like a thousand little white raindrops were raining down around me.

A book bag slammed into my back, knocking me out of my thoughts, and I looked around, disoriented.

"*Puto*," I grumbled, pushing my way to the exit when I saw we were at my stop.

I lowered the music in my ears, pushing my headphones off my head and letting them hang off my neck as I focused on being more aware of my surroundings and getting home. No place was safe enough when you were a woman.

Only when I turned the lock on my front door, my body inside my apartment, did I allow myself to relax.

"You're finally home!" Alejandra said from the couch.

I moved away from the front door and walked the short distance to our living room. I all but threw myself on the couch next to her. I looked toward the TV and grimaced when I saw she was watching *The Bachelor*.

"I don't know how you watch this every week."

"It's so good." She picked up the remote to fast-forward through the commercials. "Don't tell Yari I'm watching without her. I couldn't wait until tomorrow for her to come over."

I chuckled, shaking my head. "She's going to kill you."

Alejandra pressed play on the remote, and the sounds of the contestants speaking filled the room. I lay there on the couch, closing my eyes as I allowed myself to just relax—no angry music, no thoughts about work, just me, my sister, and the sound of the TV playing softly in the background.

I wasn't sure how much time had passed as I lay there before I felt someone poke me softly on the shoulder. I opened my eyes and took notice of the TV paused on the credits. I looked over to my right to see Alejandra slightly hovering over me, a nervous look on her face.

"What's wrong?" I asked, voice groggy with sleep.

I sat up, realizing suddenly that I hadn't even bothered to take my coat off before lying down on the sofa. I frowned, quickly standing up to hang it on one of the coat hooks by the front door.

"I wanted to talk to you about something," she said nervously. "And before you say anything else, it's a good thing. It's … exciting, actually."

"Okay," I said, curious. "Tell me."

"I've figured out my dream career," she said in a rush of words. "It's something I've been thinking about for a while now, a few years really, but I've always been a little bit scared to admit it. But I took the leap, and I got a contract with a company, so—"

"Whoa, whoa." I watched her with furrowed brows. "Slow down. What's the career? What contract?"

"I want to be a model," she said, standing tall. "I've got the following on social media and the height to pull it off. The best part is, a modeling agency contacted me a few weeks ago, and they want me to come into their office to talk about signing with them!"

I stared at her with wide eyes, disbelief and shock racing through me. Out of all the things I'd thought she'd say, this was definitely not one of them. Alejandra was beautiful, so I had no doubt that she'd gotten the attention of a modeling agency, especially with the thousands of followers she had on social media and the fact that she was five-ten and had legs for days. But the last we'd talked, she'd said she was thinking of becoming a vet or maybe a teacher.

"You can't be serious," I blurted. "What about school?"

She shrugged, arms crossing across her chest. "What about it?"

"You need to stay in school!" I exclaimed. "Aleja, modeling is not a forever career. What are you going to do when you get older and the modeling gigs die down?"

"I never said I was going to drop out of school." Frustration seeping into her voice. "Why can't you just be happy for me and not tell me all the reasons why it won't work?"

"I ..." I trailed off, trying to pick my words carefully. "I want you to be successful. Modeling is—it's not something you've ever talked about before."

"Because I knew you wouldn't understand," she shot back, face flushed with anger. "You've always been the one with the big dreams, and I've never felt like I could have them too. Why is it you get to chase your dream, but I can't chase mine?"

I stared at her, mouth dropping in shock. "Aleja—"

She shook her head, long dark-brown hair shaking around her oval-shaped face. "Don't even bother. I'm done talking with you right now."

She tossed the remote onto the sofa and all but stomped to her room, leaving me alone in the living room. I heard her door close quietly a moment later, and I sighed heavily.

What a freaking day.

The next day dragged.

No matter how many texts I'd sent my sister last night or how much I'd knocked at her door, she wouldn't answer. She was really mad at me, and I was at a loss as to how to fix things. To top it off, I'd come into work today with an email from Will, requesting that we meet after work to go over preliminary details for our song.

Our song. I still couldn't believe that I would be working with Will for the next three months to create a song. Two parts of my life intersecting in the most bizarre, alternate universe, where I would be creating a song with the one guy I couldn't stand. I guessed it was true what they said—you couldn't have a piece of heaven without going through a little bit of hell.

When I stepped into the emptying finance department, it wasn't hard to find Will. He was standing outside his office, talking to Derek, one of the assistants from his department. Will looked up when he saw the door open, eyes not leaving mine as he said something to Derek before turning away from him. I watched as Derek scurried off to his little desk at the front of the room, and with a quick, relieved wave, he walked out.

I raised a brow. "So, I guess harassing assistants is your kink, huh?"

"You're here," he said, somehow sounding both surprised and pleased.

"Where else would I be?" I replied with a forced smile.

I was trying really hard to be cordial, to not start the partnership already ready to fight. One look from him, and I could tell this would take every piece of patience that I had, and after working all day, I couldn't say that I had much left.

His eyes dropped for a second before he turned wordlessly and walked into his office. I grumbled under my breath but followed after him, a part of me curious about what his office looked like. I'd seen it from afar when I came in here to chat with Cora, but most times, he had his office door closed.

My first impression now was that looking into this room, I would assume no one used it at all. The room was designed with simple decor. A big desk took up most of the room and had multiple monitors on it. He had a desk chair that looked ten times more comfortable than the cheap desk chair I had at my desk and a big window that filled the entire wall behind it.

There was a chair across from his desk, but Will surprised me by moving his desk chair out from behind the monitors and rolling it over so that we were sitting side by side, the chairs angled to face each other head-on. He laid a hand out toward the chairs, and I walked over and plopped down on his desk chair, holding back my groan of pleasure at how comfortable his chair was. He made a small, rough sound, but when I looked up at him, his face was impassive, and he moved smoothly to the empty chair, taking a seat like nothing had happened.

"So …"

"So," he replied, "according to the email, we only get two sessions in the studio. The rest is up to us. What are your thoughts on doing most of the song on our own and using those two studio sessions to put final touches on our demo?"

I frowned in thought. "I have studio equipment at home. I guess I could bring some stuff to work when the time comes."

"I have a small studio at my apartment," he said.

My head jerked back against his seat at his words.

"It's nothing too fancy, but I have few instruments, some mics, and plenty of space to work on our song."

"Whoa, whoa. I'm not going to your place," I blurted, eyes widening. "What are you trying to do, move me to a different location so you can murder me?"

He pressed his lips into a line, looking unamused. "I'm trying to win a contest."

"So am I," I refuted. "What's wrong with making the song here, in this office?"

I knew the answer the moment I finished the last word. The acoustics in this room sucked—not to mention, the cleaning crew came shortly after we closed, so it wouldn't be the quietest space. I sighed heavily, trying to think of another solution. We could do my place, but the only thing worse than going to Will's place was having him invade my own. But even so, spending time with Will outside of work? At his place? That sounded crazy.

"We could do a trial period," he offered. "My place is only a few stops from work, so it wouldn't take long to travel, but if at any time you don't feel comfortable, we'll figure out a different space to work."

I stared at him, slightly suspicious. He was being oddly … fair.

What was his motive?

To win, you idiot, I reminded myself, nearly rolling my eyes at myself.

"Okay, fine."

He nodded shortly. "Let's talk scheduling. I think we should meet after work as much as possible."

I grimaced, even as I reluctantly agreed. "Three times a week?"

"Four," he replied, shifting in his chair so that he was angled closer. "Does Monday through Thursday work? We can do a few hours each night."

"It's never taken me three months to finish a song, especially if I'm working on it that consistently," I pointed out.

"Good. So then, we'll have plenty of time to tweak it and make sure that it's absolutely perfect before the deadline," he answered definitively.

Madre de Dios, he was so bossy.

"Four days a week?"

I sighed but nodded. "Fine." The faster I finished the song, the faster I could get away from him.

"We'll start on Monday," he said, standing up from his chair.

I caressed the soft leather of the chair in a soft good-bye and stood up too. "Fine."

I stood there for a second, unsure. But he was packing up his stuff, back toward me, and I realized belatedly that I had been dismissed.

I was tired of this partnership, and we hadn't even really started yet.

When I got home, Yari was eating in the kitchen.

"*Hola, chica!*" she yelled over the sound of the dishes clattering into the sink.

I dropped my stuff by the door and walked over, giving her a kiss on the cheek in greeting. "I thought you were going out to the mall with your mom after work?"

Yari turned off the water in the sink and dried her hands on a towel. "She wants to go tomorrow instead because she's worried it'll rain, and you know how she is about going outside when it rains."

I nodded. My tía had a thing about bad weather being a bad omen. Every time there was a thunderstorm, she used to tell us that it was God looking for someone to punish for their bad deeds. I'd never met someone so afraid of Mother Nature the way my aunt was.

I opened the fridge, looked inside, and closed it, all in the span of five seconds. Sometimes, you just knew before you even opened the fridge door that it was going to disappoint you, and yet you still opened it, hoping there'd be something in there that would surprise you and be exactly what you were craving.

The microwave timer went off, and Yari pulled out a plate with mangú, her face giddy. "God, I love your mangú."

Mangú was a traditional Dominican breakfast dish—though it could be eaten for lunch or dinner too—and it was one of Yari's favorite comfort foods. I knew without her saying anything that something had to be bothering her, but I also knew that she only talked about things when she was ready.

I shook my head. "I have a feeling you only come over here because you like a free meal."

Yari threw me a wink. "Not true. You know I come here to escape my mom. Your food is the second reason I'm always here."

I laughed. "Love you too."

I followed her into the living room and joined her at the couch as she put her plate on the coffee table.

"How was work?" she asked, taking a bite into her food.

I shrugged. "It was fine. I had to meet with Will today about the contest."

Yari threw me a consoling smile. "How did that go?"

"Surprisingly, it wasn't the worse conversation we'd ever had," I said, leaning back against the sofa. "He was his usual arrogant, bossy self, but we managed to agree on a place to work on the song and a schedule."

"Wow," she said, looking impressed. "So, what are the deets?"

I hesitated. "We're going to be working on the song four times a week … at his place."

"Damn, girl, you move fast," she joked, wagging her eyebrows. "Next thing I know, you'll be telling me that you're having sleepovers, where you make a song based on your lovemaking."

I fake gagged. "Ugh, please don't make me sick. It's nothing like that at all. He has a space for us to practice, and he lives close to the job. It just makes sense in terms of time. Besides, I'm just trying to write the best song and record it with him, so I can win this contest and then never have to see him again."

"You know you'll probably still see him, right?" she asked, putting her spoon down. "Especially if you win. He's probably going to be in so many promotional ads and videos that you'll be seeing more of him than ever."

I huffed in annoyance. "You know what I mean."

She hummed but said nothing for a long moment as she went back to focusing on her food. "Hey, what's going on with you and your sister? She texted me, saying she's doesn't want to go to the movies this weekend if you're going."

I sighed. "She's mad at me because I didn't react … well to her career announcement last night."

"Career announcement?" Yari asked, brows furrowed in confusion. "Did she choose a major?"

I shook my head. "Not quite. She's decided that she wants to be a model."

Yari nodded slowly. "I could see it. She's incredibly beautiful and always getting stopped when we're out."

I quickly filled her in on the rest of the story, about everything that had been said last night and especially about Alejandra's words about my dream versus her own. When I finished, I looked at her and asked uncertainly, "Do you think she's right? That I'm not being fair?"

"Do you think you're being fair?" she asked bluntly.

I thought about my words, about the situation and why I'd reacted the way I did last night. "I just want to make sure she's going to be okay. That she'll be able to take care of herself. Modeling doesn't offer many options for her to fall back on. If she had a backup career—"

"You mean, like you did?" Yari pointed out with a tilt of her head.

I opened and closed my mouth, stumped. Technically, that was what I had done. I'd double majored in music technology and business not because I necessarily wanted to work in the business field, but because I felt like I needed a backup, something that I could fall back on in case my dreams tanked. But what was wrong with that? I was being realistic, and the reality was that it was expensive to be a human on this earth, especially in New York City. I'd wanted to make sure that I was going to be okay, that I was going to be able to afford food and a home, no matter what.

"Maybe it's not about what's a better career option, but about what makes her happy," Yari said softly, somehow always knowing what I was thinking before I say it. "Going to college isn't a guarantee for success or happiness. And Alejandra's not saying she won't go to college—you jumped to that conclusion all on your own."

"You think I'm too hard on her," I said flatly, averting my eyes as guilt began to eat me up inside.

"You *are* too hard on her, but she needs it," Yari admitted, and I must've perked up because she quickly added, "*Sometimes.* But she also needs for you to just be her supportive big sister, who believes in whatever crazy dream she wants to chase next."

I stayed quiet at that, thinking. Was Yari right? I thought I'd gotten so stuck on being Alejandra's mom that I sometimes forgot to be her sister. I knew I'd hate for anyone to remind me of how crazy my dreams were or how unrealistic they were, yet here I was, doing it to my own sister. That guilt came crashing back tenfold.

I had known what I wanted to do since I was a little girl, and even though it was an impossible dream, no one told me that I couldn't do it. My father had encouraged my dream since the moment I held an instrument in my hands, and my family had always supported my dreams like they were their own.

But here I was, doing the exact opposite with Alejandra. She'd found something she felt passionate about, and instead of supporting her, I'd told her that her dream was a waste of time. I cringed, just thinking about my stupid words, the way that she'd flinched away and shut down so quickly, like a part of her couldn't handle hearing me say them.

I had to fix this.

True to her word, Alejandra canceled on movie night and then sent a text the next night that she'd be spending the next few days at James's place and not to worry. Even though I wanted to go over there and force her to talk to me, I knew my sister well enough to know that if I did that, it would only make her madder.

"You'd better tell me everything," Cora said, zippering up her puffy red jacket. "I'll be checking all local news stations for murder or house fires."

"Ha-ha." I glanced toward her department door down the hall.

The elevator dinged loudly, and a moment later, the doors opened.

Cora walked over, turning to look at me when she stepped into the elevator. "Remember, this is the day that you'll look back on when you're a big and famous music producer. The beginning of everything. I can *feel* it."

I couldn't help the small laugh that escaped from my mouth as I let her words wash over me. Damn Cora and her never-ending bouts of optimism. I could feel her energy trying to draw me in, to make me drop my skepticism and wariness and join her in the land of excitement and joy.

"We'll see," I said instead, giving her a wave as she stepped fully into the elevator and the doors slowly closed.

I was left alone in the hall, the soft hum of the elevator my only company in the otherwise quiet space. I leaned against the wall and sighed, glancing once more at the glass door to my left. Was he gone? I shook my head, immediately dismissing the thought. Will was a lot of things—a lot of things I hated—but there was no way he was dropping out of this contest. Despite my every wish for him to do so.

A moment later, I saw him exit from his office, long legs eating up the space between us in only a few strides. His face was set in that carefully blank expression that he always wore around me, his way—I'd always thought—of containing his true irritation and dislike of me. He was a lot better at not showing his emotions on his face than I was, but his words always said more than his face ever could.

His eyes took a quick, clinical perusal of me, stopping on my foot that was bouncing lightly. I stood up straight and pushed away from the way wall, making the short trek to the elevator to press the down button.

"You're late," I said evenly, trying to keep the accusation out of my tone.

I heard him shift beside me, but I kept my gaze on the closed elevator doors.

"Last-minute conference call that went over," he responded shortly.

We stood there in silence as we waited for the elevator, and when it came, we got on without a word. That was my quota of forcing small talk with someone I didn't like. Will must've had the same thought because he didn't say a single word as we walked out of the building and I followed him to the train station. I kept my gait fast as I walked beside him, moving through the crowds of people rushing to their own destinations after a long day of work.

The underground platforms were crowded, but we managed to squeeze ourselves onto the six train. I squished between Will and a stranger who kept stumbling into me. I kept my head down to avoid the man breathing on my face, counting down the minutes until I could get off this crowded train. After the sixth time of this guy bumping into me, his hand brushed against the arm of my jacket, fingers almost touching my wrist. I flinched away, bumping my back against Will's side and stepping on his foot. I glanced up at Will, who was scowling darkly at the man across from us. His dark eyebrows were furrowed in the deepest frown I'd ever seen on his face, a dark look flashing across his face. The man held up his hands and backed up a small step, eyes slightly wide in fear.

I stepped away from Will, now able to keep my head up without fear of having that man's breath in my face. My head turned toward to look behind me, watching as the stranger pushed and squeezed himself to the middle of the cart before looking back at Will.

"Not a fan of crowded trains?" I asked, an apology on the tip of my tongue.

His shiny black shoe now had my footprint against the front of it, and his foot no doubt had to be in pain.

He looked down at me, scowling. "We're the next stop."

I looked away, a flush creeping up my cheeks. I didn't know why I'd broken my silence in the first place.

When the train stopped at the next stop, I quickly pushed my way through, blindly walking to the nearest exit. I had just put my hand on the turnstile to exit when I heard Will speak up behind me.

"You're going the wrong way," he grumbled. "My exit's on the opposite end of the platform."

I growled under my breath, hand squeezing into a fist before I turned around and silently walked the other way. Will walked steadily beside me, his feet hardly making a sound on the concrete floor—unlike my own, which were making a decidedly loud clap with each step of my suede ankle boots as I all but stomped to the other exit.

When we exited the underground station, the cold air slapped me clear across the face, and I tried to push my face more deeply into the neck of my coat as we walked down a long block. New York winters were the worst, and I could only hope that the spring weather would come soon and, with it, the warm breeze and longer sunny days.

We walked quietly for a few blocks before Will turned toward a shiny, tall apartment building that had a doorman stationed outside.

"Good evening, Mr. Kobayashi," the man greeted with a smile.

"John, how are you doing?" Will greeted with a nod, face softening a bit as he looked at the older man.

"Can't complain," John said jovially. He glanced toward me and nodded. "Good evening, miss."

"Evening," I said with a small smile.

Will walked inside, and I followed behind, taking in the open, beautifully decorated lobby. There were mailboxes lined up on one side of the wall when you first walked in and a front desk, where a young woman was seated, tapping away at her computer. The floor was an exquisite shade of gray, like if you held up the color to the sun and the light reflected through it, and the rest of the interior matched it perfectly with white accents throughout. There were a few small couches and a table stationed around a fireplace near the elevators, but Will didn't stop as he walked straight to the elevators.

The inside of the elevator was a golden yellow, and I stood on one side, trying not to touch anything. I wouldn't be surprised to find it was real gold, and the last thing I needed was Will accusing me of damaging anything in his luxury apartment building.

I watched as the numbers in the dashboard went up and up until we stopped on the eighth floor, the doors opening with a soft beep.

Will glanced at me before stepping out of the elevator, and I followed him down a short hall that led to one apartment door. I looked behind us and saw another door farther down on the opposite side of the elevator, but it looked like that was the only other door on this floor.

A moment later, Will opened the door and flicked a light switch before entering. "Do you mind taking your shoes off by the door?"

I watched as he put his shoes on a rack, his feet slipping into his black house shoes. I'd call them slippers, but they really didn't look like the slippers I typically used or saw. They almost looked like shoes, except the back of the shoe was open and it looked like the material was leather.

I silently slipped off my shoes and stood uncertainly at the door in my unicorn-themed socks.

Will passed me a wrapped-up pair of slippers, brand-new in the packaging. "These should fit you."

I blinked, a million questions and thoughts running through my mind, but I pushed them away as I gingerly took the slippers from him and put them on. They were a light red color and were a lot softer than I'd expected. "Thanks."

Will nodded, and then he walked to a little closet by the door and took out a few hangers. I quickly took off my coat and passed it to him, and after he put both of our stuff away, I followed him farther into the apartment.

The short hallway opened into a spacious living room— high ceiling, wide-open space that somehow managed to feel minimalist even though there was a lot going on in the room. On one end of the room, there was a huge flat screen TV hanging on a wall, the thing big enough to rival a movie theater and definitely bigger than anything I had at home.

My family would have a field day with this TV, I thought to myself.

If one of my uncles bought a TV this big, the party would probably last for weeks.

Underneath the flat screen was a table holding a surround sound system, and along the walls on either side of the TV were shelves upon shelves of DVDs and what I thought were some CD albums, maybe some vinyls as well. There was a black sectional sofa that just from one glance, I could tell cost more than probably anything in my entire apartment.

On the opposite end of the room, I saw a small dining room table with a few chairs sitting not far from where the kitchen entrance was. The kitchen itself looked a bit smaller and had an open window and countertop with a few stools outside of it, the ivory-white countertops and cabinets shining against the lights.

It appeared that the living room was the main room, as there were doors on all of the three remaining walls, which presumably led to the other parts of the apartment.

I counted four additional doors before I noticed that Will was watching me take in his place, and I quickly stood up straight, making sure my mouth was closed and not opened like a guppy fish in surprise.

"Do you want a tour of the place?"

I looked toward the stack of CDs sitting on the coffee table across from the sofa before shaking my head. "Maybe some other time. We should probably get started."

He nodded and continued walking toward a door in the right corner of the living room. Despite my extreme dislike of this man, I couldn't help but be curious. My eyes were raking in every detail, moving from wall to wall, noticing a Jimi Hendrix poster hanging by one door, a painting of a cheery blossom tree hanging by the next. My eyes snagged on the painting before noticing that the white door next to it was open a crack.

I was so busy deciding between looking into the room and reminding myself not to be a creep that I didn't notice that Will had stopped walking and I slammed right into his back. I bounced back a bit, and I looked up after I got my bearing to find Will already looking down at me. He had turned his body so that he was leaning against the closed door, his leg bent so that his foot could rest on the door, his arms crossed across his chest. His eyes moved from the half-opened door to me with a small smirk. I scowled to hide my embarrassment, trying not to register the fact that his face was attractive as hell when he looked at me like that.

"Is there a reason we're standing out here and not in your music room?" I asked coolly, crossing my arms across my chest too.

"I just wanted to give you enough time to … take in the apartment," he answered smoothly, but the way his mouth hitched at the corner let me know he was teasing me and much too pleased with himself. "Are you ready?"

"Are you?" I shot back, waving my hands in front of me. "The only thing I'm interested in seeing is where we'll be practicing and making music."

He cocked his head slightly, as if to say, *You are a lying liar*, but he stayed silent. Instead, he moved off of the door and turned to open it, ushering me inside.

The room didn't appear very big, but that could be because there were instruments pretty much surrounding all four corners of the room: a few guitars—acoustic, electric, and even a ukulele—a drum set, a keyboard on a stand. The only non-musical instruments were the computer on the desk with some soundboards and two couches on opposite sides of a small table in the middle of the room.

"You can take a seat by the table," he said, closing the door behind me.

I took in the room, fingers itching to touch everything. This was like my dream space—what I wanted when I could afford my own apartment. "Do you play them all?" I blurted out, unable to stop myself from lightly touching the keyboard as I walked by it.

"Mostly guitar, but I've dabbled with pretty much every instrument at one point in time," he answered as he took a seat, resting his elbows on his legs. "You?"

"Same," I answered, taking a seat on the opposite side of the table.

We looked at each other for a long moment.

"So," he said, "the song."

"The song," I repeated. Then, because I was trying to be cordial, I added, "Do you have any ideas?"

"I have plenty," he said readily.

I rolled my eyes. "Thanks for that helpful response. In the past, I've—"

"I'm not interested in hearing what you did in the past," he replied briskly. "We need this song to be unique, something that will make us stand out among the other contestants."

"I agree," I said between gritted teeth. "I didn't say I was going to use something I'd done in the past. I was trying to explain how I've worked on songs with musicians in the past."

Will stared at me blankly. "And how was that?"

"Well, depending on how involved the musician wanted to be in the process—"

"I want to be very involved," Will said, cutting me off once again, making my blood pressure spike. "Every step of the way, I want to be there, giving feedback, adding my own ideas to the song."

Of course he did.

"That's fine. What I usually do is work with the musician to figure out either what we want our sound to be or what we want the song to be about."

He nodded shortly. "I think we should do a love song."

I grimaced. "No, everyone will do that."

"Love songs are popular for a reason," he argued. "People like love songs, and it's something universal that can attract a wide audience."

I shrugged. "That doesn't mean we should do it. Love songs are the easy way out. I thought you wanted to win."

"It's *because* I want to win that I'm telling you, we should do a love song," Will responded, voice hard.

On and on we went for the next hour. Every point I made, Will had a counterargument until it felt like we had both lost sight of the actual contest and were just arguing for argument's sake. Half the crap coming out of my mouth didn't even make sense, but the point was, if I didn't start putting my foot down and making sure my ideas were being heard, then I had no doubt that Will would take control of the entire thing.

"There's nothing wrong with some heavy metal influences in a traditional pop song," I argued, butt half off my chair as I threw my hands up in the air in frustration. "Haven't you ever heard Ozzy Osbourne's cover of 'Stayin' Alive'? Or Guns N' Roses' cover of 'Live and Let Die'?"

"Yeah, and there's a reason why those covers aren't well known," Will shot back. "It's not disco if it's got a heavy metal guitar riff in it. Now, it's just a rock song, which defeats the entire purpose of the song."

I groaned, looking away from Will and toward the small window behind the guitar stands. It looked really dark outside, and I noticed in the silence that there was the heavy sound of rain pelting the window.

"Crap, what time is it?"

A quick glance at my phone told me that I'd been here for nearly two hours. We'd spent nearly two hours arguing about every single piece of this potential song and gotten absolutely nothing done. The only thing we'd managed to agree on was that we both had very different ideas on just about everything when it came to music. Will thought country music would be the next big international sensation; I thought it was a tired-out genre that used the same sound regurgitated into a million songs about pickup trucks and broken hearts. When I said we should think about making our song be about perseverance and never giving up—since it was an album for medical research—he said that was corny and a too-obvious choice. Which, okay, fine. Maybe it was the obvious choice, but so was his stupid love song idea!

"Well, this was a waste of time," I said, sighing heavily as I stood up. My back ached from not moving for so long, and I stretched my hands above my head, ignoring Will, who got up and looked outside the window.

"It was a waste of time because you wouldn't listen to any of my ideas," he answered.

"You wouldn't listen to any of mine!" I protested. "I admitted one of your ideas wasn't that bad, but you shot down every single thing I said."

Will gave me a sardonic look. "You said, and I quote, 'That's not the worst idea you've ever had, Willy. On the list of ideas that will guarantee we lose, this is a solid four.' "

I shrugged. "That was me being nice. Really, it was more of a six, but I deducted two points for originality."

Will shook his head, taking another look outside his window. "It's raining outside."

"Yes, I'm aware," I said slowly.

"Let me drive you home," he said, turning his head to look at me from across the room.

I immediately shook my head. "I'm good with the train."

"You're going to get soaked," he growled. "Stop being stubborn and just say yes."

"I'll be fine," I said, giving him a weird look. "I've walked home in the rain before. I won't melt if I get a little wet."

He looked like he was ready to argue some more, but I ignored him, heading to the door and making my way to the closet with my stuff. It didn't take long for me to get my things together and to slip my feet back into my boots by the front door.

Will opened the door, and I quickly stepped out. I wanted to keep walking, to not stop until I got to the elevator and out of this building, but ingrained manners forced me to turn around.

Will gave me a pointed look, like he knew what I'd been thinking, and I scowled. "Good luck in the storm. If I don't see you tomorrow, I'll look for you in the puddles of water near my building."

I rolled my eyes. "Good-bye, Willy."

I turned around and began walking.

"Stop calling me that," Will said from behind me, and I smiled, secretly pleased that my nickname was bothering him.

"No," I replied, "I don't think I will."

"Okay," Will said. And then after a short pause, he added, "Buttercup."

I scowled, stopping at the elevators and pressing the button. I turned to him. "That's not my name."

"And Willy is not mine," he responded easily, leaning against his open door.

I stared at his form, at the arrogant confidence on his face, the small tilt of his mouth, like I'd no doubt had on my own when I thought I had the upper hand just moments before. His white button-down was still perfectly crisp, not a single wrinkle despite the very long day we'd had, his shirt stretching across his broad shoulders.

I narrowed my eyes when I saw his lips extend a bit higher, an almost smile on his face.

"I don't like you," I said just as the doors to the elevator opened.

His smile dimmed slightly. "I'm aware," he said almost bitterly.

I stepped onto the elevator without another word, not making a single sound until I saw the doors close in front of me. It wasn't until the elevator began moving that I let myself exhale roughly, hands running through my hair.

"He's driving me insane," I groaned out loud.

Nobody answered, my reflection on the golden door my only company.

The next day, we met after work for yet another failed session.

I should've known that things weren't going to go well when the first thing Will said when he saw me was, "Oh good. I don't have to call the police to file a missing persons report."

I'd been five minutes late.

He was in a bad mood, face sketched in an almost-permanent frown, his responses short and more blunt than usual. Thirty minutes into this meeting, and I was questioning what the point of meeting today even was, other than Will driving me to early gray hairs.

"Honestly, what is your problem?" I snapped after my third idea was shut down the moment the last word was out of my mouth.

"I have no problem," he replied shortly, fingers clenching the arm of his chair. He looked away, a scowl on his face as he drilled a hole into the instruments on the wall beside him.

"Well then, why do you keep shooting down all my ideas?" I asked, exasperated. "And don't say you're not because I just used an idea you had come up with yesterday, and now, all of a sudden, you hate it."

Will shrugged, shoulder tight. "People change their minds. I just don't like any of the ideas you're coming up with. I'm not going to say yes to a bad idea just to placate your feelings."

My eyes narrowed to angry slits, and I reminded myself to take a deep breath before responding. "Okay, well then, what are your ideas?"

I waited in the silent music room for Will to talk, to say anything, but he didn't. He just kept staring at the wall of instruments, brooding. I sighed heavily, leaning back in my chair, and looked across the room, toward his recording equipment.

How could Will afford all of this stuff? I knew he probably made more than me, but was there really that big of a discrepancy in pay between us that he could afford a luxury apartment in the city with a music room filled with up-to-date equipment and instruments?

I didn't think I'd ever get used to this apartment or the ways that it was strikingly clear how differently our lives were outside of work. I would probably never be comfortable with that much money—hell, I'd probably never make enough to afford a place in the good part of Manhattan. The closest I'd get to moving from Queens into the city would be to Spanish Harlem.

Another few minutes went by, neither of us talking, just staring at anything but each other.

"So," I said, voice loud in the quiet room, "are you going to say anything, or are we going to spend the rest of this hour just sitting in silence?"

Will's phone lit up on the table, and unconsciously, my eyes moved to the screen. From what I could see, it looked like a notification of a work email. I tried to look closer to see more when his hand snatched the phone off the table, making me flinch back in surprise.

"Let's end early," he suggested, voice rough and low.

I stared at him in shock, but he ignored my gaping face and smoothly got up from his chair.

"What happened to taking this competition seriously?" I challenged, unable to help myself.

Will finally looked at me, and I blinked at the powerful emotions that flickered across his face for a moment before it disappeared. But for the short moment that it'd been there, he'd looked frustrated … and a little sad.

"I thought I could practice today, but I can't," he said, voice calmer than it'd been all day. "I'm sorry."

I bit my lip to hold in the questions on the tip of my tongue, shocked and—to my surprise—concerned. I wanted to ask what was wrong, but that thought alone had me standing up and quietly walking to the door.

He's not your friend, I reminded myself. *You shouldn't care.*

It didn't take long for me to get my stuff together, and this time, there were no words hurled at each other as I waited for the elevator. I couldn't help but peek at him a few times while I waited, at war with myself. I casually turned my head to look down the hall and glanced at Will, who was still standing silently at his door, a faraway look on his face.

The elevator made a loud ding, and I turned away, waiting for the doors to open. I took one step, paused, and debated on saying good-bye, but before I could turn to look at him, he'd closed his door with a soft click.

"Broody man," I mumbled, taking my headphones from my light-brown bag, and hanging them around my neck. I began to scroll through my playlist on my phone until I found the one I had been looking for and clicked on it. The music blasted from my headphones around my neck, so I could hear the melancholy sounds of the viola playing.

When the doors opened to the lobby, I walked out, passing the woman at the front desk, and thanked the doorman as I exited. It didn't take me long to walk to the train, and it was a surprisingly smooth ride home on the train. I even managed to get a seat, which was rare at this time of day.

I walked into my apartment to the sound of the television blasting in the living room, and the lights were on in the hall and kitchen even though no one was there. I turned off the hall light as I looked into the kitchen, which was near the entrance, confirming my suspicion, and shut off the light in there, too, before turning into the living room.

Alejandra was lying on the sofa with Yari, both of them laughing at something on the screen. They looked up when I walked in, but only Yari greeted me.

"Hey, how was the session?" Yari asked, tossing Alejandra the remote.

She caught it easily, and she looked at me with curiosity in her eyes, but when she saw that I saw, she looked back at the TV and continued ignoring me.

"It was fine," I said, standing awkwardly at the entrance.

The room was tense with unsaid words, and Yari looked between us, sensing it. She gave me a pointed look but pulled out her phone and became engrossed in her Solitaire app.

"Alejandra, can I speak with you?" I said, cutting off the silence. I tilted my head toward the bedroom. "It'll be quick, I promise."

She nodded and got up from the couch. She brushed past me and strode into the hall and to her room. She sat down on her bed, one leg tucked under her butt, and she leaned back on her hands as she watched me.

"What's up?" she asked.

"I wanted to talk to you about the conversation we had on Monday," I started, sitting down next to her. "About modeling."

"What about it?" Alejandra questioned warily, her face guarded.

"Tell me more about it," I said earnestly. "If this is something you really want to do, I want to support you."

"Really?" she asked skeptically. "Because you didn't seem excited or even remotely happy when I told you last week. What, now, you suddenly think I'm pretty enough to be successful?"

"Whoa, wait. What?" I said, confused. "When did I ever say I didn't think you could do it because you weren't pretty enough? Alejandra, you are *gorgeous*. Of course you'd get scouted by a big modeling agency; anyone would be crazy not to want you as their client."

"But isn't that why you were so against it? Because you think I won't make enough money with just my looks?" Alejandra said, a bitter look on her face as she looked up toward the ceiling. "I know that's what Mom will say, probably the whole family."

"That's not true," I argued. "Everyone will be happy for you, and I know you'd make good money. You're beautiful, Aleja; don't tell me you don't know that."

She was five-ten, skinny but fit with the slightest curves. Long dark-brown hair and light-brown eyes. A face so beautiful that she'd stop traffic with just one look. Literally, it'd happened before. A car had nearly crashed and caused a collision because the driver had been so busy staring at Alejandra when we were standing at the crosswalk. Alejandra had everything and more to become a model. I had no doubt that she'd take the world by storm and make it big.

That was never my problem.

My concern was what the media would do to my sister's already-fragile self-confidence. My concern was that her working in a field that was so obsessed with an ideal image of beauty instead of looking at beauty as a prism would make her feel like she needed to look and be a certain way. I was worried that the industry would take my sweet, strong, but slightly sheltered and naive sister and break her. And I couldn't let that happen.

"It's kind of hard to remember that when your family is always criticizing you," Alejandra said dejectedly. She continued in a higher pitch to sound like our aunts, "Oh, Alejandra, you'd be so much prettier if you stopped getting so dark. Why don't you put on some sunblock when you go out? You're too tall, Alejandra. Why do you insist on wearing heels so much?"

My family could be very critical but especially of each other. It was like because they knew us, they felt they could be hypercritical about everything, and we were just supposed to be okay with it because they were family. And while my family liked to critique the fact that I was perpetually single and not interested in settling down anytime soon, they loved to critique Alejandra about things that were completely out of her control. She was one of the tallest girls in our family and had a darker skin tone compared to many of our other cousins. Her skin was a warm brown, the kind of brown people spent hours in the sun trying to achieve.

For as long as I could remember, my family always made comments about Alejandra having darker skin than almost everyone else. I could remember years of them plastering sunblock on both of us but especially Alejandra, telling her not to be outside for too long because she didn't need to get any "darker." They swore they had only the best intentions, but their rhetoric said otherwise.

The lighter a woman's skin color was, the more beautiful she was, according to some of my older family members. This wasn't something they just believed on their own though. The colorism in Dominican Republic and their constant disbelief of its existence would only continue to have astronomical effects on many Dominican people for generations to come. It frustrated me to no end how so many of my relatives refused to listen or own up to how harmful their words were. They loved to scream that they weren't racist, and yet in the same breath, they'd base a woman's beauty or chances of marriage on her looks.

There were many things that I loved about being Dominican, but the blatant skin-color bias was not one of them.

"They are a bunch of idiots who can't stand that you're young and beautiful and they're old and … frumpy," I said, stomping my foot like an agitated five-year-old.

Alejandra cracked a smile, and I felt my heart squeeze, relieved that she was listening, that she was giving me a chance to talk and not shutting me out.

"I know their words hurt, but you can't let what they think have any power over how you feel about yourself. They will always find something wrong with you because they can't stand just how irrelevant their opinion really is."

"It's not that easy when they're always making me feel so insecure," she responded with a sigh. "They don't make comments about your body or the way you look—"

"Just the occasional comment about my weight," I cut in dryly. "They stopped making comments about the way I look because they know I won't change or try to change to make them happy. Instead, they put all their focus on my self-worth being entirely tied to being in a relationship. Such a fun feeling, don't you agree?"

"Well, I'm in a relationship; otherwise, I'm sure they'd add that to the list of things I'm doing wrong," Alejandra pointed out.

"Regardless," I pressed, "they should have no say on whether or not you do modeling. So, tell me the details and keep nothing out."

Alejandra smiled. "Okay, well, I was scouted by someone who works for Elite Model Management." She laughed at my shocked expression. "Yeah, I was just as surprised as you. Anyway, he told me to send over some headshots, and we exchanged emails, and … well, that was that."

"Did you send over the headshots yet?" I asked, trying to think about how I could squeeze a few extra hundred dollars for her to get some professional photographs taken.

I mean, it was Elite Model Management! They'd had models like Heidi Klum, Tyra Banks, and even Cindy Crawford at one point. This place was no joke, and if she could actually get represented by them, she would have a real chance at making it.

"I could probably spare two hundred this week, but anything more would have to wait."

"No need," Alejandra said merrily. Now that she saw that I was taking her seriously, she was back to her usual upbeat and excited self. "One of James's friends did the shots for me for free. He's a photography major, and he's really, really good. I sent the headshots yesterday, and now, I'm just waiting to hear back from him."

I nodded. "So, even if you don't hear back from them, this is something that you want to do?"

"I think so," Alejandra said, looking hesitantly at me. When she saw that I was smiling, she nodded more strongly. "Yes, I really think so. It's the first time I've felt excited about something in a really long time. I feel like I'd be good at it, and I could make some real money from this. I could help with the bills, maybe even move out."

"Don't worry about the bills. I have everything handled," I said. "Do this for yourself and save the money if you do it. But don't do this if you're only looking for a way to give money to me because I won't accept it."

"Genesis, I want to do this, and I want to help you with things around here," Alejandra argued. "It is only fair. You shouldn't have to work so much."

"It's fine." I waved off her argument. "I don't mind doing it. Besides, with college, you probably won't be able to make much money off of it right now, so you should use the money for yourself or put it in savings."

Alejandra gave me a quizzical look. "Genesis, I'm … never mind."

"What?" I asked, leaning back on my hands.

"Nothing, nothing," she answered with a shake of her head. She turned her body closer to mine and smiled. "I'm just happy you're on board with this. You are on board, right?"

"Yes, of course," I said, giving her a hug. "If it's what you want, then I want it too."

Alejandra squealed, hugging me tighter until I chocked on my laughter and had to push her away. "Do you want to see the headshots? I was showing them to Yari in the living room just before you arrived."

"Yes, show them to me," I said with a smile.

We went back to the living room, and when Yari saw that we were both smiling, she grinned.

"See, I told you everything would work out," Yari said, and I couldn't tell if she was talking to both of us or just me, but we both nodded.

"I'm going to show Genesis the headshots," Alejandra explained, plopping down next to Yari and pulling the laptop back on her lap.

"They're really good," Yari said to me, making space on the sofa so I could squeeze in.

"I have no doubt they are," I said, and Alejandra beamed.

It was moments like these, where I knew that there wasn't much that I wouldn't do to make sure my sister was happy. And Yari too, for that matter. They were my family in every sense of the word, and they meant more to me than anything else. Through everything that happened in my life, they were the two constants in my life.

Even music had left for a while after my dad passed away. Music for me was so deeply connected to him that after he died, I couldn't even play without crying. I'd play one note on the piano, and even at the age of twelve, I felt like I was going to die from the pain it brought. There were times when I'd sleep on the piano bench, my head resting against the fallboard that protected the keys, because it was the only way I felt close to him. But I couldn't play. It was our thing, the one thing that he had given to me and that we had done together. To keep playing when he wasn't there anymore, it felt too much like moving on, and I wasn't ready to do that.

But like my father used to always tell me, music was a part of our souls, and we couldn't go too long without feeling the call of the music. And eventually, no matter how hard I tried to ignore the call, I had to play again. Because not playing was starting to hurt even worse than the pain of not being able to play with him. And I'd realized, nearly a year after his death, that playing again wasn't me saying I was letting go of him, but rather holding on to him and keeping his memory.

Sometimes, I wondered how differently our lives would be had he not died that Wednesday morning. Who would I be had he not left me when I needed him so badly? Would I be the same? Or would my future have been etched in stone, no matter what circumstances brought me there?

And Alejandra had only been six when he passed away. She barely had memories of him. She wasn't musically inclined, so she didn't even have those memories of him to hold on to. I was sure she had her own set of memories with him, but she had been so much younger than me. I couldn't imagine losing him at that age. How had his death affected her?

I knew that his death had made me so much more protective of her. My parents used to tell me all the time that I needed to look out for her and be her protector, but I used to get annoyed by it and by her. Alejandra would always try to be my shadow, and it would irk me to no end when I was a younger. She would follow me, try to be like me, always ask me for help for the simplest things. All I wanted to do was play my music. So, of course, Alejandra would try to play, too, but she was so bad at it and would often get bored very quickly and start whining, which would make me frustrated and annoyed with her. I couldn't even remember how many times we had gotten in fights because she wouldn't leave me alone, and I'd make her cry because I told her I didn't want to play with her.

But after our dad had passed away and our mom had turned into a ghost, she was the one that I'd clung on to harder than anything. I realized that we only had each other and that I needed to be that big sister that my father had always asked me to be. Not for him, but for her. Because she needed me. And perhaps, a part of me had needed her.

It was funny how things like that worked out. For the longest time, my sister had clung to me like I was her lifeline, and now that she was ready to let go and live her own life, it was me clinging to her. I didn't know if I'd ever be ready to let her go. But I knew that sooner or later, I would have to.

I wasn't ready to face that day though. Not today.

But maybe tomorrow.

13

The party is loud, and I laugh with my cousins as we run around the room, playing freeze tag as my father and his band play on the stage at the front of the venue. Today is my cousin Louis's birthday, and my dad took Aleja and me to his party in the Bronx even though my mom said she didn't want us taking the train to that neighborhood. She had to work, or otherwise, there's no way she would've let this happen.

Time speeds by in the way that it always does when you're a kid, and I eventually stop playing to find the bathroom. I walk down a carpeted hall outside the room my tío rented at some party venue and follow the signs for the bathroom. The closer I get to the bathroom, the more intense the urge to go becomes, and by the time I reach the door, I'm squeezing my legs together to hold in my pee. But when I go to turn the door, it won't budge. I notice a moment later that there is a small sign that says Occupied, and I sigh heavily. I begin to move away from the door when I hear a deep, familiar voice that stops me in my tracks.

"Te amo, mi amor," my dad says, and I hear a woman make this weird sound, like a pained moan.

My heart begins to beat hard in my chest, and unconsciously, my feet bring me closer to the door as I strain to hear more. I hear this weird wet *sound, and I realize a moment later that it reminds me of the sound my parents make when they kiss.*

"Javier," she says.

I step backward and away from the door. I slam into the wall behind me, heart beating in my ears—

I woke to the sound of my alarm going off in my ear, my eyes opening slowly as my dream faded and I became cemented in reality. *Dios*, I hated that dream, and I hated that my subconscious wouldn't let me forget that moment in time so many years ago.

I sat up in my bed, shirt sticking to my back, feeling hot and uncomfortable. I pulled my hair off my sweaty neck and tied it up with a scrunchie from my bedside table, turning off my alarm on my phone a moment later.

"Fuck," I muttered, rubbing my eyes as I stared at the time.

I'd managed to sleep through almost all my alarms, and now, I was at my *oh shit, you need to move NOW* alarm that I always set just in case.

Despite managing to get to work on time, I spent the whole day completely disoriented. I walked into wrong meetings. I left my lunch in the microwave too long and nearly started a fire. I even walked into our glass entrance door and spilled coffee on my skirt. To say it was a long day would be an understatement. By the time it was five o'clock, I was ready to fall face-first on my bed and give up on this day. But unfortunately, my day didn't end just because I clocked out.

When I walked off the elevator at work, I stumbled into Will, who was already waiting for me.

He frowned. "Are you okay?"

"Peachy." I wrapped my gray scarf around my neck, yanking my wavy, dark hair out of the way. My eyes snagged on his hands, covered in the black gloves from the Hershey's Kisses game from the holiday party. I looked away, shoving my own hands in my coat pockets. "Ready to go?"

We walked in silence to the train, the cold January air biting at my face and skin. I imagined warm places, like sitting in front of a fireplace or the feeling of cozy heat when you first stepped into a hot, steaming shower to try and keep warm. Unfortunately, my imagination was no match for the mind-numbingly cold winter air.

The underground station was marginally warmer, but that probably had to do with the crowd of people waiting on the platform for the train.

"I wanted to apologize for ending our session early yesterday," Will began, voice deep and clear despite the loud clanging of the train speeding through the express track.

I shrugged. "We weren't getting anything done anyway."

"I wanted to talk to you about that."

I looked over at him and waited.

"I think we should try to be ... friends."

"Friends?" I asked slowly, the word sounding foreign from his mouth.

His cheeks, red from the cold, seemed to deepen, turning his skin a distracting color of strawberry red. Will cleared his throat, and I darted my eyes up to his.

"So far, this partnership has not been going well."

I couldn't help the snort that released from my mouth.

He continued, undeterred, "For the sake of the contest, I think we need to start fresh and really try to get along."

That was easy for him to say.

I felt my face scrunch up, and I knew without a doubt that it was reflecting exactly what I felt in this moment. "I thought we were doing a pretty good job, all things considered."

Will gave me a look. "If we keep things up the way they've been going, then we might as well both drop out of the contest now because there's no way we'll have a song ready by the end of April, much less one that will help us win."

I stayed silent at that, hating that he was right. It'd been a week since our initial meeting, and we were still at the very beginning stages. We hadn't been able to agree on a single thing, and time was of the essence right now.

We got to Will's stop and got off the train, silently making our way toward the exit and up the stairs to begin the short walk to his place. All the while, I could feel Will staring at me, but I kept my head down to fight the cold, my mind on his words from the train ride. I couldn't turn off my distrust of him just because he wanted me to; it wasn't that simple. But I also knew that if I wanted to win this contest, we were going to have to change the way we worked with each other because no matter how much I hated to say it, he was right. Again. We needed to stop looking at each other like the enemy and instead remember that we were on the same side and wanted the same thing—to win.

"Fine," I managed to say right as we turned onto his block. "But the moment this song is finished, then so is this so-called friendship."

Will shrugged tightly. "If that's what you want."

We walked into his building and up to his apartment, the silence like its own orchestra of suspense. I could feel it—the tension and questions swirling between us. For me, it was, *What now?* and, *Can I really look past two years of bitter resentment to make this song with him?* I really didn't know. It was one thing to say you would try to be friends—or at the very least, friendly—but it was another thing to actually put your money where your mouth was.

There was a time when I'd wanted to be his friend. Even after that first meeting when he completely ignored me, a part of me made up excuses, tried to rewrite what had happened in my head, and still held out hope that I could make a friend in him. I didn't even know why I'd wanted to be his friend so badly back then, and thinking about how much I had been hurt when I realized I wouldn't be just made me cringe in embarrassment now.

It was so stupid. *I* was so stupid.

We were so different, and time had only shown me how lucky I was that I'd walked by that conference room that day and overheard him and his friends talking about me. I knew now who he really was and what he thought of me, and I'd come to terms with that. What was more, I knew that I'd dodged a bullet. I had Cora, who was the truest friend and best person I'd ever met. I got along with most people in my department, and I worked hard every day despite the few opportunities given to me to move ahead in this company.

Regardless of what Will and his friends might think of me, I was exactly where I was meant to be right now. Working as an administrative marketing assistant might not have been my ideal job within the company, but that didn't mean it was my end goal. I was going to do bigger things in my life, bigger than working in this department, in this company. It might not happen tomorrow or even five years from now, but one day, this whole thing would be a distant memory.

"In order for us to work together, we need to trust each other."

I looked away from Will's wall collection of guitars and toward his voice. He was sitting across from me with his back straight and his dark eyes staring intensely in my direction.

It really is unfortunate that he isn't hideous-looking, I mused to myself as my eyes traced his features.

His almost-porcelain skin looked soft to touch, in such contrast to his sharp cheekbones and jawline. Smooth yet deadly.

It wasn't until I heard Will softly clear his throat that I realized we'd just been staring at each other, and I never responded.

"What were you saying?"

"In order to write a song together, we need to trust each other," Will repeated. "I don't think I have to explain to you how ... intimate it can be to write a song with another person."

Writing a song with another person was intimate in many ways. You had to open yourself up to that person. You shared about yourself, your music, your ideas and hopes and dreams, and you had to trust that they would give that back to you and respect you and your craft. When you wrote a song with someone, it was no longer just you in a dark, empty room, laying your most vulnerable pieces on the table to rearrange into words by yourself.

It was easier, in many ways, to write a song by myself. I had no one watching me as I worked through my feelings, as I cried or screamed or threw the hundredth paper in the garbage, as I tried to figure out what I wanted my song to say. When you worked with another musician, you were showing them pieces of yourself, hoping that they would like what you had to say and that you could trust them to take what you shared and create something beautiful with it. If you didn't trust your music partner, then you wouldn't be able to dig deep, to be vulnerable with each other so that you could write a song that was meaningful to you.

The idea of trusting Will, of being vulnerable with him, had my body locking up tight, my eyes looking for the nearest exit. How could I trust someone who had taken one look at me and decided I wasn't good enough and had spent the last two years reminding me of that every chance he got?

Will stood up abruptly, pulling me from my thoughts. "Stand up."

I warily looked up at him. "Why?"

"If we're going to trust each other, then we need to do some trust activities," he explained, and I couldn't help the short laugh that tumbled out of my mouth.

"Yeah, that's not going to work," I declared firmly.

He stared patiently at me, feet not budging from his position across from me. I could read his facial expression clearly, and I knew from the way his arms rested lightly by his sides, chest rising and falling softly as he continued to watch me, that he would wait for me just like this for as long as it took.

I sighed and slowly stood up. "Fine, Dr. Genius, what's your idea?"

"We do trust activities all the time during work trainings. This will be no different," he said firmly. "Let's start with a trust-fall activity."

I was shaking my head before he even finished his sentence. "That's not going to work."

"Why not?" he asked, impatience seeping into his tone.

"Silly trust games don't work," I said simply. "I don't trust people I don't know, and I don't know you, and you don't know me."

He stared at me for a long moment, thoughts seeming to swirl in his dark brown eyes. "I know you," he said. I opened my mouth to argue, but he continued talking. "I know you like to listen to music at your desk while you're working, and when you think no one is looking, you will mouth words to a song stuck in your head. You get this happy little smile on your lips whenever you are eating something sweet, but almost always, you go into a sugar crash afterward and become cranky if you don't have something to snack on afterward. You almost never smile at work, but sometimes, when you're with Cora, I can tell you really want to. But for some reason, you're always holding back, like you can't let yourself be comfortable enough at work to let loose. I sometimes wonder what it would look like if you did."

I blinked in surprise, heat rushing up to my cheeks. That might have been the longest Will had talked to me that didn't include an insult in some way. And I absolutely didn't know how to process any of his words—especially since it meant acknowledging the scary fact that maybe Will knew me.

And so, I didn't.

"All I'm saying is," I said with a shrug, effectively brushing his words off, "I could turn around and fall backward, and I know you'd catch me, but that doesn't mean I trust you. Trust is earned; it's not something I give out freely to every person I meet."

He nodded slowly, eyes assessing me in a way that had me fidgeting in my spot. I didn't like him looking at me like that, like he was learning something about me that I maybe hadn't meant to share. "I agree."

We continued to stare at each other silently, our words hanging in the air around us. This time, I was the first to look away.

"Look at us, already agreeing on something," I said sarcastically, trying to fill the space with words, with anything to move on from whatever was happening. "Maybe there's hope after all."

Will's mouth tipped ever so slightly on one side. "Maybe there is."

The next day, I waited for Will by the elevators.

I'd received only one text from him very early this morning.

Bring sneakers for after work.

I'd texted back, asking why, assuming he was texting me in a half-awake state of delirium, but he wouldn't answer.

Even when I had seen him at work in a meeting, he'd refused to explain. I walked up to him as he was leaving and tried to ask him what the sneakers were for.

He'd only blinked at me, shook his head, and mumbled, "I'll explain later," before walking away.

So, here I stood, a quarter after five, in my black sneakers and work clothes, bundled up in my jacket, wondering what the heck sneakers had to do with making music. Will walked out of his department a minute or two later, and I immediately noticed that he did not have a change of shoes on. He wrapped his scarf around his neck, nodding hello to me as he walked down the hall to where I was standing.

"Why aren't you wearing sneakers?" I demanded immediately. My mind instinctively jumped to a negative outcome, assuming he'd done this as some sort of prank. I'd had to bring my bigger purse in order to fit my sneakers, and if he'd made me change into my sneakers for no good reason, I was going to—

"I'll be fine in my shoes," he answered easily.

He pressed the button for the elevator and looked at me, lips pressed together, like he was trying to hide his amusement. I, on the other hand, was not amused at all and felt my scowl intensify, foot tapping impatiently.

"You don't like surprises, do you?"

"I don't like surprises from someone I don't trust," I said with a pointed look, still on edge. "Now, tell me why I needed sneakers, and you don't."

"I thought we could use today's session to do another trust activity," he said, and I nearly groaned out loud. "You said you need to know someone in order to trust them, and I agree. So, let's spend today getting to know each other."

"No," I blurted out and then clamped my lips together with wide eyes when I realized I'd said it out loud.

Will stared at me with a guarded expression, lips turning down into a small frown.

"I—I mean, I don't understand. What does this trust activity have to do with footwear?"

Will studied me for a moment. "We're going to visit my favorite record store in the city, but it's a bit of a walk. I figured your feet might hurt in your boots, so …"

So, he'd requested for me to bring sneakers.

I glanced down at my feet, waiting for the guilt and embarrassment to wash away. "Oh."

The elevator dinged its arrival before Will could say anything else. Will was trying—really trying—to make this partnership work. First, with yesterday's truce, and now, today, with another activity to help me feel more comfortable after I admitted I didn't trust him. I didn't doubt that he still disliked me, but he was making an effort, and I couldn't help feeling guilty that I was not. I might have agreed yesterday to the truce and to being "friends," but I didn't actually intend on trusting Will or giving him that opportunity. Yes, I knew I'd have to learn to trust him to an extent in order to write this song, but spending time talking and getting to know each other had not been on the list of ways that I would do that.

We stepped out of the building, the tall New York City skyscrapers and bustling sidewalks a comfort against the awkward silence and forty-degree weather.

I cleared my throat, pushing a piece of my dark brown hair behind my ear. I looked at the buildings we were passing by as if it were the most interesting thing in the world. I prayed that Will would think my cheeks were red because of the cold and not because I was feeling embarrassed and nervous.

"What's so good about this record store?" I cringed, hating my inability to make small talk and not sound like a robot. I might as well start talking about the freaking weather, which really was the icing on the cake of awkward small talk.

Even though I could see my breath in the air as we walked, I didn't feel cold. As a born-and-bred New Yorker, even though you hated the cold, a few minutes outside, and your body became accustomed to it.

"They have a lot of rare LPs," he answered as we crossed the street.

He signaled that we would be turning, and I followed, walking around a family standing in the middle of the sidewalk.

I nodded, thinking about the crates I had seen in the living room and his music studio. "Are you a collector?"

A cloud of cold air streamed from his mouth like a puff of smoke as he looked at me. "A little bit. What about you?"

I shrugged. "I would if I had the space. I keep most of my collection digital."

Will didn't answer, and a few minutes later, we arrived at the store. It was called Johnny's Record Store and was a dingy little store in between a Sketchers and an upscale boutique. The building was painted this mustard-yellow color and had blue awnings over two small windows on opposite sides of the entrance.

When we walked in, the door made a ringing sound, and I was instantly hit with the smell of coconut and a distinct basement smell. Like when you found a box of old things that you'd forgotten you had, and it was all dusty and collecting spiderwebs.

"Oh my God," I breathed, stopping in front of a blue crate and quickly pulling out a vinyl from the stack. "They have Madonna's *Make the World Go Round* vinyl!"

I couldn't hold in my wide grin as I looked at the back of the vinyl and read the list of imported and unreleased tracks.

"Big Madonna fan?" Will asked from beside me, and I glanced over at him, instantly on guard. But he wasn't looking at me with his mocking smirk or like he was teasing me at all; instead, he actually looked curious as he tried to peek at the LP in my hand.

"I went through a Madonna phase when I was ten and trying to find my sound," I admitted, hugging the record to my chest. "One of my mom's friends introduced me to her music, and I instantly fell in love with her sound, her style." I laughed, mind lost in a memory. "Honestly, it was crazy how obsessed I was with emulating her back then. Once—" I cut myself short, snapping my mouth closed.

That was more of myself than I'd ever planned to share with Will. I'd just gotten so lost in my excitement at finding this rare LP that I forgot for just a moment who I was with.

Will was still looking expectantly at me, like he wanted to know the rest of the story, but I just shrugged and began to walk down a random aisle.

"What genre of music do you like to listen to?" I asked over my shoulder.

"A little bit of everything," came his reply to my left, and I nearly jumped out of my shoes. Will began to look through a crate, fingers slowly thumbing through each record like he didn't want to miss a single detail.

I stepped toward the crate beside his and began to look through, my Madonna LP still in hand.

After a few moments of silently looking through our crates, Will tilted a Kiss vinyl toward me and asked, "Love or hate?"

"They're a New York rock band from the '70s," I answered easily. "There's no way I'd hate them."

Will nodded as he put the record back in the crate and pulled out another record, this time of Led Zeppelin's *Coda* album. "Best Zeppelin album?"

"*Led Zeppelin IV*." I shifted slightly to look at him. His shoulders were hunched, head tilted down to avoid the low-hanging lights. "Favorite Zeppelin song?"

He tapped his knuckle lightly on the record in his hand, mouth pursed in thought. "'The Rain Song.'"

I nodded my head approvingly and looked back at my crate. I saw a copy of a Spice Girls record and pulled it out. "Best girl band of the '90s?"

Will tilted his head from side to side. "Best pop girl band of the '90s? Spice Girls, without a doubt. But nobody was changing the scene like Destiny's Child was back then."

"I agree," I said, eyes widening as I realized I'd just said those two words when talking to Will. "What's your favorite song?"

Will glanced at me from the corner of his eyes, a small smirk playing at his lips. "'Cater 2 U.'"

I rolled my eyes, putting the record back in the crate. "Typical."

Of course he'd love a song that was all about a woman catering to her man's every want and need. I did love that song though, the vocals alone and the way they harmonized—

I shook my head, focusing back on the stack of records in front of me.

"Johnny Cash," Will said after a few minutes of silently looking through crates. "Overrated or not given enough credit for his contribution to music?"

And on and on we went. We didn't talk the entire time; there were plenty of moments of silence as we got lost in looking at albums, but there were plenty of moments of conversation. Not all of it was amicable, and Will had me biting my tongue more times than I could count at some of his answers, but it was probably the longest we'd talked to each other without truly fighting in … ever.

After I paid for my Madonna record, we stepped back outside, and I realized with sudden dread that he might ask me to pick a place to share next. It would only be fair since he shared this record store with me.

"Want to get something to eat?" Will asked before I could say anything, and I nearly deflated in relief.

I nodded, and after a quick discussion, we decided on food from one of the halal carts parked on the corner. After walking for a few minutes, we found an empty bench in front of a small park, and we sat down.

"Are you sure you'll be okay, eating outside?" Will asked skeptically, eyes tracing over my cheeks and nose.

I had no doubt that they were red from the cold, even with my brown skin. Will's much lighter skin was a bright red, his ears the color of an apple.

"Will you?" I challenged, opening up my container of food.

"I've never felt warmer," came his smooth reply. He took a bite from his chicken gyro, looking as calm as can be.

"Same," I sniped, unable to help myself.

I looked away from Will and picked up my fork. One bite of my lamb over rice, and I was lost to the delicious taste and nearly forgot about anyone and anything else around me.

I loved the bustle of the city, the way that life never stopped moving, no matter what was going on. It might be cold outside, but that never stopped people from doing what they needed and wearing what they wanted. A woman walked by, wearing a short dress and a leather jacket, looking cool as can be. Even though she had to be freezing, you wouldn't be able to tell by looking at her.

"Your bio for the contest said you perform at bars?" I asked abruptly, trying to keep my tone casual and not at all like I'd had to force the words out of my mouth.

Will nodded. "I do some gigs at a few places—sometimes with a few friends, but mostly on my own. Mostly covers, but I have a few original songs I like to play, depending on how long the set is and what the management allows."

"What's your sound?" I asked, curious.

Some people wore their music as part of their identity, but for the most part, I'd learned that people could really surprise you. I'd worked with a girl once who presented as this tough heavy-metal gal, but when she sang, her voice was the softest thing I'd ever heard, and she played mostly folk music.

"I like to cross genres," he answered, wiping his mouth with a napkin. "Mostly pop and soul. I have a YouTube channel that's got a pretty high following. A few of my covers have gone viral in the past few years."

My mouth dropped; I was stunned. "And you've never been offered a contract?"

Will shrugged, looking uncomfortable. "It'll happen when it's meant to happen." He turned his face away, watching the city around us and effectively shutting down the conversation.

"I really love brownstone houses," I blurted out after a long minute, cringing the moment the words came out. I had been so taken aback by his discomfort that I'd said the first random thing I could think of, and now, I was regretting it big time.

Will turned his head toward me, brows furrowed in confusion.

"Ever since I was a kid, I used to walk by those beautiful, distinctive homes with the long staircases leading to their front doors, and I'd dream about the day that I could live inside one of them. I imagined sitting on the stoop, breeze in my hair, and in all my daydreams, I was so happy. So content." I snapped out of my daydream, shaking the image of the brownstone from my mind. *Dios*, this was the second time today that I'd gotten lost in my thoughts and shared more than I'd expected to. Awkwardly, I finished, "When I get my first big paycheck from music, I want to buy a brownstone."

"You'll do it," he said strongly, like my rambling, embarrassing story had made any sense at all and he believed in it.

He was probably just pretending to be nice because of the contest, which was fine because that was the only reason I was even talking to him. For the contest.

Don't let him see you feeling embarrassed, I reminded myself.

"I know I will," I answered confidently, sitting up straight.

Will gave a short laugh, shaking his head. He cleaned up his food and nodded toward mine. "Are you done?"

I nod. "Nothing beats a good meal from a food cart in the city."

"One of the things I love most about New York City," Will agreed. "Besides the energy of this city, which is unmatched."

I had nothing to compare it to, having lived here my whole life, but I knew what he meant. People always talked about how even though there were plenty of cities all over the world that looked like our city, there was nothing that compared when you looked at its substance, the people, the energy. I didn't know if I'd live here forever, but I knew that wherever I ended up in life, I'd never spend too long away from this city that was so much of who I was.

"This small little island's one of a kind," I said. "There's so much to do here, so much to see and explore. I love that every day when I leave my house, I have no idea what New York will offer me on my way to work. Dancers, singers, angry people, sad people, moments of kindness in the quietest of moments. I've seen it all."

A man walked by just then with a boom box on his shoulder, blasting "Empire State of Mind" by Jay-Z, featuring Alicia Keys, and I nearly laughed out loud at the timing of it all.

"I've never been to the Empire State Building," he shared, nodding toward the man and his song. "Feels like I'm not a real New Yorker until I've been inside one of the iconic buildings of this city."

"Not at all," I replied. "Only tourists have been to all of those places. I've never been either, but I've passed by it plenty of times. Real New Yorkers are too busy and unimpressed by tall buildings to stop their day to wait in long lines."

Will chuckled softly. "New Yorkers are so busy that they'd let their life pass them by if they're not careful."

I shrugged, not denying his point. The truth was, to make it in this city, you had to hustle. It was expensive as hell to live here, and it wasn't a place you could survive if you weren't willing to work for it. But it was also a beautiful city, and there was something about this place that made you feel like anything was possible.

I looked toward the row of tables set up along the sidewalks, people trying to sell various New York paraphernalia and art to people passing by.

"I'll be right back," I said, standing up and walking quickly toward one of the tables.

The man was older, maybe in his late sixties or seventies, bundled up and sitting in a small chair as he rearranged his figurines on the table.

"Hello there," he said with a smile.

I smiled back, picking up a silver figurine at the front of the table. "Hi. How much for this?"

"Twenty dollars, but for you, I'll make it fifteen," he said with a wink, and I laughed, passing over a few bills.

When I turned back around, small brown bag in hand, Will was staring at me with a confused frown on his face. The closer I got to him, the more I started to realize my idea was actually a stupid one—not to mention, it wasn't as funny as I'd originally thought it would be.

"Here," I said, shoving the bag toward him.

He peered inside and pulled out a figurine of the Empire State Building.

"It's not the real thing, but now, you can't say you haven't seen it."

"Thank you," he said, a small, surprised smile on his face. "I think if I take your advice, this'll have to be good enough if I want to be considered a real New Yorker."

I shrugged, feeling a little embarrassed still, even as a pleasant warmth spread through my body at the sight of his smile. "You can always go see it on your day off. Just be ready to wait in line for two hours."

"I think I'm good for now," he said, slowly turning the figurine in his hand, eyes thoughtful. "But maybe when the contest is over and we have more free time …"

He lets his sentence trail off, eyes moving to mine. I looked away, heart skipping a beat.

Did he want to go together? Or would he go by himself? Why did I care?

I wouldn't go with him, I reminded myself.

This whole truce was temporary. When the contest was over, so was this little friendship. Besides, this didn't change the things he'd said about me or the way he'd treated me since I started. We weren't real friends, and outside of this contest, we never would be.

I ignored the part of me that felt disappointed and leaned down to pick up my bag from the bench. "It's getting late. I should probably head out."

Will stood up, picking up our garbage from our seat. "Yes, of course."

We stood awkwardly in front of the bench, just looking at each other before I cleared my throat and threw a thumb behind me. "Well, I'm going this way. See you Monday."

He nodded. "See you Monday, Genesis."

I gave him a quick wave and then turned around and started walking to the train. It wasn't until I got halfway down the block that I realized with a jolt that this had … surprisingly been a good day. We hadn't torn each other up, and while he got on my nerves a little at the music store, I'd had a good time today. And just saying that to myself felt bizarre enough that I immediately reminded myself once again of all the things that were annoying about him.

He's arrogant, and he thinks he's better than me, I thought to myself. *And don't forget the way he purposely goes out of his way to make you mad at work.*

I took a deep breath of the cold city air, inhaling it in my lungs as I recentered myself. Once I felt better about admitting that maybe today hadn't been a complete waste of time, I pulled out my headphones and connected them to my phone. I had a long ride home, and now that I knew Will had music on the internet, I needed to scope out what I was working with for this contest.

I listened to his music the whole ride home, mind racing in shock as his hauntingly beautiful voice sang song after song in my ears.

"Fuck, he's really good," I muttered to myself.

His voice was deep yet soft, and whether he was singing a cover of a silly song or a sad one, he made you feel like he was baring his soul to you and you had to stop everything to listen to what he had to say. I felt goose bumps race down my arms as I listened to an original song called "Enough." The video was a similar setup to most of his videos with just him, his mic, and his guitar on the screen in what I knew was his studio. But when he sang this song about a girl that made him want to be good enough, his whole body rocking from the force of his emotions as he sang, I had to clench the pole on the train a little bit tighter from the way that it affected me. I didn't think I'd blinked once the entire time I watched his videos or listened to his songs, but one thought kept replaying in my head over and over as I stood on that crowded train on my way home.

He's going to make it big.

With or without me, he was going places.

The weekend had flown by in the way that it always did when you had no work, and in what felt like a blink, it was Monday.

"What you're saying makes no sense," I argued, voice echoing in the quiet hallway.

"It doesn't have to make sense; it's my opinion," Will said with a pointed look.

He pulled his keys out of his jacket pocket, and I fought the urge to snatch them out of his hand and toss them down the hall like a petulant child.

"Okay, well then, change it," I said.

Will chuckled. "I'm not going to change my opinion just because you tell me to."

He opened the door, and I walked in behind him.

"You can't say that Star Trek is better than Star Wars when you've never seen either and you have no real basis for your opinion! If you're going to say something that offensive, at least have some respect and watch the movies."

Will watched me as I slipped my shoes off and slid my feet into the slippers already waiting by the door. I passed him my bag and jacket a moment later, and he put both in the closet for me—all the while, an amused smirk played at his lips. I knew he was saying these things not because he really cared, but because he knew I did. And yet even though I'd told myself not to get riled up, that it was what he wanted, I couldn't help myself. It seemed when it came to Will, I didn't know how to be anything, except loud. Even so, this argument felt different. It didn't feel like he was making fun of me—well, maybe a little. But it didn't feel like those times where he was looking down on me or what I said. It felt almost playful in the way that he teased me. Which was so strange and foreign to me that I immediately rejected the idea. Yes, Friday, we had made progress in our temporary truce, but I wasn't going to forget who he really was just because he had been nice to me for a few hours.

"You are aware that there are many people who do not like Star Wars, right?" he asked with a quirked brow as he looked at me over his shoulder.

I rolled my eyes. "Yes, and those people are entitled to their wrong opinion *if* they've actually given it a fair chance."

Will shook his head, a smirk on his face as he turned to look in front of him. We entered the living room a moment later, and I nearly bumped into Will when he stopped walking abruptly.

"What—oh."

I looked around Will's tall body and saw there was a man lounging on the couch, a long bong standing on the floor next to him. The guy had long blond hair that he had up in a man bun and one of those stubble beards that was long enough to be considered a beard but not so long that it ventured on caveman territory. My eyes traveled over the rest of him, taking in his broad shoulders and naked torso before quickly glancing down and sighing in relief when I saw he had sweatpants on. Even though he was lying down, I could tell from his build alone that he was well over six feet.

"Hey, you must be Genesis," the man greeted with a small smile, voice deep and sweet like honey. "I'm Callum, the much more talented roommate."

I quirked an eyebrow at that, glancing at Will, but he looked unbothered by Callum's comment. So, Will had a roommate. This place was fancy and expensive, but something told me that he made more than enough money to afford something on his own. And Callum as his roommate? Just from the thirty seconds that I'd shared air with Callum, I could tell he couldn't be more different from Will. For starters, Callum was disheveled and looked like he enjoyed being a couch potato, and I'd bet Will didn't even own a pair of sweatpants.

How did Will know him? Were they actually friends or just two random people who lived together, like many people did here in the city when you needed to make rent and didn't have many options?

One thing was for sure: Callum was inviting me to rag on Will, and there was no way I'd miss out on that opportunity.

"I wish I'd known this before I agreed to work with Will," I joked.

Callum's smile widened, and he glanced at Will before sitting upright on the couch, eyes dancing with amusement. "Looks like you'll have to settle."

"I suppose you're right," I sighed dramatically, throwing a wink at Callum, who gave a short bark of laughter.

"I like you, Genesis," he said, grinning.

He reminded me of a harmless golden retriever when he smiled, and I got the strange feeling in my gut that he was one of the good ones. Dangerous when it came to the ladies, but a good man overall.

He looked over at Will and added, "I get it, bro."

"Enough," Will said, placing his hand on my lower back and applying pressure to maneuver me toward the music room. "We'll be working, so don't bother us unless it's urgent."

I began to walk toward the studio, if only to get Will's hand off my body and for the weird tingly sensation to disappear on my lower back. I threw a wave toward Callum, who watched us with a big grin. "Nice to meet you!"

He nodded, picking up the bong. "Feel free to come hang out with me if Will starts to drive you crazy in there."

"She'll be fine," Will answered for me, throwing his friend an exasperated look.

We walked into the studio, and he closed the door before joining me at the table.

"Callum seems fun," I said, leaning back in my chair.

"That's one way to explain him," Will agreed in a dry tone.

"And he's your ... roommate," I stated, curiosity making it impossible for me to keep my mouth shut.

Will didn't strike me as the type to willingly share his space with anyone, especially someone like Callum.

Will raised a brow, face relaxed. "Is there a question in there?"

"I guess I'm just surprised." I shrugged nonchalantly.

"Which part surprises you exactly?" he asked. "The part where I have a roommate or that it's someone like Callum?"

"Both?" I said with a shrug. "You've always struck me as someone who likes his space. Cora told me you don't let many people into your office at work, and you're always so ... put together."

"You asked questions about me?" Will asked with a small grin.

I rolled my eyes, and he chuckled.

"Callum's my best friend. He's one of the most genuine people I've ever met. I can afford to live on my own, but I choose to live with him."

I nodded. "I get it."

"Do you live alone?" he asked, ankle resting on his knee.

Everything about his body language screamed casual, almost lazy. Like he didn't care one way or another if I answered, but his eyes gave him away. There was a glint in those dark brown eyes. I couldn't read it exactly, but it instantly put me on alert.

I slowly shook my head. "I live with my younger sister."

"That must be nice," he commented.

I narrowed my eyes. "I can afford to live on my own, but I choose to live with her."

He raised a brow at my words, a near copy of his own a few minutes ago. I couldn't tell if he'd made the comment to judge me, but our history made it too easy for me to jump to that conclusion. It was the reaction I was most comfortable in because it was easier to assume Will was being a dick than to give him the benefit of the doubt.

"I have a younger sister," he shared, eyes never leaving mine. "And even though we're nearly ten years apart in age, we're very close. I think about moving back to be closer to her all the time."

I understand, I wanted to say. Because there had been so many times when I thought to myself that it was time to move out, but the thought of not seeing my sister every day was the first thing to make me pause. She was my little sister, and I always wanted to be there for her. If I moved out, I could miss those opportunities with her. It was already so hard to spend time with her with our busy schedules. If we didn't live together, I had no doubt in my mind that number would diminish.

The part of me that was still wary of Will wanted to brush off his words, to pretend he hadn't extended that olive branch. But I couldn't do it. He'd shared, and a stupid part of me wanted to know more, to share.

Just so we're on even playing field, I told myself.

He'd shared, and so would I. Couldn't have him saying he was being a better "friend" than me.

"From my experience, being the oldest often means being the parent," I said, regretting the words almost as soon as they left my mouth. One glance at his piercing, dark eyes, and I could tell I'd once again shared more than I'd meant to.

Ugh, why did sharing feel so ... wrong? Like I'd just admitted something on national television, and now, the laugh track would be going off as everyone pointed and looked at me.

I fought the urge to squirm and instead began to think of all the ways I'd eviscerate him with my words if he so much as smirked at me.

"Were you changing your sister's diapers and feeding her bottles when you were still young enough to need training wheels on your bike too?" he asked, lips tipping into a small smile.

I felt a laugh bubbling up inside me, but I forced the sound down. Will didn't make me laugh—that was not what we did.

"I used to dress my sister up as my own life-sized Barbie doll," I admitted, smirking despite myself. "And I used to sing her lullabies that I'd make up on the spot. There was one called 'Aleja the Red Ladybug.'"

"I would pay good money for you to sing it to me right now," Will said, grinning widely.

I blinked, stunned for a moment by how bright his smile was. It really lit up his face. His sharp cheekbones and strong jaw looked heightened as his full lips pulled back in a grin. And his eyes ... they twinkled. That was the only way I could explain it. I'd seen him smile at people plenty of times, but he'd never smiled at me like that. No, usually, his smiles were tipped with sarcasm or irritation whenever he looked at me. It was always a shit-eating grin that told me he enjoyed pissing me off, but this felt different.

I didn't like this. And I didn't like that my first thought hadn't been to wipe that smile off his face, but instead to figure out how to make him smile at me like that again.

"Not gonna happen," I said flatly.

He nodded, looking unsurprised by my response, which just irritated me even more.

"I've always loved Céline Dion," he said randomly.

I looked at him, brows furrowing in confusion as I tried to keep up with the random change of topic.

"I remember the first time I heard 'The Power of Love' when I was seven years old. I nearly cried."

"It happens to all of us," I joked awkwardly, unsure where he was going with this.

"She's one of those artists that no matter what she sings, her voice gives power to her words," he continued, undeterred. "That woman can hold a note—not to mention, she can project her voice in all registers and maintain vocal agility throughout each octave."

"So, basically," I said with an amused smirk, "you have a thing for Celine Dion."

Will shrugged, a grin on his face. "I have a music thing for her, sure. You're telling me you don't have that one artist that every time they sing, you feel emotionally attacked in the best way?"

I hesitated for a moment before admitting, "Yes. Marc Anthony."

His eyes furrowed for a moment in thought. "He's a ... salsa singer, right?"

I nodded. "His voice is drenched in passion and warmth. The way he makes you feel his emotions with every word ... I don't know a single person who has listened to his music and not fallen a little bit in love with him immediately afterward."

"I'll have to check out his music," Will said, fingers twitching on his thigh, like he wanted to do it right now.

"Okay." I shrugged, telling myself I didn't care one way or another if he did.

"That's what I want for our song," Will said, voice deepening slightly. "I want our song to make people pause when they hear it. To want to listen to the story I sing with my words and to make them feel moved even if they've never experienced the feelings I'm singing about. *Especially* then. I want this song to make them want to experience our message, for them to want to have a person to dedicate our song to."

I nodded, his words washing over me like a soft tidal wave. I wanted that too. That was the beauty of music. People came from all over the world, had so many different lived experiences, but when it came to music, it was the one place where you could connect on such a personal level with a complete stranger and not feel like they would judge you for it. It was one of the things I loved most about live performances too. The way complete strangers could hug each other, belting lyrics at the top of their lungs and feeling so free in that moment. There was no judgment or feeling of vulnerability because everyone in that room was experiencing the music with you, and there was comfort in knowing you were not alone.

Will's leg began to shake slowly, and my eyes zeroed in on it. *Swish, swish, swash.* I listened to the sound of his pants rubbing against the seat of his chair, a melody forming in my head.

"*Closer to you,*" I sang under my breath, standing up and quickly walking over to the keyboard. I was lost in my thoughts, a small idea growing in my brain that I didn't want to lose. I caressed the keys in a silent hello before I played a few chords over and over, mumbling the words, "*I want to be closer to you …*"

I felt Will stand behind me, and a moment later, he began to hum the melody with me. His deep voice was a soothing balm to my choppy melody as I continued to tweak it, trying to find the right key.

"*I want to be closer to you,*" he sang quietly, moving to stand beside me. "*I'd risk it all for five seconds with you.*"

I looked away from the keyboard, heart in my throat as I smiled breathlessly at Will. "That's it!"

"That's it," he agreed softly.

His arm brushed against my shoulder slightly as he reached over to tap his finger ever so gently against my fingers still on the keyboard. I watched with wide eyes, heart beating quickly as he tapped out the melody on my fingers before I glanced back at his face. He looked like how I imagined I looked right now—excited and high off the feeling of finally finding a piece of our song. But there was something else brewing behind those eyes, something I couldn't quite read.

"I knew we would be magic together," he said, his words a deep promise.

"**I** *knew we would be magic together.*"

Words that stuck with me all night and well into the next day. I couldn't stop thinking about our song, about the way Will and I had seamlessly supported each other in finding that tune, those beginning lyrics. Yesterday was our first successful music session in the three weeks since we'd started, and it hadn't been the disaster I'd thought it would be. Will continued to surprise me every day, and I didn't know what to do with that information.

Maybe we really could do this. I felt optimistic for the first time in weeks, and when I met with Will later that next day, for once, I wasn't dreading it.

The cold wind pushed against us as we walked up his block, and I cursed myself for not tying up my hair before leaving work. My dark brown locks kept blowing across my face, making it almost impossible to see in front of me, and I had no choice but to squint and look through strands of hair as I tried to walk around people.

"Watch out," Will said somewhere in front of me, amusement in his voice.

A moment later, I bumped into his arm and stumbled back.

"Sorry," I grumbled, pushing my hair back away from my eyes.

We were standing in front of his building, and I noticed a moment later that John, his doorman, was grinning at me as he tipped his head in hello.

My already-red cheeks got hot with embarrassment as I grinned sheepishly. "Good evening, John. You should really stay indoors; it's too cold out here."

"I'll be fine, miss," he said, still smiling.

I pushed against Will's back, who looked at me with an amused glint in his eyes but started walking into the building.

"Stay warm, John!" I called out as I walked behind Will.

It didn't take long for us to get up to his apartment, and I sighed in relief as the heat from his place snaked around us the moment we walked in.

"God, I can't wait for spring to come," I sighed.

I rummaged through my bag and pulled out my music journal and some papers I'd printed out at the end of work. Will glanced at the items in my hand but said nothing as he took my oversize bag and hung it up with my jacket.

"Hello, beautiful," Callum greeted from the kitchen.

"Hello to you too," Will said, coming to stand behind me as I paused by the kitchen entrance.

Callum grinned as he stuck a fork into his bowl of food. It looked like he was having rice with beef, but it didn't look like a dish I'd ever had, and it certainly smelled different too. My stomach grumbled quietly as I inhaled the sweet smell of different sauces and deliciously spiced food.

"You know I think you're a handsome motherfucker, Kobayashi," Callum said with a wink. "But you don't make Aphrodite jealous of your beauty when you walk into a room the way Genesis does."

"Aww, gee," I joked, grinning. "If you don't stop showering me with compliments, I'm going to start crushing on you."

"I see nothing wrong with that," Callum flirted, megawatt smile stretched across his face.

He really was a handsome guy and a tall one too. He was a little bit taller than Will, and his shoulders were a bit broader, but for whatever reason, my mind—and body—immediately categorized him firmly in the friend zone.

"You ready to work?" Will asked gruffly. "Or do you want to spend more time flirting with my roommate?"

I narrowed my eyes at Will, not his tone. What was his problem anyway? I thought he'd be happy that I wasn't insulting his best friend and was making an effort to be friendly with him. I could've been rude and just ignored Cal; after all, I was only here for the contest, but I'd been raised to always greet people in their houses, and I liked Callum and his easygoing nature.

"Ouch, man. I thought I was more than that to you," Callum joked, an easy smile on his face. Will didn't smile back, and Cal raised his hands up. "Relax, man. I was just being nice. I didn't mean anything by it."

I felt my irritation rocketing as Will turned wordlessly and began walking into his music room.

"What crawled up his butt?" I muttered, following behind him with a quick wave to Callum.

"I have a few ideas for our song," Will said the moment I closed the door to the music room. He pulled a guitar onto his lap and nodded to the empty chair across from him. "Tell me what you think."

Okay, so I guessed he was going to just jump into the song and pretend he hadn't been a dick back there.

"Fine." I sat across from him, putting my stuff down on the table between us.

Will also had a notebook on the table, and a quick look at the open book showed scribbled lyrics and a few chords written in the margins.

Will glanced at his notebook as he began to strum softly on his guitar. I immediately heard the chords we'd created yesterday as Will hummed along, eyes closing as a gentle peace washed over his face. I watched with rapt attention as the music seemed to flow through him, his entire body language changing with each strum of his fingers on the guitar.

He gets it, I thought to myself. *He feels the music the way that I do.*

The song went past what we'd worked on yesterday, and I felt my heart race at the rich sound of his voice as he sang a new set of lyrics. My mind immediately began thinking of what to fix, what to add, as he started from the beginning and sang the few lyrics on a loop; each time his voice sounded a little bit grittier, more emotion packed into his words, until I felt like they were words being ripped from his soul.

Without thinking about it, I started to hum the song the next time he played it from the top.

"Try the G7 chord at the end," I said.

Will didn't outwardly react to my suggestion, but a moment later, he got to the end and changed to the G7, and it made all the difference.

"Write it down," Will said, eyes opening. He watched as I jotted down the new chord into my notebook. "What do you think of the stuff I added?"

"I like what you added," I replied, looking up from my journal. "And I like the version where the beginning starts off very slow, and your voice has this almost mournful and bitter quality to it. I think we should start the lyrics about ten seconds into the song and use that beginning part as an intro and tweak it a bit. Maybe add a few other instruments, or maybe I can play around with an analog synthesizer ..." I trailed off, wheels turning in my head.

"Okay, yeah," he said, nodding, his fingers idly strumming the guitar. "I was thinking something similar. But I could also see these lyrics working later in the song too."

"I like it in the beginning, but maybe when we finish the song, it'll sound better somewhere else?" I answered with a shrug. "For now, I say, leave it. I'm more concerned about finishing up that first verse. It needs to tie into the chorus seamlessly because it'll be the first time the listener is introduced to the title of the song."

"The title, huh?" he asked with an arched brow.

I nodded, shooting him a guilty smile as I realized I'd forgotten to even ask him. "Yeah. I think it should be titled 'Closer' or something along those lines because that's what our song is about, right? Wanting to be close to someone who is always out of reach?"

"Yeah," he answered, tone soft as his eyes spaced out like he was lost in thought. Will cleared his throat, placing his guitar back on the stand. "I'm going to go get a drink. Do you want something?"

"Uh, sure," I said, watching him as he fidgeted with his tie.

He saw me watching him, and he smoothed his hand over his tie before moving his hands back to his sides.

"I'll take water, thanks."

He nodded, and without another word, he left the room. I stared at the door with furrowed brows for a moment before shrugging and picking up my journal. I flipped through the pages, at the endless songs that I'd created in the last year— some finished, most unfinished. Finally, I found my printed list that I'd made especially for today, and I pulled it out, quietly reading over it to myself.

When Will returned, he handed me one of the bottles of water in his hand, glancing down at the sheets in my hands as he walked to his seat. "What's all that?"

I sat up straighter in my seat. "I've been working on some lists for us. So that we make sure we stay on schedule and get everything done in a timely manner."

Will laughed. "You're joking."

"I'm not," I responded, putting the sheets of paper down on the table as I looked at him. "This is a great idea."

"Genesis, a schedule won't work," Will said with a shake of his head. He looked down at one of the sheets and slid it toward his side of the table, so he could read it. He gave another laugh and shook his head as he kept reading, like he found it more and more ridiculous.

"What's wrong with my schedule?" I asked calmly, reminding myself to not shout at him even though this was a soundproof room.

"You should know that music doesn't work so well when you force it into a schedule," he answered. "It's a good idea in a broader sense, but the way you're setting this up is only going to lead us to fail."

"What?" I huffed, annoyed. "How am I leading us to fail? I'm giving us weekly goals to meet so that we have something to work on each week. I also gave us monthly goals so that we will get everything done with enough time to fix up anything at the end."

"But if we miss even one of these weekly goals, this entire schedule is fucked," he explained. "I don't like the idea of having this hovering over my head. It will only add more stress to this process and mess with my creativity. I'd rather go at our own pace."

"We can't go at our own pace," I snapped, even as a part of me felt bad about it.

Suddenly, flashes of us missing the deadline played before my eyes. I saw us having a half-finished song, Harrison and Pratt telling us that we were disqualified from the contest—yet another missed opportunity for me.

"We only have a few months, Will! We need to get things done, and we *need* a schedule."

Will gave me a worried look as I no doubt looked like a maniac with wild eyes. He raised his hands up, like he was trying to placate me. "Okay, okay. Calm down. I know that we can't take our time on this but—"

"There is no *but*," I cut him off, voice trembling with emotions. "I can't lose."

God, how embarrassing.

Will would probably call me emotional and think I was too difficult to work with, but I couldn't help it.

I nearly jumped out of my seat when a moment later, I felt a hand cover mine and squeeze. I looked up with startled eyes and watched as Will's hand moved over mine, his thumb brushing my knuckles as he gently pulled my fingers away from my arm and onto the middle of the table. My forearm had crescent-shaped marks, the skin a light red against my light-brown skin. I'd been unconsciously digging my nails into my skin, and yet I'd felt nothing. Will's thumb moved over my knuckles, and I focused on the sensation of his long, callous fingers on my skin, a pleasant tingle spreading across my body.

Why was he touching my hand? And why wasn't I stopping him?

I wanted to pull away, but for some stupid reason, the feel of his hand on mine was the only thing keeping me from crying.

I'll pull away in five more seconds, I told myself, eyes following the soft brush of his thumb as it moved up and down over each of my knuckles.

I felt almost in a trance, the only sound in the room our quiet breathing. I couldn't even bring myself to look at him. To see those dark brows furrowed, mouth pinched tight in the expression he made when he didn't understand something but didn't want to say it out loud.

Will's fingers squeezed mine gently, and I felt that squeeze in my heart, tingles jolting up my arm and straight to my stomach, spreading like wildfire. "We can keep the schedule."

I pulled my fingers away and put both hands in my lap. I forced myself to look at Will, my breath nearly catching in my throat at the intensity in his eyes. It was like he wanted nothing more to grab me and force me into his space. The scariest part of all was that that for a long moment, I wanted that too.

I shook the thought away and let out a shaky breath. "I thought you were so against it."

"I am," Will said, voice gentle but firm.

I watched as he slowly pulled his hand away from the table and clenched his fingers around the arm of his chair.

"I don't need your pity," I said, shaking my head. "Don't agree to something if you don't really want it."

"I have no reason to pity you." His broad shoulders shrugged casually, his eyes losing some of their heat. "And I'm only agreeing to the monthly schedule, I'm still saying no to the weekly one."

I stared at Will as I tried to figure out if he was lying or not. Finally, I nodded slowly, not quite trusting him. "Fine, a monthly schedule."

"Fine," he agreed simply.

We sat in silence for a long minute, and I unintentionally found myself in a staring match with Will as we both seemed to be sizing each other up from across the table.

"Stop staring at me."

"I like looking at you," he replied in a teasing tone, not denying it. He had a mischievous grin on his face, his sharp cheekbones on display.

I felt my cheeks get hot, but I rolled my eyes at him. "You mean, you like messing with me. I bet every time you look at me, you're thinking of the next way to drive me crazy."

"I could say the same about you, Buttercup," he responded, smile widening as he watched my eyes narrow at him.

I hated how attractive he was when he smiled. Or when he stared at me. Hell, even when he blinked or did nothing at all. It was all unfair. The guy looked like his face and body had been carved by the Greek gods, and he had the beautiful voice to match his already-too-perfect package. I thought about his hand in mine, how those strong, rough fingers had been so gentle as he'd held my hand in his. I looked down at my hand and lightly rubbed my thumb against my palm, trying to rub away the memory and sensation he'd left behind.

"I don't think about you at all," I lied. "And I never stare at you. In fact, I bet I could go the rest of this session, not looking at you once."

He tapped his index finger on his chin, a thoughtful look crossing his face. "Is that so?"

I nodded, throwing a smug look his way. "I won't even bother asking if you could do the same because we both know you'd just lose."

"You're probably right," he said simply, and my head jerked back in surprise.

He wasn't supposed to agree; he was supposed to take my bet. That was how this went, how it always went. One of us made a ridiculous bet, and the other either succeeded or had to admit defeat.

I pursed my lips in thought, watching him with skeptical eyes. "What's your angle here, Kobayashi?"

His lips tipped up slightly at the sound of his last name. "No angle, just admitting you're right."

I hesitated, at a loss for words. What now? I wasn't even going to touch his words or the fact that he didn't think he could go an entire session without looking at me. It meant nothing and was probably just another antic to get under my skin. Even so, I couldn't look at him as I felt my cheeks get hot.

"Yes, well, I'm always right," I declared, still not looking at him as I snatched my music journal from the table. I needed to move on and far away from this conversation that had completely gone sideways. "Anyway, we have a verse to finish. Come on. Chop-chop."

I heard Will chuckle under his breath, but he wisely didn't say anything as he picked up his guitar once more.

Contest. Contract. Dream job. I silently said those three words in my head over and over until everything else faded, and I was able to look at Will without feeling any of those uncertain, annoying feelings. *You're exhausted, and your brain is not functioning at its normal capacity*, I reminded myself.

Will was still the same frustratingly arrogant man that I'd always hated. Nothing had changed. He might not be the scum of the earth that I'd originally labeled him, but he was still a dick who I'd deal with for this contest but not a second more.

"Okay," I said, taking a deep breath, feeling better, feeling in control. "Let's continue."

17

For the next two weeks, we worked tirelessly at the first verse.

I'd thought I'd wake up that next morning after our fight and want to avoid Will at all costs or be mad at myself, but surprisingly, I'd felt neither. Will had made me feel safe that day, and even though a part of me still felt embarrassed about the whole thing—the *thing* being the fact that I almost cried in front of Will and he responded by comforting me—but I was just going to chuck the whole encounter in the bin filed *Random Things That Make No Sense* in my brain and keep moving along.

"I say, we move past that part for now and continue on." Will stood up from his chair to stretch.

I leaned back from the keyboard, stretching my fingers out. My head was a fog of melodies and chords and trying to put words to the feelings the music was speaking to me. Making music was its own language, and it was one that I was most comfortable speaking. It was my way of communicating to people, the only time that I knew how to be my most honest. When I really got into the zone, it felt like an alternate universe, like I was outside of myself, creating these beats and beautiful lyrics to a feeling I hadn't even known that I felt or experienced.

My experiences, my emotions, came from so many outlets. A sad movie, the news, a favorite TV show or fictional couple, watching a random couple walk by in the street and wondering if they were always happy together—it all influenced me, and I never really understood just how much until I was sitting here with my music and it was telling me a story in the only way I knew how to listen.

I loved creating music, and the unbelievable part was, I was having a great time, creating music with Will too. He was talented, and he had a lot of really great ideas. We were so in sync in a way I'd never really felt while working with other music creators. It was strange, but I thought this truce was actually working, and every second we spent working on this song, I felt more and more confident of our chances to win.

"I think I can tweak that last section by the end of tonight," I said, writing notes in the margins of my music journal. A strand of my dark hair fell forward, and I curled it behind my ear as I hummed the song under my breath. "The beginning is the most important part of the song. If we don't entice them from the beginning, we'll lose them."

"Maybe that's why we're having such a hard time with it," Will commented. "Too much pressure. We need to go back to when we weren't feeling the pressure to make something great. It'll just come to us while we're working on a different part."

"You don't know that," I argued halfheartedly. Truthfully, I knew he was right, but I still wanted to keep at it.

"I do actually," he said simply. He took my pen from my hand and gently closed my notebook. "Let's take a break. We can order some food, and afterward, we'll go back to the song."

I wavered, looking back at the notebook and instruments. But after a moment, I sighed and nodded in agreement. "Okay, but I say, we go back to the beginning next week to see if we can fix it."

"Deal," Will said with a pleased smile. Then, like it was nothing at all and a completely normal thing to do, he grabbed my hand and pulled me up so that I was standing up next to him. "I have some menus in the kitchen, but anything in particular you're craving?"

I looked down at my hand, which was loosely tangled in his, and I frowned, shaking my head. "No. No preference. Why are you holding my hand?"

"Because I don't trust that you won't run back to the computer if I let it go," he responded simply.

I opened my mouth and then closed it again, knowing he was probably right. He smirked and started walking toward the door, and I trailed behind him, our intertwined hands in front of me as he guided me out of the room. Once we got to the kitchen, he let go of my hand, and I let my arm drop to my side, heart racing.

Why did I let him do that? Why didn't that feel as crazy as it should've? I did not hold hands with Will Kobayashi. I didn't even like him as a person. Okay, well, that wasn't completely true, but I still didn't trust him completely.

Will opened a drawer by the fridge and pulled out an assortment of takeout menus. He spread them out on the counter, and I moved closer to take a look at the options. Chinese, a few Japanese restaurants, a pizzeria, and one Indian cuisine flyer. The great thing about New York was that you could literally get anything that you were craving at pretty much any time of the day. It could be one in the morning, and you could probably still get food delivered to your front door.

"Do you like Japanese food?" he asked, and I nodded. "There's this really great restaurant that delivers here. The food isn't quite as good as my mom's home-cooked meals, but it's the closest I've come to authentic Japanese food in Brooklyn."

"Do you miss California?" I asked. I didn't know why I was asking him personal questions, and I didn't know why I wanted to know the answer so badly. Why I wanted to know *him* so badly.

"Yes, and no," he said, picking up the other flyers and putting them all in one pile. "I miss my family, and I miss the West Coast weather, but I don't regret coming here."

I nodded, not wanting to ask anything more. But my mouth had a mind of its own. "You grew up in California?"

"Born and raised," he said proudly. "My parents came here from Japan when they were about eighteen or nineteen, and we've been here since. They aren't fans of how cold it gets on the East Coast, so they prefer to stay where it's warmer."

"Makes sense," I agreed. I picked up the Japanese restaurant flyer and opened the pamphlet. "So, is there anything you recommend from here? I've only had Japanese once, and it was chicken teriyaki."

Will raised an eyebrow at that. "Let me guess. Sarku Japan?"

I grinned sheepishly. "Guilty."

He groaned exaggeratedly, looking anguished. "You're killing me, Genesis. That's not real Japanese food. That's not even close to the real thing! That's like saying Olive Garden is real Italian food."

I laughed, the sound leaving my mouth before I could hold it in. "Sorry! I didn't know any better, and it's just so good. I can't resist it."

Will crossed his arms across his chest, and I tried not to stare at how his biceps bulged in his white button-down. He stared at me with a look of deadly seriousness and said in his deep voice, "That's it. You don't even deserve to try food from this restaurant after saying that."

He snatched the pamphlet from my hand, and when I went to grab it, he raised it above his head and thus completely out of my reach. I gasped in mock outrage, trying to reach on my tippy-toes for the pamphlet, one of my hands resting on his shoulder for balance.

"Give me that flier," I growled, jumping slightly to reach for it above his head.

"Not a chance, Buttercup," he said with a grin. "You lost the right to taste real Japanese food after what you just said."

I stepped even closer to Will, my front brushing against his, and I narrowed my eyes in triumph as my fingers brushed against the flier. I heard Will grunt softly, a small gasp leaving his mouth, but just as I turned my head to look at him, I tripped over his foot, and my eyes widened in panic at the painful fall I knew I had coming.

Will quickly placed his hand on my back and maneuvered us so that my back was pressed against the counter and we weren't both flat on the ground. I looked up at Will with wide eyes, heart still racing from my almost fall.

"Okay, fine, you win. I will never go to another fast-food Japanese restaurant ever again."

Will looked down at me, gentle smile playing on his lips, and it was then that I realized how close we were standing together. It felt like the whole apartment was dead quiet, and only the sounds of our heavy breaths could be heard. I squirmed at the sudden tension but stilled when I felt my leg brush against his. Will's eyes fell to my lips, and I unconsciously licked them, breath hitching when I saw his eyes go nearly black, his gaze like a warm burn as he leaned slightly into me.

My mind was screaming, *What the hell is going on?!*

But my heart was beating loudly in my ears, each beat like an incessant chant of, *Kiss him, kiss him, kiss him,* that had me staring at him in uncertainty and confusion.

Will moved back, his eyes still dark but he'd lost some of the shimmering heat I'd seen there only moments ago. He smiled again, though this time, it looked more like a grimace, and he roughly ran his hand through his hair.

He cleared his throat and waved the pamphlet. "Since you conceded, I will allow you the honor of trying the delicious food from Kumo Japanese restaurant."

I blinked, feeling slightly dazed. *Was I really about to let Will kiss me a few seconds ago? What the hell is going on with me?*

I cleared my throat. "Thanks for the show of good sportsmanship."

"If it's okay with you, I'll order for us," he said, leaning back against the opposite counter, looking the picture of relaxed and unbothered as he flipped through the flier. "You don't have any allergies, do you?"

"Nope," I answered, voice shaking slightly. I pointed toward the music room and quickly added, "I'm just going to go check my phone while you order."

I barely waited for his nod before walking away. When I got into the room, I walked to the table where I'd left my phone, mumbling to myself the whole way.

"What the hell was that?" I asked myself, resisting the urge to smack my palm against my forehead. "Stupid, stupid, *stupid*."

I couldn't believe I had really almost let him kiss me. Me!

I glanced at the notifications on my phone, scrolling through all the emails and social media notifications and pausing on the texts. Looked like Alejandra and Yari had both been texting me, a long thread of missed texts filling my screen.

> *Aleja: What time are you coming home? James is here, and he wants to make everyone dinner. :)*

> *Aleja: Hello? Stop yelling at your cute music partner and answer!*

> *Aleja: Okay, well, now, James is just going to make whatever Yari wants, and you know she won't leave any leftovers :)*

I chuckled, quickly typing out a response and trying to ignore just how off the mark her text was about me and Will.

> *Me: I'll be home by 8 or 9 at the latest. I'm eating dinner here, but try to save me some.*

> *Me: And tell James I said thank you.*

I wasn't surprised that James was making the effort to cook everyone dinner. It wasn't that this was something he did often, but James was always helpful and willing to go the extra mile. Every so often, he'd cook dinner or take us all out somewhere just to show that he cared. I thought Alejandra might have something to do with it, but it was still a nice thought.

I pushed down any guilt I felt for missing out on the dinner and clicked on Yari's messages.

> *Yari: So, apparently, James is going to be cooking dinner tonight. Please tell me you're coming home in time because I don't want to be a third wheel to their lovefest.*

Beneath the text was a picture of James and Alejandra snuggling on the sofa. James's arm was circling my sister's waist as he kissed her neck, and Alejandra had the biggest grin on her face. It made my heart ache, seeing her that happy. I was happy that she was happy, but it also just reminded me that she was going to leave soon. I could feel it; she was ready to be on her own. As it was, she was barely home, always sleeping over James's place I could only imagine what it'd be like when she started working part-time with the modeling. I wanted what was best for her, and I wanted her to be happy—those were my two priorities. And even though it killed me, I knew that she was achieving them on her own and with James.

> *Me: I'm not sure if I'll make the dinner, so you're on your own with this dinner thing.*

> *Me: And tell James to stop pawing at my sister.*

Will walked into the room, and I looked up from my phone, locking the screen.

"The food will be here in a half hour," Will said, taking a seat across from me. "Do you—"

"We should probably continue practicing until then," I said, eyes glued to the computer in front of me. "We can continue working on the lyrics, if you're tired of playing."

Will studied me, and I kept my face as light and neutral as possible. If I wanted things to go back to normal, I needed to make sure that these meetings were strictly about the music. I was the one who'd started this by asking him personal questions about his family and life in California.

He's the one who held your hand, I reminded myself. *He started this.* Or maybe it was me because it wasn't like I had pulled my hand away or told him to stop at any time.

"So frustrating," I mumbled under my breath.

"What is?" Will asked, and I flinched in surprise.

Shit, I hadn't meant to say that out loud.

"The music," I said quickly, picking up the guitar and setting it on my lap. "I was just thinking about the fact that our song is nowhere near finished."

"We'll get there," Will said, taking his seat across from me. "Don't worry."

"You obviously don't know me very well," I joked halfheartedly. "Worrying, stressing, and freaking out over things that I have no control over are pretty much my specialty."

Will nodded, looking thoughtful. "But you don't need to. You can share them with me. Your worries are my worries; your stress is my stress. I want to help you in every way I can, Genesis—not just with creating the music, but also with all the worries and doubts and stress that come with it. Trust me to help you. Trust me to be your partner."

My heart skipped a painful beat, and I looked down, pretending to be fixing a string on his guitar.

Why was he making hating him so hard? I didn't want to like him, and I didn't want to trust him, but, *Dios*, he had been making it hard lately.

Trusting someone was never an easy thing for me to do, but looking into Will's eyes earlier, I'd had a feeling it would be the easiest thing in the world if I let myself do it.

But I couldn't do that to him. I wouldn't.

"You don't know what you would be signing up for," I finally said with a laugh that fell short.

"So, tell me," he said simply, eyes never leaving mine.

I stared back, feeling myself getting pulled into him again. Into the possibility of being actual friends with Will, what that could mean.

I roughly shook my head, shaking away those thoughts like a swarm of pesky flies. "Maybe some other time. I'd rather play some music right now."

Will stayed quiet for a long minute, and I began to pluck at the strings and slowly play the chords, pretending to be reading the notes on the music sheet so I didn't have to look at him. Finally, when I started to play the first verse, Will began softly singing the song, and I exhaled in relief. We got lost in the music, and before I knew it, everything else melted away.

"I can't let you pay for me," I said. "It wouldn't be fair."

"You're a guest," Will argued. "I'm not letting you pay for your dinner."

"Well, too bad," I said with a shrug, a smile tugging at my lips. "Because I already put the money somewhere in this room, and I'm not telling you where. You'll find it eventually, and it'll be like a surprise gift."

He walked to the table and put the brown paper bag on the table. He sighed but gave me a reluctant smile. "You are one stubborn girl."

"So I've been told," I said, still grinning. "What did you order?"

Will opened the bag, sticking his hand inside. "I might have gone a bit overboard because I wasn't sure what you'd like, so I bought a few different options."

"You didn't have to do that!" I said, feeling bad.

"I got you a chicken katsu dinner box," he said, ignoring my protest and handing me a plastic container filled with food. "But I also got you a side order of chicken teriyaki—the real kind because I couldn't let you not have the real thing and keep going to those fast-food chains."

He placed the small order of chicken teriyaki next to the dinner box. My mouth was practically watering at the smell of all the delicious food, but I forced myself to wait until he sat down before I started digging into my food.

"Wow, this all smells really amazing," I said, glancing at the food he was pulling out of the bag next. "What did you get?"

"I got shrimp yaki udon," he said, tilting the container for me to see. "It's a noodle stir-fry dish and has vegetables and soy sauce."

"Yaki udon," I said, trying to pronounce it as he had. "And you said I'm having chicken ka—"

"Chicken katsu," he pronounced slowly, a small smile on his face. "I think you'll really love it. And the other items in the dinner box are miso soup, salad, shumai—which is a type of dumpling—white rice, and a California roll."

"I don't even know if I'll be able to finish all of this," I said, eyeing all the food. I opened the container, and the smell of the delicious food hit me even stronger, making my stomach growl loudly.

Will laughed. "I think your stomach is willing to argue that it can."

I blushed. "Yeah, well, my stomach needs to stop being so hungry all the time because my hips are paying for it."

"You are perfect. You have nothing to worry about," Will said distractedly. He was searching through the brown paper bag for something, eyebrows furrowed.

"Thanks," I said faintly, telling myself not to think too much into his words.

He was just trying to be kind. I mean, he'd have to be an idiot to tell a girl anything besides "you are perfect" unless he wanted to get a plate of food thrown at his head. Regardless, my heart skipped a beat as I replayed what he'd said, and I had to bite down on my lip to hold in my smile.

Finally finding what he was looking for, Will pulled out some chopsticks. When he saw that I hadn't started eating yet, he nudged my plate closer to me. "Go on, try it. I want to know what you think of it."

I picked up the plastic fork and took a stab at one of the pieces of chicken before bringing it to my mouth. "Oh my God," I mumbled around my food. "This is so good."

Will grinned, looking pleased. "I knew you'd love it."

He started eating his food, and I could hardly remember to swallow before I started digging into the rest of my food. I tried a little of everything, and I found that I loved every single item in the box. It was all seasoned so perfectly, and even the soup tasted really good. But try as I might, I couldn't stop looking at Will's shrimp yaki udon. It just looked so good, and I really wanted to try some, but I didn't want to take his food. Besides, he'd already bought me so much, and I hadn't even tackled the chicken teriyaki yet. I'd just have to order Japanese food at home one day and try it then.

When I directed my eyes away from Will's food and toward him, I found that he was already looking at me. *Crap.* I gave him a small smile and shoved more food in my mouth, pretending I hadn't just been salivating at his dish.

He didn't notice, I told myself. I'm pretty sure it was just in my imagination that my mouth was open just a little while I stared at it.

"Do you want to try some of my yaki udon?" he asked, and I cringed internally.

"Uh, no, it's okay," I lied, swallowing the food in my mouth. I opened the chicken teriyaki container and put some of it in my container. "I have plenty here." I ate some of the chicken teriyaki and instantly moaned at the taste. "Holy shit, that is so good."

"Better than your fake Japanese food, right?" Will said smugly.

"Yeah, yeah, you win," I said with a wave of my hand. "I have to get Alejandra to try this. She's going to die when she tastes how good this is."

"Alejandra's your sister, right?" he asked, picking up his chopsticks again.

I nodded. "I might take the rest of this food home, so she can try it."

"Go ahead," said Will. "But before you leave, I want you to try some of my food."

I looked up from my food and saw that he was holding his plate toward me, chopsticks in hand. "No, I couldn't. It's your food."

"I insist." He tossed me a playful smile, and I marveled at the way he made even that look sexy. "Plus, I know you're secretly dying to try it."

"Am not," I scoffed.

"Are too," Will returned, smile widening.

I huffed, rolling my eyes, but I couldn't help the smile on my face as I took his bowl into my hands.

Will handed me his chopsticks, and I faltered for a second, wondering if I should just use my fork to eat it. But I didn't want to make a big deal out of nothing—because it was nothing—so I used his chopsticks to pick up some of the noodles and placed them in my mouth.

"What do you think?" he asked, watching as I chewed.

I swallowed, licking my lips of any sauce that might have been left over. Will licked his own lips, too, eyes a little dazed, as if he were lost in thought.

"I definitely need to eat out more because I've been missing out."

"I'll eat you out whenever you want," he said hoarsely, and I froze. He blinked and cleared his throat, his cheeks turning pink. "I mean, take you out. Er, order takeout. For when we practice. For the contest."

"Right," I said tightly, heart racing in my chest. *Holy shit, did Will just ...*

Heat pooled between my thighs as I replayed his words, and I'd never felt more betrayed by my body than right now. Even now, cheeks still tinted pink, he never looked away from me, and damn, if that confidence wasn't sexy as hell.

Shit.

This was getting complicated.

My phone vibrated on the table, and I quickly picked it up, so I could avoid Will's eyes for a few moments longer.

*Yari: Where are you? We're about to marathon some
Caso Cerrado on the DVR.*

I looked at the time and cursed. It was already a quarter to
nine. *Where did the time go?*

"I didn't realize it'd gotten this late," I said, pushing away
from the table. "I need to get going."

Will looked at his phone and winced. "I'm sorry. I didn't
realize the time. Let me drive you home."

I shook my head, putting my leftover food in the bag. "No,
it's okay. I'm going to take the train."

Will helped me put the food away, dark eyebrows
furrowing in the deepest frown. "Genesis, it's dark out there,
and it's at least a ten-minute walk to the train—"

"Five minutes if you're a New Yorker," I joked with a
distracted smile. Will looked unamused, so I added, "Don't
worry; I've had to walk home later and in scarier
neighborhoods. I'll be fine."

"If this is about what I said," Will started, fingers fidgeting
with his tie, "I'm sorry. I really didn't mean to make you
uncomfortable—"

"It's not," I said. "You didn't."

"Then, let me drive you home," he said firmly. I hesitated
for a second, and Will quickly moved to the door, calling out,
"I'm already out the door. I'll meet you at the elevator!"

"*Carajo*," I cursed under my breath, hurriedly following
behind him.

Time seemed to fly by in a blur of work and music.

If I wasn't at work, I was at Will's place, working on our song. And the times that I was at home were spent in my room, picking at our song at my much smaller workstation, eyes glued to my computer as I messed around with different sounds. This song consumed me, and I loved every second of it. I was in love with the song, the pieces that we'd created, and where we envisioned it going.

Soft drumbeats played in my head even now as I sat with Cora at a frozen yogurt spot, somehow able to completely ignore the upbeat pop song playing in the background for my more favorable beats in my head.

"... and I just don't want to go because I know she'll complain the whole time," Cora finished with a sigh.

Her brown skin, not much lighter than my own, was glowing as the sun reflected off the side of her face in the small shop. I never understood how someone so beautiful and so kind could continue to stay that way, even when life tested her in ways that would drive a saint crazy. But not Cora. She just kept smiling and kept trying.

"Tell her you're sick," I suggested, sticking my spoon in my cup. I'd ordered a Dreamy Dulce de Leche flavored yogurt with way too many toppings, but I couldn't help myself when I was presented with a buffet of candies.

"I can't do that. She's expecting me to come," Cora replied, shaking her head. "I'll just go and see what happens. Maybe this guy will be the one."

I scoffed. "Your sister always sets you up on dates with the grossest men. Do you remember that last guy who stared at your breasts the entire date even though you were wearing a turtleneck and were showing no cleavage whatsoever?"

Cora winced slightly. "Yeah, that was … not fun. But how was she to know he'd be a level-five creep? Besides, she means well, so the least I could do is try."

I shook my head. "Cora, you have more patience than anyone I know. I'm ready to disown my family the moment they even bring up the R-word with me. They know better than to even try setting me up with anyone because I would scream bloody murder."

Cora smiled. "You're lucky my mom hasn't tried to set you up yet. She's always asking about you."

I cringed. "You know I love your mom, but I will never go to your family's parties if they start trying to set me up with your cousins."

"No promises," Cora sang with a laugh.

We'd gone shopping for a new date outfit for Cora before going to the yogurt shop. I was exhausted in the way I always was when I spent more than thirty minutes at the mall, but I was glad I'd spent my Saturday afternoon with Cora.

We hung out at the yogurt shop for a little bit longer before eventually leaving, so Cora could go on her surprise date tonight. It felt good to spend time with her and catch up when it wasn't just us meeting for a few minutes before work every day.

When I got home about an hour later, I found the house in a bit of chaos. Which seemed to be its typical state since Yari had been staying here most days and Alejandra had been making more of an effort to be here. Granted, she almost always brought James to have dinner with us or just hang around, but I'd take anything at this point.

"What's going on?" I asked over the music playing from the stereo in the living room.

Yari looked up from her laptop, which was hooked up to the speakers. Her blonde hair was tied up in a high ponytail, and she had on a crop top and some workout pants.

"We're having a Saturday night jam session," Yari explained, her pouty mouth wide in a grin.

"Who's we?" I asked, still standing by the living room entrance.

The house smelled good, like someone was cooking, but when I peeked inside the kitchen, I didn't see anyone.

"Just me, you, and Alejandra," she answered. "She's in the bedroom, I think."

I raised my eyebrows in surprise. "No James?"

Yari shook her head, still smiling. "No James."

I nodded, watching as Yari frowned at the computer screen. "Yari ... is everything okay?"

She looked up from the screen. "Yeah. Why?"

"You know you can move in here, and we'd welcome you with open arms," I started gently. "But you've been spending more and more time here with us and less at home."

"I'm moving out of my parents' place," she all but blurted out, and my eyes nearly fell out of their sockets.

"*Qué?! Qué?!*" I nearly shouted.

It was something Yari had talked about for years, but I honestly thought she'd never move out unless she got married because of how much guilt her mom put on her whenever she brought the topic up.

"I love my mom, but if we continue living together, I'm afraid I will start hating her," Yari admitted. "We fight all the time, and these last few months, she's been more controlling than ever, constantly wanting to know what I'm doing and getting mad when I don't ask her permission even though I stopped doing that when I started going to college and working."

"Have you told your mom yet?" I asked, still shocked and trying to process what she was saying.

Tía was going to be upset—that was for sure.

"Not yet," Yari said. "I'm waiting until I find a place before I tell her. But that means I might be spending a lot more time here until then."

I nodded. "Let me know if you want me to look at places with you."

"Of course, *chica*." Yari winked, smile back on her face. "Maybe we can start looking for a place for you too."

"Hmm," I said, tapping the side of the entrance. "I'm going to go change into more comfortable clothes. What are you cooking?"

"Some rice and beans with breaded chicken," she said, giving me a look before diverting her attention back to the computer. A second later, the song changed to an upbeat Spanish song, and she moved her shoulders to the beat, nodding her head along.

"That's Alejandra's favorite meal," I noted. "I'm sure she'll be very happy."

Yari nodded but didn't say anything else, and so I made my way down the hall, stopping in front of Alejandra's room. I found her sitting on her bed in leggings and a bra, her hair up in a towel as she typed away on her phone.

I lightly knocked on her door. "Hey."

She looked up from her phone and smiled, "I was wondering when you'd get here."

I walked in and took a seat at her vanity table across from her bed, dropping my bags on the floor. "Trains were delayed, as always. I had to get off one stop early and just walk here because we were stuck at the station."

Alejandra winced in sympathy. "That sucks. This is why we should get a car."

"With the way parking is in New York?" I scoffed. "I'd probably spend half the night just looking for an empty spot."

I'd gotten my driver's license years ago, but that was mostly so I could help drive on family trips. Once a year, a bunch of my family got together and did a road trip to South Carolina, and ever since I'd been old enough, I did most of the driving. I didn't mind it, especially since my family tended to drive like a bunch of maniacs and I couldn't trust them not to engage in road rage at the slightest thing. But other than the occasional trip or errand for family, I didn't really drive. Like most New Yorkers, I relied on public transportation to get anywhere in the city.

"True," Alejandra conceded. Her eyes traveled toward my bags. "Your phone is lighting up like crazy over there."

I rummaged through my open purse and pulled out my cell phone.

> *Will: Hey, I think we got our music journals mixed up. Yours is sitting on my table, and mine is missing.*
>
> *Will: I wouldn't bother you if it wasn't important, but is there any way we can meet tonight to swap? I have a gig tomorrow, and I need it to go over something with Callum.*

I left all my stuff in Alejandra's room and walked to my room. I grabbed my bag and quickly looked through it. Crap, I did have his book. He had my music journal, which was basically my diary. My journal had songs that I'd written that were so personal that it was as if I'd written them straight from the deepest, most hidden parts of me. I still had a hard time showing a few songs to Yari and Aleja, and they always heard all of my songs whenever I wrote one.

"What's wrong?" Alejandra asked when I walked back into her room, unwrapping her towel from her head and letting her long, dark hair flow down her back.

I rubbed my index finger against the leather-bound book, tempted to open it and read through it. But I wouldn't, not without his permission. "Will and I got our music journals mixed up at practice, and he wants to meet up to swap tonight."

"Aren't you going to see him on Monday?" she questioned. "Can't you give it to him then?"

"He has a gig tomorrow, so he needs it tonight," I said with a sigh. "I don't really feel like going back out, but I guess I could meet him somewhere in the middle."

"Why don't you just tell him to come here and pick it up?" Alejandra asked with a shrug.

"I can't make him come all the way over here," I said with a shake of my head.

"Why not? He's the one who needs the book so badly," Alejandra volleyed back. "It doesn't hurt to ask. Besides, we're having girls' night! You can't leave now."

The thought of going back out sounded unbearable.

"All right, I'll ask," I said, and Alejandra grinned triumphantly.

> *Me: Is there any way you could come to my place to pick it up?*

> *Will: Definitely.*

> *Will: I'll be there soon.*

"So, what did he say?" Alejandra asked, tossing on a baggy gray tee that said *I'm only happy when it rains.*

"Why are you wearing my shirt?"

"Because I like it," she answered easily. "Now, stop avoiding the question. He said he'd come, didn't he?"

"Yeah," I replied with an eye roll. "You can stop with your smug little smile. You were right once. Get over it."

Alejandra laughed, skipping to her bed before jumping on it. "Nah, I like how annoyed it makes you. I think I'll be right more often. It's a good feeling."

"You're annoying," I said, reluctantly smiling. I picked my bags up from the floor and started heading toward the door.

"I'm taking a shower. Go make sure Yari doesn't put any sad songs on and turn this jam session into a downer party."

Alejandra lay like a star on her bed, all four limbs spread, but she raised her right hand and saluted me with a grin. "Aye, aye, captain."

What a goofball, I thought with a grin.

We were just getting ready to eat our late dinner when I heard our buzzer going off. I went to reach for my cell phone to tell Will that I'd be right down when Alejandra pressed the intercom by the door and buzzed him in.

I huffed but got up and walked to the door, the music journal in my hand. "You don't have to hang around in the hallway."

"I just want to say hi," Alejandra said with an innocent smile that I was definitely *not* buying.

"I bet you do," I replied sarcastically.

The doorbell went off, and I quickly stepped in front of my sister and unlocked the door, pulling it open.

What. The. Fuck?

"Hey," Will said with a soft smile.

I stared at him silently, my eyes trying to take in what I was seeing.

"You cut your hair," I finally blurted out, eyes wide. "And you're wearing jeans."

He gave me a strange look, his smile turning teasing. "Did you think I only wore suits?"

I looked at him, drinking in the new Will in front of me. One who apparently wore jeans and got haircuts that made his already-too-perfect face even more handsome. He hadn't cut too much of his hair, but he'd left more hair on the top of his head, and something about the haircut displayed his sharp cheekbones in a way that had me itching to reach out and touch him. I moved my eyes over his open jacket and saw that he was wearing a dark sweater that seemed to stretch across his chest.

"Genesis?" Will asked, brows furrowing in concern as he took a small step toward me.

I started rubbing my eyes harder, hoping against hope that when I opened them again, I'd find a less hot version of Will standing in front of me. Hopefully one with a few warts growing on his face.

"Hi, Will!" Alejandra said behind me. Not that she could've stayed hidden for long since she was so much taller than me. Seeing her stand next to me with Will across from us only heightened the fact that I had been surrounded by too many tall people in my life lately. "I'm Alejandra, Genesis's sister."

"Yes, of course," Will said, shaking her hand, serious. "Genesis talks about you all the time."

Alejandra grinned, bouncing lightly on her toes. "Genesis told me you're a phenomenal singer. We go to karaoke bars a lot. You should come one day."

Will nodded, giving me a quick glance. "I'd love to."

"Here's your book," I said, effectively shutting down their conversation.

We exchanged books, and I carefully took my journal back with two fingers at the edge to make sure I didn't accidentally touch Will. He watched me, eyes twinkling, like he found me amusing.

"Thanks for coming down here to pick it up."

He pulled slightly on his navy scarf, which was hanging loosely around his neck, and nodded. "I'll let you guys get back to your night."

"You should come inside!" Alejandra offered, making my neck snap quickly to her, my eyes wide in panic. "We're just about to eat some dinner, but there's plenty for you too."

"Oh, I don't want to interrupt your night," Will said, glancing at me again.

I quickly neutralized my expression so that I looked indifferent instead of a mixture of panic and annoyance.

"It was supposed to be a quiet dinner, just us three. I don't know if Yari would be okay with that—"

"Come in, Will!" Yari shouted over me from the kitchen.

I turned my head to see her standing in the hall outside the kitchen door, a grin on her face. "I've been wanting to meet you for years now. There's plenty of food for you; don't worry."

Will looked at me questioningly. He was obviously waiting for me to say it was okay, but how could I tell him that I didn't want him to come in because this felt like getting too close? It'd been getting harder and harder to remind myself of all the reasons I didn't like him, and I was worried I was getting too comfortable with the idea of him being in my life.

My sister coughed loudly behind me and pressed her finger hard into my back. I jumped slightly, throwing her a look behind me before nodding to Will.

We moved back so that Will could walk into the apartment. Alejandra skipped down the hall and into the kitchen, and I didn't see the look she shared with Yari, but from the way Yari looked at me, I knew they were going to be teasing me about him for the rest of the week.

"Can I take your jacket?" I asked, pointing to the coat rack by the door. "It's really hot in here, so you'll probably melt if you don't take that off."

Will took off his scarf and jacket and handed them to me with a soft smile. "Thank you."

I nodded silently, and after I hung up his jacket, we moved toward the kitchen and Yari.

"Will, this is my cousin Yari. Yari, this is Will, my music partner for the contest. He works with Cora in the finance department."

Yari was sizing Will up, her eyes moving over him as she held her hand out for him to shake. "It's nice to finally put a face to the name I've heard so much about."

Will nodded and shot me a pleased look, which I ignored since I was too busy shooting daggers at Yari. "It's great to meet you too. Genesis mentioned to me once that you were her favorite cousin and best friend."

Yari pinched one of my cheeks, and I promptly smacked her hand away with a scowl. "Aw, she's so sweet."

"Stop being annoying," I said, which only made her laugh.

"No way," she said with a shake of her head. In Spanish, she finished, "This will probably be the one and only time you bring any guy home. I need to embarrass you as much as I can since I won't get this opportunity again."

I rolled my eyes at that. "*Puta.*"

Will laughed. "Okay, now, *that* word I know."

Yari smiled. "Sorry about that, Will. My cousin tends to get a bit grouchy if she hasn't eaten."

Will turned around to look at me and gave me a wink. "Oh, I know. I keep her well fed during our music sessions to avoid getting my head bitten off."

"Gee, thanks." Suddenly, it'd become *pick on Genesis* day in this house.

"Well, the food is just about ready. Genesis"—she turned toward me—"why don't you show Will where the dining room is?"

"Okay." I nodded, liking that we were treating Will like a guest. Maybe that meant she and Alejandra would both be on their best behavior and not try to embarrass me after all. "Follow me, Will."

He smiled at Yari before walking with me down the hall. "Your place is really nice."

"Thanks," I said. I turned into the small dining room. "You can take any seat you'd like. Can I get you a drink? We have beer, juice, soda, water."

"I'll take some water." Will put a hand on the back of a chair. Coincidentally, he had chosen the spot right next to my usual seat. "Thanks again for inviting me for dinner."

I shrugged, like it was no big deal. "It was about time you tried some real Spanish food anyway. It's only fair since I tried Japanese food."

Will face lit up with his smile, and I felt my heart skip a beat. "Very true. Though I never tried to say commercial fast food was better than the real thing—unlike some people."

"Oh, come on," I said, my earlier worries dripping away as I smiled up at him. "You're never going to let that go, are you?"

"Nope." His smile got bigger as he leaned slightly toward me. "I'll probably be teasing you about this for the rest of your life, so be prepared."

I knew that he was just joking, but the idea of knowing Will for the next year—much less the rest of my life—made my stomach feel weird in a new way that I didn't like.

"I'll be right back with your drink."

As I turned to walk out of the room, Alejandra entered. She gave me a quick thumbs-up, and while still looking at me, she said aloud, "Hey, Will, just out of curiosity, are you single?"

I briskly rushed out of the room, silently promising to cut holes in all of Alejandra's shirts, à la Regina George style. Though it'd probably backfire on me, just like it did in the movie, but still.

I walked into the kitchen and walked straight to the fridge. "You guys need to stop treating Will like he's my boyfriend," I said in a hushed voice.

"Stop being dramatic," Yari said with an eye roll, her voice matching my own. "We're just having a little fun."

"And no third degree," I continued, pouring some water into a glass. "He's just a ... friend. A coworker. A coworker friend."

"A friend that you like to casually eye-fuck while he stands outside the apartment?" she asked with a saucy grin. "No wonder you've been coming home later from practice. Will is fucking sexy!"

I laughed at Yari's wagging eyebrows, shushing her. "I was not eye-fucking him. I was just surprised by his casual outfit. He never changes out of his work clothes when we practice."

"And you never told me about those dreamy eyes," Yari continued, like I hadn't talked at all. "You seriously downplayed how attractive this guy is."

"I did not," I refuted.

"You totally did," Alejandra piped up from right behind us. "We'll have to Facebook-stalk him later see if we can find any pictures of him shirtless."

"Ooh, yes, good idea," Yari whispered, excitedly turning to Alejandra. "Why haven't we Facebook-stalked him yet? We need to see if he's single."

"Already asked him, and he said he is," Alejandra said proudly.

I was just standing there in the kitchen, watching as I was rapidly losing control of the situation with each word. "He said he hasn't been dating anyone either. I bet it's because he spends *all* his free time with Genesis."

Both girls looked at me with expectant expressions on their face.

I gave them both an unamused look. "What? This isn't anything surprising. We want to win. I'm not dating anyone, and it has nothing to do with him, so I doubt his dating options have anything to do with me either."

"You're not dating anyone because of your fear of intimacy, you little ice queen," Alejandra said with an eye roll. She took the glass of water from my hand and gave me a pat on the head, like I was a sad puppy or something, as I stared at her with my mouth opened in shock. "I'll give this to Will. You can make his plate for him and bring it into the dining room."

"I'm not his girlfriend. He can serve himself," I said to her retreating back. She didn't bother stopping to respond to me, and I looked at Yari with raised eyebrows. "See? This is what I meant when I said you guys are getting ahead of yourselves."

"Oh, shut up and make his plate," Yari said not unkindly.

She passed me two plates, and I took them despite my complaining. In Dominican and most Latinx culture, you always served the men first before you served yourself or anyone else. When I had been growing up, my mom would always make my father his plate and drink, and only once that was done were we given our food and allowed to eat. Finally, once everyone was eating and comfortable, then my mom would sit down and enjoy her food. It was a bit old school— not to mention, sexist—and any other time, I would've said hell no because I hated the idea of a woman serving a man. But I wanted to do it this time because I wanted to mix the different sauces in the way that I knew would give the most delicious bite. I wanted to prepare the perfect selection the way he'd done for me at his place all those weeks ago.

I made our plates, making sure to put lots of food on Will's, and when both Yari and I were done, we walked out of the kitchen and into the dining room. I immediately became suspicious at the sight of Alejandra and Will talking, big smiles on their faces. My eyes darted to the bottle of wine Alejandra must have brought out at some point, and I noticed she'd served herself a glass that was filled to the top.

Yari put Alejandra's plate of food in front of her before sitting down beside her. I walked toward Will and placed his plate in front of him. I took the empty seat next to him and across from Yari.

"And I told him not to." Alejandra dramatically waved her hands in the air as she told her story. "But if there's one thing James likes to do, it's prove people wrong."

"And did he?" Will asked, eyes lit with amusement.

"Well, he was able to jump out of the second-story window," Alejandra said, picking up her glass of wine. She raised her glass to her mouth, but before she took a gulp, she continued with a grin, "But his pants also got stuck on something on the way down and ripped right down the middle."

Will laughed, the sound deep and seeming to bounce off the walls and straight into my veins, like a dose of happiness. I couldn't tell if the smile on my face was from her story or from watching his reaction to her story.

Yari picked up the bottle of wine and poured herself a glass before tilting it toward me and Will. "You guys want some?"

"Nah, I'm good with my water," I said, lifting my glass and taking a sip.

"Party pooper," she teased before turning to Will. "What about you? You gonna be a party pooper, too, like Genesis, or are you going to join in on the fun?"

"Sorry, but I'm joining Genesis on this one," Will said with a grin. He gently elbowed me on the side, and I felt my stomach flutter at the touch. "I guess we're just a pair of party poopers."

"Boo," Alejandra said, giving us a thumbs-down.

"Okay, let's just eat," I said with a heavy sigh, giving both girls a pointed look. "And try not to get too drunk."

I felt like because I'd said not to get drunk, they, of course, proceeded to get super drunk.

After dinner, we all ended up in the living room, talking and listening to music that Yari had picked from one of her many playlists.

"We should play a game!" Yari shouted excitedly.

I groaned, but I was pretty sure it got lost in the sounds of Alejandra's and Yari's squealing and loud debate over which game to play.

"Scrabble! Scrabble!" Alejandra started chanting. She continued her chant as she walked across the room and to our small collection of games in the cabinet beneath the television.

"Afraid you'll lose?" Will murmured into my ear.

I jumped slightly and narrowed my eyes at the smirk playing across his lips. He looked calm as could be, leaning his arm against the top of the sofa, body relaxed as he watched my sister and cousin set up the game on the coffee table. My eyes traced his strong jawline, and for a fleeting moment, I wondered what it would feel like to press my lips against them before I shook the thought off.

"Against you?" I scoffed. "Not possible."

It was bizarre, seeing Will here, in my home. I could only imagine what he thought of our modest apartment. It was definitely a downgrade in comparison to his fancy place, and even though I kept waiting for Will to make some kind of comment or to look like he wasn't comfortable, he never did. In fact, he looked almost too comfortable, like he was here all the time, and it was strange, the way he seemed to just ... fit right in.

"I don't know," Will hummed, tilting his head as he looked at me. "Looks like you're a little nervous over there. I won't judge you if you're only capable of making three-letter words."

I rolled my eyes. "When I win, try not to cry too many tears and stain our coffee table."

Will barked out a laugh, and I couldn't help the warm, pleasant feeling that flowed through me as I watched his head toss back, his strong neck on display as he laughed up toward the ceiling.

"Stop laughing," I grumbled, hating that I couldn't take my eyes off of him as he kept chuckling. "Let's just play this stupid game."

"Buttercup," he said softly, a smile still on his face as he studied my face.

I turned away from him, determined to ignore him and his stupid smile.

"Buttercup?" Yari asked, eyes lit with curiosity as she sat back down. "Like the Powerpuff Girl?"

I felt my face get hot as I shot him an indignant look. "I told him to stop calling me that."

Will shifted on the couch, his arm brushing against my shoulder for a moment. "You can certainly be hotheaded like the cartoon character, but that's not why I call you Buttercup. You've got a hard exterior with the people you don't know, but secretly, I think you care more than you want anyone to know. You're passionate and so damn beautiful. Sweet and incredibly softhearted. I love that only people who know you get to know that about you."

I was pretty sure all three of us were staring at him in surprise because Will's cheeks reddened slightly, but he did not look away as he continued, "Buttercup just felt like the perfect nickname."

"Wow," Alejandra breathed.

I glanced between her and Yari and saw them swooning with hearts in their eyes while Yari looked at Will with a big grin on her face that made me nervous.

"Um"—I cleared my throat—"Buttercup was always my favorite Powerpuff Girl as a kid, so … thanks."

Will held my eyes for a long moment, and I felt like he was reading every single thought and emotion that I didn't want him to know. His words … I felt like my heart was going to be permanently pumping at this fast pace, my body humming in pleasure. I gave him a nervous smile and looked away, trying to bring everyone's attention back to the game and far away from me or Will.

"Aleja, you go first," I said, taking one of the brown letter racks and drew seven letter tiles from the pile in the middle of the table. I moved from my spot next to Will on the sofa to sit across from him. When I saw the look of confusion on his face, I said, "I'm not letting you cheat and look at my letters."

He smirked but didn't say anything as he grabbed his own set of tiles and set himself up. As the game got started, I focused entirely on my tiles and the board and trying to find the best way to win. I didn't mind losing to my sister or Yari, but I needed to end this game with more points than Will.

"*Azido*," Will said, throwing me a wink. "Fifteen points."

I ignored him, waiting for my turn. "*Bozo*. Fifteen points."

I threw him a triumphant look, but Will didn't look bothered at all. He gave me an easy smile and watched as Yari put down her word, cheering her on for her five-point word.

"*Zack.* Nineteen points," Will said, putting down his tiles. He looked at me beneath his dark lashes as he reached for more tiles. "Getting nervous?"

"Not even close," I said with a defiant look at him.

The next twenty minutes of the game passed by in a blur of word tiles. It seemed that every time I thought I was in the lead, Will would come up with a word that earned him a triple score or double-digit points, and even though I told myself to stop getting so mad, the competitive side of me that always seemed to come out around Will just got stronger and stronger. The more Will looked confident and calm, the more competitive and determined I got to win.

"*Jack.* Seventeen points," I said to Will.

He smiled. "*Jagg.* Thirteen points."

I narrowed my eyes. "Is that even a word?"

"We can pull out the dictionary if you want to check," he offered, leaning back into the sofa with a cocky smile.

I hesitated but let it go. "*Hung.* Eight points."

And on and on we went, only looking away from each other to put down our next word. I didn't even know how much time had gone by as we played. It could've been minutes; it could've been hours. I was running out of tiles, and so was Will.

I sat up on my knees as I watched Will place his next word down on the board.

His eyes bounced between my own as he said softly, "*Love.* Seven points."

I couldn't help the triumphant grin that spread across my face. "Ha!" I all but shouted as I quickly picked up my tiles and put them across the board. "*Za.* Sixty-two points! I win!"

I grinned, arms up in the air as I began to wiggle from side to side.

Will watched me, an amused look on his face as he slow-clapped. "Congrats."

"Well, *diablo*," Yari said with a low whistle. "You two just straight-up forgot all about us—"

"But we're not complaining," Aleja chimed in with a wide grin as she looked between Will and me. "You two are entertaining as hell."

I felt my face drop slightly as I realized I'd completely forgotten all about them as we were playing. I couldn't even remember the last time they'd gotten a turn.

"I'm so sorry," I said, sitting back down on the floor. "I might have gotten a little carried away ..."

"A little?" Yari and Aleja said at the same time and then immediately started cracking up.

I glanced at Will, who gave me a knowing look, and I huffed, crossing my arms across my chest.

"Okay, so I got carried away," I admitted. "But for the record, I won."

Yari shook her head in amusement, standing up. "I'm getting another drink. Does anyone want anything?"

Yari walked away with the promise to bring more water for me and alcohol for Alejandra, who I made a face at. She ignored completely as she leaned toward Will.

"So, Will, I hear you have a gig tomorrow," Alejandra said, taking another drink from her glass. "What kind of music do you play?"

"A little bit of pop, some soul," Will answered, leaning back against the couch. "I mostly do small gigs at cafés or bars, nothing serious. But I like getting the experience and exposure."

"You have a YouTube channel, too, right?" Yari asked, walking back toward us, hands filled with drinks.

Will turned his head to look at me, but I kept looking right at the small table in front of me, pretending like I couldn't see his amused smirk.

"Yeah, I have a bit of a following on there. But it's mostly for my cover songs."

"And now, you're writing a song with my talented sister." Alejandra grinned, swaying from side to side. "Which will kick ass and no doubt win the contest. I can't wait to say that I knew you before you became famous."

"Thanks," Will said with an almost-shy smile. "It takes a lot of work, but I'm hoping to become known for more than just my cover songs. My originals don't get half as many views as those videos."

"I really liked 'Redemption,'" I said as I took a seat back on the sofa beside him. Our arms brushed as I leaned back against the sofa, and it took me way too long to pull away. "The beat alone was really great and captured my attention, and the lyrics were amazing."

"Thank you," Will said, gently knocking his knee against mine. "It doesn't seem fair though that you get to hear my originals and I've yet to hear one of yours."

"Oh, Genesis doesn't let anyone hear her originals," Alejandra said, vigorously shaking her head. After a few seconds, she had to put her hand to head, as if to forcibly stop her head from moving, and I chuckled. Clearly, she was well on her way to drunk. "They're really personal to her. It takes a lot for her to let anyone hear them."

"That's not true," I said. "I let people hear my originals that I make for clients all the time."

"I don't want to hear the ones you write for other people. I want to hear the songs you keep in that journal of yours," Will said, eyes locked on mine.

"Did you look through my music journal?" I asked, not really believing he would have but having to ask anyway.

"You know I wouldn't," Will said with a shake of his head.

I nodded, tapping my knee against his before looking away.

"I wish I could have your kind of determination for chasing my dreams," Alejandra said wistfully.

I could feel Will's stare still on me, but at her words, he looked away and focused on her words. "What's your dream?"

"I want to be a model," Alejandra said proudly. "I've been scouted and everything, but it's been over a month, and I still haven't heard back from the scout. I think that door has been closed."

"You can't let one person stop you from doing what you really love," Will said kindly but firmly. "Send him another email, and if he still doesn't reply, start sending your headshots to other modeling agencies. You're in a city that is filled with agencies. Trust me, you'll get the call."

Alejandra perked up, her smile brightening. "You really think so? I was scared that since I hadn't heard back from this guy that I shouldn't bother trying again."

Will shook his head. "The last thing you should do is give up. You're gorgeous, Alejandra, and you're going to rock the modeling world. Don't give up. You'll get there. Nothing that is really worth it is earned so easily. We have to work for it—really hard. And there will be times where it feels impossible, but once we get through those times, the reward is so much sweeter."

His words of encouragement to my sister meant so much to her, and my heart warmed as I looked at him. I could tell from her face that he'd given her the boost of confidence that I hadn't even known she needed. I'd had no idea that she was starting to lose faith in herself or this dream, and I felt guilty that I hadn't noticed.

Was I not making enough time for her? I tried to talk with her every time she was home, but sometimes, I did get stuck in my own head, especially since things had been so hectic lately.

"Thanks, Will," Alejandra said with a sloppy smile. "You should look into being a motivational speaker if the whole singing thing doesn't work out. But you're too good for it to not work out, so …" Her "so" was drawn out, her eyes widening and making Will chuckle.

He ran a hand through his hair, and I watched in avid fascination at the way his bicep flexed with the simple move. "Uh, okay. I'll make it my backup plan."

"Woohoo," Alejandra cheered, dancing in her seat.

Will looked from Alejandra to me, a grin on his face. I could tell he was all too amused by my sister's drunken excitement, and I shrugged halfheartedly, as if to say, *What can you do?*

"Feel free to change that backup career at any time," I informed him.

Alejandra gasped dramatically, her hand to her chest. "Genesis! He can't just *change* his backup career. This was my most genius idea yet. I mean, honestly! Are you hearing this, Yari?"

I rolled my eyes at her, and Yari nodded along in agreement. "Alejandra always has the best ideas, Genesis. You know this."

"Oh my God, you both are drunk," I said with a reluctant smile. "Am I the only one who remembers Alejandra's last inspirational idea?"

Will looked from me to the girls, amusement clear on his face. "I'm hurt. Are you telling me that my backup career is not Alejandra's greatest idea ever?"

I grinned. "Sorry to disappoint."

"Somehow, hearing the bad news from you makes the disappointment hurt less," Will replied, turning his body toward mine. "But then again, I don't think anything could sound bad, coming from your mouth."

"Okay, wow," I said with a laugh, even as my body felt flushed with pleasure from his words. "Are you sure there isn't vodka in that glass instead of water?"

"Cute," Will said, lips tilted slightly as he stared at me.

"Um, hello?" Alejandra said, snapping her fingers toward us. "You guys can go back to being flirty in a minute, but, Genesis, what inspirational idea were you talking about? Because all my ideas are amazing."

I looked away from Will. "Your last idea was that Yari should join the European circus, and when I pointed out that she didn't have any kind of training, do you remember what you said? You said—"

"That she should pay people to watch her twerk her ass onstage," Alejandra finished, looking proud. "That was a genius idea. Not everyone can move their body like she can. Plus, she can belly dance! She could make some serious bank."

"Yeah, there's already a profession for that. It's called stripping," I pointed out, laughing.

"Hey, I just want to point out that I'd be the best freaking stripper there ever was," Yari proclaimed, and a moment later, "I'm in Love with a Stripper" by T-Pain was blasting through the stereo.

She stood up and started swaying to the beat, and I groaned, covering my face as I started to laugh.

"Yes, girl!" Alejandra said, standing up too. "Dance party!"

I laughed hard as they both began half-dancing, half-singing to the song, moving to the middle of the room. "Oh my God, you two are ridiculous."

"Wow, she really does know how to twerk," Will said, looking half-impressed. After a moment, he turned to me, and with a crooked grin, he said, "Are you going to join them? Because that is something I'd die to see."

"I don't twerk," I said with a shake of my head. I paused, thinking about my many nights out with Yari, and amended, "Well, not unless there's a lot of alcohol involved."

"Well, the next time you decide to go out dancing, invite me," he said, turning his body more on the couch to face me.

"You dance?" I asked with an arch of my brow.

Will tilted his head to the side a bit. "Depends on what you call dancing, but yeah, I can handle myself on the dance floor. No twerking or ass-shaking though."

I grinned. "Aw, and here you had me actually contemplating inviting you out to dance next week."

The song changed to a salsa song, and Yari and Alejandra somehow seamlessly switched from twerking against the wall to moving into formation, so they could dance together.

Yari looked toward us and shouted, "Get up, you two! The rule of the dance party is that everyone has to be dancing!"

"Yeah! Get up, you two!" Alejandra shouted, spinning out of Yari's arms before moving back in to continue dancing.

Will looked toward me, amused grin on his face. "I'm down if you are. But you'll have to teach me how to salsa."

I looked toward Alejandra and Yari, who were both dancing and singing loudly between bouts of laughter as they argued over what the actual lyrics of the song were. I felt happy and carefree, and I didn't want to ruin that by being the person who was always overthinking everything.

"Yeah, let's do it," I said, standing up and reaching a hand down toward Will, not letting myself think too hard.

He put his hand in mine and squeezed gently, just looking up at me for a second. Then, as if nothing had happened, he got up and led me to a space in the middle of the living room, where we could dance without bumping into anything.

"Okay, so first, you need to put your right hand on my back and pick up my right hand like so," I said, picking up his left hand with my right hand and holding it up a bit. He placed his hand on my back, near my shoulder blade, looking down at me as he waited for the next instructions. "Salsa can be really confusing and hard to learn, so I'm going to keep the dance moves as basic as possible. You ready?"

Will nodded. "I'm ready."

He had such a look of utter concentration on his face that I couldn't help but smile, imagining him making that face whenever he had to study for test as a kid. "Okay, so starting with your left foot, you're going to move it like you're taking a step forward and then move your right foot like you're taking a step in place and end it by bringing your left food back to the starting position. Then, we'll do that but moving backward. Here, watch me."

I showed him what to do, doing each step as slow as possible so that he could get the rhythm of it. After watching me do it two more times, he started copying my moves, trying to do it on his own. He stumbled a few times at first, but by the time the second salsa song came on, he was able to keep up pretty well with the song.

"You're doing great," I said, grinning up at him. "Looks like you've got some Latin blood in you."

Will grinned back at me. "I'm concentrating so hard on my steps right now."

I laughed. "It takes practice, but if you keep at it, you'll be able to do it without even thinking about it."

Will nodded, watching me as I danced with him. If there was one thing I loved about my culture, it was the music. Dancing was one of my favorite things to do at family parties because it was the one thing that everyone, no matter how old or young, could do, and we all had such a great time.

When the song ended, it switched to an Aventura song, which was bachata, a different kind of Latin music and dance. I quickly showed Will the moves, which he picked up much easier since it was very simple and something almost everyone figured out in the first two minutes. This dance could also be a bit more intimate, as your bodies tended to be closer, his hand on my waist and his leg between mine as we moved.

Maybe it was the music, or how much fun I was having tonight, or the fact that my body hadn't stopped tingling since the moment his hand had slid into mine, but I found myself dancing closer to him than was probably necessary. From the way Will's hand moved slowly from my waist until his fingers were caressing my lower back, his eyes on my hips as they swayed to the beat, I would say he didn't mind at all. I watched him watch me dance, and the more he watched me, the more I moved against him until it felt like I was basically dry-humping his thigh between my legs. My hand on his shoulder squeezed until he looked back at me, his eyes dark and his chest rising a little bit faster than normal.

I licked my lips, trying to focus. "You're doing great. Dancing, I mean."

His hand moved from my hips down to my outer thigh, caressing up and down until his fingers were dangerously close to the curve of my ass. "I have the best teacher. The way you move—"

I swirled my hips, and Will made a choking sound, his rhythm off for a moment as he watched me with rapt eyes.

What am I doing? I practically screamed those words at myself, but I didn't stop dancing, and when his hands gripped my hips, bringing me closer to him, I eagerly moved towards him.

We both looked down at our hips, our foreheads brushing against each other as we got lost in the way our bodies moved together. And, damn it, I hated myself for it, but I was turned on. By him, by the way it felt to have his hands on me, and by the look of barely restrained control in his eyes.

"Oh shit!" Alejandra said, and suddenly, I felt something cold and wet splash on my back and the side of my sweater.

I jerked away from Will and glanced down, seeing a red stain start to trickle down the sleeve of my sweater, and I could feel it seeping into my back as well.

"I'm sorry!"

I stepped away from Will and bent down to pick up the now-empty cup of wine. "It's okay," I said, handing her the cup with a shaky hand. Alejandra looked sad, and I rubbed her shoulder, giving her a small smile. "Don't worry about it, Aleja. I'll just go to the bathroom and clean up."

I didn't look at Will as I quickly walked away, heart racing in my chest. When I got to the bathroom, I didn't even bother turning on the lights. I put shaking fingers on the sink and squeezed, closing my eyes as I tried to slow my racing heartbeat.

"It was just a dance," I told myself quietly. "You're fine. It meant nothing."

I stood there for a few minutes until I heard the sound of knocking on the bathroom door. "Yeah?"

"It's me," Will's deep voice answered behind the door.

I hesitated for a moment before opening the door. He stepped into the bathroom, a shirt in his hand, and he frowned as his eyes darted over my face.

"Yari got you a shirt." His arm stretched out toward me.

"Thanks," I replied softly, clutching it in my hands.

We stared at each other in the dark bathroom, only a silver of light seeping in from the nearly closed door. I could see most of his face, but he was shadowed in the darkness of the room. My eyes moved over him, tracing the lines of his cheeks and nose and stopping on his full lips. I could feel his eyes mapping out my face as well, and even though we both had no reason to be in this bathroom together, neither one of us moved.

Slowly, Will took a step forward, and the room was so small that it put him instantly in my personal space. His arms reached out and landed on either side of me, caging me in against the sink as he leaned his head down until I felt his nose brush my cheek, his breath a soft puff of air that had me gasping in the quiet space.

"You have no idea …" His whispered words trailed off, like a half-spoken confession into the darkness.

My heart jumped into my throat, and I felt certain that he could hear my heartbeat, like a siren's call. My body, being the traitor that it was, thrummed with desire and want, and I had to squeeze tighter onto the shirt in my hand to stop myself from reaching up and touching him.

His lips brushed ever so gently against my ear as he continued, "But I won't."

My body stiffened, confusion and disappointment rushing through me as he leaned back slightly to look at me.

"What …" I stumbled on my words, not sure what I wanted to say or not say.

"When I finally kiss you, it's going to be more than a hidden kiss in the dark," he said, eyes dark with emotion. His hand reached for my chin, and he tilted my head up toward his own, eyes never leaving mine. "And right now, something tells me that you'll kiss me with the lights off, but when the lights come on, you'll go running."

My heart was beating so hard in my chest that I thought for sure he could hear it. I stared at him in silence, not answering him, but somehow, I got the feeling that my silence gave him all the confirmation that he needed.

He nodded and took a step toward the door. "I'll go check on your family."

He left a moment later, and I was alone, exhaling a shaky breath as my mind raced into overdrive. My eyes snagged on the shirt in my hand, and I quickly changed into it, trying to push all the confusing thoughts to the back of my mind. I'd deal with them later—when I was alone and had more time to think.

When I stepped out of the bathroom, the music was still playing, but I couldn't hear anyone. I walked into the living room and stopped short when I saw both Yari and Alejandra asleep on the couch. I looked around the room, which was messy with scattered drinks and game pieces from Scrabble strewn everywhere for reasons I wasn't sure of. I stepped around the mess and peeked into the kitchen, watching as Will stood at my sink, sleeves pulled up to his elbows as he cleaned the dishes from tonight's dinner.

"You don't have to do that," I said softly.

I didn't know how to look at him after what he'd said. He'd been more real with me tonight than I'd ever been, and I wasn't sure how to handle that, how to handle Will hinting at having any sort of feelings for me that weren't negative.

"I wanted to help," Will replied easily, turning off the faucet shortly after. "Besides, I'm already done."

I nodded in thanks, glancing behind me. "My sister and cousin are knocked out."

Will chuckled. "Yeah, I saw." He walked toward me, and my heart nearly paused in my chest, but he didn't stop. He kept walking, and I followed as he stopped at the entrance of the living room. "They crashed hard."

I walked toward the couch and picked up my sister's arm, which had been hanging off the couch, and put it to her side. "I guess I should leave them be. I can only imagine the hardship Alejandra would give me to get her to her bed."

"I could carry her there," Will offered.

"No, it's okay. She'll be fine there," I replied with a shake of my head. "I'm just going to get them a glass of water and some medicine for when they wake up later. I'm sorry about all this. You don't have to stay—"

"I'll help," Will said, already walking toward the kitchen. "I'll get the water, and you get the medicine?"

For the next fifteen minutes, we worked side by side, fixing up the living room and tidying up the place as much as possible. The only times we spoke was when I kept saying he didn't have to stay and clean and Will refusing or when he'd ask where to put things.

After we were done cleaning up the living room so that it was back to its spotless self—with the exception of the two drunk girls on the couch, both now covered with a throw blanket—I gestured to the front door, and Will nodded, taking his jacket and journal with him. I watched as he put his jacket on, bundling up for the cold that no doubt waited for him outside. I played with my fingers, feeling unsure and shy.

"Hey," he said softly, finger and thumb on my chin as he gently tilted my face up toward his. "Thank you for letting me spend the night with your family."

I nodded, mouth dry as I tried in vain to look away from him. He pulled away, and with a wave, he opened the front door and stepped out into the hallway.

I watched him turn to leave, and without thinking, I blurted out, "Text me when you get home?"

Will turned back to look at me, and I felt my face get hot in embarrassment, feeling like I'd said way too much with those few words.

"I will," he promised, eyes staring at me with a look I couldn't decipher. "See you Monday."

When I got to work on Monday, I knew almost immediately that I would have a bad day.

Clements's shouting could be heard from the front door of our department as I walked swiftly to my cubicle, shooting a quick wave to the few people who looked up from their desks.

"He's asking for you," Kevin, a marketing associate who sat a few cubicles up from me, called out as I walked by. He gave me a pained smile. "Good luck. He's on the warpath."

I grimaced. "Is it too late to call in sick?"

Kevin chuckled. We both paused as a man came rushing out of Clements's office and across the room. I wasn't friends with the guy, but I remembered that he worked on the floor below us, in the HR department. Phil was his name, I thought.

I dropped my stuff at my desk and grabbed my notebook, and with a quick, bracing breath, I made my way over to his office.

"Enter," he barked the second I finished knocking.

The moment I stepped inside his office, I took a quick study of his face and body language. He looked to be at a level seven on his usual scale of one being he was mildly irritated to ten being he would fire you on the spot if you so much as blinked at him.

I ignored his impatient expression and cluttered desk and took a seat in the empty chair across from him, keeping my face calm and neutral. "Good morning."

"It's about time," he snapped.

I was thirty minutes early to work, as always. I'd learned quickly that the best thing to do in these moments was to do nothing but wait him out. Nothing I could say would make him happy, except complete compliance, and while a part of me wanted to snap at him, I knew that wouldn't do any good.

"I need you to make fifty copies of the Jefferson contract but not before you go to Starbucks and get me ..."

On and on he went.

My morning was the busiest it'd been in a while. What made it worse was that Clements had me go back and forth to the 3rd Avenue office throughout the entire morning for little errands instead of just telling me all of them at once. And it was raining. And I had no umbrella.

I watched the rain smack against the window, hair slightly damp from my latest run from the cab back to my building and lying against my back in a frizzy mess. A sharp beep from the machine in front of me had me turning my head back to my task, and I collected the last of the papers from the printer.

Cora: Want to eat lunch in the cafeteria today?

I sighed, ignoring my growling stomach. After juggling the stack of papers to my left hand and balancing it on my side, I quickly sent out a reply.

Me: I can't. Clements wants me to manually alphabetize all the contact information of the clients. I'll probably skip lunch today. :(

Cora: Whaat? You can't!

*Me: I have to. Clements is in a mood. Pray for me and
my angry stomach.*

I spent the next thirty minutes working on the Excel sheet
at my desk, music pouring into my ears from my headphones.
I tried not to blast it too loud and to still be aware of my
surroundings on the rare chance that Clements came over here,
looking for me, but once "Formation" by Beyoncé came on, I
couldn't help but to turn the music up and start dancing in my
seat a bit.

I bobbed my head from side to side, mouthing the words
as I typed away. I inhaled the smell of pizza as I deleted some
numbers on the screen, and I tried my best to ignore it and
how jealous I and my stomach were. I spun in my chair, singing
the lyrics under my breath, and nearly screamed when I saw a
figure standing by the entrance of my cubicle, a smirk on his
annoyingly handsome face.

"Will," I breathed. I yanked my headphones down around
my neck and took in his casual stance against the wall, eyes lit
with humor. "What are you doing here?"

He lifted his hands, and it was then that I noticed he had a
box from Rosa's Pizzeria. "I got you lunch."

I frowned slightly, confused. "Lunch?"

He raised a brow. "Yes, lunch. Come take a break from
work and eat with me."

I glanced at the spreadsheet on my laptop screen,
hesitating. But probably not as long as I should have. "Okay."
I stood up, taking the headphones from around my neck and
placing them on my desk. "But only because that pizza smells
so good."

Will nodded, a small, amused smirk on his face. "Of
course."

I walked out of my cubby, Will standing to the side so I
could step out first but the space was so small that our arms
brushed. I sucked in a sharp breath at the zap of electricity that
raced up my arm at the contact. I didn't think I'd ever get used
to that feeling.

"Follow me," Will murmured, head tilted down so that he was almost speaking into my ear, his hand pressing ever so lightly against my back.

I nodded silently and hated myself for feeling disappointed when he stepped away and started walking down the narrow hall between the cubicles and toward the exit.

I had replayed Saturday night in my head more times than I cared to admit. The way that he'd touched me, his words, how he'd fit in with my family so seamlessly. Every time I thought about him, my body went haywire. My brain was constantly yelling at me to protect myself, to not get too close, or to care because he would only hurt me. The rest of me loved the way I felt when I was around him and wanted him closer.

I saw a few people look up as we walked, and though I refused to make eye contact with any of them, I could feel the surprise in their gaze as they no doubt wondered what the heck we were doing within five feet of each other. Will, being the well-liked guy that he was, had more than one person popping their head out of the cubby to say hello, all smiles and respect in their eyes as he confidently maneuvered through each of their conversations with quick hellos, always checking back to make sure I was still with him even though he'd never stopped walking once.

"You are the king of small talk," I whispered to him as we finally stepped out of my office space and into the quiet hall near the elevators.

Will shook his head, his lips pressed tightly together, like he was irritated. "No talking until you get some food in your system."

I shook my head, bemused, but continued walking with him until we made it to the empty staff lounge that almost no one used.

He pulled out a chair for me with one hand, the other placing the pizza box down on the table, and he once again ordered me in that deep voice of his, "Sit. Eat."

"So bossy," I mumbled, but again, I did as he'd asked.

Will took a seat across from me and opened the box, and my mouth practically watered at the sight of the half-chicken-and-bacon, half-chicken-and-broccoli pizza. Will picked up a chicken-and-bacon slice, put it on a paper plate, and silently passed it to me. Chicken and bacon were my favorite toppings on a pizza … but how did he know that?

My question must have been written on my face because Will casually said, "You mentioned once that chicken-and-bacon pizza was your favorite."

I took the plate from him with a soft thanks as I tried to remember when I would've said that. "I did? When?"

"It was a while ago," Will answered vaguely, eyes dropping to my plate. "Eat. Please."

I took a bite of my pizza and nearly moaned at the greasy deliciousness on my tongue. "Oh my God, this is so good."

I took another bite and then another and all but devoured my slice in two minutes. I had known I was hungry, but sometimes, you didn't realize just how hungry you were until you took that first bite. I took my last bite of my slice when Will plopped another one down on my plate, a satisfied glint in his eye as he nodded at me, taking a bite of his own pizza.

"How was your gig on Sunday?" I asked a few minutes later. I wiped my mouth on a napkin and watched as Will frowned slightly, eyes glancing at my empty plate. I shook my head. "I'm full, really. Thank you, Will. I just want to hear about your gig."

My face got hot as I realized what I'd said, and Will smiled softly, nodding.

"It was great. I played a few covers, a few originals. After the show, I went home and worked on a song I'd been stuck on for a while."

"What's the song about?" I asked, curious.

"That's personal, Buttercup," he chided lightly, an amused grin on his face.

I shook my head, a small smile on my face. "Fine. Then, why didn't you hang out after the gig with your friends? Most musicians like to chase the high of a performance after it's over."

Will shrugged. "Don't get me wrong; I like to have a good time, but I don't need the parties and the people around me like that after a performance. I actually prefer to be alone most times."

I hummed. "You might change your mind when you make it big and are invited to celebrity parties."

"Is that what you would do?" Will asked, face open and curious.

I shrugged. "I mean, I wouldn't say no to going to a mansion party or two if I was invited."

"When I get my first invite to a celebrity party, you'll be my plus-one," Will said firmly, a twinkle in his eye.

I rolled my eyes, smiling. "Sure, buddy. You'll be saying *Genesis who* the moment you get that contract."

"That would never happen," he replied flatly, all traces of amusement fading.

I blinked once and then twice. I studied Will's face, the way his brows furrowed slightly, his mouth tipped down on the sides as he all but scowled at me.

"Are we friends?" I blurted out and then immediately winced in embarrassment.

Will watched me for a moment. "We are whatever you want us to be."

"Whatever you want us to be."

I felt my heart kick-start in my chest as I replayed his words in my head.

A month ago, I would've said I wanted absolutely nothing from Will. I hadn't let myself even think about him being anything more than colleagues who barely tolerated each other. But after this past month … I couldn't deny that things felt different. Lines felt blurry. I felt too much, and yet at the same time, I didn't know what any of it meant. If it was all in my head or heightened because of our history. I knew that I was happy when I was around him, but did that mean anything?

I heard the sound of his chair moving back and watched as Will's shiny black shoes got closer to me. A moment later I felt his finger under my chin as he gently tilted my head up until I was looking at him.

His eyes were warm, tone soft as he asked, "Do you want to be friends?"

My mouth being the traitor that it was whispered the word I didn't want to admit, "Yes."

He nodded and took a step back. "Then, yes, we are friends."

I felt butterflies swarm in my stomach as I watched him step away, and his words echoed in my head. I couldn't deny that this past month had already shown me a whole different side to Will, but was I going to just ignore the past two years in favor of this new Will? Could I do that?

"Will?"

He turned to look at me, brow raised slightly.

"I need you to answer something for me."

He nodded, eyes curious.

I took a deep breath and reminded myself that no matter what he said, I couldn't let myself get upset. Not in front of him and not at work. I tried to think about what I wanted to ask him, how I wanted to word it. Ah screw it. "Why did you ignore me when we first met?"

Will's head jerked back slightly, and he stared at me like I had two heads. "What are you talking about?"

I fought not to squirm in my seat, embarrassment and uncertainty setting in. "My second day of work, I walked up to you and introduced myself to you, and you just stared at me like I was an idiot," I explained, my words rushing out of me. "And then, even after that, you never talked to me even though you talked to everyone else in the room."

A pained look crossed his face. "Genesis, I never meant for you to feel ostracized."

"Could've fooled me," I scoffed, old bitterness rising.

"The truth is," he said, "I saw you that day, and I didn't know what to say. Despite how easy it might seem for me to talk to people, when I saw you, my mind went blank. It was like I couldn't remember how to form words, and I felt like I was a kid again with no social skills. The awkward kid who never said the right thing." His lips twisted in a sardonic half-smile. "It's a feeling that hasn't really gone away, and I'm beginning to learn I almost never say the right thing when I talk to you.

"I didn't know how to talk to you," he continued. "I'd see you around work, and the same thing kept happening. By the time I figured my shit out, you'd started hating me, and I knew you didn't want to be friends, so I let it go. In a way, it was easier because when you were hating me, at least you were looking at me. And it didn't matter what words came out of my mouth because you were never going to look at me the way you'd looked at me on that first day."

My heart was beating quickly in my chest as I tried to process everything he had said. "I hated you because of what you thought of me."

"What I thought of you?"

"I heard you, Will. Talking with the guys. I heard you tell them that I didn't belong on the team, and then they—" I broke off, blowing out an angry breath. I hated that embarrassed tears threatened to fill my eyes. "And then they started talking about me like I was nothing more than something good to look at, and I realized then that you thought I wasn't good enough to work here. Certainly not good enough to be respected as an equal at this job, and even though I didn't know you and your opinion of me shouldn't have mattered, for some reason, it did, and I hated you for it."

He stared at me, eyes burning with emotion. I watched him with cautious eyes as he walked over to me and slowly took my hands in his. "I respect you more than anyone else in my life," he said fiercely, head dipped down to my eyeline. "What you heard, it wasn't what you think."

I scoffed, trying to pull away but he tightened his hands around mine.

He continued, "I never agreed with those assholes, and what you didn't hear was the reaming of a lifetime I gave them after. I should've done more to defend you in that moment, and I'm sorry for that. But what I said that day"—he blew out a frustrated breath as he shook his head—"I wasn't saying you weren't good enough. It's quite the opposite. I watched you around the office, and I saw how hard you worked; it drove me crazy, how undervalued you were. One of the few women on the team, one of the few minorities, and I knew they were setting you up to fail, and it made me so angry. Because you deserved better—you still do. You are so much better than the team you're on with a bunch of sexist white men who make you do all the work while you reap none of the benefits." His voice was deep with anger, and I watched him with wide eyes. "You are too good for this job and too good for me. I knew it from the first time I saw you."

I stared up at him, overwhelmed. All that he had said ... it changed everything I'd thought I knew about him.

He defended me.

I didn't know how to put into words how I was feeling right now, and I knew that it was something I'd need time and space to fully process.

Will went to pull his hands away, but it was my turn to squeeze, not letting go. He looked down at me, an almost-guarded look on his face.

I said softly, "You're wrong. I'm not too good for you, and I'm certainly no better than you or anyone else. I deserve better than this job—it's true. But then again, so do you. It's why we're chasing our dreams, right?" I gave him a small smile and another squeeze on his hand before letting go.

He nodded tightly, eyes never moving from my own as he swallowed.

I continued, "Thank you for having my back, even when I didn't know it. From now on, you can count on me to have your back too. I mean it."

Will stared at me, emotions swimming in his eyes. But he didn't respond to my words or even acknowledge them past a tight nod as he stepped away. "We'd better get you back to your desk. You have work to do."

I opened my mouth but then closed it with a quiet sigh and nodded. I wasn't good with words, and I doubted he needed them from me anyway. I quickly tossed our trash from lunch into the garbage bin, fighting a scowl as I berated myself for not being able to give Will the words that he needed. I took a step toward the door, but I stopped when I felt Will's hand close around my upper arm. I didn't even get the chance to blink before I felt him pull me into his body, his arms circling around my back and my cheek resting on his firm chest as my hands gripped on to his back in surprise.

"Thank you," he whispered into my ear, one hand softly running through my long hair as his other arm squeezed me tighter to him.

All my embarrassment, my disappointment, disappeared like a puff, and I hugged him back. I pushed my face more into his chest, and even though I tried to hide it, I couldn't deny the smile that spread across my face as I stood there in his arms.

"Genesis," Clements snapped from across the room a few days later.

I jerked my head away from the stack of papers I'd been collating and watched as he waved his hand in the air. I'd hoped his bad mood would have subsided by now, but he'd been in a foul mood all week, and it made the hours drag by.

I left the papers on the table and walked over to him at his office door. "Yes, Mr. Clements?"

"You're presenting in tomorrow's meeting with Popify," he replied shortly.

I blinked, mouth falling open. "I'm—"

"Here's their file." He tossed it at me, and I scrambled to catch it. "This is a multimillion-dollar client. I don't have to explain to you what will happen if you mess this up."

"I won't." I nodded confidently, even as I began freaking out on the inside.

Holy shit, Clements was finally letting me present in a meeting. But did it have to be such a big client? If I fucked up, I knew that he'd use this as an excuse to keep me in my current position, and it'd get brought up in yearly evaluations.

You won't fuck up, I told myself. *You'll show him exactly what you're capable of and prove him wrong.*

I spent the next two hours at my desk, working hard on the presentation and trying to organize all the information from our team about our sales numbers and top-selling artists. It was a lot of work, and even though I hardly blinked, time flew, and it was the end of the day before I knew it. I knew that I needed to keep working on this no matter what, but I felt a twinge of guilt and disappointment at knowing I wouldn't be able to meet Will for practice tonight.

I shot a quick text over to him and explained that I'd need to cancel for today before focusing once again on my presentation in front of me.

"Why the heck do we need to present all this information to them?" I grumbled under my breath as I moved bullet points around on the slide. My computer froze, and I started smacking the side of the screen like that would solve anything other than my frustration for a few seconds. "Stupid. Freaking. Computer!"

"Buttercup, how many times must I remind you that violence is not the answer?" Will commented from behind me.

I spun around in my chair and found Will standing at the front of my cubicle, an amused smirk on his face as he ran a hand through his hair. I watched his fingers run through the strands, my own hands clenching on my chair as I felt my heart skip in my chest.

Do not look at his biceps, I chanted to myself in my head. *Do not look at him at all.*

After our conversation in the staff lounge a few days ago, I'd been doing nothing but thinking. I'd thought about the last two years, and I felt like I was finally seeing things through new eyes. I remembered times during meetings when he would call me up to answer a question or he would volunteer me to work on presentations or make comments about my job performance. So many moments where I'd thought he was trying to sabotage me. Now, I wondered just how wrong I'd been about him.

I spun back toward my computer, which was still frozen but now had a spinning circle where my mouse should have been. I sighed, shaking the mouse uselessly. "I can't meet tonight. Didn't you get my text message?"

"Why are you fighting your computer?" He stepped into my cubicle and ate up every inch of remaining space in this miniscule cubicle.

This office was tight enough when it was me and Cora. With Will, who was over six feet tall, it was a lot like a bull in a china shop as he tried to peer down at my computer screen.

I quickly explained to him my conversation with Clements's earlier today, trying to keep the nerves out of my tone as I felt the gravity of this presentation weigh on me, the longer I talked. My fingers inched toward the mouse of my computer once more, and I sighed in relief when I saw that the screen was no longer frozen.

The sound of wheels rolling behind me had me turning my head away from the computer, and I frowned in confusion when I saw Will with a desk chair in front of him, his body barely fitting into this small space with me and the chair.

"What are you doing?" I asked.

Will stopped next to me, his leg brushing against mine as he sat down. I watched as he began to uncuff his white button-down sleeves, rolling them up to his elbows.

"I'm going to help you with your presentation."

It took me a moment to pull my eyes away from the muscles in his forearms and the image of those arms wrapped around me, picking me up—*coño*, what was wrong with me? I shook the images away and tried to focus on what he'd said.

"Wait, no, don't do that. You should go home, relax, and get far away from this place."

Will gave me one of his calm *shut up, Genesis* looks. "Your boss hasn't given you a chance to lead in a meeting in nearly six months. This is big." He moved his hand slightly so that it was hovering near my notebook, filled with notes I'd started writing to help me organize my thoughts on where to start for tomorrow. "I'm going to help you, if you'll let me."

He wanted me to succeed.

He's always been on your side, I reminded myself.

I yet again found myself thinking about our conversation a few days ago, and the thought made a warm feeling rush through my veins. I ever so slowly lifted my hand and gently pushed my notebook toward him, that soft, warm feeling still coursing through me as I said, "Okay."

Will jumped straight into work mode. I always knew he was tenacious, and his work ethic was one of the things I begrudgingly admired about him. Not only did he focus with an intensity that could be intimidating, but he also never once made me feel like he was taking over things or trying to make my presentation be exactly like he would do it. He offered feedback, showed me different ways to present information, and even helped calm me down as I freaked out over the many ways that I could get fired for messing this up.

Time seemed to fly in the way it always did when I was with Will.

At some point, Will had gotten up to use the bathroom, and I'd been so wrapped up in rereading through my slides that I didn't realize how long he'd been gone until I heard him clear his throat behind me.

"You need to stop feeding me all the time," I said, eyes greedily landing on the box in his hand.

"I like feeding you." Will put the box on the desk next to me and nudged it toward me. "Come take a break."

I opened the box and saw two footlong subs from the sandwich shop a few blocks over, two bags of chips, and a small bag with snickerdoodle cookies.

"These are all my favorites." I looked up at him with a surprised smile.

He handed me a paper plate. "I've worked with you for almost two years. I know what you like."

"I guess you do," I admitted with a shy smile. I picked up my sandwich and put it on my plate. "Thanks."

Will nodded, taking the other sandwich from the box and unwrapping it. He'd gotten himself a Philly cheesesteak sandwich, and I watched his jaw with fascination as it clenched while he ate his food.

After a minute of my full-on staring, Will looked up, and I quickly looked away and back toward my own food. My face felt red hot, and I just had to pray that he couldn't tell I was blushing or that he'd caught me staring at him eating, like a creep.

"When I was growing up, my mom used to make me bento lunch meals every day."

I looked up at his words, surprise and curiosity in my eyes as I silently watched him.

"She put so much time into making sure I had these lunch meals for school every day," he explained quietly. "But then kids at school started teasing me about my lunch, making fun of the food or saying that it smelled weird. And like an idiot, I cared more about what the kids at school were saying about me and not about what those meals meant to my mom, to me. I told her to stop making me lunch and asked to buy lunch from the lunchroom instead. It wasn't the first time that I'd let my family down, but it was one of the first times that I really hurt my mom in a way that I'd never forget."

I understood all too well the struggle of wanting to fit in, especially when people made you feel like you were not good enough because you were different. My heart ached for young Will who had gotten picked on for his food and God knew what else. If his childhood had been anything like mine, he'd probably heard criticisms about the way he talked, looked, and any number of stereotypical and racist comments that people said "as a joke," which wasn't funny at all.

"I bet your mom understood," I said softly. "She understood how hard it was for a little kid to stand out when all the kid wanted was to fit in."

"Maybe," Will agreed with a shrug. "It took me a long time to figure out who I was and how to juggle being Japanese and American without feeling like I was less of either. To not feel guilty when I asked to eat pizza for dinner, but to also not blink when I pulled out the next volume in my favorite manga while hanging out with my friends."

"I wish I had known you back then," I said with a soft smile. "I didn't have many friends as a kid, but I have a feeling we would've been great ones. Two first-generation kids trying to navigate school and life." I chuckled lightly. "What a pair we would've been."

"Sometimes, it feels like I've known you my whole life." His dark eyes stared deeply into my own, and in that moment, it felt like we were saying everything we couldn't say with words.

Sometimes, I wanted to say, *I hope that I never stop knowing you.*

"I'm glad we're friends, Kobayashi," I said.

Will smiled that half-smile that did funny things to my heart. "Me too, Buttercup. Me too."

21

"I'll now send it over to Joseph from social."

I kept my smile on my face, even after I sat back down on shaky legs beside Clements. I had done it. I'd led for my team in a meeting with important clients, and for better or for worse, I'd made it to the end.

I glanced across the conference table at Cora, who threw me a bright smile, practically bouncing in her seat like she wanted nothing more than to jump out of her seat and reach for me. I looked quickly at Clements, whose expression hadn't changed once since the meeting had started.

What was he thinking?

At this point, I wouldn't be surprised if he told me to pack my things and go home at the end of this meeting.

The crazy part was that the one person I wanted to talk to right now was Will. And I didn't know what to do with that feeling. I also couldn't concentrate on the rest of the meeting because now that I'd done my part of the presentation, all I could think about was the fact that Will would've received the thank-you gift I'd made for him.

I'd been regretting it since almost the very second after I asked Derek, the accounting department assistant, to deliver it to him whenever he went on lunch break. I didn't know why I had done it. I told myself that any positive emotions related to Will was only because we were making music together and we worked well together. He was a friend, yes. But it was different. He was different. It wasn't like my friendship with Cora or even other musicians I'd worked with in the past.

It was simple and complicated and perfect. And right now, that was all I needed to know.

When the meeting finally ended, I had to force myself to not run back to my desk to see if Will had texted me. I picked up my things and turned toward Clements, wondering if he'd chew me out right here or have the decency to wait until we were in his office, where there were less people.

But Clements only nodded at me and walked away. Just walked away! Didn't give me the usual long list of inane tasks to do or bitch at me about incompetent workers. Was this a good thing? A bad thing? I was so surprised by his quick exit that I didn't see Cora rushing over to me until she basically collided with me, her voice in my ear.

"You kicked major butt!" she squealed, practically hugging my arm as she bounced on her toes. "Your presentation was so engaging! I think it was the first time that everyone in the room didn't look like they wished they were anywhere but here."

I smiled. "Thanks, though I can't take all the credit. Will helped me out with the presentation last night. Can you believe he stayed late with me at work to make sure I was ready to present today?"

"That doesn't surprise me at all," Cora replied. "That's exactly the kind of guy that Will is. Always the first to help anyone out. What *does* surprise me is that you took him up on the help."

I shrugged and began picking up my papers again from the table. "I needed the help—that's all."

Cora studied me for a quiet, long moment. "Is there something going on between you two?"

"No," I immediately responded, all but shouting. Her eyebrows went up at that, and I took a quick breath and made a concerted effort to lower my voice. "We're just friends."

"Since when are you friends with Will?" she asked, surprise coating her voice. "You hate him."

We began walking toward the door, the conference room just about empty at this point.

"Yeah, I might've been wrong about him," I admitted with a guilty smile.

Cora jerked to a stop in front of me. She turned around, and with an almost-accusatory look on her face, she stated, "You like him."

I guffawed, giving her a strange look. "No, I don't. I just told you, we're friends."

She slowly shook her head. "I knew something was different, but I just thought you'd say something." She began talking under her breath, face contemplative as she walked in front of me. "Will has had a thing for her for *months*—years?— so it's been hard to tell if his puppy eyes were any different lately, but how did I not see *her* puppy eyes?"

I stared at her, bewildered. "What the hell are you talking about? Will does not like me."

Cora gave me a blank look so reminiscent of the face my mom used to give me when I tried to lie to get out of a punishment as a kid that I nearly ran out of the room. "Of course he likes you! I've been telling you he's been halfway in love with you for years, but you never listen."

"Stop. I don't want to hear this," I said, shaking my head and all but plugging my fingers into my ears.

Cora watched me with this soft, almost-pitying look on her face. "Genesis, how long are you going to keep running from love?"

I shrugged, feeling seen—and not in a good way. I crossed my arms across my chest and said, "I'm not interested in a relationship. Ever."

Cora smiled sadly. "I wish you were."

Me too. The words floated on the roof of my tongue.

For just one second, I let myself imagine being in a relationship with Will, and I thought of us sharing space together the way that we already did. How we could share things about ourselves and know that there was no judgment or just sit in silence and know that there was no pressure to be anything other than ourselves. I thought about being with someone who made me feel safe, even as I was feeling terrified of the unknown.

And then I thought about the moments we'd never experienced together but could if we were together. Intimacy. Sharing a bed together and feeling him around me as he slept or waking up the next morning and his face being the first one that I saw. Holding hands in private or outside as we walked to the grocery store or had a date in the park. Kissing and exploring each other's bodies. Knowing what it felt like to smell him all over me and be so full of him that it ached when I moved the next day.

My heart stuttered, just thinking about it, my thighs wanting to squeeze together at the need that coursed through me. Not just need, but longing. Longing to have those things and to have them with him. The intensity of my longing began to scare me, and I knew that I needed to shut down my thoughts right now and forget I'd even entertained the idea for a moment.

At this point, I didn't know if I'd ever be capable of letting someone in that way. After my dad had died, I'd realized that things weren't permanent. People weren't permanent. Someone could be in your life one day, and the next, they were gone.

What was the point in opening myself up to someone when they would just leave me and I'd be left alone again?

At least right now, I still had Alejandra and Yari. I had Cora. They were enough of a risk, but I loved them too much to not have them in my life. But I wouldn't do it again—and not for a man. Because something told me that if I ever fell in love and they left me—by choice or not—I would never get over it. And the thought of letting someone have that kind of power over me was the most terrifying feeling in the world.

"I'm happy with the way my life is now," I promised her, giving her a reassuring smile. "I have so much love in my life. I really don't need anything else."

Cora didn't look convinced, but she knew me well enough by now to know that I wasn't going to change my mind suddenly. We parted ways by the elevators, and I walked slowly back toward my desk.

"Great job in the Popify meeting today!"

I looked up and smiled at Kevin, who was sitting at his desk, munching on a snack while scrolling through some Excel sheets on his desktop. "Oh. Thanks!"

A few other people smiled at me when I looked at them, and I realized I'd been so stuck in my own head that I didn't even notice that people were looking at me like they were happy for me. It was weird.

When I made it to my desk, I plopped down and pulled my phone out from my top drawer. My heart nearly stopped in my chest when I saw that I had two text messages from Will, one of which was a photo.

Will: Thank you.

I clicked on the photo he'd sent. It was a selfie, his arrestingly handsome face on display. I spent a long moment studying the hard lines of his face and the way his full lips in that small smile seemed to almost soften his face. He didn't look like the arrogant, unruffled douche that I used to hate so much. My eyes finally trailed down from his face, and my heart fluttered in my chest when I saw that he was holding the bento lunch I'd made for him, more than half of it gone.

After last night, I couldn't stop thinking about our conversation while we had dinner. He'd stayed with me until nearly eight o' clock, going over my presentation with me, and he didn't complain once. The entire ride home, I kept thinking that I wanted to do something nice for him to show him that I appreciated his help and his friendship. When I'd walked past the twenty-four-hour grocery story two blocks from my house, and I had known what I was going to do before I let myself think about it for too long.

> *Me: My presentation was a success. The lunch doesn't begin to cover what I owe you. :)*
>
> *Will: You owe me nothing. I'll always be here to help you.*
>
> *Me: That's what friends are for, right?*
>
> *Will: Right.*

I clenched my phone in my hands, still standing in my small cubicle as I waited to see if he would say anything else. But after two minutes of no response, I put my phone down on the desk and finally slid into my seat.

Two days before our first session in the recording studio, and we were falling behind schedule.

"We'll figure it out," Will promised as we walked down the hall.

I could hear the television blasting from the living room, and a moment later, my suspicions were proven correct when I saw Callum lounging on the couch with a bag of chips, a mountain of paperwork spread out on the cushion beside him.

"Genesis," Callum greeted with a lazy grin. "Care to watch some TV with me? I'll even share my Cheetos with you."

"You know I'd love to," I answered, "but I have to practice. Besides, I've seen this episode already; it's not that good."

Callum gasped, looking outraged. "How dare you say that about *Bob's Burgers*! Every episode of *Bob's Burgers* is a masterpiece. If you want to keep coming to this house, you need to remember that."

I laughed. "Are you really going to kick me out if I don't like every episode?"

He shrugged his broad shoulders. "I might. It depends on whether or not Will would kick my ass for doing it."

"I would," Will responded, standing by the music room door. "Especially since we both know *Family Guy* is way better."

"Facts," I said, raising my hand so that Will and I could high-five.

He shook his head at me, laughing when Callum groaned loudly.

"I can't even look at you two," he said, and I rolled my eyes. "Go into that room and leave me in peace, so I can watch my show without judgment."

"You are so dramatic," I said, taking a few pieces of chips from his bag. He lunged—either for me or the bag, I wasn't sure—but I quickly rushed toward the music room, shouting, "Have fun watching the second-best show!"

Will chuckled behind me, closing the door to whatever Callum was shouting. "You just love messing with him, don't you?"

"Eh, he loves to do it to me too," I said with a shrug, grinning. "Besides, he is too easy to rile up. And too cocky for his own good."

"Oh, you have no idea. After our gig yesterday, he went home with two girls," Will said, grimacing and taking a seat at the table. "Let's just say that not even my headphones could block out that crap, and I'm now running on four hours of sleep."

"Two women?" I asked, raising an eyebrow. "That sounds ... excessive."

"Callum loves the music, but he loves the women and the attention that come with it too," he answered, running a hand through his black hair. "And the women love him. Almost every gig we do together ends in the same way."

I wanted to ask if it was the same for him, if he loved the women and attention. If he took up the offers from the many women who I knew were probably throwing themselves at him after his gigs. But I couldn't. Not without feeling like I was asking something I had no right to ask.

Still, I found myself saying nonchalantly, "You can't say that you haven't taken advantage of the attention from women a time or two yourself. Most musicians do."

"Maybe." Will shrugged, and I felt a sharp pang in my chest that I actively tried to ignore. "But it's not my preferred way of meeting a girl."

"Oh?" I asked, forcing a smile on my face. "And what is your preferred way?"

"For one," Will said, leaning back in his chair, "I prefer to know more than her first name."

"How chivalrous of you," I joked, trying in vain to push away the urge to ask the higher beings for the power to erase every one of his past experiences from his memory.

"I'm a gentleman in the streets but a freak in the bed," he agreed, nodding sagely.

I shook my head at his twist on an old pop song, smiling so hard that my cheeks hurt. "Okay, Ludacris, let's not get ahead of ourselves here."

Will barked out a laugh, his eyes shining. "Nice. I wasn't sure if you'd get the reference."

"Of course I did," I scoffed, grinning. "My sister had the biggest crush on Usher when we were kids. That song was one of his many songs that got played on repeat in our house."

"Who was your celebrity crush?" he asked, a small smile playing on his lips. He tapped his finger to his chin. "Wait. I want to try and guess."

I leaned back in my seat, knowing without a doubt he wouldn't guess correctly. "Go ahead."

"Was it ... Justin Timberlake?" he asked, and I shook my head. "Adam Levine?"

"Nope," I answered. "Romeo Santos."

"Who?" Will asked, eyes furrowed.

"He was the lead singer in a bachata band called Aventura," I said, smiling at the memories playing in my head. "Yari and I had such a huge crush on him. We got in this huge fight once when we were kids because she kept saying that she was going to marry him and I was determined that we'd meet and write these beautiful Spanish ballads together and fall in love and get married. We were so ridiculous."

Will chuckled. "That's really cute. I could imagine a ten-year-old you demanding that Romeo was going to be yours because you both were performers."

"Yeah, that was pretty much how it went," I said, smiling. "How about you? Who was your first celebrity crush?"

"Jessica Alba was my first celebrity crush," Will replied. "But in terms of singers, I think my first was Shakira. Or maybe Britney Spears."

"Nice," I said with a nod. I glanced down at my phone to check the time and realized we'd spent the last twenty minutes just chatting and joking around. "Okay, ready to get back to work?"

Will nodded, and for the next two hours, we were all business. Most of our practices were about tweaking and reworking the stuff we'd done the previous day. I wished I could say that it was so much fun and about something new each day, but most of the work was in rewriting, trashing, and crying over music sheets. I mean, we'd spent the past month writing and rewriting the same verse. And I had a feeling we'd be revising this song until the night before the deadline. We were both perfectionists when it came to our music, which was great because I never had to worry about him being annoyed by my meticulous rechecking and questioning of every note and beat.

After changing the lyrics countless times in the last two weeks, we'd built the foundation for the song, but it was still missing that special something. We needed to make sure that the music itself was strong on its own and that the lyrics would only add to the magnetism of what they were hearing. There was nothing worse than listening to a song with a shitty beat or melody but good lyrics. Or vice versa.

But on the other hand, music was all about a mood, so we had to take that into account when we were creating our sound because whatever melody we decided on, the lyrics were going to have to work with that mood that we were setting. Luckily, that was one of our easier decisions. Everyone wanted a song that would bring them to tears. Move them in a way that made them feel changed, like it was an experience.

It was the way I'd felt the first time I heard my father play "Nuvole Bianche" when I was just a little girl. I didn't even understand what I was feeling, but while watching him play, his whole body moving with the song, like the music was flowing through him, tears clouding his eyes, I sat there and cried silent tears. I felt like I was seeing a piece of my father that I hadn't known before, like I was getting this secret, hidden part of him. It was only later that I'd realized that feeling only came when you were quite literally giving a piece of yourself with the music you created or played.

"*Won't you let me in?*" he sang, paused, and then sang the chorus again with a small frown. After a moment, he looked up from his guitar. "We're missing something."

I nodded. "Problem is, we can't figure out what needs to change."

Will put the guitar on the stand. "I'm going to get some water, stretch my legs. Do you want anything?"

I nearly smiled at the fact that he didn't ask if I wanted to join him. He knew me well enough to know that I wasn't moving from my spot until I figured out the song. "I'm good, thanks."

I watched as Will walked out of the room, telling myself that I didn't want to join him. That I didn't want to be near him nearly every second of the day.

I shook the thoughts away, focusing on the notebook in front of me and the song we needed to perfect in just a few short months. I picked up his guitar and began strumming the chords to the chorus, singing the words to myself—at first quietly, no more than a whisper. But slowly, the more I sang, the more I let myself really let go, touching emotions that I never touched unless I was touching music. It was my safe space; it always was. When I was making music, when I was singing, nothing else mattered. It was my safety, my therapy, and my home, all wrapped in one.

"*I can't let you in, baby,*" I sang, eyes closed as the words seemed to flow from somewhere deep inside of me. "*I'm a puzzle that can't be solved. I want you, but you can't know. And I'll never tell. My secret desires.*"

I let the last word drag out, my fingers playing the melody as I hummed the song, swaying softly in my seat. I sang the song from the beginning, mouth lifting into a smile, the longer I played. I loved this, and I loved this song.

"You are magnificent."

My fingers slipped on the string, and I made a rough sound on the guitar as I abruptly turned toward the door, heart in my throat. Will stood there, a look of determination and something tender in his eyes as he watched me. I quickly placed his guitar back on the stand, face flushed and feeling caught in a way that both made me feel warm with pleasure and embarrassment at the same time.

"I think I figured out some lyrics to add to the chorus." I kept my eyes locked on the table in front of me, pretending to be looking at the lyrics written on the paper in front of me. "I think that if we tweak the chords a bit on the second chorus—"

"You have to sing with me." He moved from the door and walked over to his seat, eyes never leaving my face.

Even though I tried hard to pretend I didn't notice or hear him, my body was entirely attuned to him, and I felt my body tense as I fought with myself to not look at him, heart beating wildly in my chest.

"Your voice is beautiful."

I shook my head. "I don't want to sing. I produce. I'm a music producer. A songwriter. But not a singer."

He studied me for a long moment. "Buttercup, look at me."

I wanted to ignore him, but that soft tone, steeped in a command, had me looking up before I even had a second to think about it.

"Talk to me."

And I did.

"Singing is just for me," I explained carefully. "I give a piece of myself in every one of my songs that I create, and I want that. To share that with the world. It feels so good to make music, but I don't want to be onstage. I want to be in the studio, helping people make music. In the background, working behind the scenes, I get to be heard but not seen. And I love that. They can have my words, but they can't have me."

It was the one difference between my father and me when it came to music. My father had loved music more than anything in the world, but his problem had been that he was so obsessed with the idea of being famous, of everyone knowing who he was, that the music stopped being enough. I didn't need everyone to know who I was, to be on billboards or on television. I wanted to work in the studio and help artists create songs that put into words how they were feeling. Whether that meant splicing together a track or creating the lyrics to a song for them. I loved sitting with an instrument and creating new sounds or taking something familiar and putting my own twist to a beat. I wanted to create music, but I had no interest in being a performer.

Will leaned over the table, his hand hesitating over my hand for a moment. I gave him a small nod and he engulfed my hand in his with a tight, comforting squeeze. "You will never be in the background. Not in your career in music and never with me."

I stared at Will, confused. "I don't—I want to be in the background."

He laughed humorlessly, shaking his head. "You don't even see yourself, do you? When you walk into a room, you light up the whole place. When you speak, everyone stops to listen and hear your words. And when you write a song ... it doesn't matter if the words aren't being sung out of your lips; people are going to want to know the woman who wrote a song that put a piece of their soul out on display."

I watched him with glassy eyes, a gasp escaping my lips as his other hand clasped the side of my face gently, his rough fingers sending a shock wave of tingles and heat across my entire body.

His face was mere inches from my own, eyes dark with heat as he whispered his words across my lips. "You are so fucking beautiful, and you will *never* be in the background."

My eyes closed of their own accord, his words hitting my heart like an arrow. I exhaled, feeling shook to my core.

Dios, the way he saw me … he never hated me, did he?

His forehead brushed my own in the softest caress, his thumb sweeping gently over my cheek before he pulled back and I lost the heat of him completely. I blinked, opening my eyes, and released a shaky breath. I felt rattled, and I had the sudden fear that if I looked at Will right now, he would see every single confusing emotion on my face.

And so, like the chicken that I was, I didn't look at him.

"Thank you." I laughed awkwardly at the floor, pretending to fix my sock even though it was perfectly fine and not off-center at all. I picked up my journal and tried to steer us back on course. "So, about the song, I came up with some new lyrics that I think could be intertwined into the chorus after the second verse."

"I have a better idea," he replied smoothly. "I think you should sing in the chorus with me." I immediately began to protest, and he held up a hand and gave me a strong look. "The song is about this man who wants to be with a woman who is unavailable. It would take the song to the next level if in the chorus, he's singing a plea to her, and she's singing one back. Besides, from a marketing perspective, duets do pretty well, especially when it's a love song."

Damn it, he was right. I sighed, leaning back in the chair and looking over at him. He was leaning back in his seat, a look of confidence across his face, as if he knew I would agree with him and was just waiting for me to catch up to the plan.

"You could use a stage name in the credits, so no one knows it's really you," Will reminded me gently with a soft look. "But at the end of the day, I don't want to do this if you're not comfortable with it. If you don't want to sing, you don't have to."

"Let's do it." I nodded strongly. "I'll sing in the chorus."

Will frowned. "Are you sure?"

"In the chance that we do win, just know that I won't be singing onstage," I joked. "This contest means everything to me, and I need to win, but I'm a producer and songwriter, not a performer."

"I need to win just as badly as you do," Will reminded me. "It's just as much my career on the line as it is yours."

"Yeah, but if you don't win, you have a backup career," I pointed out. "Not to mention, a growing music fanbase and parents who are more than supportive."

"My parents aren't as supportive as you think," Will said, running his hand through his thick hair. "My father is a strict man who doesn't believe in careers that don't offer guaranteed security. He indulges my music, but that's only because I have a nine-to-five job."

"What are they like?" I asked, unable to hide my curiosity.

Will stood up. "Come with me."

I followed him, half-expecting him to open a door in his apartment that led to his family or something. But instead, he opened a door to a bedroom. I stopped at the door, taking in the room with wide eyes. My eyes pinged around the room, trying to capture every inch of the room, but my eyes kept moving back to the massive bed.

Will moved an item on his dresser, and the loud sound pulled me from my musing about his bed. I noticed he had a photo in his hand, and I immediately walked into the room toward him.

"This is my family," he shared as I stepped closer to him.

It was a picture of him when he was a kid with an older couple, the woman holding a little girl against her hip.

I studied the photo—at Will's bright smile; the crying little girl, holding a pink doll; the stern, serious face of the older man; and the small smile on the woman's face, even as she looked tiredly at the camera. This had to be his parents and his sister. Will looked so cute with his mushroom haircut and bright smile. He looked like a kid who had never been unhappy a day in his life. I knew that probably wasn't true, but even then, even as a child, he had the kind of smile that made you think everything was going to be okay.

"We were on a trip to Disneyland in that photo," he said, making me glance from the photo to him.

"You look so happy," I said softly, fingers gently tracing the edge of the photo.

"We were," he said simply. "That was the last family vacation we took. It was right before my dad's business made it big."

I studied the photo again, looking at his father's stern face. He had a full set of hair in the photo, hair the same color as Will's, and they had the same eyes and strong jaw too. I wondered idly if I was looking at a photo of what Will might look like in twenty years. His father looked to be in his late thirties or early forties; it was too hard to tell, and I'd never been good at guessing people's ages.

"What kind of business does your dad have?" I asked, not looking away from the photo.

Will sighed, and I heard him shift beside me. "He has his hands in a little bit of everything. He likes to invest in things, but he's the CEO of a shoe company."

That made me look up from the photo. "Which company?"

"Excels," he answered, and I felt my eyes widen in shock.

Excels was one of the hottest shoe companies out there right now. They were right up there with Nike and Adidas. I didn't own a pair, but that was mostly because my budget couldn't afford those shoes. I shopped wherever the bargain was, and chances were, Excels weren't there.

"Your family must be really rich," I blurted, putting the photo back on the dresser.

"Yeah, but we don't live a life of excess. My father always made sure of it."

"How did your dad make sure of it?"

"We had a small house in the suburbs. We lived with the minimum and nothing more or less." Will shrugged. "Even though my dad was this hotshot who made tons of money, I never really realized it, growing up, because we lived like we were any other middle-class family. I won't say I didn't have some privileges because I did. I went to private school and took music and singing lessons since I was a kid, and for that, I'll always be grateful to my parents. But I was never handed things. I had to earn them. My first car was some beat-up ten-year-old Camry that I had to work a summer job to make the money for."

"What about college?" I asked, unable to stop myself from wondering about his life, his family. "Were they happy that you came all the way across the country to study music? There are plenty of great schools in California."

"NYU was always my dream school. Partly for the amazing music department, but also because of where it is," he explained. "I wanted to study and make music in the Big Apple. I wanted to live the clichéd tortured-musician lifestyle, playing gigs in shitty bars and writing cheesy love songs about food."

I cracked a smile at that last part. "And did you?"

Will nodded, a small grin on his face. "Everything, except the cheesy love songs. Well, at least so far anyway. There's still time to write love songs once you finally cook for me."

"Who said I was going to cook for you?" I teased, poking him on his stomach. It was solid and toned, so really, all I did was hurt myself. I doubted he'd even felt it. "And how do you know it'll even be good? I could be a terrible cook."

"It could taste like dirty feet, and I have a feeling I'd still think it was delicious if you cooked it," he said, making me roll my eyes, even as I laughed. He laughed with me, tugging on a piece of my hair so I'd look back at him. "What, too cheesy for you?"

"Maybe just a little," I teased.

"What about your family?" he asked.

"My family is supportive," I said, shrugging tightly. Will watched me silently, and after a moment, I shared, "My father was a musician, so music has always been a part of my life for as long as I can remember. He taught me how to play the piano and the guitar. He even helped me write my first real song."

"Sounds like you have a really special bond with your dad," he said with a kind smile.

"Yeah." I nodded, heart aching slightly as I thought about my dad. "But having a musician as a father taught me a lot about the music industry and about love."

"Like what?"

I started picking through his other photos on his dresser. "How hard it is to make it in the industry. My father loved music and being on the road. Sometimes, I think he loved it more than he loved being with his family." I chuckled sadly. "He certainly loved the women that came with music."

Will's hands covered mine as I rubbed at the corners of a photo of Will's family. "I'm sorry, Buttercup."

"Don't be." I swayed slightly toward him, like my body wanted his comfort, even as my words denied him. "Like I said, my father taught me a lot."

I pulled my hands away from Will and carefully set his photo back on his dresser. I had so many more questions about his family, about his life, but somehow, this had become about my life. I didn't know how he did it, but he'd had me sharing more with him than I'd ever shared with anyone else.

"You don't believe that all musicians can't be faithful, right?"

I looked back at Will. "No, of course not. That's ridiculous."

He nodded. "It's a stereotype, but it's one that has stuck the longest."

"Being faithful isn't a musician issue; it's a relationship issue," I joked. "If you don't want to get hurt, then just don't put yourself in a situation to get hurt."

"It's that simple, huh?" he asked, face impassive. He watched me with those intense, dark eyes, and I got the feeling that he had me all figured out. "Come on. Let's get back to work."

When I got home after work on Friday, the place was quiet.

I dropped my bag into my room and sat down at my desk, letting out a tired sigh from the long day. I'd gotten so used to the sound of the television greeting me as soon as I walked through the door that it was strange to come home to silence.

I debated on texting Alejandra or Yari to find out what they were up to but quickly shook that idea away. Even though I wanted to be a worried hen and check in with Alejandra, I needed to let her live her life and not pester her about spending time with me just because I had some free time for once. It was hard to not be a worried hen about Alejandra though. I'd been taking care of her for so long now that sometimes, I had to remind myself that she didn't need me the way she used to when she was younger.

When our father had died, Aleja had only been six years old. Our mother was so overcome by her grief when he died that at the age of twelve, I had to push my grief to the side and be the parental figure for her. I took control of our lives in any way that I could. I started picking her up from school, making her lunches, and signing her school permission slips. I took her to her doctor appointments, held her when she was sad, or let her sleep in my bed when she got scared. As we got older and the years passed, my mom pulled herself together again, but I never stopped taking care of Alejandra. At that point, it had just been second nature. I loved my sister, and that would never change. Whether she was six or sixty, our connection was one that could never be broken.

I shook the memories away and pulled my laptop closer to me on the desk. I opened up my work email, planning on getting ahead of some work, when I felt my phone vibrate in my pocket.

Will: What are you doing?

My mouth curved up into a smile, and I tried to ignore the pleasant butterfly feeling in my stomach as I stared one second too long at his name on my screen.

Me: About to catch up on some work.

Will: Want to come over? Callum left for the weekend to visit family, and I'm thinking of doing a Star Wars marathon.

Will: Finally see what you love so much about them. ;)

It took me all of five seconds to make my decision.

Me: I'll be there in an hour.

I slammed my laptop closed and jumped from my desk. After a quick shower, I pulled on some yoga pants and a light knit sweater and threw my jacket on.

After throwing my wallet and keys into my purse, I wrapped myself up tight in my scarf and a blue Giants hat. I closed my bedroom door behind me and walked down the hall and past the empty living room, smile never once leaving my face.

It didn't take me long to get to Will's place.

I walked into the building and onto his elevator, reminding myself again and again that we were friends, that we could hang out and it didn't mean anything.

I stepped off the elevator when I heard a door open, Will's tall body waiting for me down the hall. My eyes took him in with almost-greedy gulps, like I hadn't spent the whole day at work catching glimpses of him in the halls.

"Hey," Will greeted, a lazy smile on his handsome face. He moved beside the door so that I could walk in and continued, "I was just about to start the movie without you."

"Start movie you can't," I teased, trying my hand in Yoda speak.

Will laughed, eyes lit with happiness. "I'm in for a lot of Yoda talk tonight, aren't I?"

"Yep," I agreed, grinning. "Better get used to it now because I will be full-on geeking out."

"I can't wait." His soft smile made me blush, and I had to look away, even as I couldn't stop the goofy grin from overtaking my face, feeling slightly flustered by this flirty, confident Will.

It was hard to come to terms with how easily Will could go from friendly to smoldering without a second thought. One minute, I thought that he might be the sweetest guy I'd ever met, and the next, I was fighting the urge to jump his bones. I was just so attracted to him, more so than I thought I'd ever been attracted to a guy before. And it wasn't only when he was flirting with me or teasing me with those soft touches. Sometimes, I'd watch him biting the back of his pen while staring at our music sheets or when he stared at the restaurant pamphlets with such concentration, as if he was really thinking through every option available on the menu and not going to get the same thing each time, and I'd have the sudden urge to lean over and just kiss him. It drove me crazy how he talked softly and surely through every single one of my annoying questions about our song, always listening to my opinion and never telling me that I was being ridiculous. Or when we'd talk about music, and we couldn't figure out how to explain what we were thinking out loud, and yet we were able to finish each other's thoughts, as if the same music flowed through both our souls, like we were kindred spirits that were connected forever through music.

I sometimes wondered if he knew me better than anyone else, and the thought both terrified me and made me feel safe.

The DVD menu was playing on a loop on the TV screen, and I saw that Will had a bowl of popcorn and chips on the coffee table in front of the sofa. He had chosen *Star Wars: Episode IV* to start the supposed marathon, and I saw that he had the other Star Wars movies stacked on the coffee table by the snacks.

"You don't watch them in order?" I asked, plopping down on the couch. It felt weird, sitting here when almost every time I'd come here in the last two months, Callum was sitting on it, either smoking weed, watching TV, or both.

"I read somewhere that it's a better experience if you watch them in order of timeline," he said, walking to the kitchen. He called out over his shoulder, "What do you want to drink?"

"Water's good," I said, eyes looking through the other movies on the movie stand by the TV. They had a huge collection, and from what I could see from the sofa, it was mostly action or horror films.

He returned a moment later, putting two glasses of water on the table before sitting beside me on the sofa. "Do you watch the movies in a different order?"

I shrugged. "I don't usually have time to binge-watch stuff, so I usually just watch whatever my hand pulls out from the stack first. My favorite so far is *Episode V*, I think."

"How come?" he asked, turning his body on the sofa so that our knees were almost touching.

"I don't think it has so much to do with the movie itself, but the memories I have of watching it," I explained.

Will nodded but waited patiently, like he knew I was warring with whether or not I should say more.

Finally, with an exhale, I continued, "I used to watch the Star Wars movies with my dad. He would get all into them; he knew all the words and everything. We watched all the movies together, but for some reason, *Episode V* is the one that I have the most memories of watching with him. He would do all the voices.

"One time, after watching the movie the night before, he came home in a wampa costume to scare us, and I remember my mom almost peed herself in fright because she was cooking in the kitchen and didn't know he'd gotten home. My sister and I laughed so hard, and after that, we got into this tradition of dressing up as the characters of the movies every time we watched them together.

"My sister wore her Princess Leia costume for a week, and even though my mom complained, my dad insisted on letting my sister wear it if she wanted. She was only five, and she loved the idea of being a badass princess like Leia. It was really cute."

He smiled, eyes soft. "What did you dress up as?"

I laughed, thinking back to my costume and how much work I'd put into getting into character. "I was Yoda. I would speak like him for days at a time. It drove everyone crazy because I'd even do it at school. I think one of my teachers wanted to throttle me during that time."

"How long did you guys do that?" he asked.

I felt my eyes start to sting, but I pushed the feelings back. "He actually died not long after we started the tradition."

His face turned soft with sadness. "I'm so sorry, Genesis."

"He died suddenly," I blurted out, needing to say it. To share it. Share my dad with someone. "One minute, he was walking us to school, and the next, he was on the ground, dead."

Will's eyes widened. "Shit."

"Ruptured brain aneurysm," I said, giving a shaky laugh. "He was dead before the ambulance came."

I fought to take a deep breath, trying to get my emotions under control. This was the first time I'd talked about my father's death out loud in years. Sometimes, I'd talk about my dad with Yari, but it was mostly about how I missed him or of memories we had of him. But his death was something no one wanted to talk about, and my family especially didn't want me or Alejandra to. They wanted us to forget it, and while Alejandra had a very hazy memory of that day, I remembered everything in painstaking detail. The sound his body had made when it connected with the concrete. The way Alejandra's giggle had turned into a scream, my father's joke long forgotten by both of us. The way I'd stood there, frozen, not knowing what to do. It wasn't until later—when my voice was hoarse and my throat burning as I sat in the empty hospital room with my sister and mom, staring blankly at the white walls—that I'd learned that I'd screamed the entire time. From the moment he'd hit the ground until the ambulance arrived nearly fifteen minutes later. I'd temporarily lost my voice from it, but even if I could've spoken, I didn't think I would have said anything right then.

I didn't even know who had called the ambulance, and for some reason, that one nagging question always bothered me. I remembered everything about the morning he'd died. I even remembered the outfits we had been wearing—me in some denim jeans, a green turtleneck, and my favorite black sneakers that had stripes on the side, my puffy black jacket protecting me from the cold March wind. My sister had been wearing a cute purple-and-pink polka-dotted dress, white stockings, and cute black flats that had bows on the front, a matching black jacket, and she also had a pink hat on to cover her hair, which was in low pigtails. My dad was in his usual black work overalls; he worked as a mechanic at a mechanic shop a couple of blocks from our school.

And yet I couldn't even remember who had called the ambulance.

I knew it wasn't a big deal, and many people had probably called because I remembered there was a crowd surrounding us, people shouting things over my screaming and Alejandra's crying. I guessed I wanted to know because I wanted to thank them. For at least trying. Even if it was all for nothing. Even if their act of kindness couldn't save my father.

"Genesis," Will said in an anguished whisper, and before I knew what was happening, he pulled me into his body across the couch, his arms hugging me in a tight hug.

My face was against his shoulder, and without much thought to it, I wrapped my arms around his waist, needing his comfort. His arms, which were around my shoulders, tightened when I hugged him back, his cheek resting on the top of my head, and we sat there quietly for a long time. I breathed him in, pressing my nose against the side of his neck, and closed my eyes. I wanted to cry, but at the same time, I really, really didn't. Because I knew that if I did, I wouldn't be able to stop, and I couldn't deal with that right now. I couldn't deal with the grief of a person who had died over ten years ago but who was still, to this day, haunting me in a way that made me incapable of moving on. But I also didn't want to move on. Because if I stopped hurting, would that mean I'd stop forgetting? I didn't want to forget anything, not even that day.

I didn't want to forget, but right now, I did. I wanted to forget the grief and hurt for just a little while.

I moved my face an inch so that my lips brushed softly against his neck, and I felt him shiver. My heart began a fast beat in my chest, tingles of desire and want flashing yet again through my body. But this time, all the reasons I'd told myself not to, the lies I'd told myself to ignore these feelings, did not cross my mind. I pressed my lips against his neck again, this time a little harder, my hands moving slowly from his back toward his chest.

"Genesis," he murmured, pulling away to look at me, indecision flashing in his dark eyes. "You—"

I kissed him, and the feeling of my lips against his set off an explosion of lights behind my eyes, my body tingling like fireworks exploding into the sky. I gasped against his lips, eyes flying open, and he stared at me, eyes black with heat and desire.

"Genesis." He sounded winded, chest heaving as his eyes locked on my lips.

I'd never experienced a kiss like that, and it had only lasted a few seconds. What would it feel like to really kiss him? To have his hands on my body?

"Please," I whispered, fingers shaking as they crawled up his chest and around his neck. I didn't know what the hell I was doing, but for once, I wasn't letting myself think about the consequences.

"You need this." His voice was rough as he watched me with those dark eyes. His hands traveled down my arms around his neck, down my shoulders, and to my waist, where he gripped me firmly, pulling me onto his lap until I was straddling his legs.

"Please," I repeated, tightening my hands around the back of his neck. My fingers played with the soft hair at the nape of his neck, and I felt him shiver, watching me with half-lidded eyes.

"I told myself I wouldn't kiss you until you were ready, until you really meant it." He laid his forehead against my own, his lips brushing my nose in the softest of kisses. "But I can't help myself. Just one kiss. And then we'll stop."

I was nodding my head, eyes closing as my body clenched in anticipation. "Yes. Yes, just one kiss."

His mouth touched mine, and my body exploded in a kaleidoscope of lights. His lips moved against my own like he owned them, owned me, and the thought alone had me clenching my thighs around him. His tongue plunged into my mouth. I moaned as one of his hands held the back of my head, and he just took and took what he wanted, giving me everything I hadn't known I needed.

How had I lived my entire life and never known a kiss like this?

I needed more. I wanted him imprinted on me so that I'd never breathe in air that wasn't his as well.

His hands never strayed below my waist as he kissed me, our tongues dancing together in a slow dance that felt a lot like fucking. I moaned, putting my hand over his cock, hard through his pants, and began rubbing him as we kissed. The anticipation of more, of feeling his hard cock between my legs, of feeling his hands on my naked body had me squeezing him, breathless sounds rushing from my mouth as I tried to infuse our bodies together until there was no space between us. I felt his answering groan vibrate into my mouth before he tore his mouth away from mine, a short expletive leaving his mouth.

His hand closed over my wrist, and he slowly lifted my hand off him, his other hand reaching toward my thigh. He gently lifted me and placed me on the sofa next to him. I watched him with wide eyes, breath heavy as my body pulsed with need.

"Will," I said on a gasp, trying hard not to squirm in my seat.

"One kiss," he reminded me, voice tight with barely restrained control.

We watched each other silently, the sound of our breathing loud in the quiet room. It took a long moment for my breathing to even out, but eventually, reality came crashing back down, and I felt an overwhelming surge of embarrassment and uncertainty wash over me.

What the hell is wrong with me? Did I really just practically beg Will to kiss me and try to grope him on his sofa?

Oh God, how was I ever going to look at him again, much less make it through this movie marathon?

The answer was, I couldn't. I had to finish out the contest, so I'd have to figure out how to make music and not look at him, but I didn't have to stay for the movie. He probably wanted me to get the heck out anyway after I'd thrown myself at him like a wanton hussy.

I began to scoot away, trying to think up an easy excuse to get the hell out of there and spare us both the awkwardness, when I felt the sofa shift slightly. A moment later, I felt Will's hands on my waist as picked me up as if I weighed nothing, and he put me in his lap before lying down. He situated me on his body—and I let him—until he was lying on the sofa on his back, and I was lying on top of him, my leg in between his, my head resting on his chest, like he was my own personal body pillow.

"What are you doing?" I murmured, bewildered, wondering halfheartedly if I should protest.

"I'm getting us comfortable for our movie night," he explained easily, reaching his hand down onto the floor and picking up the DVD player remote.

I could feel his long dick pressing against the side of his thigh, so I knew he was still very much turned on. And yet, he'd taken one look at my face and known what I needed. He pressed play on the movie, his hand resting on my lower back, which was rubbing small, soothing circles. He paused the movie a moment later, and I felt his head turn to look down at me on his chest.

"Unless you don't want to watch this movie? I know what this movie means to you, so we can watch something else."

"No." I shook my head against his chest, heart squeezing at his thoughtfulness, mind racing to keep up. "No, it's okay. I want to … with you."

"Okay," he said, lips brushing a kiss against the crown of my head before pressing play again.

The next few hours were amazing. We watched the movie together, making commentary throughout on our favorite scenes and making jokes about the plot when it had gotten a little crazy. And when that movie ended, we quickly moved on to the next episode in the Star Wars franchise, my earlier uncertainty and embarrassment completely forgotten. My heart kept skipping a beat every time I thought about our kiss, but lying here with Will felt so natural that I didn't even have to remind myself to not run because for the first time, the fear never came.

It was fun, watching the movie with someone who enjoyed it as much as me. We laughed so much. I loved how every time Will laughed, I could feel his chest and stomach move against me, and because I had my face pressed against his chest, I could hear his laugh almost vibrate through me. It made me smile every time he did it. I wanted to listen to his laugh like that every time now.

And when the movie was over, Will insisted on driving me back home. I kept trying to argue with him that it was pointless for him to go out when it was so late and cold—plus, it'd take him double the amount of time to get home—but he didn't want to hear it.

"I invited you over so late. I want to make sure you get home safe," he said firmly. "I'm not letting you go out there by yourself, Genesis."

I let it go because secretly, I didn't want our night to end just yet.

"Wait, how can this song possibly make you happy?" I asked incredulously.

We were listening to Sarah McLachlan's "I Will Remember You" in his car as he drove through the light traffic.

We listened one of the many playlists Will had on his phone, and he was explaining certain memories or facts that he knew about each song. It felt like every song that Will listened to, he had a story for it. He was the type of guy who loved all kinds of music, so some of the music on his playlist was a bit out there—I would've never pegged him as a McLachlan fan; that's for sure—but when he explained the song to me or told me about the first time he'd heard it, it'd make me instantly love the song.

"The song is sad, yeah, but it's more than that," he argued, making sure the light was still red as he turned more in his seat toward me. "It's also hopeful, and it's about remembering the good memories you have with someone and not regretting that even if your time is over with them. Her voice is so soothing. When I hear this song, I think of friends and people I've met through the years who aren't in my life anymore, but I still have all these great memories of them, and it just makes me feel good. Sometimes, it's a bittersweet happiness, but still, I don't regret my memories."

"That still sounds crazy," I said even if I did understand his viewpoint. "I get it, but her voice is just so sad; she's basically the reason I'd cry at all those ASPCA commercials. It was bad enough that I felt bad for the dogs, but then she'd start singing, and I'd be bawling and feeling guilty that I couldn't adopt all those dogs."

Will laughed loudly, the sound immediately sending happy sparks straight to my heart. "I forgot about those commercials. They used to get my little sister all the time. She'd beg my parents to let us adopt a dog, but they were not having it."

I smiled. "Your sister is in high school, right?"

"Yeah, she's going to college next year," he said. "She's the biggest pain in my ass, but I love her. Even if she's always texting me at all hours of the night just to tell me about her high school drama."

"Sisters are really good at being annoying, but loveable," I joked. I started scrolling through his playlist, looking for the next song to play before deciding to just click on the first song my finger landed on. I pressed on a song called "The Milky Way" by Kokin Gumi, and soft instrumental music started playing.

Will smiled, a sad, almost-nostalgic smile. "This is one of my mom's favorite songs. I love listening to this when I'm feeling homesick. It reminds me of lazy days at home during vacation as a kid, watching my mom clean and move about the house with this music playing quietly in the background."

"I get that," I said, nodding. "I love listening to Spanish music because it reminds me of my family. There isn't a single family gathering that happens without Spanish music playing in the background pretty much at all times."

"Funny how the sound of a song can bring back all sorts of memories, huh?" he asked with a small smile.

"It's part of the reason why I love creating music so much," I agreed, fiddling with his phone. After a moment, I looked back up at him. "I love creating music for so many reasons, but most importantly, I can't *not* write down the music that plays in my head. I want to create something that makes people feel even half the emotions I've felt while listening to music."

"You do," Will said. "Your music means something. Never forget that."

I nodded, feeling oddly shy. I thought about tonight—about the kiss, of course, but also about the way that he'd been there for me. He'd always been there for me, always open to listening and talking, to giving me whatever I need.

"Thank you for inviting me tonight," I blurted, forcing myself to look at him, wanting him to see the sincerity in my eyes. "And for listening earlier. It's not easy for me to talk to people, to share, but when I'm with you, it feels like the easiest thing in the world."

"I'll always be here for you," he replied. "Anytime, Genesis. I mean that."

I smiled softly and nodded, words stuck in my throat that I wanted to say but couldn't. Will looked away to continue driving, and I clicked on a song I knew from the playlist.

I shot Will a grin as the upbeat bass pumped through our ears. "The Pussycat Dolls? Really?"

Will chuckled, and with a shrug, he said, "They were a great girl band."

I shook my head in faux disappointment. "Just when you start to think you know someone ..."

"Don't pretend you and your cousin weren't singing 'Don't Cha' when you were kids." He laughed at my exaggerated scoff. "That song was basically every girl's anthem. I can't even tell you how many times Kata used to sing that song, and she was only six the first time she heard it."

I chuckled. "That song is pretty old, but it's definitely a good early 2000s hit."

"So, I was right then," Will said, looking pleased. "Just out of curiosity, is there any footage of you singing and dancing to that song? Because I'd love to send that in to *America's Funniest Home Videos*."

I lightly smacked him on the stomach with the back of my hand, heart light as I grinned up at him. "Well, even if there were footage, I certainly wouldn't show it to you now."

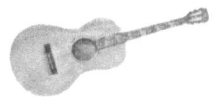

Time passed by in a blur of music and Will. February turned into March, and with it, the cold winter weather seemed to be holding on for dear life as we neared the beginnings of spring. We spent nearly every day together, working on our music but also talking for hours about everything and nothing. Sometimes, Will made me laugh so hard that I'd cry, and other times, we'd just sit together in silence, sharing space in the way you only could when you felt so completely safe with someone.

And with Will, I did. I'd never felt this way about another person before, especially a guy. I woke up, and I wanted to text him, to tell him about my crazy dreams or the song that had popped into my head as I was brushing my teeth. When Clements drove me crazy, he was the person I wanted to talk to because I knew he'd make me feel better, just by being there. But more than that, I loved getting to know Will. When he talked, I didn't care about anything else but what he had to say.

It was insane. It made no sense how two months ago, I hated him, and now, I couldn't imagine a day without him. I could've never seen this coming, and yet I wouldn't change it for a thing. His friendship meant everything to me now.

I finished work a little bit early today. Clements had surprisingly been going easy on me lately with the workload. Recently, he'd been letting me join more meetings with him, and he hadn't made me go on a ridiculous errand the whole week. It definitely had me on edge a little bit, waiting for the other shoe to drop, but Cora had told me I should see the positive in it, that maybe Clements was trusting me with more serious work.

Since I was done a little early, I decided to pick up some pastries from the staff lounge for Cora and Will. They'd both had busy afternoons in and out of meetings, and I imagined they could use the pick-me-up.

I balanced the pastries in my hands as I walked down the hall to their department, biting down on my lip to hold in my smile as I thought about Will's face once I handed him the blueberry muffin—his favorite.

"What the heck?"

I paused at the glass entrance door, watching as Jameson Harris—the CEO of the company—walked out of Will's office. Will stood by his entrance for a moment, an unreadable expression on his face, before turning back into his office and closing the door behind him. Mr. Harris did a quick glance around the office, and I hastily hid by the side of the wall, heart pounding at him nearly catching me at the entrance, like a creep. If he asked, I had no work-related reason to be over here at this department, and the last thing I needed was for him to kick me out of the contest when we were so close to being done.

I debated with myself for a minute on whether or not I should just run back down the hall, but I was curious. I wanted to see what Mr. Harris was doing in there. After taking a quick breath, I peeked my head out and looked back into the office. He had his back to me, but I frowned when I realized that he was now standing in front of Cora's desk. I stepped out a little bit more until I could see Cora, who was sitting at her desk, a big smile on her face. She looked completely at ease despite the fact that the freaking CEO—who looked like an overgrown lumberjack in an expensive suit—was staring down at her.

I watched as Cora opened up her top drawer in her desk. She pulled out her secret stash of goodies and held up a chocolate chip cookie. His head turned slightly; he had an almost-dazed look on his face, like he didn't know what was happening, and yet he didn't walk away. He held his arm out, and Cora dropped a few cookies in his hand, her mouth moving a mile a minute, her eyes friendly and bright.

I stepped away from the wall and started walking back to my desk. I had no idea what Mr. Harris was doing, talking to Will—or Cora for that matter—but I knew that I absolutely couldn't get caught outside their office like that. I'd have to ask them about it later.

"Hey, Genesis. Could you help me locate the Cassidy file for tomorrow's pitch meeting?" Kenny, a new intern from a local college asked.

"Of course. I'll be right there."

I dropped the pastries off at my desk and walked over to my coworker's cubicle. A half hour into helping my coworker, I sent Will a quick picture of me in front of a stack of files with a sad face and texted him.

> *Me: Please get me out of here. Kenny is about to suffocate me with these files.*

Will texted me back almost immediately.

> *Will: Cute. Meet me in five at the elevator.*

I grinned, staring at the text for an extra second before sliding my phone back into my back pocket.

"Here are the files, Kenny." I dropped a giant stack on his desk. "Good luck!"

"Wait," Kenny called out. "Genesis, I could really use your help—"

I was gone like the wind.

"Why is this verse so hard?" I huffed, tossing the music sheets onto the keyboard and leaning back into the seat.

We were so close to being done with the song, so of course, we'd be hit with an intense creative block.

"It's because we're thinking about it too hard," he answered. "It'll come to us."

Will strummed on the guitar, playing the riff of an old '80s pop song called "Take Your Time" by The S.O.S. Band, and even though I didn't want to, I began to smile.

"Okay, first of all, why do you even know how to play that song on the guitar?" I asked. "And second, I'm pretty sure that song is about sex, which has nothing to do with our current dilemma."

Will threw me a wicked smile but didn't stop playing. "I once did a wedding gig in Long Island, and they wanted us to play only '80s pop songs."

I raised an eyebrow. "You played at weddings? Did Callum play with you too?"

"Yeah, the whole band did," he replied. "This was back during my undergrad when we'd pretty much take any gig that was thrown our way. Wasn't so bad though. We got to meet new people, got free food and booze."

Did you meet women there? I wanted to ask, but I bit my tongue and kicked those stupid, jealous thoughts away.

Whatever Will had done in the past was none of my business. Hell, even now, he could screw whoever he wanted, and he didn't owe me a single thing. We were just friends. Only friends.

The fact that even the thought of another woman touching Will made me feel like I had been sucker-punched was completely normal. Plenty of people felt that way about their friends. It was natural … right?

"Sounds nice," I said, turning back toward the keyboard so he couldn't see the jealousy written all over my stupid face.

I began playing the melody again, not bothering to sing because I knew at this point, it was fruitless. Maybe if I just kept playing the melody over and over, words would miraculously pop up in my head.

"Buttercup."

I glanced behind me, fingers still moving across the keys. "Yeah?"

"Stop playing. I have an idea." He stood up and began to push the chairs and table toward the opposite wall near the door.

I watched him, turning in my seat. "What are you doing?"

Will walked to the window and closed the blinds in his music room, shutting the room off from almost any of the remaining winter light. "Come lie down on the floor."

"The floor?" I stared, feeling confused. "Why did you close the blinds? I can't see the keyboard or—"

"Buttercup."

Funny how he was able to say so much with just one word. I stood up and blindly made my way toward the empty floor in the middle of the room. I could see Will's figure walking toward the computer he had set up by the window, and a moment later, the light from the screen illuminated the room a bit.

"Whenever I'm feeling burned out, I sometimes get on the floor and just lie there with some music on."

I sank to the floor, loosely wrapping my arms around my bent legs as I watched him. "That sounds ... relaxing."

Instrumental music began to play softly from the speakers, and I watched as Will made his way over to me, keeping about six feet of distance between us as he joined me on the floor. He lay completely on his back, legs stretched out and hands behind his head, like he was tanning at the beach and not lying in a dark room. I lay down slowly, resting my arm beneath my head like a pillow as I stared up at the ceiling. It didn't take long for me to get lost in the darkness, in the music.

"Have you ever listened to a song and remembered *exactly* how life used to be when you first heard it?" His voice was low and deep, and for a second, I almost thought the voice had come from inside my head.

I stared across at him, the light from the computer illuminating the side of his face. His sharp jaw looked almost gentle in the soft light, and I ached to reach my arm across the floor and cup it in my hand, to trace his jaw with my thumb and see how it felt.

"The last time I saw my grandpa, we went on a car ride to the ice cream shop, and I remember that 'Born to Be Alive' by Patrick Hernandez played on the car radio. My grandpa lit up and explained that he remembered this song from his first visit to America, after my father had come. It made me laugh at the time to see my grandpa—who barely spoke a lick of English—choppily sing along to this song, windows down in the car, like he didn't have the slightest care in the world."

I smiled softly, imagining a young Will laughing wildly as his grandpa sang this song, the innocence of anything bad happening to people unknown to him. "It sounds like a beautiful memory."

Will smiled sadly. "It was. A few weeks later, we got the call that my grandpa had passed away in his sleep. I remember thinking about that song and how I'd spent so many days learning to play it on the guitar for him. I had been so excited to play it for him when I saw him again. He never got to hear me sing it."

"I'm so sorry," I whispered, turning onto my side so I was facing him.

"He was the first person to believe in my music." He turned his head to look at me, eyes somber. "He gave me my first string instrument, a ukulele. Listened to me play all these American songs even though he didn't understand any of the words. He would sit in his chair and listen to me sing for hours, the proudest smile on his face, and it made me feel so special."

I looked at him in the dark, able to see his shape even if I couldn't make out every line of his face. I knew it well enough by now to have it memorized. I didn't need the light to know that Will had that furrow between his brow, the one he got when he didn't want to show that something bothered him. My heart ached for him, like it wanted nothing more than to jump out of my chest and into his. I wanted to chase away his pain, but I also wanted to sit in it with him, to let him know that he wasn't alone in it either.

"When I play, I like to think that the sound of my music reaches him wherever he is and that it brings him peace." His voice was hushed, like his words were for my ears only. "I miss him every single day, but I'm so grateful for the ten years that I got with him because he shaped me into who I am today. I'll never forget him, and I never want to forget."

My eyes watered, and I felt such an overwhelming need to comfort him, to feel his body in my hands that I slowly scooted closer to him, heart beating wildly in my chest. My head was screaming at me to go back, that I was going to get hurt, but my heart was pulling me toward him, needing to make sure that he knew he wasn't alone. He watched me wordlessly, eyes never leaving my own as he stretched out his arm in an open invitation to come closer.

I gently laid my head on his shoulder, and I felt his body exhale, like he had maybe been hoping and waiting for me all this time. I didn't want to completely encroach on his space, so I made sure my legs did not knock into his own as I placed my hand on his chest. I slowly moved my hand back and forth in what I hoped was a comforting touch.

"He must have loved you so much, Will," I said softly into his chest. "I wish I could have met him."

"He would've loved you." His arm curled around me, a silent request for me to stay, and I scooted closer to his body, our legs touching.

We lay there in silence, Will gently caressing my hair with a featherlight touch as I laid my head between his shoulder and beneath his chin, my thumb rubbing against his chest in slow, even movements. The music continued to play from the computer, though the screen had long since gone into sleep mode, turning the room almost pitch-black. I listened to Will's breathing, feeling the rise and fall of his chest on the side of my face, and for a single second, I allowed myself to imagine waking up every day like this.

I whispered my secret into the dark room, eyes feeling heavy with sleep. "I don't want you to leave me, and that scares me. You mean something to me ..."

I felt myself drifting off, but right before sleep completely took over me, I could've sworn I'd heard him whisper something into my hair, his lips a soft balm to my fractured heart.

"You mean everything to me."

I woke suddenly, mind racing and music still playing in my head. I noticed almost belatedly that Will's arms were around me, my leg on top of his, and I wanted to freak out about our cuddling session and the fact that we'd fallen asleep together, but I couldn't because I'd figured it out.

Finally.

I sat up, and Will woke immediately, his eyes alert and worried, fingers reaching for me.

"I figured it out," I whispered down at him. "The song."

He sat up with me, jumping to action. We worked seamlessly as I shared my ideas out loud, Will quickly writing them all down as I picked up the guitar.

Ten minutes later, I played the chords, and he sang the bridge, tweaking it slightly in the moment. I sang the outro, a growing smile on my face that was nearly painful by the time I finished singing.

"We did it," I said, laughing.

It wasn't perfect yet, but we finally had a whole song.

"We have our song." Will said, eye shining with a kaleidoscope of emotions. I couldn't identify all the sentiments

I saw studied him in that moment, but I had a feeling they were the same emotions that were written all over my face.

And for once, I didn't even try to hide them from him.

I couldn't stop thinking about Will.

All weekend, he kept popping into my head. His face, his lips, the way that he looked at me sometimes when I was talking to him. It'd been three days since that night in his apartment, where we had fallen asleep together, and I still couldn't get the feeling of being wrapped up in his arms out of my mind.

These last few months had altered my life so completely. Feelings that I'd held captive inside me, suffocating them so I'd never have to acknowledge them, were now out and written all over me. I couldn't hide what was so glaringly obvious, and now, I was trying to figure out where that left me.

I liked Will. A lot. I wanted to be with him, but a part of me was still scared. What if he'd changed his mind? What if I was too much for him, and he wanted something easier, someone who didn't have so much emotional baggage?

My door swung open, banging loudly on the wall, and I nearly jumped out of my skin as Alejandra raced into my room, hair flowing wildly around her face.

"I got a call back from the modeling agency!" she shrieked.

I dropped the guitar onto my bed. "You what?" I asked, trying not to get too excited. "Did they say they were taking you on as a client?"

"Yes!" she screamed, jumping up and down. "Yes, of course, they said yes! Oh my God, I can't believe it. They said yes!"

I jumped off the bed and pulled her into a hug, laughing as she continued cheering and rambling. "I'm so happy for you," I said, pressing a kiss to her cheek. "Congratulations, Aleja."

She squeezed me into another hug before pulling away. "Thank you. Okay, I'll be back. I need to call James and let him know."

I blinked in surprise. "You didn't tell him first?"

"No, silly." She smiled. "I wanted to tell you first."

I smiled, trying not to show how much that meant to me. I guessed I wasn't doing a good job of it because she huffed, throwing me a playfully exasperated look.

"You know you're basically my mom, right? I'm always going to come to you first. I love you."

This time, I couldn't even try to hide as my eyes watered. "I love you too."

She blew me a kiss and left, walking back to her room, her mind no doubt back on her amazing news. I watched the door absently for a second before sitting back on my bed and picking up my guitar.

I was halfway into playing one of my old songs when I got a text from Alejandra.

> *Alejandra: We're doing a celebratory breakfast for dinner at Denny's on Northern! Be there or be square.*

> *Me: Why are you texting me when I'm literally right across the hall from you?*

> *Alejandra: Because it's easier this way, duh. It's at 9, so don't be late.*

Me: Okay, lazybones. Congrats again. I'm proud of you.

Alejandra: I know you are. :)

I'd been so lost in all my music stuff that I'd nearly forgotten all the stuff happening with Alejandra, about her career change. Even though I was still skeptical about the modeling industry and I was scared to see her get sucked into it all and get over her head, I couldn't *not* be immensely happy and proud of her too.

It was about time that my sister started believing in herself again.

Later that evening, we all got dressed up to celebrate Alejandra's blossoming career. Even though we were going to a diner, Aleja demanded that we dress as fancy as possible since we were now in the presence of a model. I nearly rolled my eyes at that comment, but since it was her day, I just nodded and put on my nicest sweater dress that offered me warmth in the late March night.

Fortunately, we were seated quickly, and the place wasn't too packed. Yari scooted down in the booth, so I could sit next to her, and Alejandra and James sat across from us. I saw Alejandra glance behind me before taking her seat at the end of the booth, and I gave her a quizzical look.

"Just checking out the family that just walked in," she said brightly, taking a menu. "You know how I get distracted when I people-watch."

"Do you want to swap seats so that your back is to the door?" I asked, pausing in taking off my jacket.

"Oh no, it's okay," she said quickly, giving me a smile. "I'll be fine. Hmm, what should I order?"

She raised her menu onto the table and opened it up so that her face was covered as she read. I shook my head, a small smile on my face as I finished taking off my jacket and passing it to Yari to put at the end of the booth. This booth could've easily have fit three people on each side, so it gave us ample space to put our stuff.

I opened my menu and scanned it halfheartedly, already knowing what I'd get. I was obsessed with their ham and cheese omelet. It was my go-to breakfast food whenever we used to go here when I was a kid, and that hadn't changed, even as an adult. I turned to Yari to see what she was going to order and saw that she was texting on her phone, a small frown on her face.

"What's wrong?" I asked.

She looked up from her phone and sighed. "I've been looking at apartments to move into, and this place I wanted in Forest Hills fell through."

I squeezed her hand. "I'm sorry. You'll find a place."

Yari's been taking the steps to finally move out of her mom's place, which her mom still didn't know about. Her plan was to tell her after she already had a place set up so that her mom couldn't guilt-trip her into staying when they both knew she needed to go.

Yari shot a look at Alejandra and James, who were both giggling over something on her phone, before she continued in a lowered voice, "We fight almost every day. I really don't know how much longer I can do it. I love my mom, but living together is ruining our relationship."

"Hi. Good evening." A waitress stood in front of our table, little notepad in hand. "My name is Jen, and I'll be your server for tonight. Are you guys ready to order?"

"Actually, we need a few more minutes," Alejandra said, giving her a distracted smile, her eyes straying to the doors.

"No problem. Can I start you guys off with some drinks?" Jen asked, moving her gaze to the rest of the table.

We all ordered our drinks, and after promising to be back in a jiffy, the waitress walked away.

James began talking to us about one of his classes this semester, but I couldn't help but look at Aleja, whose eyes roamed behind me again, looking distracted. This time, I turned behind me, but there was no one there.

I turned back around and asked, "Why do you keep looking behind me every other minute?"

"It's nothing," she lied, brushing her hair over her shoulder. "People-watcher, remember?"

"It's more than that," I pressed, pulling her menu down when she tried to hide behind it. "Seriously, what's up?"

Alejandra hesitated, looking at Yari. I frowned, looking toward Yari, who quickly picked up her phone and pretended that she wasn't listening to our conversation. It didn't take a genius to figure out that they were up to something.

"What? Just tell me," I demanded, starting to worry.

"I invited Will to come out tonight," Alejandra blurted, and I felt my eyes widen in shock. She quickly continued, "But I guess he isn't coming, so it's not a big deal."

I felt like my heart was going to bang out of my chest, but I tried to remain calm as I asked, "Why would you invite him to dinner?"

"Because he's important to you, and I wanted him to be here," she answered without pause.

"You didn't have to invite him to your big celebration."

Alejandra rolled her eyes. "Are you seriously still riding the denial train?"

"No, I'm not," I responded at the same time as Yari said, our words clashing, "Yep."

I turned to shoot her a glare, but she wasn't even looking up from her phone, so it was pointless.

"I hate both of you," I grumbled, folding my arms across my chest.

"I don't get the big deal," James said, speaking up.

I arched an eyebrow as I stared at him, wondering where he was going with this. He usually stayed out of our little arguments, knowing that there was really no point when we'd probably just outvote him.

"If you like him and he likes you, then why all the games?"

"There are no games," I snapped. "How about you mind your own business, hmm?"

James raised his hands up in surrender. "Shit, excuse me for trying to help you out. Girls are always making things more complicated than they need to be."

"That's not just girls," Yari said, finally putting her phone down and coming to my defense. "That's life. Nothing is ever as simple as boy likes girl, girl likes boy, and they live happily ever after. People come with baggage, experiences that hinder and complicate that perfect little fairy tale we all want to achieve."

"Will!" Alejandra suddenly shouted, rising half out of her seat and waving.

I felt my heart rate triple, and I nervously rubbed my hands on my thighs, not looking up from the table. It was one thing to be in my bubble with Will when it was just us, but this was my family. They'd have opinions, and they could read me like a book. I wasn't ready to admit whatever this was with Will to them when I hadn't even talked about it with him myself.

"Oh my God," Yari whispered into my ear. "You *like* him!"

"Shut up!" I whispered back, eyes wide with panic. "Just … shut up!"

"You made it," Alejandra said with a big smile.

I could feel Will standing at my side, could smell his subtle but strong masculine cologne, but I refused to look up. I started to move around my utensils, pretending like I knew which order they should actually be in. After doing that, I moved on to opening and refolding my napkin, putting it on my lap before putting it back on the table.

I was such a mess.

"Yeah, sorry for getting here a little late," Will said, his voice like music to my ear. "I got lost, trying to find the place."

"No worries," James said, slapping his hand against Will's in some weird, universal bro handshake as he introduced himself. "We haven't even ordered yet."

I looked up, mostly because I couldn't *not* look at him. He was nodding at what James had said, his profile the first thing I saw. His sharp cheekbone caught my attention, and I fought the urge to raise my hand and cup his face. His cheeks were a little red from the cold, his hair mussed from the hat he must've just pulled off his head.

"Hey," I said, clearing my throat. I moved over in the booth, accidentally bumping into Yari.

He looked down at me, an easy smile on his face. He nodded, his eyes gazing at me for a second before looking away. "Hey, Buttercup."

He sat down next to me, his knee bumping into mine beneath the table as he began to unbutton his topcoat. I studied him for a second, studied his strong, long hands as they moved across the buttons and pockets of his coat before shaking myself out of my stupor. He was wearing a fancy suit, dressed up just like the rest of us, and I couldn't stop staring as I drank him in.

Just then the waitress returned and started passing out the drinks to everyone, pulling my eyes from his body as she passed me my own.

"Are you guys ready to order?" she asked, eyeing Will.

I looked at Will, who had taken my menu and was looking through it. "Are you ready to order? We can have her come back in a few minutes—"

"No, you guys go on ahead," Will said, giving the waitress a comforting smile.

She smiled back, looking relieved. She probably didn't want to have to keep coming back to our table, especially since it was getting busier and she had other tables to take care of.

"I'll put my order in last."

Alejandra clapped her hands, grinning. "Great. I'll go first. I'll have the Belgian waffle with scrambled eggs, and can the sausage and bacon be turkey instead of pork?" The waitress nodded, her hand moving rapidly to write everything down as Alejandra continued talking. "Also, can I have a side of hash browns with that? Ooh! Does this come with toast on the side?" She paused for a second and looked at the waitress. "I want toast."

"Damn, girl," Yari said, whistling. "Is there even going to be space on this table for the rest of our food?"

We all laughed as Alejandra pouted.

When I looked over at him, he was already looking at me, a soft smile on his handsome face. His eyes traced my face, and I wanted to close my eyes at the overwhelming urge I felt to press my lips against his.

His callous fingers gently touched my hand in my lap, and without hesitation, I flipped my hand around and clasped his hand in mine, squeezing lightly. I exhaled quietly, my body settling now that I had his hand in mine.

"Need help ordering?" I asked.

He watched me with a growing smile, his thumb caressing my knuckles.

"What are you getting?" he asked, tilting the menus toward me.

I flipped back to the earlier pages, my arm brushing his, and I pointed to the omelet combo. "Alejandra wants this to be a breakfast-for-dinner thing, so naturally, I went with my go-to breakfast platter."

"Omelets are pretty good," he mused, nodding. "Maybe I'll get one of those. Callum makes a really good omelet though, so I doubt this place will measure up."

"He makes breakfast for you guys?" I asked, surprised. "Half the time when I come over, he looks like he just woke up."

"He only does it once in a while," Will admitted, smiling. "He usually just takes half of whatever food I made for myself in a half-sleep stupor and then drags himself back to his room to sleep. Sometimes, I think he's sleepwalking, and he's just led by his nose whenever he smells food."

I chuckled, imagining that scene. "For some reason, that does not surprise me at all. He seems like the type who would steal food in his sleep and not even know it."

"Oh, you have no idea," he said, shaking his head ruefully. "This guy is just as much trouble when he's asleep as he is awake."

"Genesis, it's your turn to order," Yari said, nudging me softly.

I looked away from Will and toward the waitress, trying to ignore Alejandra's blinding grin as she looked back and forth between me and Will.

"Can I have the ham and cheese omelet, please?" I asked, pointing to the item on the menu.

She nodded and then turned to Will. "And for you?"

"I'll have the Ultimate Omelet, please," Will said, pointing to a photo that had an omelet with egg, sausage, bacon, and a bunch of vegetables as well as cheese inside of it. It also had a side order of hash browns and bread. It looked delicious, and I felt my mouth water slightly, the longer I stared at the picture. "And can I have a glass of water whenever you get a chance?"

"Yeah, of course," the waitress said with a smile. She collected all the menus from us, and with one last glance at my sister, she said, "I'll go put your order in and be back in a bit."

"Aleja, tell us everything about this modeling agency," Yari said eagerly. "Do they have a gig lined up for you already?"

"No, they want me to come in this week to take some headshots with them and fill out some paperwork," Alejandra replied, bouncing in her seat with excitement.

I took a sip of my water. "Do you want me to come to the meeting with you? When is it?"

"It's on Thursday morning," she answered.

I nodded, taking a sip of my drink. "I'll be there."

Alejandra grinned, looking like she was floating on air.

The conversations around us smoothly moved from topic to topic, never a quiet moment at our booth. Will was so great at keeping conversation, and it felt like he had been friends with everyone for years. He was able to keep up with everyone, even when we went off on tangents or changed the topic three times in one story, which Yari tended to do. Even when the food came, the conversation continued to flow, and I found myself laughing more than once as Will told us story after story of all the craziness he'd gotten into when he moved to New York his freshman year.

"And then this guy came up to me on the train, and at first, I thought he was being nice to me," Will explained, taking a sip from his drink. "He started making conversation about the trains, complaining about all the construction, but then, suddenly, the conversation was about what I could do for our Lord and savior Jesus Christ—"

I busted out laughing, and everyone else laughed with me, already knowing where this was going.

"You met your first religious converter three weeks into moving here," I said, still chuckling. "I'm surprised it didn't take longer."

"At least they don't ring your doorbell every Sunday at nine a.m.," Yari said dryly.

"They still ring our doorbell every once in a while, but they stopped coming around as often after Callum answered the door naked once with two naked girls behind him."

Yari choked on her food, coughing roughly. I patted her hard on the back, chuckling, even as I was silently thanking the universe that I hadn't seen that scene. I liked Callum, but the last thing I wanted to see was his naked body even if he was by all accounts a really attractive guy.

"Your roommate sure sounds like … a character," Yari said, coughing lightly into her fist before taking another sip of her drink.

Will chuckled. "That's one way to describe him. He's really cool though, and he's my best friend. He's been there for me and helped me out with the music scene so much, especially when I first moved here and didn't know much."

I gave him a soft smile, nodding. "Callum is a great guy. I think you'd like him. He's really funny and would have you dying."

Yari wrinkled her nose, looking doubtful, probably still thinking about Will's story about him from moments before. "Maybe."

"We need to try that one time," Alejandra piped up, earning a raised brow from James. "I bet if we opened the door, looking all sexed up, they'd leave us alone for a while."

"Anything to help the cause," James said with a grin.

I snorted. "Yeah, no, thanks. The last thing we need are the neighbors bitching about your loud sex sounds again."

Will raised his brows. "That really happened?"

"More than once," Alejandra said proudly, and I rolled my eyes.

You'd think a girl would be embarrassed about being loud enough to wake the entire floor, but nope, not Alejandra. Her brazen confidence weirdly made me love her even more.

James's cockiness, however, didn't.

"Okay, James," I started, "either wipe that cocky little grin of yours off your face or I'm going to do it for you. With my knife."

James winced and quickly stopped smiling. "Shit, sorry. You know I love Alejandra."

"Yeah, but that doesn't mean I want to hear, talk about, or see you two having sex," I said dryly.

"Genesis, let him be proud of how good he is at sex," Alejandra said, grinning. "The first time we had sex, he didn't even last twenty seconds. He's come a long way."

We all cracked up laughing, except James, who turned bright red. After a moment, he shrugged and smiled, throwing an arm around Alejandra's shoulders so he could squeeze her to his side, and he lightly nipped at her cheek. She laughed, and he started whispering something in her ear. Whatever it was, it made her face turn soft, and a dopey look crossed her face, and … yep, they were kissing again.

I peeked at Will from the corner of my eyes. *I wish that were us.*

The entire night, Will fit in so seamlessly with my family. They loved him, and I loved seeing him with my sister and cousin. He was patient with them, so caring and thoughtful, and I could hardly keep my eyes off him the entire night.

After the dinner, Will drove us back home and even joined us upstairs when Alejandra declared that the night wasn't over. Of course, she then proceeded to blast music from our stereo and promptly decided that we should have a fashion show in the middle of the living room.

I could still hear the loud music pumping and cheering coming from the living room as I took a break from it all in my room. I was having a great time, but I just ... when I looked at Will, it was like I couldn't breathe. I didn't know how to be in the same room as him and not blurt out my feelings.

I heard the door open behind me, and I watched as Will walked in, eyes glancing around my room for all of a second before focusing entirely on me.

"I think I'm going to head out."

I watched him, confused and a little disappointed. "Oh. Is everything okay?"

He took a step into the room, closing the door behind him. "Everything is fine. Except for the fact that you are clearly uncomfortable with me being here. And I want you to enjoy tonight, so—"

I shook my head. "Will, I'm not uncomfortable with you being here. I *want* you here."

"Then, why have you been avoiding my eyes for the last hour? And every time I try to touch you, you practically jump out of your skin and move away."

I walked toward him until our shoes were nearly kissing. I looked up at him, taking one of his hands in mine. "I want you to stay."

He watched me silently. His hand that wasn't being held in mine lifted, and he curled a piece of my dark hair behind my ear. "Why?"

"The lights are on," I whispered.

His eyes flashed, remembering our conversation all those months ago in the bathroom.

"The lights are on, and I'm asking you to stay."

"You're so beautiful," he whispered, his hand softly tracing my face.

My heart stuttered in my chest as I felt the full impact of his stare on me.

"Kiss me," I whispered back, my hand resting on his chest.

His face lowered toward mine, his eyes never leaving mine until I had to close them at the intensity of his stare. I felt his hand gently cup my cheek, and a moment later, his lips softly brushed against mine. My tongue peeked out, wanting to wet my lips, but the moment my tongue touched his lips, tasting him, feeling his breath hitch slightly, I moaned lowly in need.

Will's lips slammed down on mine, gentleness gone as his mouth devoured mine. His tongue plunged into my mouth, tangling with mine, the kiss somehow soft and hard, all at once. My hands wrapped around the back of his neck, pulling him closer until my breasts were pressed against his chest, our lips never stopping. The kiss went on and on with little breaks just to breathe air before going right back, like we were two magnets that couldn't stay separated for long.

"Will," I sighed, opening my eyes for a moment to stare into his.

His eyes were dilated, his breath just as rough as mine, and he tightened his grip on the back of my neck, pulling me back into the kiss.

The kiss grew hungry, and soon, we were tearing each other's clothes off, our hands clumsy as we raced to get naked. Will softly pushed me down on the bed, his hands pulling my bra off as I lay down. His hands soon followed, playing with my nipples, tweaking and pinching with expertise as I writhed on my bed, trying in vain to pull him closer.

My hands reached out blindly and latched on to his buckle, and I struggled between wanting to get it unbuckled and wanting his weight on top of me. One particular suck of his mouth on my nipple had me moaning loudly, and when he traveled to my neck to continue the onslaught, I pulled him on top of me, forgetting all about his buckle. He paused after a long minute and pulled his shirt off, tossing it on the floor. His eyes perused my body with hunger, eyes nearly black with lust, which had me squirming beneath him.

My eyes landed on his chest, firm and toned, like he spent hours at the gym. Without much thought, I leaned forward and kissed along his chest, licking his nipple lightly. He made a sound deep in his throat, and so, I did it again, this time moving to his other nipple and sucking lightly. I moved my hand up his leg until I was rubbing his erection through his pants, my lips still trailing kissing all over his chest. He groaned low, undoing his belt and pants quickly before lying on top of me on the bed. His hands traced up and down my body, chest brushing against mine, as he pulled my face to his in a fierce kiss, his hips between my legs.

"Are you sure you want to do this?" he asked, pulling away after a second. "We don't have to have sex tonight."

"I don't want to wait, Will. I just …" I leaned my face into him, nose bumping gently into his, lips brushing as I whispered into his mouth, "I want to be with you."

I wrapped my legs around his hips and ground my lower half along his, eliciting a moan from both of our mouths. I was soaked, I could tell without even touching that he had me wetter than I'd ever been with any other guy.

I continued to grind slowly against him, and I almost cried in relief when he pressed against me, his hand lowering to the part of me that needed relief the most. He played with my clit as two of his fingers entered me, fucking me with his fingers until he had me crying out for him.

My hand wrapped around his cock as I tried to guide him into me. He was so incredibly hard and thick, and I worried for half a second if it would hurt but I wanted it too badly to care.

"You want me inside of you?" he murmured into my ear, his fingers moving faster inside of me, his thumb pressing against my clit. "Don't you want to come on my fingers?"

"No," I moaned, my fingers locked in his silky black hair as I pulled him down for a hard kiss, sucking on his tongue. "Please, Will."

He pulled his fingers out of me, and I moaned at the loss. But a moment later, I heard the sound of a condom wrapper, and I saw the outline of his hand as he wrapped himself up. His hand moved between my inner thighs, and he pulled my legs more widely apart before lying between them.

Will's face hovered above mine, his hair lightly brushing against my cheek as he peppered kisses across my face. "You're the kind of girl who's going to turn my whole world upside down, aren't you?"

I stared up at him, his words ringing in my ear. I kissed him softly, my tongue tracing his lips as he slowly started to enter me. My breath hitched in my throat at the feel of him inside of me, and when he was seated to the hilt, he started to grind himself against me slowly, eliciting a cry from me and a deep groan from him.

I wrapped my legs more securely around the backs of his thighs, the best I could do with how widely he had me spread, and tried to move myself on him, needing to feel him on me. As if he knew what I wanted, he placed his hand on my waist and slowly pulled out before slamming back in. He did that again and again, grinding down on me with each thrust, his groans accompanying every time I tightened against him.

"Will," I cried out, my nails digging into his back with each thrust.

Never had sex felt like this. I was ready to climax already, and that never happened for me. Ever.

I started meeting him thrust for thrust, kissing every part of him I could reach as he continued pumping into me. His hand gripped my ass as he angled me to get deeper, his mouth latched on to my neck.

Sweat glistened on his chest, making him slide easily against my body with each passing minute, his thrusts never stopping, never slowing, and I could feel the signs of my orgasm getting closer and closer.

Yes, I chanted to myself. *Yes, yes, yes*.

I bit down onto his lip, sucking it roughly into my mouth before letting it go to cry out again as he changed his angle, somehow moving *deeper* inside me.

"Genesis, *fuck*," he grunted as his thrusts gained momentum, and I moved with him, my arms wrapped around his shoulders, moaning loudly. His hips slapped against me, the sound loud in the quiet room filled with our moans.

"Will!" I moaned loudly. "I-I need—"

His hand reached down, rubbing against my clit as his thrusts got quicker, rougher, and a moment later, I felt myself let go, losing myself in the bliss, my head tossed back as I writhed uncontrollably against him. Shortly after, I heard him groan lowly as he planted himself deep inside me, his mouth taking mine in a sloppy kiss that I felt down to my toes, the aftershocks of my orgasm still running through my body.

After a few seconds of labored breathing on both our parts, loud in the now-quiet room, Will moved off me, but after taking the condom off and disposing of it, he threw his arm around my stomach, keeping me close to him.

"Don't go," I breathed hard, overwhelmed with how much I was feeling right now. I turned to hide my face in his chest, legs tangling with his.

His arm tightened around me, and I felt his lips on my forehead. "I'm not going anywhere, Buttercup."

We lay in each other's arms for a long moment, and I realized suddenly that in our rush to be together, I'd never actually said to Will exactly how I felt.

I sat up slightly, rustling Will, who looked drowsy and content. "Will, I need you to know something."

He wrapped his arms around my waist, trying to pull me in for a kiss but I stopped him. "What is it?"

"I want to be with you," I blurted, watching his eyes soften and his lips tilt into a soft smile. "I like you, and I'm realizing that I might have liked you for a while now, so if you are still interested in being something more—"

"You are it for me," he said firmly. "You've been it for me for a long time now, Buttercup. I'm yours if you'll have me."

My heart stuttered in my chest, and I felt overwhelmed with happiness and love as I cupped his cheek in my hand, forehead resting against his. "I want you, Will. You mean everything to me."

His eyes flashed with emotion, and a moment later, he kissed me, hugging me tightly to his chest.

And in that moment, I'd never felt safer.

26

When I woke up the next day, it took me a moment to remember.

My mouth was smiling before I even opened my eyes, and I blindly reached my arm toward the other side of the bed. Except there was no one there.

I opened my eyes and looked around the empty room.

He left.

I shook the thought away as soon as it entered my mind. That wasn't Will.

Last night played on repeat in my head—his words, his touch, how he'd held me in bed as we kissed and whispered to each other until we fell asleep. But more than that, the one thing I knew about Will was that he never said something he didn't mean.

I reached for my phone, which was still in my pants pocket on the floor. There are a few unread messages on my phone from Yari, which I click on.

> *Yari: Alejandra and I are going out shopping. P.S. You two are so cute together. ;)*

Beneath the text was a photo of Will and me sleeping in my bed, obviously taken from my door. Will was wrapped around me like a koala, his face cuddled into the back of my neck, his naked chest pressed against my back.

"That crazy *puta*," I muttered to myself, smiling despite how freaking weird it was that she'd taken this photo of us this morning.

I heard a loud clang from outside my room, and I lifted my head from my phone. It sounded like pans or pots, something metal moving around. I stood up and looked on the floor for a T-shirt, stooping down to pick up Will's T-shirt. I pulled it over my head, and the shirt stopped mid-thigh, slightly baggy. I lifted the shirt to my nose and sniffed, smelling his cologne and spices.

I quickly pulled a pair of underwear on and opened my bedroom door, the smell of bacon and delicious breakfast foods permeating the air. I walked down the hall and into the kitchen, where Will was scooping some eggs onto two plates, bare-chested and wearing boxer briefs.

He looked up when I entered, his eyes scanning me from head to toe in a way that had me remembering last night all over again. "I like you in my shirt."

I smiled, walking closer. "I like you in my kitchen."

He put the pan down on the stove and pulled me into his body, arms circling my back. "Good morning."

"Morning." I kissed him, leaning up on my tippy-toes to get closer. I pulled back a moment later, embarrassed and trying to cover my lips with my hand. "Wait, I have morning breath—"

"I don't care." He pulled my fingers away from my mouth and pressed his lips back on mine.

We stood there in my kitchen, lips moving softly over one another, and for the first time since I'd woken up, I felt at ease. Will pulled away, pressing kisses to my cheeks, nose, and lips, and I smiled, keeping my eyes closed.

"Are you hungry?"

I nodded, tilting my face up for more kisses.

I felt his smile against my neck before he pulled away. "Let's eat."

After using the bathroom, I met Will at the dining room table, a full plate and an orange juice waiting for me in the seat across from him.

"This looks amazing." I rubbed my bare foot against his leg. "Thank you."

Will leaned over the table, his hand cupping the back of my head as he pulled me in for a deep kiss. His tongue played with mine, and I moaned, leaning closer and nearly sticking my whole hand into my plate of food.

He pulled away, a glint of hunger in his eyes. "If you touch me, we won't make it through breakfast. And I need you to eat before I fuck you again."

I exhaled, licking my lips. "Again?"

"Again and again," he confirmed, pressing a kiss to my throat before sitting back in his seat. "If I have it my way, I'll have my girlfriend all to myself today."

Girlfriend.

I couldn't stop the grin that spread across my face as I sat back in my seat. "That can be arranged."

"One more time," I gasped into his mouth, straddling him as I ground against him, gripping the couch cushion behind him.

"Fuck, I'll never get enough of you," he groaned against my lips, his fingers digging into the backs of my thighs. His forehead leaned against mine for a second, both of us breathing heavily as we tried to catch our breath. "God, how did I last this long without you?"

"Will," I said like a breathless plea. My thighs tightened against his waist, and I kind of ... unconsciously ground my pussy against his lower stomach. "Oh, that feels so good."

I did it again, my breath coming out in pants against his lips as I watched my hips undulate in his hands, my lower half rubbing scandalously against him. Will shifted me in his arms a bit, his hands now on my ass, and he took control of my movements. His hands moved me roughly over him, and I nearly moaned out loud when I felt his hard cock beneath me. We were both still naked from the last round, our clothes scattered around the apartment after breakfast almost two hours ago. I should've been exhausted, but all it had taken was one brush of my hand against his body or one look from those dangerously sexy eyes, and I had jumped him.

"I want to fuck you just like this," he growled against my lips, and my eyes shot up to his.

But he wasn't looking at me.

His eyes were glued to my wide hips, to watching me dry-hump him, his rough hands gripping my ass tightly. His eyes closed tightly a moment later when I pressed down hard against his erection, and he groaned loudly. "Oh fuck."

More than loving that Will was able to set my body alight was being able to see how much I affected him and watching him become overcome with passion. I thought it turned me on more, seeing how responsive he was to how I was making him feel. It made me feel sexy that I could get him so turned on that he couldn't control the sounds he made, couldn't control the words he said.

Such dirty words. I would've never thought Will was someone who liked to talk during sex, much less talk dirty during sex, but he was. And, oh, how I loved it.

I became entranced with watching him watch me. I wasn't thinking about the stretch marks that covered the tops of my thighs or the way that I had just enough fat on my thick thighs and ass that they jiggled with every glide or slap of our bodies moving against each other. My body felt like it was on fire, and I could feel myself losing control.

"Lift your hips, Buttercup," he murmured against my lips.

I complied, my breath hitching in my throat when I felt his cock slide against the seam of my pussy. My fingers wrapped around his shoulder as I looked down between our bodies to see where we were about to be one.

We'd already talked with each other about both being clean, and I was on birth control, so we'd decided to forgo condoms, wanting to experience each other without anything between us.

He teased my entrance with his cock until I was writhing above him in half-desperation, nearly moaning if it weren't for my clenched teeth holding the sound inside.

"Will," I breathed, tightening my fingers in his hair until he looked up at me.

His eyes gleamed hungrily as he licked his lips. "How do you want it?"

"Huh?" I asked, distracted by the way his tongue traced over my lips before entering my mouth in a kiss so filthy that I felt myself getting wetter as I imagined his thrusts mimicking the exact rhythm of his tongue.

"Fast, hard, slow, deep?" he asked, pale fingers tracing along the curve of my waist and gripping my hip in his large hand.

My light-brown skin had patches of red from his mouth and grip, and I loved knowing that I'd have these reminders of him all over my body for the next few days.

"Yes," I pleaded, pulling him in for another kiss.

Will groaned against my lips, and a moment later, I felt his cock push against my entrance as it began to slowly enter me, inch by inch.

"You're mine," he gasped out his demand, wonder shining in his eyes beneath me. Like he couldn't believe he got to say those words, and it made my heart clench, even as I felt myself fading already to the overwhelming feeling of his cock inside me.

His fingers gripped my ass, and he controlled my movements, how fast or slow he impaled me on his cock. It was the sweetest torture—the way he would start a fast pace, and just when I was close, he'd jerk my body to a stop, his hands slowly moving me up and down his cock as his mouth wrapped around my dusky-brown nipple.

After a few minutes, I couldn't take the teasing any longer, and I tightened against him. Will cursed, his grip turning tight, and he held me in place as he thrust into me roughly from below. Nothing in the world could stop me from screaming out, my orgasm coursing through me, his groans like music to my ears as he followed me over the edge.

I lay on his chest, breathing quickly as I tried to catch my breath. His fingers traced patterns on my back, his other hand lazily caressing my ass, like he couldn't help himself.

I picked my head up off his chest and found Will staring at me with a cocky smirk.

"Your legs are twitching."

I huffed, playfully rolling my eyes. "Someone's feeling mighty full of themselves."

"I'm full of something," he murmured, thrusting lazily into me, already half-hard.

I moaned but pulled away. "No. My vagina needs a break from your dick."

"One day into our relationship, and you're already asking for a break," Will teased, leaning up to speak against my lips. "I'm hurt."

I chuckled, taking a deep breath and exhaling as I moved up and off of Will. "We can kiss and make up later."

I stretched my hands up in the air, arching my back slightly.

Will's hand slid up my back and around to cup my small breast before moving down to cup my pussy. "Maybe we can kiss and make each other feel better in an hour?"

"You are insatiable," I said, pretending to be scandalized.

I pulled his shirt back on and stood up, glancing down as Will sat up on the couch. My eyes landed on his dick, and I had to force my eyes away and remind myself that we couldn't have sex all day.

Will shrugged, not denying my accusation. "Going off how soaked my thighs were while you humped my leg earlier and begged for my cock, I'd say, you're just as insatiable."

I gasped, cheeks turning red. "Will!"

He stood up, pausing to kiss me on my lips. "It's okay, Buttercup. That's what makes you so perfect for me."

I shook my head, mouth twitching into a smile. "I'm using the bathroom. When I come back, you'd better have your underwear on!"

I giggled when I heard Will's groan, all but skipping to the bathroom.

When I finished cleaning up, I walked back into the living room to see Will wearing his suit pants from yesterday and smell the popcorn in the air.

"What's going on?" I asked, watching him pull the bag out of the microwave and into a big bowl.

"We're going to watch some TV together." Will finished pouring the popcorn into the bowl.

"What are we going to watch?"

He grinned. "I thought it was about time that you finally watched *The Office*."

"Is that the show you judged me for not watching back at the Christmas party last year?"

"I still can't believe you thought Dwight was Will Ferrell in *Elf*." He shook his head, a smile peeking out. "This is why this watch is necessary."

I playfully rolled my eyes. "You get the popcorn, and I'll set up the TV."

It took only a few minutes to get everything ready.

Will pressed play and kissed the side of my face before leaning back against the sofa. I was slightly worried I wasn't going to like the show, especially when the first episode was kind of cringy, and I could feel Will staring at me every five seconds to see my reaction. But somewhere between the first episode and the fourth, I became totally engrossed in it. I was laughing my ass off every few minutes, and when I wasn't laughing, I was joking with Will about what stupid thing Michael had said or done next in the show.

I was pretty sure I said, "Oh my God, he did not just do that," at least twenty times.

Two hours passed by in a blur, and I realized the time when the end credits for the episode rolled on the screen and I saw that it said the next episode was for season two.

"Holy crap, season two already?" I exclaimed, moving my head from its resting place on Will's shoulder.

Somewhere during the last six episodes, I'd gotten comfortable on the sofa. Will was lying down on his back, and I was lying against him—my head on his chest, my legs tangled with his, and my hand resting on his side. His hands had moved sporadically from my back to playing with my hair throughout the last few hours, and even though I didn't say anything, I thought he could tell that I really loved his hands in my hair. Every time he did it, I had to fight back the urge to purr, but I couldn't stop myself from burrowing deeper against him and sighing contentedly.

"Season one is a really short season," he explained. "I should probably start heading out soon."

I sat up, feeling disappointed even though I had known realistically that he'd have to go home eventually. "Okay."

"Next weekend, I have a gig," Will said, pushing my hair behind my shoulders before leaning in to kiss my cheek. "I want to take you out on a date. Come watch me play, and I'll take you to dinner after?"

I smiled, nodding. "Yes, I'd love that."

He grinned, kissing me lightly on the lips. "Then, it's a date."

"It's a date."

The Breaksters, the bar where Will was performing, was packed by the time we got there.

I'd been here a few times before, but I'd never seen it this crowded. I knew that he had a pretty big fan base, one that was only continuing to grow, but seeing its reality was a whole different thing.

More than anything, I felt proud of him. And so incredibly happy. He deserved every ounce of success, and seeing people recognize his talent and appreciate it made me feel light as air.

"Come meet the band," Will said, his hand tugging mine toward the side of the stage.

I followed his eyes and saw three guys standing together by a bunch of equipment, laughing and talking.

"I thought you were a one-man act?" I asked—well, kind of yelled really. It was pretty hard to hear with all the loud chattering and excited people.

"I am for the most part," Will answered, turning his head so I could read his lips. "But for bigger gigs, we typically play together."

I nodded, and a moment later, we stopped in front of them. The three guys turned toward us, and I immediately grinned when I saw a big hulk of a man with a familiar face.

"Callum," I shouted, pulling away from Will so I could go hug him.

Callum grinned when he saw me and picked me up in a tight hug, spinning me as I laughed. I honestly felt like a rag doll in his hold—that was how much bigger he was than me.

"Genesis, you made it."

The moment he put me down, I felt Will's chest at my back, his hand going to my waist. I looked back at him, and he smiled, his eyes happy.

"Genesis, you already know Callum. He's sometimes my bass guitarist and backup singer," Will started, and Callum gave a dramatic bow, making me chuckle. Will's hand pointed to the two guys next to Callum. "And this is Sam, my drummer and Zander, my keyboardist."

I shook hands with them both, assessing them as they either smiled or nodded back at me. Sam had a mop of red hair and the cutest smile. He had this sort of mischievous look to him, and I had the feeling he was the kind of guy that liked trouble. Where Callum looked like he liked trouble of the lady variety, Sam looked like the he liked trouble of the chaos variety. From appearance, he was probably around my age, if not a year or two younger maybe.

Zander, on the other hand, gave me a completely different vibe. When I shook hands with him, his shake was firm, and he only nodded at me and said nothing else. He didn't seem like he was mad or angry about seeing me, and I didn't feel uncomfortable by him at all. It was more like he was somewhere else. His eyes were distant, like he wasn't even here, and it didn't really matter to him one way or another what we were talking about. He had dark brown skin and short, dark hair, his build strong but not overly muscular.

After he'd shaken my hand, he had taken out his cell phone, and whatever he had seen or not seen made him bite down on his bottom lip. It was then that I had seen the appearance of two dimples on each side of his cheeks. I had a feeling he had a beautiful smile, but going off first impressions, I'd have to say not many saw it.

The guys started talking about their set, and Will put his arm around my shoulders, pulling me into his side as he talked. I wrapped my arm around his waist, half-listening as they bounced ideas off each other, my mind wandering.

I could tell they had a great bond together and that they all loved music. Their bodies were practically eating up the energy, excited to get on the stage and perform. Even Zander, with all his seriousness, was excited, his hand continually drifting toward his keyboard case.

I wondered about how they felt about Will possibly getting a contract deal and if they would be a part of it with him. I knew that Will didn't play with them all the time, but it was clear that they were a family, and I couldn't imagine Will not making an effort for them to join him if they wanted.

It wasn't long before they had to start setting up onstage, and with a final kiss, I took a seat at a nearby table. Every so often, Will would glance back at me, as if to make sure I was still there, and I'd smile each time.

"Hey, everyone. Welcome!" Will said into the mic, and immediately, the room went crazy with shouts and cheers.

I cheered along, clapping my hands and grinning, and Will glanced toward me and winked.

Finally, once it quieted down, Will laughed and continued, "Wow, thanks for that warm welcome, guys! I'm so happy you were all able to make it down tonight. For those who might not know, I'm Will Kobayashi, and I'll be your musical entertainment for the night."

"Baby, I'll entertain you all night," someone shouted from the crowd, and quite a few girls shouted agreements, making Will laugh.

I didn't even let it get to me because things like this were typical for any musician, and really, if I couldn't handle this crap now, I wouldn't be able to handle it when he was doing concerts in sold-out arenas.

Wow, look at me, thinking positively and imagining a future with someone. I surprised myself more and more each day, especially when the thought hadn't immediately set me into deep panic and made me want to run for the door.

"I have some really great songs I want to share with you—some old, some new," Will continued, "I'm going to start the night off with an original you all might be familiar with. It's called 'Kismet.'"

The song started out with a slow melody on the guitar, but before long, the drums and keyboard accompany him, and I found myself tapping my feet along to the intro. Will started singing, and as always, I was unable to look away. At this point, I knew his voice by heart, but it still blew me away every time he sang.

The song he was singing was about meeting a girl who made him feel like he belonged, and after years of orbiting each other, they finally met in a kismet clash. The lyrics were so beautiful, and even as I swayed to the beat, my heart squeezing in my chest at my overwhelming emotions for him, I wondered briefly about who this girl was.

Was it an ex? Was it a song just based on a feeling he had randomly?

I knew better than anyone that sometimes, inspiration for songs came from literally anywhere. I'd once written a tragic love song after watching a commercial about cancer patients at a local hospital. Sometimes, we wrote songs that we didn't necessarily relate to, but it was an emotion we'd felt in that moment. Composing music for me had always felt a lot like creating a story. It didn't necessarily have to be my story; it could be the story of any girl or boy, whoever I created inside my head when I thought of what I wanted to compose.

He seamlessly moved from one song to the next, always giving the crowd exactly what they needed. I got lost in just watching and listening to him perform. He was so comfortable up there, and just watching him tonight had further resolved for me that it was where he belonged.

"We have one last song for you guys tonight," he said into the microphone, smiling when the crowd began to simultaneously cheer and boo. He sat down on the stool, holding the acoustic guitar on his lap, and the lights faded to focus on him. "This is a new cover that I've never done before. It's for a girl who came crashing into my life two years ago, and I haven't been the same since. For a long time, I didn't understand her, the way she could be so strong and yet so closed off to everyone around her, and no matter how hard I tried, I just couldn't get through her walls. But with time, I learned her secret language, and I learned not to focus just on her words, but also her voice. And her voice told me everything that her words couldn't say. This song is called 'You Sang to Me.'"

Heart pounding in my throat, I watched as he began to play the beginning chords to the song, and I felt like I was in a daze. He was singing a Marc Anthony song. And his voice was … it was like he was singing straight to my soul. I listened to every note that left his mouth, and I felt myself falling dangerously in love with this man who knew me down to my core. He saw me, the beautiful and the ugly, and he liked me anyway.

I thought about his words, how he'd been trying to get to know me all this time, and he was right; I was closed off. I'd been scared to let him in even an inch, but I knew now that even when I'd been so determined to hate him, I never did. Even as I hated him, I was thinking about him. I'd seek information about him and tell myself it was because I needed to know my enemy, but really, I'd just wanted to know him.

I looked around me, and I saw that I wasn't the only person mesmerized by Will. The whole place was swaying and singing along, so many emotions across their faces. This was where Will belonged. Not in some office building, working with numbers, but up there onstage, making a difference with his voice.

When he finished the last note of the song, the place went crazy with cheers and clapping. I eagerly rose to my feet and clapped as hard and as loud as I could, a huge grin on my face, even as tears threatened to fall.

As Will and the guys waved and grinned at the crowd, I couldn't help but wonder how drastically different my life would have been if I had never been picked to work with Will. I wasn't one to believe in fate or destiny, but after years of us circling each other, it felt right. It felt like it was meant to happen for a reason. We had come into each other's lives at the right time, and even if we didn't win the contest next month, I'd know that I'd made an impact on his life, and he'd certainly made an impact on mine.

When I saw Will and the guys walk off the stage, I eagerly move toward them, pushing people out of the way as they stood to stretch and get more drinks. There was supposed to be another performance from someone else in twenty minutes, but until then, the bar had already moved back to their playlist to play through the stereos.

Will turned, his smile widening when he saw me walking toward him. The moment I was within touching distance from him, he pulled me into a tight hug, one I gladly returned.

"Will, you were so amazing," I gushed, pulling back a bit so that I could look at him.

His eyes were dark, but I could tell he was just a ball of adrenaline, the rush of the performance still coursing through him.

I leaned in and brushed a soft kiss against his mouth. "I'm so proud of you."

His eyes stayed locked with mine, and when I finished, he squeezed me tighter to him, my chest now firmly pressed against his. "I loved having you here."

I smiled at that, feeling my stomach flip at his words. "This is my favorite gig I've ever been to."

"Aww, you two are so fucking cute," Cal teased, standing to the side. "Genesis has you wrapped around her finger, Kobayashi."

Sam chuckled, running a hand through his hair, his other hand laying a cold bottle of water against his neck. "Fine by me. That means, more groupies for me."

I chose to ignore that comment and instead focused back on Will. He was watching me, a small, amused smile on his face.

"You really were great," I told him again.

"Thanks," Will replied, pressing quick, small kisses against my lips. His hands that were resting on my waist squeezed gently before he stepped back. "I need to help them put the equipment back in Zander's van, but after that, we can head out."

"Sounds good," I replied, missing his touch already.

"Nah, you guys have to come out and celebrate with us!" Cal protested, throwing an arm around my and Will's shoulders.

"I'm only interested in celebrating with one person tonight," Will said, tossing a wink my way before moving back toward the equipment.

Cal pouted, and I couldn't help the laugh that broke free from my lips.

In that moment, I felt happy in a way that I hadn't felt in a long time. Nothing about my life was the way I'd predicted it to be, but it somehow felt perfect anyway. I couldn't believe that Will Kobayashi was one of the reasons that I was feeling this happy. For years, we had driven each other crazy, but now, I couldn't imagine not seeing Will every day. For the first time in maybe my whole life, I felt optimistic. I wasn't trying to see the end or convince myself of all the reasons why this wasn't going to work.

It felt amazing. And it was all because of Will.

I awoke the next day in a cocoon of warmth.

I took a deep breath, my cheek nestled in the most comfortable pillow I'd ever laid my head on, a heavy pressure on my waist. That pressure squeezed on my stomach, and it took me a second to realize that it was Will's arm wrapped around me, my face smooshed half on the pillow, half on his forearm.

My eyes fluttered open, a part of me fighting that feeling of waking up, wanting to snuggle back into my Will pillow and go back to sleep, but the bigger part of me—namely, my bladder—did not think I could wait another minute before I needed to get up.

The first thing I saw when I opened my eyes was Will's bedside table with the little Empire State Building figurine that I'd bought him all those months ago during our impromptu outing. The sight of it made me smile and then laugh softly at the craziness of that day.

I slowly turned my head toward Will, my hair tickling against my cheek. His face was teetering on the end of his pillow, almost like he had tried to join his head with mine, his eyes still closed as he slept quietly beside me. I studied his face, the way his mouth was tilted up in one corner, like he was smiling in his dream, his face free of worries. He looked peaceful, like an angel. All sharp angles that became soft in sleep, full lips that looked as gentle as a cloud. I found myself getting lost in just staring at him, the need to pee a distant demand. I felt a pull in my chest, this yearning to be inside his dreams, to see what was making him look so content. I wanted to know what his dreams were, and I wanted to make them come true.

I cared about Will Kobayashi. A lot.

Too much, a part of me whispered. That scared part of me that didn't want to get hurt.

But I trusted Will. Sometimes, it felt like I trusted him more than I'd ever trusted anyone in my life.

Every day, that feeling became stronger, and I didn't know how much longer I could hold it in. What was the emotion for when you couldn't imagine life without someone by your side?

I carefully peeled myself out from under Will's arm and off his bed. It was too early to overthink what I was feeling, and I knew by now that starting that train was just asking to get sucked into uncertainties. I tiptoed out of his room and toward the bathroom, yanking Will's already-long shirt further down my legs in case Callum was out in the living room. But the apartment was dead quiet, Callum's door open and bed unmade. I could only assume he never came home last night.

I made the quick trek to the bathroom, my legs squeezing together as I cursed under my breath and searched aimlessly for the light. Why was it the closer you got to the bathroom, the more you felt like your bladder would just explode? I gave up on the light switch and just rushed toward the toilet, barely managing to plop down on the seat before sighing in relief.

After cleaning up, I finally found the light switch on the wall, and I turned it on. My brown eyes danced with bright spots as they became accustomed to the bright bathroom, and I blinked a few times as I waited for my face to become a clear picture in the mirror. But instead of focusing on my face in the mirror, I froze as I took in the little notes written on music sheet paper taped to the mirror.

When you see yourself, what do you see? I see an extraordinary woman who has the world at her fingertips and yet remains so humble. I see the care that the universe took in creating someone so imperfectly perfect—from your gentle soul to your silent scars.

I see you. All of you, and I love every molecule that makes up your being.

Do you see what I see?

My eyes didn't know where to focus, taking in the beautiful words that Will had written for me.
When did he do this?
It had to have been after I fell asleep last night.
To think he'd stayed up and written these notes for me to see when I woke up ...
I felt my eyes well with emotion that I fought to tamp down. My eyes bounced between the different notes—some serious, like the first one, but others silly and sweet. My eyes snagged on a note left in the middle of the mirror, almost covering where my lips would be. I leaned closer to read it, heart thumping loudly in my ears.

Wake me with a kiss, Buttercup. I want your lips to be the first thing I feel, your face to be the first thing I see, your tongue to be the first thing I taste.

I backed away from the mirror and walked slowly out of the bathroom. My head felt full with thoughts, but they were all centered on one objective—kiss Will.
I crawled up the bed on my hands and knees until I was hovering over his body, Will now lying on his back, arm thrown out toward my side of the bed. I leaned down and brushed my lips against his, moving my mouth across his cheek

to press quick, little kisses until I reached his nose, kissing it quietly while I stared down at him. I watched as his eyes fluttered open, and I bit down on my lip as I waited nervously to see his reaction.

Will's dark eyes met with mine, and I could no sooner open my mouth to talk before his arms wrapped around me and pulled me down on him, his lips colliding with mine. We kissed softly, lips brushing back and forth against each other in a silent hello. I curled my fingers in his hair as Will positioned us on our sides, his tongue pressing against my lips in a quiet demand. I opened willingly and snuggled closer to him as we continued to kiss, tongues tangling with each other.

I pulled away after a moment and looked up into his eyes. "Morning."

Will lowered his forehead on mine, gently rubbing his nose against mine. "Best wake-up kiss ever."

I laughed softly and kissed him quickly on his lips again, watching the range of emotions play through his face, as if he was accepting that kiss with his whole soul.

I pushed on his shoulders until he lay on his back, and I straddled his legs, leaning over him as I whispered across his lips, "I saw your notes in the bathroom."

His hands clutched my thighs lightly, and he murmured, "Is that so?"

I nodded, moving slowly down his body, planting kisses along his neck and chest as I spoke. "The things you wrote ... they were beautiful."

"I write what I see and what I know," he answered, breath stuttering as my lips skimmed lightly down his stomach, my hands on either side of his boxer briefs. "Genesis—"

"You make me so happy, Will," I said, feeling shy with the truth. I forced myself to maintain eye contact, wanting him to see the truth in my eyes as I whispered, "I see you too. All of you."

His eyes darkened with emotion, hands tightening on my thighs. I pulled on his underwear in a silent question, and Will lifted his hips for me, his hands gliding up my body, up my back, and to my hair, which he fisted gently.

"You make me feel," he said, voice rough. "So intensely, Genesis."

Heart racing with a million feelings, I focused on his cock, which was standing at attention a few inches from my face. God, how could a penis be so beautiful? It had to be because it was attached to Will because I'd never looked at a penis and thought it was beautiful. But the thick ridges and the way it curved just a little bit at the top toward his stomach turned me on like no other.

I leaned down and ran my tongue along its side, up and down as I gripped the base in my hand. Will hissed, fingers clutching my hair for a second before he loosened his grip, like he was trying to fight against his instincts to guide my lips where he wanted them. Typically, I might try to tease him, really take my time in putting my lips around his cock, but this wasn't about torturing Will. And truthfully, I wanted my lips on him just as much as he did.

I trailed my tongue back up his cock till I got to the head and wrapped my lips around it as I sucked, slowly moving my mouth up and down. Will groaned loudly, hips jerking, and his cock slid deeper in my mouth. I moaned, shifting my thighs against each other as I continued to suck up and down, building a steady rhythm with my hand and mouth.

"Fuck," Will cursed, and I looked up at him, mouth suctioned on his cock to see him looking down at me with a pained expression. "Oh fuck, Genesis, don't stop. You look so beautiful with my cock in your mouth."

I moaned, taking him deeper into my mouth. Will cursed loudly, his hands gripping my hair tightly as he started thrusting up into my mouth. He was so big that I knew getting all of him in my mouth wouldn't be easy, my throat needing time to open up for him. Seeing him lose control made me feel wild with pleasure, wetness coating the inside of my thighs.

Will loosened his grip on my hair after a few more thrusts, allowing me time to come up for air, and murmured, "Deep breaths, Buttercup. I want to finish in your mouth, baby. Are you going to let me come down that gorgeous throat?"

I kissed up and down his shaft, my hand massaging his balls lightly as I moaned my approval. I lifted my head and looked up toward Will and his intense, dark eyes. "I—"

"Will, wake up, you sleepy—oh shit!" a young feminine voice shrieked.

I froze, realizing a split second later that I was ass up with only a thong on, fully on display to whoever that voice belonged to. Will moved much faster than me, cursing loudly as he swiftly pulled the covers over us, yanking me up to his side.

"Kata, what the fuck?" he shouted, and I looked toward the young girl with dawning horror.

She looked like she couldn't be older than seventeen or eighteen with delicate features and short, dark hair that stopped beneath her chin. Her big, dark eyes were wide in horror, cheeks red, and she looked about as mortified as I imagined I looked.

Will's younger sister had just walked in on me giving her brother a blow job.

"I'm sorry!" she shouted, turning around quickly and even covering her eyes for extra measure. "I'm so sorry! I didn't know—I thought you heard the door—I—oh my God, I can't believe I just saw that!"

"This can't be happening," I whispered, embarrassed tears filling my eyes.

I'd never felt so embarrassed in my life, and I would pay anything, give up anything, to disappear right in this moment. I covered my face with my hands, not wanting to be seen, and I felt Will's arm wrap around my shoulders, his face pressed against the top of my head in comfort.

He said something sharply in Japanese to Kata, and she responded back, sounding defensive. They talked for a few more seconds before Kata promptly left the room, closing the door behind her. I keep my face hidden behind my hands, even as I felt Will turning his body toward mine.

"Genesis," he called out quietly.

"Tell me that wasn't your sister," I said, my words muffled by my hands still pressed against my face.

"It was," he answered, and I could hear the apology in his voice. "I'm so sorry that happened. I had no idea that they were coming over today. They weren't supposed to arrive until tomorrow."

I jerked my head up, turning to look at him with wild eyes, my voice rising to a high pitch as I squeaked, "They?!"

A look of hesitation crossed his face before he admitted, "My parents. They're here for a visit."

Could this moment get any worse?

"Will ... I can't go out there."

His family had come down for a few days to celebrate his mom's birthday in the city. It was the one gift that she'd wanted, for them all to be together since he couldn't stay in California for New Year's Eve a few months ago.

We finished getting dressed, and I could hear Kata talking quietly with someone in the living room, where we were expected to be in just a few moments.

But I couldn't do it. It was too much. How was I supposed to go out there and meet Will's parents and his sister after what she'd just walked in on? I couldn't even imagine what she was thinking of me or what his parents would think of me, knowing that I had obviously slept in bed with Will. What if they judged me or thought I wasn't good enough for their son? What if—

"Genesis," Will said, hands cupping my cheeks and snapping me out of my thoughts. His eyes bored into mine. "Breathe. It's going to be okay. They already love you."

"What?" My head jerked back a bit in confusion, eyebrows furrowing. "How could they love me when they don't even know me? They probably think I'm a groupie who isn't as serious about their career and is just working with you to ride your coattails—"

"No," he said firmly, anger coursing through his eyes, jaw tight. "Do not for even a second think that you are not talented or good enough. Don't ever give anyone that kind of power over you, especially my parents."

I shook my head, even as his words warmed my heart. "But I want them to …" *Like me,* I wanted to say, but I suddenly felt shy and stupid for even thinking it. Why was it still so hard for me to tell him how I felt? Was I ever going to get comfortable with telling people that I cared about them? It frustrated me enough that I blurted out, "I want to make a good impression."

Will smiled softly at my admission and repeated, "It's going to be okay, I promise. Trust me."

I took a deep breath and let it out loudly, nodding my head. "Okay, I trust you."

Will's smile brightened then, taking over his entire face until it felt like staring at the sun because of how brightly it lit up the room. He pulled me in close and hugged me to his chest, squeezing me tightly to him, and spoke against the top of my head. "You make me so happy."

I squeezed him back, heart thumping in my chest at the unsaid words. "Right back at ya."

Will chuckled lightly, pulling away but holding on to my hand as he nodded toward his door. "Ready?"

I nodded, focusing on my breathing as we walked toward his door and into the living room. Kata was in the kitchen with her mother, pouring water into three cups as her mom inspected the fridge. Both of them looked up toward us, but I focused on his mom, not quite ready to make eye contact with Kata.

His mom was short, probably around five-two, and had straight black hair that touched the tips of her shoulders. Her face was striking, and even though I'd told myself I didn't want to look toward Kata, I couldn't help but marvel at how much she looked like her mother. They both did. There were differences, of course; Will didn't have her delicate nose or her cheekbones, but the resemblance was there nonetheless.

"Morning," Will greeted in Japanese, letting go of my hand to wrap his mother in a hug.

She smiled and talked to him in rapid Japanese, pointing toward his fridge.

"Mom, I'm not going to talk about the contents of my fridge right now," Will said with a laugh. "We can go out for breakfast. I know a great diner in the neighborhood that makes the best chicken and waffles."

"I'm sold!" Kata cheered, passing her mom a cup of water as she hip-checked Will out of her way.

He looked down at her and pretended to wince in pain, which made her roll her eyes.

I stayed rooted to where he'd left me at the front of the kitchen, unsure of what to say or do, but Will didn't leave me hanging for long. He reached out his hand toward me, and I slowly grabbed it, giving him a nervous smile as he pulled me in front of his mom and sister.

"Mom, Kata," he started, grinning like I'd never seen him grin before, "this is Genesis."

"Hi," I said quietly, lips struggling to stay in a genuine smile as I focused on not fidgeting. "It's so nice to meet you both. Happy birthday, Mrs. Kobayashi."

I reached my hand out to shake her hand, but she pulled away from Will and reached out her arms wide as she said, "Can I hug?"

I nodded, shocked, and glanced at Will, whose grin got impossibly wider as he watched his mom pull me into a hug. I had a few inches on her, so I had to reach down a little to not make it awkward, but once I was in her arms, I couldn't help but feel such warmth and kindness.

"Wow, look at Mom, asking permission before hugging strangers," Kata joked, and when I glanced at her, she winked and added, "Mom has been dying to meet you for *years*."

Will coughed loudly, giving his sister a sharp look. "Okay, Mom, why don't you let her go now?"

His mom laughed softly but pulled away, grabbing my hands and squeezing them gently. "It's such an honor to meet you. You have made a great impact on my little boy's life."

I stared, dumbfounded, at her, mouth opening and closing like a fish. I looked up toward Will, who was now turning a bit red in the face, even as he threw me a sheepish grin. "Uh ..."

"Mom, please," Will said and then quickly glanced at me before switching to Japanese as he spoke to his mom.

"Big brother," Kata admonished, a playful glint in her eyes, "don't you know it's rude to speak another language in front of a guest who cannot understand?"

"Kata," Will started, but his mom interrupted him.

"No, Kata is right, Will," his mom said with a stern look at him. "We can talk later. You have a guest. Is this any way to treat your girlfriend? Do you want her to leave and never come back? Honestly, Hikaru."

I choked on a laugh, trying to hide my smile as I saw the wicked glee on Kata's face at getting her older brother in trouble. Will scowled at his sister, but I could tell there was no heat behind it, and instead, he kissed his mom on the cheek and smoothly walked over to me and intertwined our fingers again.

"It's okay, Mrs. Kobayashi," I said, shooting Will a smile. "My family constantly speaks Spanish in front of Will, so I guess it's only fair that he do the same now that he's with his family."

"Call me Sora, please," she said. Her phone rang, and with a quick glance at the screen, she shot me an apologetic smile. "I'm so sorry. It's my husband."

I smiled in understanding, and she stepped out of the kitchen and walked toward the front door.

"Sooo," Kata drawled, and I looked back toward her. She comically raised her eyebrows up and down as her eyes bounced between me and Will. "Should we talk about the very awkward elephant in the room?"

"Um, I'd rather we didn't," I mumbled, feeling my face get hot. I wanted to disappear, just thinking about the incident. "I'm really sorry—"

"Genesis, you have nothing to apologize for," Will stated, giving Kata a look filled with reprimand. "Kata, you know better than to just burst into someone's room without knocking. Today, you invaded not only my privacy, but Genesis's as well."

Kata looked ashamed, cheeks red and her face hidden behind her bob as she looked down at the floor. She was no longer the smiley and upbeat girl that I'd met in the kitchen ten minutes before, and that made me feel bad. It wasn't like she had known what we would be doing, and I didn't want her to get into trouble on my behalf.

"I probably should've locked the door when I got back from the bathroom," I blurted, shooting Kata a small smile. "Probably would've saved us all from that morning show, huh?"

Kata looked up from the floor and gave me a hesitant smile in return. "Yeah, but knowing me, I would've picked the lock before knocking. Sometimes, I forget about the whole privacy thing in my quest to get a rise out of Mr. Calm and Serious."

I chuckled, glancing up at Will, who was back to a relaxed expression. "Mr. Calm and Serious, huh? You should've seen him when I beat him at Uno after practice one night." My sister had been coming up the block as Will dropped me off one night and Aleja had invited him up for a game, always the nosy matchmaker. Now, I couldn't help but be grateful for it, for every single memory I had with him.

Will cracked a smile at that, eyes glued on mine as he turned fully toward me, pulling me closer to him. "And which version of the story are you going to tell her? The one where I won fair and square or the one where you cheated and had your sister deal you all Plus-Four cards?"

I immediately scoffed and exclaimed, "That's a lie! You have no proof that happened."

"I have plenty of proof," he declared confidently.

I couldn't help the grin that blossomed across my face and the laugh that came shortly after. Will's eyes moved hungrily from my eyes to my mouth to my throat, like he couldn't decide where to focus his attention. Like he wanted to look at all of me and capture my every expression, every movement, and imprint it all in his memory.

"Innocent until proven guilty," I triumphed with a squeal as he playfully growled and nipped at my ear.

"Admit the truth, you little thief," he grumbled in my ear, mouth softly kissing behind my ear, his fingers lightly tickling my sides.

"I admit nothing!" I wiggled in his arms, happiness floating from my voice like a song.

"Oh my God, you guys are so in love. It would be cute if it wasn't so disgusting," Kata declared from behind us.

I pulled away from Will, who was already shooting a glare at his sister—either for her comment or for interrupting, I didn't know.

"Disappear," he commanded, pulling me back into his arms.

Okay, so it was probably the latter.

"Will," I admonished, pulling away and turning to his sister, who was sticking her tongue out at him. When she saw I was looking, she quickly smiled and tried to pretend like nothing had happened. I shook my head and laughed. "I can just feel the love in this room between the two of you."

"Oh, you have no idea," Will drawled deeply.

The squeak of the door had all three of our heads turning toward the hall, and I watched as Will's mom—Sora—walked in with a tall older man in black slacks and a button-down shirt. The man's face was severe, and if I had to guess, I would say that he didn't smile much. He had thick, dark eyebrows that were furrowed as he glanced down at his phone, either not noticing or not caring that we were staring at him.

"Sweetie, put down your phone and come greet Hikaru and Genesis," Sora said, touching his forearm lightly.

He swept his phone into his pants pocket and looked up. This close to him, I could say that my first impressions of him had probably been a little off. I could see laugh lines around his mouth, and while he had the same sharp cheekbones and jaw as Will that made him hard to read at times, there was something kind about his eyes. They were almost soft with emotion as he looked over at his wife and squeezed her hand that was on his forearm.

His eyes turned toward first to Will, and even though that softness remained in his eyes, his mouth tightened, and I could feel Will tense up next to me. "Hikaru."

"Dad," Will responded, taking a step forward to shake his father's hand. "How was the plane ride here?"

"It was fine." He turned his eyes toward me, and I felt the full force of his assessing gaze. "You must be the Genesis that my family cannot stop talking about."

"It's nice to finally meet you, sir." I reached out and shook his hand, like I had seen Will do.

"I have heard that you are an extraordinary music producer. Someone who could really make a name for herself in the music industry."

I blinked in surprise and threw a glance at Will, whose face was surprisingly impassive. "That's the plan, sir."

He nodded and asked, "Will you be joining us for breakfast?"

I glanced uncertainly toward Will, who gave me a small smile and shrug, which I knew to mean he was leaving it up to me. I knew if I needed him to, he would make up an excuse for me to leave. And he'd never hold it against me or let me feel anyone's disappointment.

"I'd hate to impose," I started, shooting his parents a kind smile. "I know it's been a few months since you've all been together as a family—"

"Nonsense." Sora waved off my words. "We'll have plenty of opportunities for family time together."

"Come, Genesis," Kata pleaded, shooting a quick glance at her father, who was watching her closely. "It'll be nice to hear some more stories about Will losing his cool in board games."

I chuckled and nodded. "Okay. Thank you for inviting me. I'd love to come."

"Great. It's settled," his father said, glancing at his watch. "Hikaru, walk with me to this diner. I have some stuff I want to discuss with you."

Will nodded, calm and serious mask on, and walked briskly to the coat hanger in the hall, grabbing both our jackets.

I thanked him with a smile when he passed me my jacket, but when I went to grab the jacket, he did not let go.

Instead, he leaned down toward me ear and whispered, "Thank you for staying." He placed a kiss on my cheek before pulling away to help me put my jacket on.

I tried not to feel uncomfortable when I realized the hearts his mother had in her eyes as she stared at us the entire time.

Will looked toward Kata and his mom and warned with a small, amused smile, "Try to remember to breathe in between all the questions."

Kata linked her arm with mine, her grin wide. "Okay, I need more embarrassing stories about my brother, stat."

“ “That’s a wrap.”
“Are you sure I shouldn’t fix my vocals in the chorus?” I replayed the chorus, listening carefully to the vocals. “I think—”

“It’s done.” Will carefully removed the headphones from my ears and placed them down on the soundboard. “This song is perfect.”

I couldn’t believe it. After months of working on it, we were really done.

“I love our song,” I admitted quietly, a small grin overtaking my face.

Will smiled softly, pulling me in for a kiss. “I know you do. I love our song too.”

Dating Will had been perfect. We ate lunch together at work almost every day, sometimes with Cora if she was available. We spent almost every day together after work, usually at his place but sometimes mine. We went out all over the city, Will spoiling me rotten with dinner dates and surprise dates at events he thought I would enjoy. And I even stayed for some of his practices with his friends, which were entertaining as hell to watch.

For the first time in so long, I felt so happy. Like everything was perfect and exactly how it should be.

I didn't want a single thing to change.

"You forgot to add the second egg," Will called out from the fridge. I looked down at the messy counter and nearly sighed when I saw that he was right. We'd both been craving something sweet and decided to try and make brownies together and take a break from our *Terminator* movie binge. So far, we've watched the first two and even though I still wasn't a big fan, I really enjoyed the soundtrack. Will loved these movies and had done his impression of the Terminator no less than three times.

I felt his arms come around me from behind a moment later, chin resting on my shoulder as he held up an egg near the orange mixing bowl. I smiled in thanks before taking the egg and cracking it open into the bowl. "I can't wait to eat these brownies," I said, mixing the ingredients so that the egg yolk disappeared into the batter. I looked into the bowl and all it's delicious chocolate goodness and had to fight the urge to take a quick lick from the spoon.

Will moved his hand from around me and I watched as he dunked two fingers into the bowl until they were covered in batter. "Open," he murmured into my ear, finger tapping against my bottom lip in command. I did as he asked and eagerly sucked his fingers into my mouth, moaning at the taste of chocolate on my tongue. I turned my head slightly when I felt Will move closer, his body caging me against the counter as he watched me with dark eyes.

His eyes traced my lips and I slid my tongue along his fingers, drawing them deeper into my mouth. "Fuck," he groaned, pulling his fingers out of my mouth.

I smiled, teasingly. "Tasty."

His lip ticked up, despite the hot look in his eyes. "You are trouble, Buttercup."

"Only with you." I turned quickly to dip my finger into the batter and lifted onto my tiptoes and swiped batter onto his nose. Will watched me silently as I drew on his cheek with the batter, a big grin spreading across my face as I looked at my masterpiece. "You look positively delicious."

Will didn't bother to take more than a quick glance at his reflection in the microwave window across from him before dunking his own fingers once more into the batter. "My turn."

I smiled as I felt his fingers move across my cheek and watched his eyes trace my features with something that looked a lot like adoration. When he was finished, he put his fingers into his mouth and licked them clean, eyes never once moving from mine. I was about to wrap myself around him until I remembered the chocolate on my face and turned to inspect my cheek.

"You drew a cute flower," I said as I tilted my head at a different angle to see more of it. He'd written his name across my cheek with a flower underneath to match the heart I drew with my name written across his cheek.

"It's supposed to be a bulbous buttercup," he said from behind me. My heart squeezed at his words and I pulled my phone out of my pocket, wanting to take pictures.

"Say cheese," I said, holding my phone up towards his face. I quickly took the pictures, his lips barely tilting up into a smile as he reached across and swiped my phone out of my hand. "Hey!"

He pulled me closer to him and held the phone up, the front camera on so we could take a selfie. "If we face each other, we can get both of our cheeks in a picture."

I turned, my left cheek facing the camera as I looked up at him. "Like this?"

His face came closer to mine and with a hand on the back of my neck he pulled me into a searing kiss that had me clinging to his waist. I melted at the feel of his lips against mine, his tongue gliding into my mouth like a sensuous wave that lulled me closer to him. All too soon, he pulled away and I had to bite down the disappointed sound that wanted to leave my mouth.

When I opened my eyes, he was looking through my phone, finger sliding swiftly across the screen before stopping and turning the phone for me to see. My eyes widened as I looked at the photo of us kissing, our cheeks with our "art" on display. Everything about the photo was beautiful, but it was the way that we clung to each other, the intensity of our feelings for each other written all over our faces as we kissed that captured my attention.

We look like we're in love.

The thought made my heart race with nerves, but I couldn't deny that every time I looked at Will or even thought of him, I felt this warm feeling spread through my body. I felt safe with him, and yet he lit me up in a way that made me feel invincible. I didn't know how, but somehow Will had wiggled his way into my heart. Relationships used to terrify me but being with him felt so right that I couldn't even bring myself to listen to the scared voice in my head that was terrified of being hurt. Not when I knew with every fiber in my being that Will would never hurt me.

"I love it," I said, watching as he put the phone on the counter. "I should have you take all my photos from now on. Put that tall height to use."

He ignored my comment and wrapped his fingers around my jaw, tilting my face until my cheek was facing him. "Time to clean up."

I felt his tongue lick my cheek and I squealed, laughing loudly as he wiped my face clean of chocolate with his tongue and lips. "Will!" I said breathlessly between giggles, trying to move my face out of his grip.

He pulled away a few seconds later, a bright grin on his face before he pressed one more kiss on my cheek. "I love hearing you laugh."

My smile softened and I pulled his face closer to my own, fingers wrapped around his sharp jaw. "My turn to clean you up."

I pressed my lips against his cheek, his skin smooth with just the barest hint of stubble that I felt when I brushed my fingers along his jaw. I felt his hands pull me closer, one hand gripping my hip as the other moved to my ass and I exhaled a quiet laugh against his cheek when I felt him squeeze lightly in warning. I licked his cheek clean, making sure to be as silly as possible by moving my tongue in zigzags before pressing quick kisses along his face.

When I pulled away, I saw that he had the biggest smile on his face that he quickly pressed against my neck as he pulled me into his arms. I snuggled up in his arms, more than happy to stand here with him in the silence.

A few minutes later, the sound of his front door closing made us both look up. I heard Cal's deep laugh and heavy footsteps before I saw him, but surprisingly he wasn't alone. Zander and Sam were behind him, grocery bags in hand.

Cal grinned when he saw us. "Hey, what are you two up to?"

I reluctantly moved out of Will's arms and back towards our long-forgotten brownie batter. "We're making brownies."

Sam opened his mouth. "No, you can't have any," Will said before Sam could even talk, making me smile and his friends laugh. Well, Cal laughed. Zander just shook his head at Sam and put the bags he'd been carrying on the opposite counter.

"Do you need help?" I asked Zander, watching as he quietly put away cans of food in one of the taller cabinets.

He shook his head. "I'm good."

I nodded, moving to get the oven pans and lay them out on top of the stove. I listened as Will talked with his friends, and I felt a pang of guilt when I realized he was supposed to be practicing with them tonight. We'd been so wrapped up in each other that we'd lost track of time.

After I finished mixing the batter and pouring it out as evenly as I could in the tray, I carefully placed it in the oven and began cleaning up.

"Do you want me to make you a drink, Genesis?" Cal asked as he began putting out cups on the counter, a variety of alcohol and juices spread out.

"I'm probably going to start heading out," I said with a small smile. "But I can help you with making drinks for everyone before I go."

"Your leaving?" Will frowned, moving away from Sam and the collection of games they'd been looking at.

I nodded, eyes tracing over his furrowed brows and slightly down-turned lips. "I don't want to get in the way of your practice. I'll take a cab home, don't worry."

"Stay," he said, taking one of my hands in his. "I want you here."

My heart warmed at his words, but I still shook my head. "What about your friends? Won't they be annoyed?"

Will was shaking his head before I even finished my sentence. "They don't care. They like you."

"It's true," Cal agreed. I smiled, turning to watch him as he finished pouring some pineapple juice in a cup and handing me the drink. "We could use your input on one of our new songs we're working on. Besides, now Will won't end practice early to call you on the phone for a million hours because he can just talk to you here."

I looked at Will who shrugged but didn't deny Cal's words. "Will, you should never end practice early! Especially not to talk to me!"

He kissed my hand and said, "Stay, and I won't."

I grinned, even as I pretended to be outraged. "This is practically blackmail—I hope you know that."

His eyes were lit with happiness and warmth as he tilted his head down towards me and said, "There's nowhere else you'd rather be."

I smiled, even as I shook my head at his confidence. But I didn't deny his words, and when he pulled my hand to lead me into the music room, I happily followed.

"There's no doubt in my mind that you guys are going to win," Cora said, throwing out her garbage as we left the cafeteria.

It'd been three weeks since the official cutoff. The weather was warmer, officially in spring territory, but it did nothing to calm my anxious jitters about the contest. I wanted this so bad. For me, for Will. Even for his friends in his band.

"I want this really bad," I admitted. "But if we don't win, I'm still so grateful for everything I got from it."

"Aww," Cora cooed, staring at me and Will. "You guys are so cute together. I love this soft side that you bring out of her, Will."

Will smiled. "I'm grateful for her every damn day."

I watched Will, fighting the urge to lean over and kiss him. We kept things professional at work, not wanting anyone in our business. That was probably more for me than Will, who didn't care what anyone thought, but I didn't want people ruining how beautiful our relationship was with gossip.

"Oh my God," Cora said, looking at her phone screen. "Mr. Harris and Steve Pratt just sent the official email that they will be revealing the winner of the contest during a four thirty conference today!"

I looked toward Will, who suddenly looked sick, face pale.

"Hey, are you okay?" I asked, my own anxiety on pause.

Will shook his head, giving me a strained smile. "Yeah, I'm fine. I just thought we had more time to wait." He glanced quickly at Cora before leaning toward me and lowering his voice. "I need to talk to you before the meeting."

I frowned, confused. "I have a meeting with Clements at three, but it shouldn't be long. I can meet you afterward."

Will exhaled and nodded. He intertwined our fingers together, squeezing lightly. "We're going to be okay, Genesis. No matter what happens."

I squeezed back. "I know; I know."

Despite my hopes, I wasn't able to meet with Will before the big meeting. Clements kept me in his office about different clients that needed to be contacted for contract renewals. But it was okay. I was sure whatever Will had to talk to me about, we could talk about after work since I'd be going to his place to have movie night with him and Cal. We were going to watch the new Fast & Furious movie and order Chinese food, and I was excited to irritate Cal by asking him a bunch of inane questions every five seconds.

When I walked into the conference room where most of my team was meeting for Harris and Pratt's news, Cora waved me over, having saved me a space.

"I'm pretty sure I'm about to throw up," I mumbled to her as I sat down.

She squeezed my arm. "You got this. Take deep breaths."

I looked around the room but didn't see Will. It was crazy, but right now, all I wanted was for Will to be sitting with us, holding my hand. I felt like I could get through this if I had him with me, but he was nowhere to be found.

I chatted with Cora for a few minutes as we waited for the meeting to start. At four thirty on the dot, Will walked into the room and stood by one of the glass walls, just as the big TV turned on and Harris and Pratt appeared on the screen.

"Hello? Is this working?" Pratt said loudly, big smile on his face.

Harris stared stoically at the screen. "Hello, everyone. We appreciate you making the time to meet us at the end of your very busy workday."

"No better reason to come to a meeting than to celebrate," cheered Pratt, long gray hair swishing around his face as he moved back and forth, arms pumping in the air.

Harris cleared his throat, giving Pratt some serious side-eye. "Yes, well, we won't waste any more of your time. There were many talented contestants this year, many of whom we wanted to offer contracts to, but there can only be one."

"We urge you all to apply again next year," Pratt chimed in. "Or to send your demos to our talent department. You never know when your life might change."

"God, Mr. Harris looks miserable," I muttered to Cora. "Does that guy ever smile?"

Cora hummed but didn't move her eyes from the screen, likely too nervous to reply.

"Without further ado," Mr. Harris said, voice echoing throughout the room. I held my breath, eyes shooting to Will, who was already staring at me. "The winners of this year's music contest are ... Danielle Rodriguez and Jason Keppner!"

My heart dropped, and I felt Cora's hand squeeze mine tightly, her face turning toward me.

Be happy, I told myself. *Clap. Put on a happy face.*

I started clapping, trying to smile as everyone around me politely clapped.

"We would also like to congratulate another one of our employees who recently signed a music contract with us," Pratt said, grinning. "Mr. Hikaru—er, Will Kobayashi, who works in the finance department. Congratulations!"

Confusion washed over me. Time froze, and I felt like I was seeing things in slow motion, my hearing muffled, like I was swimming underwater. My eyes slowly moved toward Will, and I watched him stare at me with regret and horror.

Will had a contract. With Siren Music Records.

What does that mean? Was this whole thing just a game to him?

I couldn't imagine Will being the douche bag that I'd always imagined him to be, not after everything we'd been through these last few months. But nothing else was making sense.

I stood up abruptly, chair moving back roughly, and all at once, everything came rushing back as if it never stopped. I watched everyone cheer for Will, many people standing up to congratulate him, the sound in the room nearly deafening.

"Genesis," I heard Cora's worried voice and felt her stand up next to me, her wild curls in my periphery.

"I need to go," I mumbled and rushed to the door.

I heard my name being called, but I kept walking, rushing down the hall the moment the door closed behind me. I didn't know where I was going, but I knew I needed to get out of here, out of this building.

"Genesis!" I heard his voice a moment before I felt his hand gently tug on my elbow.

I spun around, fire blazing in my chest. God, it hurt to even look at him. I wanted nothing more than to wrap myself in his arms, but I needed to figure out what the hell was going on.

He took a step toward me, arm reaching out like he wanted me to intertwine my fingers with his.

I stared at that hand and then his face and asked point-blank, "Did you sign with the label?"

He slowed, arm falling down to his side. His face was a mix of emotions, there and gone too quickly for me to read them. He stared at me for a moment and answered, "Yes."

It was my turn to feel a rush of emotions. Happiness. Excitement. Joy. Sadness. Uncertainty. Fear. I was feeling them all, but I tried to push them away for now. I needed to know the facts first.

Reality, Genesis. It's what you base your decisions on.

"How long?" I asked, leaning against the wall between the elevators. "How long have you known? How long has this deal been on the table?"

He hesitated. I could see it in his eyes, in the way he looked almost guiltily down at the ground for a moment before looking back at me. But I knew then that his next words would hurt. I knew this conversation was going to rock my foundation, and I gripped the wall behind me tightly.

"They first showed some interest back in January," he admitted, and I felt a crack in my chest, my lips opening in shock. "But then I didn't hear back from them for months. We had the competition, and I was focused on winning … on working with you and getting you to give me a chance. I didn't even care about it anymore. It was just another label who had shown interest and then moved on. I'd been there many times."

His hands clenched at his sides, his body rocking forward, even as his feet stayed cemented to the spot across the room. Like he was at war with his body and mind. The part of him that wanted to come over here and hold me, touch me, was at war with the part of him that perhaps knew that what I needed right now was for him to give me space. I felt love for him course through me, even as the pain came in equal measure.

"And then?" I prompted quietly after a moment, shaking those soft feelings away.

"Last month, they came to one of my gigs. We talked, and they offered me a deal," he said gruffly, like he knew he had to say it like ripping off a Band-Aid. Quick and painful. "I accepted a week later."

It took every piece of strength I had in that moment to not flinch at the pain vibrating through my body. A month. This had happened over a month ago, and he'd never said a word. There had been a gig last month, a few of them.

Questions circled in my head like a swarm of bees.

Which one did it happen at? I'd just been to one of his gigs a few weeks ago. *Did his band know already? Did they all know not to talk about it in front of me? Did they know that Will was lying to me?*

His dream had happened, and I'd never even known. He'd never shared it with me, deciding to keep it to himself. A whole month. Thirty days. Maybe longer.

I blurted out, "Why didn't you tell me?"

He took a small step toward me and then stopped, eyes remorseful. "I planned to tell you, I swear. But I didn't want to distract you from the contest. It was important to give these last few weeks entirely to our song."

I stared at him, slowly shaking my head. "We'd had our song ready for a while. You didn't tell me because you didn't trust me."

Will frowned, immediately shaking his head. "That's not true. I trust you, Genesis. Completely. With my whole being. I—I knew how stressed you were about the contest, about winning. I didn't want you to feel more stressed, knowing that, win or lose, I was going to be okay. I wanted to prove to you that it didn't matter."

"Will, how can we be together if you don't trust me to stay?" I paused, a heartbreaking thought coming to my mind. "Did ... did you think I wouldn't be happy for you? That I would be angry? Resentful?"

"No," he said adamantly, voice rising with emotion. "I was always going to tell you. You have no idea how much it was killing me to not tell you every day. It wasn't real until I told you. It was what I told myself every day. But I wanted to wait until after the contest."

"Okay." I nodded, pushing off the wall.

I turned to leave. I'd gotten my information, my dose of reality, whether I liked it or not.

But then Will called out my name, his voice closer than before.

"I need space," I said, speaking to the door.

"Damn it, don't run away," he demanded, pain echoing through his words. "Let's talk this out."

I turned around at that, tears in my eyes. "It hurts, Will. That you lied to me for over a month and you didn't even blink. I ... I don't know what to feel because you made me feel like I could trust you, and now, it all feels like a lie."

I cursed under my breath, unable to stop the tear that fell down my cheek. Will made a wounded sound that seemed to have come from deep in his chest and took a step toward me, like he needed to hold me. I held my hand out quickly, pressing into the closed elevator door, and he jerked to a stop, staring mournfully at me.

"I let you in," I admitted quietly after a moment. I continued in a whisper, knowing that if I tried to talk any louder, my voice would crack, and it wouldn't be long before the sobs came. My eyes were glassy, marring my view of Will until he looked like a blurry shape. "I let you into my heart, let you know every single one of my hidden layers. And you lied to me. You hid pieces of yourself—your *life*—from me. Damn it, Will, you haven't been honest with me at all this *entire* time!"

We had spent hours together, countless hours, talking about our dreams with one another. Sharing stories about our families and upbringings. Our first experiences, how music made us feel whole in a way that no one seemed to understand. I'd cried after he told me about how playing music made him feel closer to his grandpa, feeling bonded to him through our shared loss of someone we loved. But we'd also laughed with one another. Sharing embarrassing auditions and horrible lyrics to songs that I would sooner die than play for anyone else. And I knew he felt the same.

Without realizing it, Will had taught me that it was okay to love someone even if it terrified you. For so long, I'd been closed off, but Will was always the exception. From the first day that I'd met him, I had known that he would be different for me. It was why it hurt so much when I'd thought he'd hated me all those years ago. I knew when I saw him across the room that if he was in my life, I was going to be changed in a way that I could never take back. And I'd thought that he felt the same about me.

But now, I wasn't so sure.

And the sad part—the part that made me want to fall to this floor and cry my eyes out—was that I didn't know if I could ever forgive him for hiding this from me.

"I'm going to go," I said, voice cracking. I bit my lip hard to hold in the whimper of pain that wanted to fall out.

"So, that's it then?" he demanded, voice rising with emotions. "I made a mistake—I know that. Please let me make this right."

I couldn't help the tears that fell as I turned back toward him. "I don't know how we could possibly move forward when I can't trust you to be honest with me."

He roughly ran his hands through his hair, yanking so tightly that I knew it had to hurt.

"You looked me right in the eyes every day for over a month and lied straight to my fucking face," I nearly screamed, voice breaking with emotion.

He rocked back on his heels, face jerking down to mine.

I hated that I'd lost control of my emotions, but I forced myself to keep going. "I always thought that you were the one person who would never hurt me. I trusted you. I loved—" I choked on a sob, and I pressed my palms against my eyes, trying in vain to pull myself together and act like I hadn't just had my heart ripped out.

He walked quickly up to me, cupping my face in his hands as he leaned his forehead against mine and pressed kisses to my face. "I'm so sorry." His lips brushed against a tear on my left cheek. "I'm so sorry." Another kiss. "I'm so fucking sorry."

My eyes closed as I tried to hold on to the feeling of being held by him, the sweet pain of knowing that when I walked away, I didn't know if I'd feel his touch again. I heard a loud ding, signifying that the elevator doors would be opening, and with a shaky sigh, I opened my eyes.

He stared at me with tortured eyes, remorse and so much sadness written all over his face. "I love you. So goddamn much. Don't go."

With his thumb, he gently wiped a tear from underneath my eye, and my body sighed at the comfort that only he could bring me, eyes closing as his words washed over me. I felt his lips a moment later as they brushed across my face, stopping at one of my closed eyes, seeming to hover there in the softest kiss for a long moment before gliding over the bridge of my nose to my other closed eye.

I ached to reach out for him, to wrap my arms around him and never let go. But I knew that wouldn't solve anything.

Instead, I pulled away from him. Slower than I should have because I wanted to prolong the contact as long as possible. I didn't allow myself to look at him as I turned to the open elevator doors, and this time, I walked away.

The nice thing about Clements was that he didn't care enough about whatever might or might not be happening in your life to talk about it.

Even though I was sure the building was buzzing with the news about who had won, he didn't say a word about it the entire week. He expected the same work ethic as any other day, and for once, I was thankful for it.

The weekend passed in a drunken haze. I quite literally couldn't remember it because I had gone out with Yari, drinking way too much, and ended up hugging the toilet for most of the night. Between my throwing up and crying, she held me the whole time, whispering consoling words to me. Drinking the entire weekend hadn't really helped much, but it had kept me distracted, which meant I hadn't called Will or taken a cab to his place, begging for things that would never happen.

Today, Clements had me joining him in a meeting across town at one of our buildings. We rode in the luxury black cab in silence, and I used the time to look over the contracts for the meeting and read emails that had come in from over the weekend.

The car moved slowly through Manhattan traffic, jerking to a stop every few seconds, car horns going off on all sides of the car. As a New Yorker, that sound was practically the soundtrack of your life, and you learned to tune it out. I did just that as I pulled up the Monday newsletter, frowning when I read the notice about the free breakfast and realizing I'd missed out on free Dunkin' Donuts this morning. They almost never did that, instead offering stale coffee and bagels each morning. I kept scrolling through the newsletter, skimming congratulations notices to a couple who got engaged recently and one person on floor nineteen who was expecting a baby.

I was skimming so quickly that I almost missed the updated announcement at the end of the newsletter. They'd released the official name for the album along with the album cover which was blown up so there was no way you could miss it. *Hope and Belief.* Right next to the album was a graphic with the words, *And the winner is …*

Heart slamming hard in my chest, I reread the announcement over until it started to blur in front of my face. I took a deep breath and schooled my face into a mask of indifference, and after a quick peek at Clements, who was playing a word game on his phone, I continued to read.

> *We want to once again give a big thank you to everyone who submitted for the Hope and Belief bonus soundtrack this year. There were some amazing contenders, and it was hard to narrow it down to just one song! You should all be very proud of your talent, and please know that at Siren Music Records, we feel honored to have you on our team.*
>
> *That being said, we want to congratulate Danielle Rodriguez and Jason Keppner, who have won the contest with their song, "Haven."*

For those of you who did not win, do not lose out hope! As this contest was a raging success, we will look into doing more opportunities like this within the company in the future!

Congratulations again and a job well done to all who participated!

I reread the notice from top to bottom at least ten times, trying to work through what I was feeling right now. Danielle and Jason were hard workers, and I had no doubt that their piece was amazing. I wanted to hate them for taking my opportunity away from me, but at the same time, I had known what my odds were when I entered the contest. Seeing their names in the newsletter, their pictures next to the album, I couldn't hate them. I still believed strongly that our song was perfect for the album, but what I felt didn't matter. Because the reality was, our song would not be on that album.

I told myself those things over and over, cementing the cold, hard facts into my head until the ache behind my eyes went away, my hand loosening its tight grip on my phone.

"Are you coming, or would you like for us to be late to this meeting, like you've been late to everything else this morning?"

My head snapped to the open door, and I realized with a start that the car had stopped. Clements was already waiting on the sidewalk, staring impatiently at me. I didn't know what had made him madder—that I wasn't already waiting for him on the sidewalk, like I usually was, ready to be at his beck and call, or the fact that he'd had to open the car door for me.

I put my phone back in my pocket and smoothly stepped out of the car, stack of files and contracts in arm. *Fake it till you make it.* "I'm ready."

The meeting went fine.

Truthfully, I hadn't given it my usual one hundred ten percent attention, but thankfully, no one seemed to notice or care that I was there. Also not unusual. One of the guys had asked me to pour him a coffee when I walked in, and on a typical day, that would've pissed me off to no end, but I'd just smiled and done as he'd asked.

What was the point? None of it really mattered at the end of the day.

When we walked back into our building, Clements was still rattling off a list of things he needed me to do, and I dutifully wrote each of them down, one ridiculous errand after the other. Going off his comment before the meeting about being late, I guessed he cared and paid attention to what was happening more than I'd thought.

"Did you get all of that?" he repeated.

I sighed and walked into the elevator with him. "Yes."

"Recite it for me," he demanded, pressing the floor number where HR and legal were located as the doors closed.

I pressed the button for our floor and did as he'd asked. "Write up formal notes of the recorded audio transcripts from this morning's meetings. Pick up your lunch at Bellagio's and make sure to double-check that they added the extra marinara sauce. Pick up your dry cleaning. Reorganize your files on your computer. And cancel your dinner reservation at Eleven Madison Park tonight."

He said nothing, not even acknowledging that I'd talked. I stared at the buttons on the elevator, wishing to be anywhere but here. God, I just wanted to go home.

"Quit moping about the contest," he stated bluntly.

I looked over at him in surprise, and he raised an eyebrow at me.

"What, you think I don't know how badly you wanted to win that contest? Everyone wanted to win, but there can only be one."

"Okay," I said sharper than I'd intended.

"So you'll probably be an assistant for another year," he continued with a shrug. "Or maybe they'll hire you on officially as a marketing associate. There's nothing wrong with that. You're good at it."

I stared hard at him, struggling with feeling nothing and feeling too much in that moment. "I'm good at producing music."

"A lot of people are, kid," he said simply.

I said nothing at that, looking down at my feet in defeat.

I heard him exhale, and then he snapped, "Stop it."

"What?" I asked defensively, looking up at him.

"Stop with the *woe is me* crap," he declared with a wave of his hand. "It's not you, and it's annoying. You don't want to be an assistant, then don't be an assistant. But if you've got the drive like I think you do, then you won't let this one loss stop you."

"This isn't my first loss," I admitted begrudgingly.

"And it won't be your last either," he responded. The elevator doors opened, and he began to walk out but paused, holding the door open with his arm. "You've got talent, and everyone who's met you knows it. Hell, your name has been floating around on the upper floors for a while now. They know who you are. They know your work ethic. It's up to you to decide what you want to do with that. But I'll let you know one thing, kid: no one cares about your tears. Not unless those tears will make the company some money. So, quit looking like your dog just died and prove to them that you're an *asset*."

He let go of the door and walked away, leaving me alone in the elevator.

"Fuck you too," I mumbled. The doors had already closed, my distorted reflection my only company. I stared at myself, at the blood I could feel coursing through my body and up to my face. For the first time today, I didn't feel like a zombie.

The door dinged once again and opened up onto my floor. I filed away Clements's advice and stepped out of the elevator. The floor was its usual buzz of chatter and noise. But it felt like there was an added tension to it all. I saw some people whispering as they looked over some files, and when one of them made eye contact with me, their eyes widened before they gave me a pitying smile. I knew they were whispering about the contest, Will winning and me losing. He got the dream, and I was stuck at my entry level job, forever memorialized as the girl who almost had everything but wasn't good enough.

I was so tired of losing. Of chasing a dream, a love, that constantly left me behind.

But I couldn't give up. Not yet.

I didn't remember falling asleep.

I woke to the feeling of hands moving softly through my hair, and the feeling was so nice that I pushed closer to it. I opened my eyes and blinked hard, confused.

"What's wrong?" I pulled away, sitting up in my bed.

"Are you okay?" Alejandra moved her hand to my shoulder, a worried frown on her face. Her hand gripped my chin lightly, and she peered at my face, sadness in her eyes. "It looks like you've been crying."

I moved away from her and stood up from my bed. "I'm fine. Do you need me to take another look at paperwork?"

Alejandra had received her first contract for an advertisement. It wasn't anything big. She would be modeling for a small clothing chain that had stores mostly on the West Coast, but it was still a huge accomplishment. We'd hired a lawyer to look over her contract, but there was a lot of paperwork that she still needed to fill out that was taking her a lot longer to complete than she'd anticipated.

She shook her head, lips pressed together. "Genesis, talk to me. What is going on? Yari said something happened with Will …"

I sighed, not wanting to talk about it. I didn't want to even think about Will because every time I did, I was hit with so many conflicting emotions. I missed him—so much. I missed his touch, the way it felt to be held in his arms. But more than that, I missed his friendship. I missed our whispered talks in the middle of the night or the way that he always let me choose what movie we put on, even when I'd chosen *Pride & Prejudice* for the fifteenth time in the week. I missed the way that one of us would hum a melody, and then the next thing we knew, we were playing music together, just jamming as we let the music move us, talking as we played, singing lyrics that were sometimes beautiful, but most of the time just silly, making us laugh until I cried. Will would always wipe my tears away with that soft look in his eyes, and I'd have no choice but to kiss him, so I wouldn't tell him something that terrified me, something I'd never said to someone who wasn't my family.

But things were so different now.

I could feel him staring at me in meetings, but I refused to look at him. Whenever he tried to talk to me, I all but ran out of the room, pretending to have work I needed to get done. A part of me was terrified that if I looked at him, I would run back in his arms and pretend that nothing had happened, and I couldn't do that.

Will had lied to me, and I didn't know how to trust anything that he said when he could lie so easily. How was I to trust that he wouldn't withhold important information from me again in the future if he thought I couldn't handle it? I didn't know much about healthy relationships, but I knew that they didn't work if you weren't honest with each other.

"Genesis," Alejandra whined, snapping her fingers.

I looked back toward her. "We're taking a break. Or maybe we broke up. I don't really know, and I don't want to talk about it."

Alejandra rushed over to me and pulled me into a hug. I stiffened, not used to receiving comfort from my sister in this way. Usually, it was the other way around.

"I'm so sorry."

I patted her back lightly before stepping back with a shrug. "It is what it is. It's probably for the best."

She frowned. "Don't do that."

"Don't do what?"

"Don't brush everything off like it meant nothing," she demanded. "Just because things are messed up right now doesn't mean they can't be fixed."

I knew she was right, but it was hard to feel hope because hope just felt like one more thing that could hurt me.

Right now, I needed a distraction, and I was putting all my focus into looking for a new job. Now that I'd lost the contest, I really didn't see myself lasting at this job for another year. I couldn't be an assistant for another year. I just couldn't. Instead, I'd gone home after work, determined to apply to every open position available in the five boroughs, but somehow, I had ended up falling asleep halfway into my third application.

"Genesis," Alejandra called out. I looked up at her. "Promise me that you're not going to shut down or be closed off to fixing things with Will if the opportunity presents itself."

"I won't," I promised. It was easy to make the promise when I wasn't so sure that things could ever be fixed.

And the scared part of me wasn't so sure I wanted them to be.

"Hey, I need those preliminary charts you have on Robert's album," Holland, a marketing associate shouted across the room.

"Already on your desk," I called out, effortlessly juggling the coffee and binders for Clements to look over for this afternoon's meeting with a VIP artist.

Dixinson was a Grammy-winning pop-rock artist who had recently left Jagged Pill records and signed with our company after wanting to make a switch to the country genre. He'd left his old label for multiple reasons, one of which was that he felt like they didn't understand his "sound" anymore. His country album with us had released about four months ago, and now, Jefferey was going to have to present to some higher-ups about how it was doing and the next steps.

A piece of my hair had come out of my low ponytail, and I blew a breath, trying to get it out of my field of vision, even as I continued walking toward the elevators.

"Never leave me," Holland pleaded, hands folded in prayer before turning the corner and out of sight.

I smirked, but my focus turned to the elevators when I saw that one was about to close, and chances were, I'd have to wait ages for the next one. "Hold the door, please!"

A hand reached, the doors opening wide once more, and I quickened my pace.

"Thank you so much," I gushed, a little breathless. My smile immediately dropped when I saw it was Mr. Harris, miraculously alone. "Oh. Good afternoon, Mr. Harris."

He nodded. "Miss Gonzalez. I hope you're doing well."

"Yes, thank you," I replied.

I juggled the items in my hands for a second, maneuvering them so I could press floor thirteen on the elevator board. I saw that he was going to his floor, and I wondered for a moment why he wasn't using his private elevator on the other side of the building.

"The elevators in this building seem to break frequently," he commented, and I whipped around toward him, fearing for a moment that I'd asked my question aloud and not just in my head. But he continued nonchalantly, "In the last six months, these elevators have been broken at least a dozen times, if not more. Starting to wonder if they're a death trap."

I gave a small smile. "I tell myself I'll take the stairs to avoid the elevator unpredictability, but I never do."

He stared impassively at me, not reacting at all. I'd have thought he hadn't heard me if it wasn't for the fact that he didn't look away as I chuckled awkwardly. He seemed so intimidating on the conference calls or rare meetings he'd join, but I thought maybe that was how he had to be. I was starting to think that the guy didn't have a personality past being surly and painstakingly serious.

"And how is your division doing?" he inquired, quickly glancing down at his phone screen as it lit up. Whatever he read made his mouth tighten, face wiped of any emotions. "Everyone doing well on your floor?"

I stared, confused, and answered slowly, "Yes, I think so."

He nodded, eyebrows furrowing, like he was fighting with himself to say something. He opened his mouth, closed it, cleared his throat, and said, "Good. That's ... good to hear."

We got to my floor first, and the doors opened.

"Have a good day, sir."

He nodded, though I could tell he was lost in thought and had already forgotten about me and probably our strange conversation. The whole conversation had been weird.

I forgot entirely about the conversation as I knocked on Clements's door, opening it when I heard him call out.

"It's about time," he grumbled, hand already outstretched.

I passed him the coffee, ignoring his comment since I knew I was on time and it had been no more than five minutes since he'd demanded I bring him a coffee and to bring the folder up.

"Dixinson's numbers aren't performing well." I handed him the folder, getting straight to the point. "His fans are not responding well to his switch to country with a thirty percent drop in sales since release week."

He nodded, scanning the document before closing it to look at me. "What do you think of the album?"

I raised my eyebrows in surprise but quickly masked it. "I think the songs are fine for what they are, but I think they played it safe in the studio, and it backfired."

He steepled his fingers together, watching me thoughtfully. "How so?"

"The songs are generic. They fit on brand for what a traditional country song is supposed to be, but there's nothing that really makes it stand out from other songs in the genre," I explained. "He made a switch mid-career, and that is ballsy and not easy to do while trying to maintain your followership. But one of the things people loved about Dixinson was his unique take on the pop genre. He messed around with autotune, played with multiple instruments in a way that made his songs stand out on mainstream radio. He brought together rock and pop singers in a way we hadn't seen in years. Added with the powerful lyrics that seemed to play on his voice just as much as the music, he had back-to-back hits. This album didn't do that."

"Your recommendation then?"

"Promotional tours are a possibility," I commented, brain racing to slow down my ideas enough for my mouth to catch up. "I'd recommend radio visits, podcasts, or small venues at first. After his political rant at his concert last summer, I also think it's important to have some clear rules set out if we don't want him to do any further damage to his career and our numbers. If we did another big concert, chances are, it would hurt sales more than harm it. We need to do some damage control, maybe a bonus track, or have him do a country rendition of a popular song, but this time, make it *him*, not basic cowboy."

Clements nodded, satisfied with my answer. "I agree. Job well done, Gonzalez."

I stared, trying not to make it obvious that I was shocked. He had never complimented me once in the two years I'd worked here. "Thank you, sir."

"All right, now, get out of my office," he said, turning back to his computer, tossing my file to the side.

"But what about the meeting?" I asked, confused.

"You're not going," he said, eyes still on his screen as he began typing.

I blinked. "But, sir, why not? You just said—"

"You're going to go set up a time to talk with Jacobs about Dixinson's album," he cut me off, and my heart began beating furiously in my chest.

Jacobs was the songwriter on Dixinson's album and had also written most of his previous songs, most of which had gone platinum.

"Tell him what you told me and pick three song recommendations for Dixinson to cover on a live show he'll be doing next week."

I choked on air, coughing roughly. "Sorry—okay, yes, I'll do that, but—"

"If Jacobs gives you a hard time, tell him it's a direct order from the higher-ups." He looked up from the computer and purposely looked toward the door. "Email me the song choice tonight. Now, get out and get to work."

I nodded, trying not to show my excitement and confusion on my face. I closed the door behind me and had to shove my hands in my pants pockets to hide the tremor going through them.

For whatever reason, Clements was finally letting me take the lead on something again. I wasn't going to mess this up.

I was on such a high, mind lost in the encyclopedia of music in my brain, that I didn't even notice when the elevator bell dinged, and the doors opened. I dashed on before the doors closed and went to press my floor number, only to notice a moment later that it was already pressed. I looked around in confusion and gasped when I realized I wasn't alone.

Will.

He was standing at the opposite side of the elevator, hands in his pockets as he watched me with a small, quizzical smile on his face. He looked so good. Tired but good. My eyes greedily soaked him in, taking in his perfectly combed-back black hair, the way that his suit fit him like it had been tailored for his body, and landed on his fingers that were hidden in his pockets.

"Oh!" I said, feeling flustered. I pressed my back against the wall opposite of him so that we were facing each other. It took a moment for my brain to process this new information, and I took him in, half in a daze of music, yearning, and happiness.

"You look like you're working hard up there," he commented, smile still on his face as he tapped his index finger to the side of his head.

I opened my mouth, wanting to share what had just happened, to jump in his arms and scream, let myself get visibly excited in a way I didn't let myself do often. Knowing he would be happy for me and he'd talk me down from my immediate second-guessing once it all settled in. But then I paused. I remembered.

My face fell, and I tried to look down quickly, not wanting him to see it. But he knew because he always knew. We stood there in tense silence—me looking down at my feet, him looking at me. It didn't take long for us to make it to our floor, and I nearly sighed in relief at the sound of the doors opening.

"I wanted to ask you something," Will called out over my shoulder as I took my first step out of the elevator.

I stopped and looked back at him. He looked nervous, his fingers tapping a quick rhythm on the side of his leg.

I frowned, not used to seeing that look on his face. "What is it?"

He looked around and then jerked his head to the right, toward the empty halls. "Can we talk somewhere else? I promise I won't take long."

I hesitated, knowing I needed to start thinking about what song I'd recommend to Jacobs. But I couldn't resist Will, and I needed to know what was on his mind. So, I nodded, and he immediately pivoted and started walking down the hall, turning toward the conference rooms. He stopped in the vending machine room, empty, as it usually was since they'd switched all the good snacks out with healthier options. The room had a few small tables and chairs in case people wanted to sit down here. I remembered eating my lunch here a few times in the beginning, trying to avoid Will after our first big argument back when I first started. It felt crazy how long ago that was, seeing as where we were today. Who we were. I was certainly a different girl than the one who had sat here, feeling angry and determined and trusting no one but myself.

I stepped into the room and stood uncertainly by one of the vending machines. I turned to watch Will. He stood a few feet away and ran his hands quickly through his thick black hair.

He turned to me, dropping his arms. "I told my parents about the contract deal."

My eyes widened, mouth dropping. "That's great! What did they say?"

Will smiled a sardonic smile. "My father had many questions, but overall, they are both very happy. Kata wants me to buy her a car with my first advance. My father is going to be on the East Coast for business at the end of the week, and he wants to have dinner."

I laughed, missing his sister. "But wait, you only just told them?"

He nodded, stepping a tiny step closer. "It wasn't real until you knew about it. I wanted you to be the first person I told. Obviously, that didn't go quite as planned, but ..."

I stared in astonishment at him, processing his words, not sure what to say.

"My father wants you to come to dinner," he continued, taking another small step toward me. "I want you to come."

"Will," I said, uncertain.

"I know nothing has changed from last week," he quickly added, determination in his eyes. "But selfishly, I don't want to celebrate if you're not there. This dream doesn't even feel real without you."

I stared at him, heart beating quickly at his admission. "Did you tell them ... about us?"

He looked at me, face soft and eyes hot with emotions that made my legs feel weak. "I didn't tell them because I don't plan on letting this breakup stick. I'm respecting your wishes for space, but I'm not letting you go, Genesis. I'm going to win you back."

I stared, speechless at his declaration, my heart rejoicing, even as my hands shook with nerves. I didn't know what to say to that, so I ended up saying dumbly, "Technically, I didn't break up with you."

His eyes lit with fire, and he strode toward me. I got the distant feeling that I'd just said the wrong thing. He stepped into my space, the toes of his shoes touching mine.

"Oh? So, I can touch you? Kiss you?" His hand hovered by my hip, his chest just barely brushing mine, as I took a shallow breath, overwhelmed by his sudden proximity. His lips moved down to my ear. "I can fuck you against this vending machine and feel your pussy tighten on me, sucking me in? Hear your moans in my ear, your fingers in my hair? Your nails on my scalp as you try to fight coming too quickly even though you know I'll make you feel it again and again?"

"Will," I whimpered, closing my eyes at the visual his words had brought.

He moved his head, his lips grazing my forehead. He continued softly, a hint of reverence in his tone, "So, I can whisper to you in the dark about music again? And we can share feelings that sometimes feel too scary to say in the light? Wake up the next day, not in a panic for exposing darkest parts of my soul, thinking about how to save face, but feel safe in knowing that you are my home and I am yours?"

I swallowed, eyes still closed as I listened to his words, felt his breath on my face, his hand tracing my features oh-so delicately.

"If we're not broken up," he continued softly, yearning in his voice now, "does that mean I can feel you against my chest as you curl around me, your hand always needing to be close to mine, like you're searching for me, even in your sleep? Does that mean I can watch you sleep peacefully in my arms and feel like the luckiest son of a bitch because I get to be with the woman who makes me feel alive again? Who makes me feel loved and respected, crazy with feelings that I'd never imagined in my wildest dreams were true?"

He stopped abruptly, breathing hard, and I blinked quickly, trying to rid the tears from my eyes. His words ... I wanted to taste them on my lips, to inhale them until my lungs exploded from the love I felt in every dip of his voice. I wanted to give in right now, tell him that, yes, I wanted all those things, but uncertainly stopped me once more.

Was it the right thing?

"Will," I repeated breathlessly, leaning back to look up at him.

His eyes were tracing my cheek, and he raised his hand a moment later toward it before dropping it. He moved away, frustration making his shoulders tighten in his gray button-down, his mouth set in a hard line.

He turned to look away, and I spoke quickly, not letting myself think about it for a second longer. "I'll go. Of course I'll go."

His head snapped toward mine, face stark with relief and hope. "Thank you."

I love you, I wanted to say. *How could I turn down a moment to be near you? To be with you on such an important day, especially when you need me?*

"Always," I said instead, locking those unspoken words deep inside of me.

How did one dress for a dinner with your *kind of, but not really* boyfriend and his father?

I'd already changed out of three outfits, and I still couldn't find one that I felt comfortable enough in, but I was starting to wonder if the feeling had more to do with myself than the clothes. I felt nervous for so many reasons. I was going to be spending time with Will for the first time in nearly two weeks.

I also felt nervous because I'd have to pretend like everything was normal in front of Will's dad, who was kind of an intimidating man to be around. He made me feel like he could read my mind, like every word that I said had more meaning than I'd meant to give away. I'd spent most of the time with Kata and Will's mom when they came to town, so I was surprised and nervous about Will's dad wanting me to be there tonight.

"So, we don't hate Will anymore, right?" Alejandra asked from her spot on the sofa, bag of sour-cream-and-onion chips in her lap. She had her face clean of makeup and was lounging in pajamas, somehow still upbeat, even after a nearly ten-hour photo shoot.

"We never hated Will," I sighed, half-paying attention to her as I tried to finish buttoning up my blouse.

"Good, because I've been texting with him since you broke up," she answered happily, crunching loudly on a chip.

"You've been what?" I nearly shouted, glaring at her.

Her eyes widened in faux innocence. "What? Was I not supposed to do that?"

I rolled my eyes at her antics, focus going back to the button on my shirt for a moment. "You are so annoying. What do you two talk about anyway?"

Aleja hummed happily, wide smile on her face. "Oh, just him wanting to make sure you got home safe from work or making me double-check that your alarm was turned on for work the next morning when I told him you'd fallen asleep at your desk again. I mentioned once that you hadn't had dinner because you were working on some big project for Clements, and he ordered dinner for us. Joe's Pizza was from him last week. Sorry I lied and said it was me."

I couldn't believe he'd cared enough to check up on me these last few weeks. It felt ridiculous to say that, knowing how much he cared about me, but still, every time I thought he couldn't show me how much he cared, he proved me wrong. I knew now how badly he was trying to respect my wishes while wrestling with his need to take care of me and make sure I was okay.

I stopped buttoning my shirt and sighed with frustration. "I hate this shirt. I don't even know why I'm pretending that I'll even wear the stupid thing tonight."

"Just wear the black dress with the cute little red hearts," Aleja called out to my retreating back. "You'll look appropriately cute for a parent dinner, but also sexy enough with the subtle cutout sides to drive Will crazy."

"I'm not trying to drive Will crazy," I shouted from the room.

I pulled the dress on, smoothing the skirt out over my legs. What I loved about this dress was how it managed to be both modest and sexy at the same time.

"So then, why are you putting the dress on?" Aleja called from the living room, laughter in her voice.

"Because," I said, walking back out into the living room, "it's cute, and I'm tired of trying on a million dresses. I need to start heading out soon anyway."

Aleja hummed, not looking convinced but wisely staying quiet, though her mouth was still tugged up into an amused smile that I pretended not to see.

"How was the photo shoot today?" I asked, needing to change the topic.

Aleja made a face. "It was okay. There was this makeup artist who was new and kept poking my eye with the mascara brush because her hand was shaking. But honestly, I didn't blame her because the other makeup artist was such a dick."

"Did you get to keep anything from the set?"

Last week, she had gotten to keep a purse that she'd modeled, and that thing cost half my paycheck. I couldn't deny that Aleja got some sweet perks from being a model, and it seemed like she was only becoming more and more popular. She was getting more gigs than ever before, her new agency really helping to build her portfolio and name.

She shook her head. "I left as soon as I could. I didn't like the energy on the set, so I didn't really want anything to remember it by, you know?"

I nodded, about to ask another question when I saw my phone light up on the table. I reached for it, heart squeezing with nerves and excitement when I saw it was a text from Will.

Will: Are you sure I can't pick you up?

Me: Positive. I'm going to use one of the cab apps and meet you there. 7, right?

Will: Yes, 7. Text me when you're here, so we can come in together. I'll be waiting outside.

I sent a quick *okay* and then put my phone back down. I needed to get started on my hair, or I'd never get there on time.

My sister joined me in the bathroom, standing by the door to talk to me as I used the curling iron to work my hair into soft waves down my back. After adding some hairspray to make it stay, I applied quick makeup to my face. I had some intense dark circles, so concealer had been my best friend lately.

"God, I wish I had your hips," Aleja said with a sigh. She looked down at her own body. "If only I could gain more weight, but my metabolism makes that pretty much an impossible feat."

"Be grateful for it," I said, finishing up in the bathroom. I grimaced when I realized my dress was riding up a bit in the back and quickly pulled the dress back down. "You can eat pretty much anything you want, and you don't even gain a pound."

"Yeah, well, what if you want to gain a pound?" she grumbled, looking put out. She brightened a second later. "Maybe James and I should have a kid, so my body will change."

I gave her a look. "Stop saying the first stupid idea that comes to your mind."

She laughed, nodding. "Yeah, that was pretty stupid. I like my body the way it is anyway. Besides, I wouldn't be able to fit into my favorite pair of shorts if I gained weight, and they stopped making these shorts last summer, so I can't have that."

"Someone's got their priorities straight," I joked, walking past her and back into the bedroom. It only took a moment for me to find the perfect little booties to go with the dress.

"*Ya tu sabes*," she sang loudly, making me laugh out loud.

I snagged my purse and jacket, walking back into the living room to get my phone and request a cab ride on one of the apps. The app said four minutes, which meant I should be waiting outside already because they loved to leave and cancel your rides if you made them wait more than ten seconds.

"Okay, *me voy*," I said, walking toward the front door. "I'll text you when I'm on my way home."

"Have fun!" Aleja cheered, blowing me kisses. "Try not to blink too many times when you have to lie to Will's dad. It's your tell, and he'll figure you out in a hot second."

I waved my hand, ignoring her comment. She was right though; I'd have to work hard at not making it obvious that I was lying, but hopefully, Will would do most of the talking tonight. I was here to celebrate Will's success. The stuff with his dad was all secondary as far as I was concerned.

The restaurant was bougie.

It was the only word I could think of as I looked at the host in a tux outside the front door, a stand in front of him with a reservation list. The building was beautifully displayed with twinkling lights along the awning and gave the allure of stepping into a nighttime dream.

I looked down at my outfit and tried not to second-guess myself as I looked for Will. I found him a moment later, leaning against the building next door to the restaurant, phone in hand.

He was dressed in slacks and a button-down but one I'd never seen before. It fit him perfectly in a way that you just knew that it cost money because it made him look good. But then again, everything looked good on Will. I noticed that he'd gotten a haircut, his hair shorter in the back and no longer teetering between long or short. I wondered if he'd cut it for his dad or because he wanted to keep the short hair.

He looked up a moment later from his phone, small frown on his face, and I watched as his eyes moved across the area, skimming past me for a moment and then slamming onto me again. I gave a small wave, fighting the butterflies in my stomach as I watched him take me in, his eyes hungrily scanning me up and down.

"You look beautiful," he said as soon as I was within hearing range.

His hand reached out, and he gently placed it on my elbow, leaning down to plant a kiss on my cheek. I couldn't help the small sniff I gave him, inhaling his aftershave and that Will smell that drove me crazy.

"Thank you," I said softly, body leaning closer to his as he started to pull away. I forced myself to lean back on my heels, pulling my own metaphorical chain. "Is your father here?"

"He should be here in a minute, but we can start heading in."

Will put his hand on my lower back and ushered me toward the door. I felt his hand like a hot brand, and I had to remind myself over and over to not get excited about his touch.

"Welcome to Kabul's House." The host at the front of the restaurant smiled at us both. "Can I have your reservation name?"

"Kobayashi for three," Will said, a distracted note in his tone.

His eyes were trailing along my hair and neck, a look of delicate yearning on his face. I looked back at the host, who was paying us no mind, but I still felt a bit embarrassed, so I elbowed him and jerked my head slightly toward the host.

"The third member of our party can meet us inside."

"Not necessary, sir," the host said with a strained smile as he gestured to the door. "He has already arrived and is awaiting you both. Bianca at the front desk will bring you to your table."

I looked at Will in surprise, and I saw that his jaw tightened as he nodded silently to the host. He put a little bit of pressure on my lower back to walk, and I followed along, wondering if there was some sort of confusion with his father and the time.

"He's playing a game," Will murmured as he tilted his head slightly toward mine.

His hand moved from my back and I mourned the touch. A moment later, he interlaced his fingers with mine, giving them a slight squeeze. I squeezed back, brushing my shoulder against him in comfort as we continued to walk.

"My father doesn't like to be the last person at a table. He welcomes you; you don't welcome him."

"What? Why?"

Will paused to tell the woman at the front desk, Bianca, our reservation name, and after a moment, she came out from behind the desk and started ushering us down a hall. The inside of the building was even more beautiful than the outside. It was truly like eating among the stars—something you never saw in New York City, where lights and tall buildings blocked any possibility of seeing them. Chances were, what you thought were stars were probably airplanes coming in and out of the airport.

"It's his dinner, so he has to be there first," Will continued, speaking softly. "He sees it as a show of disrespect to be late to anything and would be unhappy if I'd gotten to the table first."

"But what if we'd continued waiting for him outside?" I asked, eyebrows furrowed as I tried to keep up. "Then, we would've been late, and he would've been upset."

"Like I said, he's playing a game," Will said grimly. "My father likes those. Never outright says what he wants or expects but demands you match his expectations anyway."

I stayed silent at that, piecing together the father that Will had told me about in the past, the father I'd met just a short few weeks ago, and the one I was still getting to know.

The hostess opened a glass door, and a moment later, we walked into what looked like a private room. The decor was the same, but this was clearly meant for private parties. Mr. Kobayashi was seated at the table, staring blankly at us as we walked in. The guy had a good poker face—I'd give him that.

As we got closer, he stood from the table. The hostess quietly walked out, closing the door behind her. Will greeted his father first, shaking his hand before going in for a half-hug, both of them speaking quietly in Japanese.

"It's good to see you again, Genesis," his father said, reaching out for a hug.

I quickly stepped toward him and hugged him, surprise coating my face.

He gave me a small smile. "My wife would have my head if I did anything less. She says family deserves hugs, and you are now family, are you not?"

I looked toward Will, bewildered and unsure of what to say. That felt like a big lie to start a dinner off with, but how could I say anything else besides a tentative yes?

"I haven't proposed yet, Father," Will said lightly, a hint of sarcasm in his tone. He moved to the chair closest to me and pulled it out for me, squeezing my shoulder gently as I sat down. He threw his father a tight smile. "Let's not jump down the timeline yet."

His father nodded, waiting until Will took his seat beside me to take his seat across from us. I picked up the vase of water and poured myself and Will a cup of water, noticing that his father already had a glass.

"Very well. Your mother won't be happy to hear about a delayed wedding. She's got grand ideas for the two of you, and she's already started knitting baby clothes."

I choked on the water and put the glass down a bit too hard on the table as I began to cough, trying to mask it as much as possible. Will rubbed my back, face a mixture of concern and amusement as he passed me a napkin.

"Thank you," I croaked a minute later, tapping my lips gently with the napkin.

"Of course, with Hikaru's music career finally taking off, I suppose now isn't the right time for children," he continued as if I hadn't had a minor choking attack a minute earlier. He opened the menu in front of him, and his eyes scanned it with a thoughtful look. "Genesis, your career will be taking off soon as well, I have no doubt."

I hoped so, but with the way my luck had been going lately, I wasn't holding my breath.

"Yes, that's the plan," I confirmed with confidence I didn't have.

"We will have to celebrate when it happens," he said decisively, as if there were no room for anything else.

I glanced at Will from the corner of my eyes, watching as he looked calmly through his menu. I picked mine up as well, trying to focus on the words on the menu and not staring at Will. The menu was just a list of items, but there was no description for them, though with pasta, I guessed you couldn't really go wrong. They also didn't list the prices, which usually meant it was going to be expensive.

I'll just get whatever Will gets.

We'd eaten enough food together by now that I knew he wouldn't steer me wrong. Just then, a waitress wearing a simple black dress and black pumps walked in, a warm smile on her pale face.

"Hello. My name is Anne. I will be taking care of you tonight," she said brightly. "Can I start you off with some drinks?"

"We'll take a bottle of your recommended red for the table," his father said, and I tried to not think about how expensive that bottle might be. "We'll start with an order of the kashke bademjan. And I'll have the lamb chops with rice and salad."

She nodded and turned toward me and Will. "For you, miss?"

I panicked, looking from Will to the menu with wide eyes. "Uh, I'll have ..."

"We'll take two orders of barg, please," Will replied smoothly, gently taking the menu from my hands and adding it with his on the table. "Could you also bring another vase of water, please?"

She nodded, and after repeating the order to make sure she got it right, she left. I looked to Will and hoped my smile expressed how grateful I was in that moment. I'd had Afghan food before, but I trusted his taste more than my vague memory of a chicken kebab.

I'd have to ask Will later how he was so familiar with these dishes. Though considering how money wasn't a concern for his family, I thought it was safe to assume this wasn't the first time he'd been to such a fancy restaurant.

We made small talk for a few more minutes, though it was mostly Will's father and me talking until they brought in the bottle of wine and wineglasses.

"Let's toast," Mr. Kobayashi said, lifting his glass of red wine in the air.

We followed suit, and I turned to look at Will, giving him a bright smile. Even though everything between us was still there in the back of my mind, tonight, I was pushing it all aside to help celebrate a monumental moment. I was so proud of him. He deserved this moment more than anyone I'd ever known. He was already looking at me, lips tilted up in a smile.

"To Hikaru, who was gifted with a voice that will move mountains in an industry that makes it nearly impossible to stand out. But you did it, Hikaru, and you have made me proud."

Will looked surprised by his father's words, and he blinked quickly before looking down at his lap. I reached my hand out and squeezed his hand, trying to offer him comfort as he worked through his emotions.

"I have one other thing to add," I said, and Will looked up, eyes locked on mine. "Will—Hikaru …" Will's eyes darkened at my use of his formal name, and I continued, never looking away, "When I look at you, I see someone who embodies hard work and determination in a way that demands others to see it too. You've reminded me to demand the same things in myself, and if I want something badly enough, it will happen. And you're living in that dream right now." I paused, swallowing down emotions as I gave him a watery smile. "I am so proud of you for all that you've achieved, and I cannot wait to hold your album in my hands, to learn the sound of love all over again through your words, through your voice, and through your melody."

I gave a small, embarrassed laugh, realizing that I'd gotten too emotional, especially with Mr. Kobayashi right there. I lifted my glass and cheered, "To Hikaru!"

"To Hikaru," his father repeated, and we all took another drink from our glasses.

I nearly jumped when I felt Will's hand on my thigh under the table, and a moment later, his face was close to my own.

I slowly put my glass down and tried to slow my fast-beating heart as he whispered in my ear, "The sound of love is your voice, and I hear it every time I close my eyes. My music is nothing without you. Thank you."

He pressed a lingering kiss to my cheek, leaving me speechless as he positioned himself back in his seat, his hand back on his side of the table. Mr. Kobayashi was looking between Will and me with an unreadable expression on his face, hands steepled under his chin.

I cleared my throat. "How is Kata doing? Will told me she still hasn't decided on which college she will go to yet."

"Yes, she is between NYU or Boston University," he answered, a pointed look at Will. "Seems she is determined to be free from her parents and move to the East Coast, just like her big brother."

"I do not control what Kata wants or decides," Will replied, dismissing his father's look. "Both colleges offer great history programs that will make her happy."

"She won't be studying history," his father said firmly. "She will be earning a business degree—"

"She will be studying whatever she likes," Will warned, a sharp edge to his tone. He stared hard at his father, jaw clenched. "You will not make this hard for her the way you made chasing my dreams hard for me."

His father scoffed, immediately dismissing his words. "Don't be ridiculous, Hikaru. I allowed you to study music, did I not? And you worked your silly job at the label even though you could've been making double that had you taken the opportunities offered to you time and again."

"My job is not silly," Will corrected. "Working hard at a place that offers me the opportunity to learn about something that matters to me is not silly. And I think it's disrespectful of you to call my job silly when Genesis works for the same company. Are you calling her job silly? Are her dreams silly for not involving work for corporate America?"

"Will, I don't—" I started, trying to defuse this argument.

Mr. Kobayashi raised his hand up, cutting a sharp look at me that had me snapping my mouth closed in surprise. Will jumped out of his seat, chair screeching backward and tilting over onto the ground, and I jumped, staring at him with wide eyes.

"Don't you *ever* silence her like that again," Will said, his voice deep with barely restrained anger.

I'd never seen him this angry before, and I could tell that he was on the edge of losing that endless self-control he held with a tight fist.

"I came here tonight only because of her. You disrespect her again, and I swear to God, I will walk out of your life and never look back."

Anger bounced off Will's body like a heat wave, and I wondered for a moment if it was possible for a person to melt the walls down with their anger.

But Mr. Kobayashi was right there with him. He looked so angry and frustrated, and I knew that this was just a regurgitation of arguments that they'd been having for years: Mr. Kobayashi's need for control, to try and guide his children to what he thought was the best choice for them instead of letting them make that choice for themselves. And Will's resentment of that, of all the ways that he'd let his father control him, make him feel unsure about himself and his dreams. I knew that Will wanted to make sure that his father didn't control his sister the way he'd controlled him for so long, and I knew he felt guilt for not doing a better job of it since he was no longer in the house and could not protect her the way he wanted.

"I apologize, Genesis," Mr. Kobayashi said, voice hard. "This conversation feels inappropriate to have right now. Hikaru, we will discuss it at a later time."

"There is nothing left to discuss," Will responded firmly.

He was getting that infamous control back, his eyes no longer dilated and his fist slowly unraveling. I tried to catch his gaze, but he wouldn't look at me, instead picking up his glass and taking a hefty drink of his wine. He put down the glass gently on the table, still standing.

"As always, it's great to see you, Father, but I think Genesis and I should get going."

I silently stood up, instantly following Will's lead. I was worried about this fight, about Will leaving his celebratory dinner with his dad and what that would mean for his relationship with him. But ultimately, it was Will's choice. And if he didn't want to be here anymore, he shouldn't, and honestly, I didn't want him to be. This was meant to be a celebration of Will and his achievements. I didn't know how it'd turned south so quickly.

It had all been going so well. But then I'd mentioned Kata ...

I nearly groaned, feeling like the biggest idiot.

Mr. Kobayashi began to protest, standing up from the table. "Now, Hikaru, there's no need to act like a child. Sit down, and let's continue with our dinner."

"Mr. Kobayashi, with all due respect, sir," I began, sliding my chair into the table, "thank you for dinner, but right now, I think the best thing for everyone is to take some space."

I interlaced my hand with Will's, and he squeezed, his thumb grazing over my knuckles in silent thanks. Mr. Kobayashi didn't answer, but he nodded, face impassive. We said our good-byes quickly and stepped out of the private room, walking silently down the hall. I kept glancing at Will, trying to gauge how he was doing, but other than our hands still connected, Will looked straight ahead, as if he were on a mission alone. I kept his pace until we walked out of the restaurant, stopping and pulling on our locked hands to get his attention.

"Will," I started, worried. "What happened—"

He took a step toward me and pulled me into a hug. He pressed his face into my hair, his arms wrapped around my shoulders so that my body was pressed firmly against his. Without thought, my arms wrapped around his back, and I laid my head against his chest. We stood there for a long minute, silent and in each other's arms, the sounds of people walking past us on the streets and cars passing by a distant soundtrack as I listened to the melody of his heartbeat against my ear. It was one of my favorite songs, the way it drummed steadily in his chest like a calling card, letting me know that he was okay.

Will eventually pulled away, his hands trailing from my shoulders and down my arms until they got to my hands. He squeezed them in his own, a look of pain on his face. "I should let you go."

I studied his face, my earlier calm at being in his arms slowly fading as I replayed his words in my head. "You mean, go home?"

He said nothing for a long moment. "I'm sorry I didn't tell you about the contract."

I blinked, confusion on my face. "Will …"

"In that moment, I thought I was doing the right thing," he pressed, pushing through like he had something to say and he needed to make sure he said it. "I realize now that the way I handled the whole thing was wrong. I can't promise you that I'll never make a mistake again, but I can promise you that I'd never intentionally hurt you." His voice turned urgent as he squeezed my hands a little bit tighter, eyes bright with emotions. "I'm not that kind of person, Genesis. I need you to believe me when I say that."

"I believe you," I said, eyes locked on his, imploring him to hear the truth in my voice. "Will, you are not your father."

He stared at me like I held his heart in my hands, like I held his truth and resurrection. "I never meant to hurt you, and I hate that I did. I got scared, and I didn't want to lose you. But in trying to hold on to you, I took away your ability to make a choice of your own—for you to choose me—and I am an asshole for that."

I nodded, eyes glassy with emotions. I pulled him in for another hug, lips against his neck, as I whispered, "I believe you."

We stood in each other's arms outside of that building, whispering to each other as the busy city and people moved around us. The world kept moving, but there we stood, two people trying to take comfort in each other from pain we were trying to move past.

I didn't know where things were left with Will.

Being in his arms that night, just holding each other and bringing each other comfort, had made me feel whole in a way I hadn't felt in weeks. Being in his arms, my heart had felt like it was slowly being mended. But when we'd finally pulled away, Will had simply ordered me a cab, kissed me gently on the cheek, and with a request to text him when I got home, he'd closed the cab door and watched me drive away. We hadn't said a single word to each other. We didn't talk about the limbo we were still in or what our words to each other last night meant for us.

I felt confused. About where we stood. About how I felt.

I thought about him all weekend, about that night and these last two years and just everything that I knew about Will. About our relationship, his fears and my own. And it'd clicked for me sometime last night that even though it hurt me for him to lie, if I wanted to be with him—and I did—then I had to allow Will to be human, just like he'd allowed me that room. He wasn't perfect, and he hadn't intentionally gone out to hurt me. There was no malice or disregard for me in his actions—

quite the opposite. I'd believed him when he said he'd planned on telling me after the contest. In his head, he'd thought he was protecting me. There was some doubt, some worry, that had led him to hide it from me—I couldn't deny that. But that was something that could only be changed through time and effort on both of our sides.

I shared all of this with Cora as we got coffee on Monday morning and walked slowly to work. She had her hair pushed back with a yellow headband that matched the little yellow suns printed on her black button-down shirt, her unruly curls bouncing with her every step as she listened to me prattle on and on about my feelings, her face open and attentive.

"I also feel really bad that he hasn't had a real celebration of his contract," I finished, releasing a big breath. "I know everything is messy right now, but I was thinking … would it be insane for me to plan a little get-together with his friends and some coworkers as a surprise celebration for him?"

We stopped at the corner of the street, waiting for the light to turn red as cars sped by.

Cora shook her head, vibrating with excitement. "No, I think that's a great idea! It would be all people who want to celebrate Will and his exciting new change in his life, zero negativity—ooh! We could rent a karaoke bar! Get one of those private rooms!"

I laughed, watching as the wheels turned behind her light brown eyes. The light finally turned red, and we began walking again, staying close to each other as a crowd of pedestrians tried to walk through us.

"Okay, that's actually a good idea, but I have to get a head count first and figure out what day everyone could do."

"Do it this Wednesday," Cora suggested. "A lot of us in the finance department usually get drinks on Wednesdays, so it wouldn't be out of the ordinary if one of us invited Will. I could tell him you're going, which would guarantee him going, and then you guys could go together, and we could surprise him when you walk in."

She clapped, a big smile on her face, like she'd just solved world hunger, and I felt my own mouth curl up into a smile. It was hard not to be happy around Cora. She made you feel like every issue was minor and could be fixed so easily if you just talked it out.

"You are a genius," I stated. "And strangely really good at planning things out. Are you sure you shouldn't be an event planner or something?"

"Meh," she replied with shrug, taking a sip of her tea. "I just get all this inspiration when it comes to friends. Whenever I try to plan events for random people, I feel so uninspired and miserable."

We walked up to the building and swiped through the turnstiles, waving hello to Kirk, one of the security guards who blushed at Cora's bright smile.

"He has such a crush on you," I mumbled as we walked past him and toward the elevators. "Poor guy. I wonder if he'll ever get the guts to say something."

Cora waved off my comment. "Stop. No, he doesn't. Besides, Kirk is just being sweet; he has a wife and two kids at home. I probably just remind him of his daughter or something."

"I don't think parents blush when their daughter smiles at them," I joked, laughing when she looked at me with wide, embarrassed eyes.

It always made her uncomfortable whenever I pointed out the way men reacted to her. Like she didn't believe me, which made no sense because Cora was so pretty and so sweet. All she had to do was look at a guy, and he'd do whatever she wanted, but I didn't even think she realized that.

Meanwhile, most guys ran the opposite direction when I looked at them. But that could also have something to do with the scowl that was almost always on my face. Gotta love resting bitch face.

"Change of subject," Cora said brightly as the elevator opened.

We quickly piled on, holding hands so we didn't get pushed apart in the crowd of people. She turned toward me as we made it to the back, our sides nearly pressed to each other. I scowled at the man in front of me, who stepped on my foot, but tried to soften my face when he offered me a quick apology.

"Have you had your meeting with Dixinson yet?"

After sending Clements my song list and getting his okay, I'd spoken with Jacobs in the studio, which had gone surprisingly well. I'd thought he'd be defensive or not open to hearing my ideas—what with me being a "lowly" assistant and all—but he'd been enthusiastic to work with me and hear my ideas. We'd gotten along so well that he'd called me the next day, saying that Dixinson wanted to set up a time to talk music with me and hear my input on his sound for the shows he'd be playing.

To say I'd been shocked would be an understatement.

"It's Wednesday," I answered, biting down on my lip to hide my smile. Cora's smile brightened like she could feel my elation, and I said quietly to her, "I'm scared to be excited. But I am."

She leaned her head on my shoulder for a second and squeezed my arm. "You got this! Be excited! Because this is a great opportunity, and you're going to kill it. I mean, this is huge!"

I threw a hesitant smile at her. I knew she was right, but I just felt scared to get my hopes up when I'd been down this road before, and it never went far. I was confident in my work. I just didn't know if everyone in the studio would feel the same way on Wednesday. Dixinson was notorious for being stubborn. Once he had an idea stuck in his head, he didn't like to change it, no matter who was making the demands at him. I knew that he'd had major control over the sound choices made for his country album; he'd made a lot of demands that the label was all too happy to follow even if they now realized they'd kind of shot themselves in the foot with it.

If I went in there and told him my vision and he didn't like it, who knew how he'd react? At the very least, he could kick me out of the studio, and worst-case scenario, he could talk to Clements and demand I get fired for my incompetence.

I wished that were a dramatic scenario that wasn't realistic, but the very same thing had happened at his last label with a music tech intern.

"How are things going with Harrison?" I asked. Harrison, the AD in her department had not stopped picking on Cora's work since Christmas. If anything, he'd been worse these last few months.

The elevator opened, and a few people got off, which left us more room—thank God.

Cora made a face. "As well as expected. I've been debating on putting in a request to change teams, but I don't know. I don't want to make a big fuss. I'll probably just suck it up and hope I get promoted soon."

"Cora, you shouldn't have to 'suck it up,'" I argued, scowling. "He treats you like you're nothing more than an airhead who can do basic math when you're a freaking genius and you should be the head of the team! Even Will agrees and told me that half the team goes to you for guidance on projects."

Cora shrugged, brushing off my comment. "I like being helpful to the team, and I like my team. The guys are all great. Except for—"

"Mr. Fartface," I supplied, smiling at her exaggerated sigh.

"Harrison," she corrected, her mouth ticking up into a smile despite chastising tone. "I don't want to leave my team, but since Will is going to be leaving to be an artist on the label in a few weeks, who knows? Maybe I'll apply for his position."

I didn't like the idea of her still working with Harrison, who was a sexist pig. But I knew Cora well enough to know that she could be very stubborn when she wanted to be, and she seemed determined to stay on that team.

"What if you filed a report about Harrison," I said as the last person left the elevator, "I'm sure the rest of the team would back you, and then that way, HR would have to do something about it. He doesn't deserve to work there anymore."

"Genesis, I don't want to make waves," she said with a shake of her head. "I'll figure it out; don't worry."

I frowned but let it go for now. I wasn't going to stop bothering her about this though. One way or another, Mr. Fartface was going to get his Karma.

Today was just going to be one of those days. It seemed like no one knew how to do anything without my help. Sometimes, I felt more like their mother than a coworker with the way some of these men needed me to literally hold their hand through simple phone calls.

"Kenny," I said patiently as I went over the spreadsheet for the third time, "the red column is for the target traffic audience after seven days, and the green column is for after thirty days. You put the data in the wrong columns."

He grinned, nodding his head. "Got it! Thanks, Genesis! Clements would've had my ass if I'd sent this to the partners."

Yeah, no shit, I thought to myself but just nodded and headed back to my small cubicle.

I'd been bouncing around all day today, so I hadn't had a chance to sit at my desk at all. One glance at my watch showed that I'd almost worked through my lunch break again. I stopped at my desk, rubbing my eyes tiredly as I debated between making a quick run for lunch or just powering through to get my work done.

My eyes opened and snagged on a stack of notebooks sitting on my desk, white folded paper on top. "What the ..."

I walked closer to the pile, and my heart nearly jumped out of my chest when I saw my name scrawled in Will's handwriting. With a nervous breath, I picked up the paper, unfolded it, and began to read.

Genesis,

Loving you has been a religious experience. When you smile at me, it lights up my world. When our eyes lock, I'm weak in my knees. You speak my name, and it echoes in my ears like a prayer from the gods. I love you like the birds love the sky. When I'm with you, I feel free. Like a bird spreading its wings, in your arms, I know peace.

I want you to know me, this last secret layer. Do with my journals as you wish.

I love you. Then, now, and always.

Will

I blinked back tears, hand shaking slightly as I turned the letter over, noticing another page beneath it. This page looked like it had been ripped from one of the notebooks, the paper slightly yellowed from either age or the sun, splotches of ink scattered on the edges.

Album: The Book of Genesis

1. When We Met

2. Brown Eyes Speak to Mine

3. Take What I Can Get

4. Butterfly Glances

5. Waiting

6. Too Soon to Say

7. I Love You

8. Forever

I stared in shock as I read through the paper over and over. Will was naming his album after me. And the titles ...

I gently placed the paper on my desk and picked up the first notebook. It was navy blue and filled to the brim with papers sticking out on all sides. I opened it up and realized with a start that Will had given me every single one of his journals from the last couple of years. The first page was a scribble of thoughts and ideas about a song titled "Careful." I flipped to the next page, heart aching in my chest at the trust, the gravity of what Will had given me. He was showing me the inside of his soul, the pieces of him that he didn't share with anyone else. As I looked through each page, I found a kaleidoscope of Will—pages about his family, his friends, his loneliness and yearning for something that he couldn't quite name.

My fingers paused when I got to a page with notes for his song "When We Met." It was a mess of ideas and feelings, half-scratched out words as he had written over each line like he couldn't get the words out fast enough. The page was dated, and I swallowed thickly when I realized he'd written this song six months after I started working here.

The song spoke about a girl who stepped into his life and rocked his world on its axis with a single smile. I read through every line of the song like a secret that was meant only for me. I read and reread over and over before forcing myself to continue through the journals, finding song after song about me. They weren't all written in that first journal, instead spanning over two years. Some were silly songs wrapped in love, like the one titled "American Cuisine," which was about the first time we'd ordered Japanese food all those months ago after practice. I gave a watery laugh as I read his lyrics, remembering how we'd had our first almost kiss in that moment and wondering how differently things would have been if I'd stood on my tippy-toes and touched my lips to his in that kitchen.

All these years, I'd thought Will hated me, and I couldn't have been further from the truth. I knew that, and yet reading through these journals, knowing the depth of his affection and love for me, left me feeling overwhelmed with emotions. He'd been waiting for me. For two years, he had waited for me. Secretly helping me without ever expecting a thing in return, finding ways to be around me even if it meant sparring with me over inane things at work. He saw every single piece of me, and instead of finding me exhausting or not worth the trouble, he loved me. Quietly at first. A secret only for him but then loudly with every glance, every touch that we shared, daring me to love him back but satisfied in the feeling that he could at least be in my universe.

"Buttercup."

I looked up, not believing my ears. "Will!" I nearly dropped the journal in my hands.

He stood at the entrance of my cubicle, a nervous smile on his face.

I hugged the journal in my arms and blurted, "I read your journals. And the letter."

He nodded, eyes staring deeply into mine. "I'm glad."

I watched him, heart beating wildly in my chest as we just stared at each other for a long minute. There was so much I wanted to say, so much that was running through my head, words that I had always been afraid to say out loud but had rung true for me for a long time now.

Will stepped back. "I'll go."

"You waited for me," I blurted out, unconsciously reaching a hand out toward him. I blushed, putting my hand down, but kept my eyes on his as he watched me with quiet eyes. "All this time, you cared about me, but you never said anything."

"Genesis." He sounded winded, eyes locked on mine. "I would've waited a hundred years for you. You are all I see, all I've ever seen."

"I see you," I said softly, taking a small step toward him. "It scared me back then, the way you could light me up in a way no one else could. But in a way, I've been waiting for you too. A secret hope that I didn't dare say out loud because love had always been a scary thing to me." I took another step toward him, heart beating a calm tempo in my chest. I wasn't afraid to say these next words because I knew that this unexpected fall had always been destined from the start. "I love you. Then, now, and always."

As I repeated his words back to him, his eyes darkened, a shaky sigh leaving his lips. "Say it again. Please."

I walked closer to him, my fingers gripping his waist as I looked up at him. "I love you," I said breathlessly. It felt so good to finally say the words, to say the feeling that had been inside me for so long.

To love was to look at imperfection and find beauty in its cracks.

"I love you so much," he said lowly, voice rough. He leaned his face closer to mine, our foreheads brushing as he spoke his next words onto my lips. "No matter where life takes us, I want to get through every obstacle with you."

"That's all I want," I whispered. "I don't want you to ever hide anything from me because you don't think I can handle it. I'm your partner, and no matter what, I will always be there for you, just like I know you'll always be there for me."

Will kissed me, hands cupping my face as he poured every inch of his love into me. I grasped his wrists, eagerly returning his kiss, heart soaring with joy. He tilted my head, deepening our kiss, and I nearly whimpered at the feel of his tongue touching mine.

I pulled away with a small gasp. "I never want to stop kissing you, but—"

"You don't want to make a spectacle at work," he finished for me, breathing heavily as he eyed my lips.

I smiled so hard that I knew my cheeks would hurt from it. "

Since officially getting back together, we spent hours after work every day, just talking. Will had told me everything that was going on with the band, how they were going to be officially signing on with Will and joining him on tour next year. I talked to him about my work with Jacobs and Dixinson, how I felt hopeful for the first time in a while, but that I was still applying to other labels, just in case. In between our long conversations, Will had helped me with an Alejandra crisis after she got in a fight with her boyfriend, and I'd helped Will repair things with his father. Will had spent over an hour on the phone just talking to his dad and I think it was the first conversation they had in a long time that didn't end with any arguments.

Things were busy, but they were perfect.

"Let's skip the drinks," Will murmured in my ear from behind. His arms hugged me closer to him, and I felt his lips brush my ear as he continued, "Come back to my place."

I leaned back against him with a smile. "We can go back to your place after. I want to do drinks with everyone."

"And I want the taste of your pussy on my tongue," he said lowly, his hands moving slowly from my stomach to my hips, stopping dangerously close to my inner thighs.

"Will," I said with a breathy moan. I pulled away and turned, knowing I needed to stay firm on this even though I missed his touch and wanted it just as desperately as he did.

"Come back here," he growled playfully, arms reaching for mine.

I let him pull me in, and he reclined against my desk, moving me so that I was standing in between his legs. I wrapped my arms lightly around his neck, but when he leaned down to kiss me, I pulled back, giggling when he growled again.

"Will, we have to get going." I laughed at the adamant shake of his head before he rested his forehead against my chest. "I'll go back to your place after the bar. We can watch the next Star Wars movie and order food."

"And we'll be naked," he added, a devilish grin on his face. "Don't forget the naked part, Buttercup."

I shook my head, smiling, but added, "And we'll be naked."

He nodded, looking satisfied, but then added, "I also want to hear about how it went with Dixinson. Tell me on the way there?"

I kissed him softly on the lips. "Yes. I need you to analyze this meeting with me."

He smiled, pulling me in for another kiss. "I'm so proud of you."

My heart squeezed, and I couldn't help the smile that took over my face. "I'm proud of me too. And I'm proud of you. So, so proud and happy. My little rock star."

He groaned, letting out a small laugh. "God, no. The last thing I want is to be a rock star."

"Can I be one of your groupies?" I asked with a teasing smile.

His hands drifted to my ass, squeezing it roughly as he yanked me close enough that there was no space between us. My chest brushed against his, and I squirmed as his hands massaged my ass cheeks, a beautiful mix of sharp squeezes, followed by soft caresses.

His eyes met mine, sharp and hot. "You are the only one who matters. The only one I want to see at my shows, the only one that I see."

"A simple no would've sufficed," I joked halfheartedly, trying to hide the hearts that were probably flashing in my eyes from his words.

Will looked down at me in front of him, and I pushed up on my toes, kissing him again.

"I can't wait to watch your dreams come true."

His eyes brightened, his hands trailing up my back and into my hair. "Your dreams are my dreams, baby. I can't wait to watch us achieve everything we've ever wanted—together."

"Okay, seriously, you guys are too freaking cute."

I pulled away from Will slightly to look back toward Cora, who was standing at the entrance of my cubicle, a bright smile spread across her face.

"Hey." I pulled fully away and turned toward Cora, who was still staring at us in adoration. "Is everyone still on for drinks?"

Cora nodded, eyes never leaving mine. "Yep. Everything is good to go. Um, just one thing. Everyone has decided to go somewhere different today. Not too far, of course, but no biggie!"

I stared at her with wide eyes, trying to communicate that she needed to pull her act together. She was a bad liar, and it was obvious she was nervous about something.

"Okay, well, just send us the address," I reminded her firmly, eyebrows high with meaning.

"Yes. Yes, I'll do that." She clapped, cheerfulness taking over her nerves. "Okay, well, see you guys soon!"

With a final wave to us both, she turned back around and quickly left. I sighed, shaking my head as I turned back toward Will.

"She doesn't want to come with us to the bar?" Will asked with a quizzical look. "We're all going to the same place anyway."

"I think she has a few other things to do before going," I lied with a shrug. Man, I was going to have a serious conversation with Cora about her acting skills. "Anyway, we should probably get going."

Will sighed but nodded. Hopefully, once he saw what this outing was really about, it would boost his enthusiasm.

It didn't take us long to get out of the building and start walking to the train. We held hands the entire walk, and I couldn't stop grinning even if I wanted to. Being with him made me so unbelievably happy, and if the smiles he kept throwing my way were telling me anything, he felt the same way.

"So, Dickinson," I said once the train passed through the station, bypassing our stop and making enough noise that it probably woke the dead.

Will looked at me, giving me his undivided attention as I shared everything that had happened, every feeling I'd felt, and how I felt the meeting had gone overall.

"I'm so happy for you." He pulled me into a hug.

By now, we were on the crowded train, holding on to one of the poles as we stood.

"It sounds like you made a really great impression not only with Jacobs, but with Dickinson as well. I wouldn't be surprised if Jacobs asked for you again in the future."

I beamed, heart feeling so light that it probably would've floated away had it not been contained in my chest. "You really think so? I don't know. I mean, it was just one conversation, but Will, being in that room, talking music with them?" I let out a happy sigh, staring at him with wide eyes as I tried to express how it'd felt. "It was just … it's where I belong. I felt it in that moment, and I know that it's where I need to be. I don't want to be an assistant anymore. Not after getting a taste of my dream. I don't want to go back."

"You won't have to," he promised, kissing me on the top of my head.

I leaned my head against his chest, letting myself get lost in thought as I swayed gently with the train car. I didn't know what I would do, but in that moment, I honestly felt like I would quit if I had to continue working as an assistant. I wasn't miserable, but it didn't bring me happiness. I didn't feel fulfilled doing it, and while the marketing aspect was interesting, I knew it wasn't my true calling. I wanted my dream job, and I was tired of waiting for it.

So much so that I'd set up a meeting with Clements about it, stating I wanted to do my yearly evaluation a few months early. I didn't know what I would say next week if Clements said I was going to continue as an administrative marketing assistant, especially when I'd made it abundantly clear that I wanted to move on to different things.

I pushed the thought away as the train came to a stop, and Will and I exited. I slipped my phone out of my pocket and looked at the address that Cora had sent. It was a karaoke bar on St. Marks called Sing, Sing, and according to Google Maps, it wasn't a long walk from the train.

"Did I tell you that Callum wants to get a dog?" Will asked, mouth curving into a smile.

I chuckled, already picturing the crazy theories and reasons behind his idea. "Why does he want a dog?"

"Apparently, he's been lacking in companionship," Will said with a shake of his head, amused smile on his face. "I brought up the many women he's been with, but he said that he needed someone to relax with and that the only time he's felt relaxed with a woman is after he's … well, you know."

"God, he is so predictable," I said with a small laugh. "Well, does this mean you'll be getting a dog in your apartment?"

"I told him to wait a month and that if he still wanted a dog, then I'd be cool with it," Will answered with a shrug of his broad shoulders. "But I don't know how good of an idea it is to get a pet when he's not home much."

"I could totally see him with a golden retriever," I mused, smiling. "He and his dog would have matching hair; it'd be so cute."

Will laughed. "Don't go getting a crush on him if he gets that dog."

"No promises," I said with a wink, pulling Will toward the entrance of the bar.

"A karaoke bar?" he asked, surprise in his tone.

I shrugged and silently led him inside, telling the woman at the front that we had a room reserved. Will looked at me, questions in his eyes, and I knew I had to give him something.

"Phil said he didn't want to get outshone by anyone in public, so he reserved a private room for karaoke," I explained with another shrug. "Something about getting booed off a stage the last time he came here or something."

Will winced and then chuckled. "Yeah, that was brutal. But in defense of the crowd, he sang 'Chandelier' by Sia, and I think dogs all around the world heard him when he tried to hit those high notes."

I laughed, heart racing as we got closer to the room. I just hoped everyone was there and that he was surprised in a good way and not annoyed.

"Enjoy," the young woman said with a smile.

"Thank you," I said, putting my hand on the handle. With one final quick breath, I turned the knob and slowly opened the door.

"Surprise!"

I looked up at Will, a nervous smile on my face as I waited to see his reaction. He blinked in surprise, eyes bouncing around the room as a big smile took over his face.

"Congratulations, Mr. Pop Star!" someone yelled.

I heard a bunch of people start cheering and clapping, but I kept my eyes on his face.

"Holy shit." He laughed, grinning hard as he ran a hand through his hair. He turned toward me, surprise coating his face still. "Did you plan this?"

I nodded, biting my lip slightly. "Cora helped me. I thought you deserved a real celebration, one where we celebrated you. Are...are you happy?"

Will leaned his head down, his hand on my waist as he kissed me in answer. Everyone in the room went crazy again, screaming and whooping.

I felt my mouth turn up into a smile when I heard Callum's unmistakable voice shout, "Yeah, tongue action!"

Will pulled away, laughing with me as he wrapped his arm around my shoulders and pulled me into his side. I leaned my face against his arm as I looked up at him.

"Wow, thank you for doing this and for coming out today. I'm ... truly at a loss for words, but this means so much to me. So, thank you."

Everyone cheered again, and then someone must've turned the karaoke on because heavy bass came out from the speakers as everyone started talking again. I looked around the room, taking in the twenty or so people who had come. The room was spacious with multiple sofas with tables in front of them, alcohol bottles scattered around. I saw most of Will's team in one corner and a few other people from work that I knew Will was friendly with.

"Walk with me?" he murmured into my ear, pulling my eyes back to his.

I nodded, pulling away to hold his hand. He made his way through his friends, and I happily joined in conversations, smiling wide as I watched Will in his element and looking so incredibly happy.

"It's about time you got over here!" Cal shouted with a big grin, pulling Will into a hug. He turned toward me a moment later, arms opened wide, and said, "Come give daddy some sugar."

Will smacked the back of his head, and I laughed, stepping toward Cal and giving him a big hug and kiss on his cheek.

"Thanks for coming, guys," Will said to Sam and Zander, who were standing with Cal, drinks in hand.

Zander was wearing a white button-down and slacks, looking like he had come straight from work. He had his sleeves rolled up to his forearms, and despite the small smile he had on his face as he greeted Will, his eyes stayed their usual somber self. He had the saddest eyes I'd ever seen, and knowing him for the last few months, I'd never seen him look truly happy. In fact, it seemed the more I saw him, the sadder he looked each time. Like someone who was living their life, going through the motions but not really feeling anything. I just hoped one day, he could move on from whatever was holding him back.

"You think you could hook me up with that girl wearing the red sweater?" Sam asked, head turning to look behind Will.

I turned to look and nearly scowled when I saw it was Cora he was talking about. She was oblivious to his stares, of course, talking to a group of coworkers with a bright smile, hands animated as she spoke.

"She's unavailable," I said before Will could say anything, and Sam looked to me with a raised brow. "She's in a relationship."

Sam shrugged, undeterred. "Hasn't stopped me before."

I narrowed my eyes, biting my tongue before I said something that would inevitably lead to an argument. I'd grown fond of Zander and his quiet yet powerful presence. And Cal and his ability to make you laugh, no matter how you were feeling or where you were. But Sam? Not so much. It was clear he had no plans of ever being in a relationship, and sometimes, when he looked at me, I got the distinct feeling that he purposely said sexist shit just to make me uncomfortable. Like he wanted to see how much he could get away with until I threw a fit or left. But I'd also seen his loyalty to Will and the way he was always the first to be there for his friend, and it made me wonder if there was more to him than just a gross man-whore.

"Man, keep it in your pants for one freaking evening," Zander's deep voice boomed as he shook his head. "These are the people Will works with. Don't shit where he eats."

Sam rolled his eyes but finally turned from Cora. "Fine. It's not like I don't have a phone filled with girls' numbers anyway. This one girl I met last night has the fattest—"

Ugh. My lips curled in disgust, and I pretended to be fascinated with my shoes as I tried to tune out the rest of his words.

I felt Will's hand squeeze mine gently, and I looked over at him.

You okay? he mouthed, and I nodded with a smile.

I leaned my head against his arm and went back to people-gazing as Will talked to Zander about a new keyboard he'd found online. Jill from human resources had just finished a pretty great rendition of "Dancing Queen" when I felt a tap on my shoulder.

I turned, mood immediately brightening when I saw Yari, her face flushed like she'd run from the train.

"You made it!" I exclaimed, letting go of Will's hand to hug her. She smelled like honey and white jasmine flowers, and I touched her dark brown hair as I pulled away. "You dyed your hair back."

She nodded and then shrugged. "Turned out, blondes don't have as much fun as I thought."

"Good to have you back, *prima.*" I winked, and she laughed, shaking her head.

Yari moved around me, a big grin on her face as she looked at Will. "Here's the man of the hour. Congratulations, future brother-in-law!"

I just nearly controlled the urge to kick her in the back of the leg as she hugged Will, his face amused as he looked over at me. I widened my eyes in innocence and blew him a kiss, which only made him laugh loudly.

"Thanks for coming, Yari," Will said as he pulled away. "Can I get you a drink or—"

"Will, please," Sam said, interrupting him as he stepped closer. "You are a celebrity now; you don't serve drinks. Allow me to take care of our beautiful guest."

Yari looked over at Sam with an amused glance before taking in the rest of the guys. I could tell she was connecting the dots on who they could potentially be, but as I went to introduce them, her gaze snagged on Cal, who was staring intently at her, his mouth ticked up into a half-smile.

"Yari, these are my closest friends." Will gestured to the three men. "This is Sam, Zander, and Cal."

Cal was surprisingly quiet, offering a nod and a quick handshake in greeting, though he still hadn't looked away from her. Zander offered the same but quickly turned back to Will, showing him something on his phone as they quietly talked.

"What's your drink of choice?" Sam asked Yari with a flirty smile. "Sex on the Beach? Screaming Orgasm?"

"Get Lost," Yari answered with a sweet smile.

Sam looked at her in confusion, likely unsure if she was telling him an actual drink name or if she was telling him to go away.

"It's a drink that Genesis and I made up a few years ago. It's a little complicated, so I'll just make it myself."

She moved toward the table of liquor and juices, not looking back at him as she took her jacket off and hung it over the side of a chair. She was wearing jeans with thigh-high boots and a long-sleeved maroon crop top that showed off her toned light-brown skin. Sam's eyes nearly fell out of his head as he stared at her ass, and I snickered when Cal smacked the back of his head, shooting daggers at him.

"What the fuck, man?" Sam complained, rubbing his head. "You haven't even said two words to her. There's no way you get to call dibs."

"That's Genesis's cousin, idiot," Cal said, eyes trailing back to Yari for a moment before returning to Sam. "What part of *keep it in your pants tonight* are you not getting?"

"If I'd known this was going to be a cockblock party, I would've rubbed one out before I left home," Sam grumbled. He picked up his drink, and with a salute, he walked up to a small group of girls not too far away.

Cal sighed, watching him go before turning to me with a wicked smile. "So, about your cousin …"

"Don't even think about it," I said, lip twitching.

"What?" he said innocently, blinking his big green eyes at me. "I was just going to ask if she has any experience with dogs. I'm in the market for one, and I could use some pointers."

I hummed. "Will hasn't agreed yet."

"But he will," Cal said confidently, grinning. "He can't say no to me. I'm his best friend. Besides, getting a dog would help me feel not so lonely once we start going on tour and are constantly moving around."

"Whoa there," I said, holding my hands up with a laugh. "That won't happen for at least another year, if not longer. Besides, you know Will; he's never going to leave New York for long."

"That's what they all say," Cal said, lifting his drink toward me. "But then they get a whiff of the world, and it's *hasta la vista, New York*, and *hello, Beverly Hills*."

I frowned, trying to imagine Will in Beverly Hills. Would he like it there? Would I go with him? Or would we do the long-distance thing? We had a while before we had to start thinking about that, but we should probably be at least thinking about it, shouldn't we?

"Whoa, I didn't mean to make you upset," Cal said with panicked eyes. "Quick, start laughing, or he'll come over here and beat me up for making you sad."

I laughed. "It's fine. You didn't make me sad. And Will would never beat you up."

Cal shook his head, a small smile playing at his lips. "When it comes to you, there are very few things he wouldn't do."

"*Prima*, I made you another drink." Yari walked back to my side and passed me a cup filled to the brim with liquid.

I took one sniff and could smell the heady mix of vodka and Jack Daniel's with just a splash of a juice. Our drink was called Get Lost for a reason—a few cups of this drink, and you didn't know who you were, much less where the heck you were. The first time we'd made this drink, we were pregaming before going out, but we didn't realize how strong of a combination we'd made until we got on the train. We were so drunk that we ended up in Far Rockaway and completely lost. We couldn't even remember our addresses. It was a crazy night. Thankfully, we had been able to pull it together enough to call my sister and have her order us an Uber from our location on my phone.

"Hey, Cal. Come here for a sec," Will called, holding out his phone.

Cal nodded at us, his eyes staying on Yari's for a second before leaving.

"Shall we go say hi to Cora?" Yari asked, surprisingly not mentioning Cal's obvious interest in her.

I nodded, and we walked arm in arm to the other side of the room as Yari told me about her mom's latest scheme to get her to move back home.

"I swear it's like she doesn't realize that her schemes just make me want to run farther away," Yari said with a shake of her head. "With the daily phone calls of guilt and weekly visits, it feels like I never even left anyway. She's driving me insane."

We walked up to Cora, who squealed when she saw Yari, throwing her arms around her. "Yaya, you're here!"

Yari hugged her, petting her pretty curls as she looked Cora over. "I see you didn't wait for me to start drinking."

I laughed. Cora was a legendary lightweight. It only took a few sips of a drink for her to hit tipsy land and not much more for her to get drunk.

Cora pouted, her arms crossing over her chest for a moment before she brightened. "Now that you're here, we can do karaoke together!"

I grimaced, and Yari quickly shook her head.

"Oh, hell no." Yari lifted her drink with a raised brow. "I am not even close to being drunk enough to start singing in front of a bunch of strangers."

"So then, get drunk," Cora quipped, bouncing on her toes. "Because I'm going to put us down for a song. And, Genesis, before you object, it's mandatory that you sing with us."

I groaned. "Just do not pick a girl power song, or I swear I will leave you to fend for yourself."

"No promises," she sang and quickly walked away and toward the karaoke setup.

"She's going to make us look like idiots, isn't she?" Yari said with a sigh.

"No doubt about it," I agreed solemnly. "We'd better start drinking, so we don't remember this in the morning."

She raised her cup toward me. "Cheers to that."

Turned out that there was a bit of a line to sing karaoke, which Yari, Cora, and I used as an opportunity to drink some more and chat. There was nothing that made you feel happier than drinking with your girls. Cora spilling her drink on her shirt and Yari trying to prove that you could salsa to any song by dancing salsa to "(Everything I Do) I Do It for You" by Bryan Adams had me laughing so hard that if I didn't have six-pack abs by the end of the night, then I'd be suing.

I didn't know who I'd be suing—maybe myself.

I'd figure it out later, if the abs weren't there.

"We're up!" Cora sang, throwing her hands up in a little dance.

"Fuck," I mumbled as Yari shouted, "Let's do this, *chicas!*"

Cora clasped my hand in hers and half-dragged me to the karaoke machine right as a few guys from accounting finished the last chorus of his song. The group of guys were rowdy, riding the high of performing as they handed the microphones to us.

I took one with a soft, "Thanks."

"Why am I scared to see what song you picked?" I asked her, tapping my microphone lightly with my finger.

I realized suddenly that I hadn't seen Will in a while and looked up, eyes searching the room for him. I found him a moment later, sitting with Zander and Callum at a table, an amused look on his face. Zander and Callum gave me a big thumbs-up. Then, Callum cupped his hands around his mouth and hooted as Zander shook his head, mouth tipped into the world's tiniest smile. I scrunched up my nose and gave a thumbs-down, laughing.

"Have faith. I have great taste in music," Cora answered with a grin. She blew kisses to a few coworkers and shouted into the microphone, "I want to see everyone up and dancing with us to this song! Come on, guys. We're here to celebrate Will's big record deal. Let's make some noise!"

Everyone started cheering, myself included. Grinning wide, I looked back at Will, throwing him my own kisses with a wink. A second later, I heard the intro of our song begin to play, and I looked back toward the screen, watching as the title "This is How We Do It" by Montell Jordan appeared on the screen. I barked out a laugh, and Cora gave a proud smile, already bouncing on her toes.

This was one of our favorite jam session songs. We'd had many girls' nights and nights out to this song. It didn't matter the occasion; this song was always necessary to pump us up for socializing.

Yari started dancing, clapping her hands to the beat, and quickly, the room clapped along with her. I clapped, too, laughing hard at Cora and Yari as they seemed to dance in sync. We sang the song perfectly without even needing to look at the words on the screen, and by the first chorus, I wasn't even feeling nervous about people listening to me sing, especially since everyone was singing loudly with us.

By the end of the song, we hugged, and my cheeks hurt from how much I'd been smiling not only in the last four minutes, but also in the last few hours.

"That was so much fun!" Cora shouted.

I nodded in agreement, squeezing her into a hug as I gave her a quick kiss on the cheek.

"Solid song choice," I complimented as we walked back toward the sofa with the guys. I fanned my face with my hands and then realized almost absently that I'd left my cup by the karaoke machine. It was so hot that I'd have to ask about turning on an air conditioner in here or something.

We stopped in front of the sofa, and Cal immediately stood up, giving us high fives.

"Oh shit, that was amazing!" he exclaimed, laughing. "You guys had the whole room so hyped up. And your dance moves were fire."

"I know, right?" Cora grinned, plopping down on the sofa. She began waving her hand at her face from the heat, trying to push back her curls from her neck.

I looked toward Will, who was grinning so hard that I felt myself smiling again for the millionth time tonight just from looking at him. "Hey, handsome."

Will laughed, wrapping his arms around my waist as he pulled me in closer. "Hello, beautiful. You were shining up there. I couldn't keep my eyes off of you. Did you have fun?"

I hummed in agreement, wrapping my arms around his neck. I put pressure on the back of his neck slightly as I demanded, "Kiss."

His eyes were lit with mirth as he leaned his head down to kiss me. "Anything else?"

"Can we expect a song from you tonight?" I asked, playing with his hair on the back of his head.

"If you'll join me," he answered, eyes dancing around my face. He frowned a second later. "You're flushed. Do you want some water?"

I nodded. "Thanks. It's really hot in here, don't you think?"

Will led me to the table with a vase of clear liquid, and with a quick sniff, he poured me a cup. "They have the air-conditioning blasting in here. Come, sit with me."

He led me to the sofa, and I happily took a seat on his lap, wrapping one arm around his shoulders as I sat sideways so I could still see his face and everyone around me.

"Drink," he reminded me gently, brows furrowed.

I gulped the water down quickly, instantly realizing how parched I was. Before I knew it, my cup was empty, and I had to wipe the side of my mouth as some water had spilled down my cheek. I grinned sheepishly, but Will just looked satisfied, nodding his head as he put my cup down.

I laid my head against him, listening in as Cora animatedly explained why Cal should get a Bernese mountain dog, hands gesticulating wildly. Yari pulled out her phone to show everyone a picture of the dog Cora was talking about, and they were all talking over each other about dogs and limited space in New York City apartments.

I watched silently, a small smile on my face, content to be in Will's lap and just enjoying the night. I didn't know what life would look like for us in the next few months, but I knew that things were changing. Hell, they changed every single day. Will's career would be taking off, and that could potentially mean less time with his friends, maybe even less time with me. Cora was my best friend, and I knew we'd always be in each other's lives, but I honestly didn't know if I could see myself staying at Siren Music Records if I had to be an assistant for another year. Would things change if we didn't see each other every day at work? And Yari would always be in my life, too, but more and more every day, she was taking control of her future, and it looked like that could mean finally saying good-bye to New York. She'd always said she never planned on living here forever. She'd been saying it since we were little kids. That could change soon, which meant no more after-work drinks at her place or meeting in the park or the city, just to spend time together and vent about our lives.

"You okay?" Will asked lowly, lips brushing the top of my head.

I pulled away, so I could look at him. "Do you ever get sad, thinking about how much your life is going to change and there's nothing you can do about it? I mean, happy because it's a good change, but also sad?"

His hand pushed a strand of my dark hair behind my ear, his eyes intently on mine. "Even when you want change, you can dread it at the same time."

I nodded, soaking in his words. "I was just thinking about how life is always changing and how these moments never last. Change is good—I know it is—but there's comfort in knowing you can always count on someone to be there, always available whenever you might need them."

Will studied my face, frowning. "You know you can always count on me, right? I'm always going to be there for you. Doesn't matter if I'm an assistant or an artist at the label. You need me, and I'll be there."

I smiled softly. "I know."

He gave me a look, likely knowing that I wasn't being completely forthcoming with my thoughts. "I feel like there's a but there that you're not saying."

"Will, stop talking about butts in front of our friends," I teased. "Or at least wait till we're in private."

Will slid his hand up to my hip, gripping it lightly. "I know what you're doing, Genesis."

"I don't know what you're talking about," I replied innocently, leaning in to lay a soft kiss on the underside of his jaw.

His hand flexed slightly on my hip before he began lightly trailing it up and down the side of my leg.

"Hey, lovebirds!" Cal shouted, standing above us.

I slowly looked at Cal, giving him my best *go away* expression, to which he just grinned and said, "You're up next for karaoke."

I perked up, looking excitedly at Will. "You're singing!"

"No, *we're* singing," Will amended confidently.

I frowned, looking at Cal, who nodded and threw a thumb over his shoulder. "Go on up. We can't have a party for Will and not hear the voice that's going to make us millions."

Will rolled his eyes but gently tapped my leg to stand up. I did and immediately made eye contact with Yari, who winked.

"You don't have to if you don't want to," Will reminded me, making me turn toward him.

"No, I want to," I said, knowing in my heart that it was true. I grabbed his hand and interlaced our fingers. "Let's do this."

He nodded, and we began our trek to the front. Of course, people were patting Will's shoulder and shouting for him over the music. It didn't take long for us to get to the front and pick up the microphones from the table.

I tapped my fingers against my leg as I waited for the song to begin. After a moment, the screen turned black, and letters began to roll up from the bottom of the screen. "You're the One That I Want" from the *Grease* soundtrack came up, and I had to fight my grin as I looked at Will, who was waggling his eyebrows comically at me.

He sang out Danny Zuko's lines in the song, his voice sounding somehow both soulful and sexy, and I felt myself hypnotized by his voice for the thousandth time.

I moved my eyes from his microphone to his face, and my heart leaped into my throat when I found that he was already staring right at me, a small smile on his face.

I sang Sandy's part, moving my hips to the beat and grinning as I pointed at him dramatically.

I continued to sing the song, and like it always did, I felt my nerves and all my other thoughts disappear as I orbited around Will. It was just me and him up there. By the time the chorus came around, I couldn't stop myself from laughing out loud, especially when Will started dancing around me, like he was really playing the role of Danny Zuko.

When the song ended, it felt like the room seemed to vibrate with everyone's cheers, my ears ringing with the sound. More than one person came up to us, patting us on the back, and I gave a small smile in thanks and handed the microphone to the guy manning the karaoke machine.

Will came up to me, and I tilted my head up to see him, feeling a little dazed. He pressed his thumb into my chin, his forehead leaning on mine for a moment as he whispered roughly, "Thank you."

I closed my eyes at the rush of emotions that seemed to exhale on his breath and into my own. Was it possible to love someone more than I loved Will? With every rise and fall of my chest, I felt my love for him like it was a living thing inside of me.

A moment later, I felt someone hug me from behind, jostling me as they jumped up and down. "You sounded so amazing!"

Will stepped back, which allowed me to turn and look at Cora, who immediately threw herself in my arms, still raving about our silly karaoke performance.

"Cora, stop jumping, or you're going to make yourself throw up," I warned, putting my hands firmly on her shoulders.

She stopped but looked at me with wide eyes. "Your voice is like an angel."

Now, I laughed, giving her a half-hug as I moved us away from the karaoke machine and to the side so the next group could go. "Okay, enough drinking for you."

She nodded, touching her lip. "Yeah, you're probably right."

"Let me get you some water," Will offered, coming to stand by my side.

I smiled up at him in thanks and said to Cora, "But if you want to hear an angel sing ... you should put Sam down for a Mariah Carey song. That guy has vocals that could make the heavens weep."

Cora lit up with intrigue, and I laughed as Will shook his head at me, amusement in his eyes at my little prank.

There was nothing better than this moment, with the people that we loved. And I never wanted it to end.

I woke to the feeling of soft kisses trailing slowly down my spine.

I groaned, hiding my face deeper in my pillow, trying to block out the rays of sun I could feel beaming from behind the curtains.

"Wake up, beautiful," Will murmured against my skin, his hands tracing patterns on my sides.

I squirmed slightly, loving the feeling of his lips on my skin, even as I battled with the need to go back to sleep. His fingers trailed down to my hips, hand shaping over my ass cheeks in a soft caress, like a sculptor in awe of their creation. I jumped slightly when I felt a sharp nip on my right cheek, his lips sucking away the sting a moment later. He did the same to my other cheek, and I couldn't hide the low moan that came out or the way my hips slightly lifted of their own accord, seeking out more.

He flipped me over effortlessly, and I welcomed it, breathlessly awake as my arms reached out for him. But he didn't crawl on top of me like I wanted. Instead, he looked at me with hungry eyes, eyes that made me ache between my thighs with anticipation. He slowly slid off the bed and yanked me to the edge as he got down on his knees. He threw one of my legs over his shoulder, his mouth kissing my inner thigh, eyes never leaving mine.

"Will," I moaned, hips restless as I ached to feel his lips between my thighs.

His hands slid up to cup my small breast as he leaned in, and slowly, so achingly slowly, he finally licked me where I needed him most. He groaned, eyes closing as he leaned in closer, and I almost came from just looking at him with his face pressed against me, ravenous. His fingers began to play with my nipples, massaging one breast as he tweaked my nipple in the other, his lips and tongue playing my pussy like a beautiful symphony of pleasure. It only took one light suck of his mouth on my clit to send me off, and I came loudly, hands fisting in his hair as I rode through the waves of euphoria coursing through my body and behind my eyes.

When I came down, I noticed that we had moved back onto the middle of the bed, Will hovering on top of me as he began spreading soft kisses around my breasts. His tongue gently traced around one nipple, causing my hips to jerk toward him, a moan leaving my mouth. He hummed deeply before he took my nipple into his mouth, sucking hard. If I hadn't already been wet before, I was drenched now. I fisted my hands in his hair, legs wrapping around his as I shamelessly ground against him.

"Come closer," I pleaded.

My hands yanked on the elastic of his boxer briefs, trying to simultaneously pull him closer and pull them off him. He looked up, his lips leaving my breast with a loud, wet sound, his eyes midnight black and hair disheveled from my hands.

I licked my lips, my hand gripping his cock as I said, "I need you."

He surged up and locked lips with me, tongue plunging into my mouth. I nearly wept with relief, tongue sweeping over his in a game that I would never tire of. I tugged on his cock still in my hand, moving my fist up and down his shaft, and his groan vibrated against my lips.

"Fuck," he hissed, his hand covering mine as he yanked my hand off his cock.

I looked up, heart racing with anticipation as he put his hands on the backs of my thighs and pushed down until my knees touched my chest. He entered me swiftly, and I had to bite down on my lip to hold in my scream of pleasure, eyes rolling back.

Sex with Will was indescribable. It was dirty and pleasurable and incandescently beautiful in the way that sex was when you loved someone and they knew exactly how to make you scream. I forced myself to keep my eyes open because I wanted to watch Will as he lost control, his hands squeezing my thighs tightly, cock slamming into me over and over, his lips tight like he was in pain.

"Fuck, you're so tight," he grunted, grinding down on my clit.

I moaned, insides squeezing around him, and he cursed, eyes hungry as he watched with rapt fascination as his cock entered me.

"Look at your pussy, sucking me in. It doesn't want me to go; it wants me to stay inside you."

"Don't stop," I pleaded, spreading my thighs wider. "I'm so close."

He quickened his thrusts, thumb rubbing my clit in perfect tandem, and I nearly wept with joy as I felt myself coming for the second time. He came a few moments after me, head thrown back, and I watched as his hips jerked roughly before he collapsed on top of me, arms just barely managing to move my legs so that he could rest in between them.

I ran my fingers through his hair as I felt his heart racing against my own. There was nothing I loved more than watching Will lose control. Except maybe what came after.

Sometimes, I wondered if I loved cuddling more than I did the sex. There was something so intimate about cuddling, about bodies being pressed together in comfort without turning into sex.

He lifted his head from my shoulder and kissed me softly, tongue dancing with my own in a lazy tango. "I love you," he murmured against my lips, voice gravelly.

"I love you too," I said, lips lifting in a smile.

He kissed me again before groaning loudly and falling to the side. Arm thrown over my waist, he yanked me with him.

I giggled, peppering his chest with kisses. "Let's never leave this bed. I think we could do everything we needed right from here."

He ran his fingers through my hair, tugging me gently toward him for another kiss. "I'd love nothing more than to wake up every day with you right beside me. I'm at my happiest when I'm with you."

I wrapped my arms around him and laid my head back on his chest. I'd never felt the kind of happiness that I felt when I was with Will. I never wanted to lose that, and there was something inside of me telling me that I never would.

My phone went off somewhere in the room, and I groaned, knowing the sound of my alarm. "Nooo," I whined, tightening my arms around him. "Can we ditch work today?"

"I wish we could," Will said deeply. "But I have a big meeting in the afternoon."

I pouted. "But I just want to stay here with you. Naked."

Will grinned, hands trailing down my back. "We still have to take showers. How many times do you think I could make you come around my cock before we need to leave?"

I didn't answer with words but instead wrapped myself around him like a spider monkey and demanded, "Yes, please."

Somehow, despite the quickie in the shower, we still managed to get to work on time.

I had been lucky that I had clothes already at his place and hadn't had to stop home and delay us both. It hadn't even crossed my mind that I had a lot of my stuff scattered around Will's place until this morning.

When we got to work, I went with him to his office to eat breakfast together, quietly talking about what our days looked like. It felt good, normal, so domestic that it made me giddy.

When I left his office, I ran into Cora, who eagerly grabbed the coffee I handed her with a bright smile.

It didn't take long for me to sit down at my desk and get immediately lost in my work. There were countless emails to get through, most boring but a few from Dickinson and the producer about the cover composition I'd sent him. The email had my heart racing with excitement, especially once he told me how much he liked it and wanted to use it.

It felt good to be able to show people what I had to offer, to make music. Even if I wasn't officially on the job, it didn't matter. I just wanted to make music. I wanted to make something that people listened to and felt changed by. Whether it made them feel happy on a rainy day or angry because the characters in their favorite movie had just died and this song was playing in the background. Music was everything to me, and I wanted to share that.

My computer dinged with a new email, and I scrolled up to find an email from Clements, telling me to come by at the end of the day. I sighed, just imagining the work he was going to tack on for me to do just as I was trying to get out of here.

Anticipating that list of extra work, I focused hard after lunch on catching up on work and trying to eliminate any last-minute things for him to complain about when I saw him.

When I entered his office at a quarter to five, I walked in with my notebook in hand, confident that I'd be able to handle whatever tasks he needed of me.

"Come sit." He gestured to the seat opposite of him in front of his desk, and I did so quietly. I opened my notebook and uncapped my pen but stopped when he said, "You don't need to take notes for this."

I hesitated, confused, but put the pen and notebook down on my lap. "Okay."

Clements's attention was surprisingly entirely on me. His eyes weren't looking at his computer as he shouted demands, half-paying attention to the words coming out of his mouth as he typed up something else. His slightly graying hair was combed back in its usual hairstyle, but I noticed that it looked slightly askew, like he'd been running his hands through it before I came in. I felt nervous suddenly, like something bad had happened, and mentally ran through all the things I'd done in the last month and if it was possible that I'd messed up in some major way.

"There are some changes happening at the end of the month," he began, and I listened warily. "We have some people moving around, departments making cutbacks that are being overseen by our CEO."

I waited, wondering where he was going with this. Did he want me to make a spreadsheet about the different departments? I eyed my notebook in my lap, itching to start making a list. Once Clements started throwing out demands, you had to move quick, or it'd all get confusing before you could even blink.

"You'll be one of those people moving," he added, and my eyes jerked from my notebook toward him in shock.

My mouth opened and then closed silently. I licked my lips and then asked hesitantly, "Moving?"

God, please don't let it be sales, I prayed silently.

I couldn't stand that team, and I knew from looking at their files on our shared drive that they were unorganized and a mess. I didn't know who was in charge down there, but they had been slacking ever since Juliet had gone on maternity leave, and it was a wonder the whole department hadn't gotten fired yet.

"The company would like to offer you a contract to produce an album," he answered.

I nearly choked on my own spit, eyes widening.

"I-I don't ..." I stammered, at a loss for words and completely confused. "I don't understand. They want to offer me a contract?"

"Yes," he said, strangely patient. "They have a new artist that they want you to work on an album with. I can't talk money or what the contract will look like, but someone from HR will contact you with all the information by the end of the week."

How could this be happening?

My heart raced in my chest, and yet I felt like I was not fully processing what I had been told. I had come in here, expecting to get a list of menial tasks to do, and instead, I'd been told that they were offering me a contract to produce someone's album.

"I don't understand," I said dumbly. I wanted to kick myself for not just immediately jumping on the offer and saying yes, but my brain was working at a slow speed, and honestly, a part of me was wondering if I was still asleep and this was all a dream. It was the only logical explanation for this conversation.

"They were very impressed by the work you submitted in the contest," he said slowly, staring at me with raised brows. "While you didn't win, it had nothing to do with the quality of your work. You've made it no secret that you are trying to make a name for yourself in this field, and your work these last few years has shown that. You don't think this contest was the first time they'd heard about you or your work, do you?"

"They want me to produce an artist's entire album?" I asked, skipping over his question. I couldn't think about what he was implying right now.

He nodded. "It'll be you and another producer, but he'll mostly be there to oversee."

"What about my job here?" I asked another dumb question yet again.

"We'd hire someone else to take over your position," he said. "Of course, I'll expect you to help train them before leaving. But again, this is all stuff to worry about later. The important thing to know right now is that this offer is on the table. I know how much you love being my assistant, so I imagine this will be a hard decision."

Was he making a joke?

I looked at him incredulously and couldn't help the laugh that barked out when I saw his smirk. "I'm sorry. This all has just surprised me. I'm still surprised. It's what I've always wanted."

"It's a hard business, but if anyone can handle it, it's you," he said kindly, and I blinked in surprise. He threw another smirk at me. "Besides, you already know the artist, and with your help on the Dickinson cover, you've shown that you can work across genres."

"Wait, who's the artist?" I asked in confusion.

He looked at me like I was stupid. "Will Kobayashi. Truly, Genesis, this is getting a little tiresome."

I listened to him as he explained a few more details, not bothering to talk anymore because I clearly wasn't capable of comprehending anything right now anyway.

When I walked out of his office, I immediately pinched my forearm to make sure this was real and not a dream. I winced a second later at the sharp pain I'd just inflicted on myself, but even though I knew this wasn't a dream it still didn't feel real. I walked to my desk and found Will waiting for me, just like we'd talked about. He took one look at me and stood up from my desk, walking right up to me.

"What happened?" he asked calmly.

It helped ground me, and I held on to his forearm as I rasped, "They offered me a contract."

He continued watching me, eyes never leaving my own. "What kind of contract?"

"They want me to produce a new artist's album," I said in a rush of an exhale. I couldn't help the tremble of excitement and maybe even a little nervousness in my voice as I added, "They want me to produce your album."

His smile lit up his face, joy and happiness spreading across his entire being, and he pulled me into a hug, his arms wrapping around me. I hugged him back just as tightly, and with my face against his chest, I let myself smile for the first time since I'd gone up there.

I pulled away a moment later, bouncing on my toes as I looked up at him, and let out a disbelieving laugh. "I don't know how this happened, but they want me! And we'll be working together. Did you know? Did they tell you?"

He smiled at me, like my excitement and happiness brought him happiness and I knew that to be true. "I was one of the many who put in a good word for you when I first signed my contract. But considering I'm a new artist, I'm not sure that I had much to do with it." He cupped my face in his hands and smiled gently down at me. "When it comes down to it, your music spoke for itself, and they knew that they'd be stupid to not offer you a contract."

I leaned up and kissed him softly, heart melting at his words. "You make me so happy. I've always believed in myself and my music, but your belief in me makes me feel like I can soar to the sky. Like nothing is too impossible of a dream for me."

"This is just the start of our forever," he promised deeply.

I held one of his hands in mine and squeezed. "Promise to catch me if I fall?"

He smiled, squeezing my hand back. "Always."

The End

Epilogue

One Year Later

"I can't believe this is your new place."

I glanced behind me and watched as Alejandra walked into the room and carefully placed a brown box on the floor. Her long dark-brown hair was hanging down her back in a French braid, face slightly red from exertion.

Moving in the summer heat in New York City was no joke. If the humidity didn't suffocate me, all the boxes currently surrounding me surely would. But even with that, I couldn't muster an inch of misery.

The sound of laughter echoed in the empty house, and I smiled as I heard my friends and family talking in one of the many rooms of the four-bedroom brownstone that I would now be calling home.

I felt so happy, and I had been feeling this way for a long while now.

"Thank you for all your help today," I said to her, our shoulders brushing as she plopped down beside me on a box.

"Are you kidding?" she answered with a smile. "I can't wait to help you decorate this place. It's huge!"

She wasn't wrong.

This place was bigger than any place I'd ever lived in and had cost a pretty penny to buy. But with Siren Records signing me on as one of their music producers for the next three years and Will's music career blasting off, we could more than afford it.

The Book of Genesis, Will's debut album, had soared through the charts and blown the entertainment industry away. The tour had been a huge hit, and after one celebrity had raved about Will's single "Waiting" on their social media, everyone had suddenly known who he was. His song was playing everywhere. Social media, bars, department stores—there wasn't a place in the world that wasn't playing his music or talking about this new artist who was singing his way into every man and woman's heart.

Life for the both of us had changed so much.

I was working with artists in the studio, creating music and learning so much about the music industry and improving on my craft every single day. Even though it was the job of my dreams, it wasn't always easy. Working with all types of artists and people had its challenges, especially when paired with the impossible demands of a multibillion-dollar company that was constantly breathing down your neck to create a hit. But even on my worst day in the studio, I would never do anything else.

I stood up from the box I had been resting on and waved my sister toward the door, wanting to see what everyone else was up to. We walked out of the empty music room and down the hall into the spacious kitchen.

My eyes immediately connected with Will, who was standing in front of the fridge with Cal, a pack of beer in hand. Happy shivers spread through my body as I stared at him, eyes devouring him like it'd been months since I'd last seen him and not just a few minutes. His sharp features and dark eyes still made my heart skip a beat even now, and I couldn't help myself as I walked up to him from behind and wrapped my arms around his waist. His hand immediately touched my forearm, and I squeezed, pressing my lips gently against his back.

Will lifted my arms and turned, placing them around his shoulders. His face leaned down toward mine, eyes bright with love and amusement. "I was just about to go looking for you."

I smiled. "I was trying to organize the boxes for the music room, so things wouldn't be so impossible to set up later."

He hummed, not looking surprised. His fingertips traced my cheek before curling a stray piece of my dark hair behind my ear, eyes flickering across my face. "All the boxes are in our house. Now, we relax with our friends and family. We drink, eat, and if we're lucky, we'll get to christen at least one of the rooms in the house before passing out for the night."

I grinned, pressing a kiss to the corner of his mouth. "This countertop looks pretty inviting to me."

His hands moved from my waist to grip my hips, teeth gently biting down on my earlobe. "Don't tease me, Buttercup. I'll send everyone home right now."

"Dinner's here!" Yari shouted, front door slamming shut.

"Saved by the bell," I teased and nearly laughed out loud at the unamused look on his face.

With us both being on crazy schedules the last few months, Will had become a little bit possessive of his time with me. There were weeks where we only saw each other a few nights, one of us always coming or going for work. Things were finally getting back to normal now, and I was very much looking forward to waking up every morning with the man that I loved beside me. I didn't sleep as well when he wasn't there with me, and I knew from Will's complaints about being on the road that he felt the same.

Yari and Cora walked in, carrying boxes of pizza, Zander and James behind them with brown bags filled with paper plates and snacks. The volume in the kitchen picked up as everyone moved to congregate around the pizza. Alejandra shouted that she wanted first dibs on the pepperoni pie, which caused Sam to start complaining that he had carried the most boxes and should therefore get first dibs.

Will rolled his eyes, small smile on his face as he moved back and took my hand in his. "Ready?"

"I'm ready for anything," I said, thinking about so much more than tonight.

His eyes flared, understanding and devotion shining through as he watched me intently.

"I want it all with you."

"I'll give you the world," he promised, pressing a kiss to the back of my hand.

"I don't need the world." I softly brushed my lips against his knuckles, looking up at him with my heart written all over my face. "I just need you."

His smile gentled, and he pulled me into his arms, lips brushing against my own. "You have me. Yesterday, today, tomorrow—"

"Forever," I finished on a gasp, eyes closing as our lips brushed.

And he gave me exactly that.

Forever.

Acknowledgments

I can't believe that I've finally written the book of my dreams and it's out there for the world to read. Writing stories has been a dream of mine for as long as I can remember, but it was a dream I thought I would never fulfill. To know I'm here now, having written my first book, I feel such immeasurable joy. But this book would have never seen the light of day if it wasn't for so many people in my life.

First, I have to thank my good friend, Sonia, who without her words of encouragement and support, this book would've never been finished. Thank you, Sonia, for always being an open ear and answering my many questions and talking me off the ledge and just being an altogether great friend.

Thank you to Laura who has always been one of my greatest friends and greatest supporters when it comes to my writing. Your help and support mean more to me than I could ever explain. Big thanks to Melanie aka Melania, for always being there for me and being supportive and answering my questions about so many little aspects of my book.

Thank you to my family: Alyssa, Mar Bear, Rosemary...I am lucky enough to have a big family who have always accepted me for exactly who I am.

Thank you to Melinda, Najla, and Jovana who helped shape my book into the book it is today. I could not have done this without you and your hard work and dedication to making my book the best it could be will stick with me for the rest of my life.

Finally, thank YOU! The reader, the person who took a chance on my book and kept reading to the end. Thank you, thank you, thank you! I hope you stick around to see what comes next but if you don't, I'm grateful to have shared this story with you.

About the Author

Anna Salcedo is a lover of all romance, but especially ones that make her heart skip a beat. Her stories are for people who are looking for diverse romances and who love a good HEA.

Website: www.authorannasalcedo.com

Facebook:
www.facebook.com/authorannasalcedo

Twitter: www.twitter.com/annaswrites

Instagram:
www.instagram.com/authorannasalcedo

Goodreads:
www.goodreads.com/author/show/
21587812.Anna_Salcedo

Pinterest:
www.pinterest.com/authorannasalcedo

Email: authorannasalcedo@gmail.com